Redwood Writers
2016 Anthology

From the Deep
Part of the
Well

# Redwood Writers 2016 Anthology

# UNTOLD Stories

## From the Deep Part of the Well

A collection of poetry and prose
from members of the Redwood Branch
of the California Writers Club

Editor: Roger C. Lubeck

REDWOOD WRITERS Press

WRITERS HELPING WRITERS

2016 Redwood Writers Anthology
*UNTOLD STORIES*
*From the Deep Part of the Well*
Roger C. Lubeck, Editor-in-Chief
Copyright © 2016 by Redwood Writers

LCCN: 2016946235
ISBN-10:0-9977544-0-0
ISBN-13:978-0-9977544-0-7
Second Edition, October 12, 2016
365 pages.

Cover Art
Artist: Edward Hopper (American, 1882-1967)
Title, Date: Automat, 1927
Medium: Oil on canvas
Dimensions: 36 x 28 1/8 in. (91.4 x 71.4 cm.)
Complete Credit Line: Des Moines Art Center Permanent Collections; Purchased with funds from the Edmundson Art Foundation, Inc., 1958.2
Photo Credit: Rich Sanders, Des Moines, Iowa.

Cover design by Roger C. Lubeck and Joelle B. Burnette.
Interior design by Roger C. Lubeck.
Interior graphics by Roger C. Lubeck, Joelle B. Burnette, John Compisi, Pamela Heck, and Leena Prasad.

Published by: Redwood Writers Press
P.O. Box 4687
Santa Rosa, California 95402

REDWOOD WRITERS ANTHOLOGY SERIES

*Stolen Light* (2016)

*Journeys: On the Road & Off the Map* (2015)

*And the Beats Go On* (2015)

*Water* (2014).

*Beyond Boundaries (2013)*

*Vintage Voices: Call of the Wild* (2012)

*Vintage Voices: The Sound of a Thousand Leaves* (2011)

*Vintage Voices: Words Poured Out* (2010)

*Vintage Voices. Centi'Anni: May you live 100 years* (2009)

*Vintage Voices: Four Part Harmony* (2008)

*Vintage Voices: A Toast to Life* (2007)

*Vintage Voices: A Sonoma County Writers Club Harvest* (2006)

*I learned never to empty the well of my writing, but always to stop when there was still something there in the deep part of the well, and let it refill at night from the springs that fed it.*

—Ernest Hemingway, *A Moveable Feast*

# TABLE OF CONTENT

# INTRODUCTION

*Untold Stories: From the Deep Part of the Well* is a collection of eighty-one stories, memoirs, and poems from sixty members of Redwood Writers, the Redwood Branch of the California Writers Club. The stories and poems in this collection reflect the diverse experiences and rich imaginations of the Redwood Writers. I especially like Jean Wong's poem "The Thirteen Ways of Looking at Blackberries," and Harry Reid's "Millicent, My Millicent," a hair-raising but humorous tale of experiments in primate behavior at St. Ole College that go awry.

For practical reasons, this anthology is divided into three sections: poetry, memoir, and fiction. In the poetry section there are twenty new poems from our poets. These are followed by twenty-seven memoirs and thirty-four new works of fiction. In each section, the pieces are ordered alphabetically by title. In essence, they are arranged by topic and the imagination of the authors.

The poems and stories in this work span decades and reflect the ages and cultures of the Redwood Writers. There are tales of "Bird Watching in Ecuador," "Being Down and Dirty on the Mekong River," and the comfort of "Mint Tea."

For the Baby Boomers, there are stories that will help you remember or rediscover California in the 1960s. You will be entertained by personal memories of earlier times and different lands. There are stories set in Asia, South America, the Middle East, a ghetto in Cleveland, a Mississippi Delta, and the cold of space and stories that reflect on life, death, love, betrayal, and murder. Powerful stories and poems that illuminate the deepest parts of the well of human experience.

The title of this collection, *Untold Stories: From the Deep Part of the Well,* came from several sources. In *A Movable Feast,* Ernest Hemingway wrote, "I learned never to empty the well of my writing, but always to stop when there was still something there in the deep part of the well, and let it refill at night from the springs that fed it."

The quote regarding untold stories is usually attributed to Maya Angelou. "There is no greater agony than bearing an untold story inside you." According to club member Abby L. Bogomolny, a faculty member in the English Department at Santa Rosa Junior College, this phrase first appeared in *Dust Tracks on a Road,* the autobiography of Zora Neale Hurston, published in 1942 by J. B. Lippincott Company.

It is likely Angelou was influenced by Hurston and simply requoted the earlier writer.

Finally, I want to thank all the writers who shared with me their untold stories. Sixty writers shared their talent, imagination, and their lifetimes of remarkable experiences. I have come to appreciate and depend on the professionalism, volunteerism, and goodwill that exists among the members. Writers helping writers are evidenced on every page.

Roger C. Lubeck,
Editor-in-Chief

# ACKNOWLEDGMENTS

This work is the result of a team of dedicated member volunteers. The annual anthologies would not exist except for the club members who submitted original poems, memoir, and fiction. Thanks to all who submitted pieces, and congratulations to those finally selected.

A team of fifteen dedicated associate editors worked on this anthology. Without them this book would not be possible. The poems and stories in this work were chosen after a detailed evaluation by our team of judge/editors: Fran Claggett, Susan Gunter, Eugene McCreary, and Janice Rowley. A team of developmental editors then worked with the authors in this collection to finalize their poems, memoirs, or pieces of short fiction. The editorial team included: John Abbott, Robbi Sommers Bryant, Catharine Bramkamp, Joelle B. Burnette, Fran Claggett, Marlene Cullen, Cristina Goulart, Susan Gunter, Crissi Langwell, Juanita J. Martin, Eugene McCreary, Jan Ogren, Helen Sedwick, and Janice Rowley. These editors performed brilliantly.

Additional thanks goes out to Joelle B. Burnette for her work with me on the cover. Thanks to Joelle B. Burnette, Pamela Heck, and Leena Prasad for adding to the interior graphics, and John Compisi for his photo of Valledolmo.

A special note of thanks goes to those editors who worked to proofread and finalize this book: Robbi Sommers Bryant, Joelle B. Burnette, Fran Claggett, Crissi Langwell, Belinda Riehl, and Janice Rowley.

Finally, this book would not exist except for the oversight by the Branch's president and board of directors. Thanks to President Sandy Baker, board members, and special thanks to Linda Loveland Reid for her guidance and advice.

# POETRY.

Whenever the question "What does poetry do?" or "What is it for?" is raised, I have no hesitation in replying that poetry is central to our culture, and that it is capable of being the most powerful and transformative of the arts.

—John Burnside, 2012

# Thirteen Ways of Looking at Blackberries

## Jean Wong

a white plate
under a blackberry
loneliness

pricked fingers
caps wet with sweat
cooked fruit under a crust

my answer fell
like a frown
bruised blackberries at my feet

blackberry eyes
like caviar
but sweet

two blackberries
you cannot have them all
but I will share one with you

sunlight on a striped awning
the din of the marketplace
Blackberries for Sale

if I had a blackberry
I'd place it on your tongue
and listen to you swallow

an old wound
bleeds from memory
blackberry stains

searching,
blackberries unseen
turning home, they wink

a thicket of blackberries
a wooden plank
rapes the bush

sprayed blackberries
glistening in the heat
a tart poison

shriveled fruit
a bear lumbers by
and heads for his nap

blackberries spilled on the ground
I stooped
to pick up my life

# *Archaic*

## Leigh Jordan

turn the tide of thought
to unseen inchoate words
whispered in a flow
pulled by first-human
from the toe of consciousness
as he gropes to tether
sound to meaning
        this fire he makes
        burns white to scorch
        its enduring pattern
        in the design that made him

# *Attending Mary Oliver*

## Valerie Kelsay

Attending Mary Oliver
Luther Burbank Center, Santa Rosa
December 2008

The gray hair, bald pates, and glasses
In the audience affirm

How long it sometimes takes
To appreciate the simple, natural things

How belatedly we remember
Our first, pure joy.

The house is filled
With those who do.

Those who have driven through the early dusk
Navigated stop lights and Christmas decorations

Ascended the stairs with their walkers
—some with grandkids—

Who peer expectantly at the podium
That single spot where they know
They'll hear the echoes of their souls.

All have come for words they
Cannot sing or write
And now—not being metaphysicians—
Endeavor just to hear.

# *Bittersweet*

## Mary Lynn Archibald

It is the first sunrise in eleven years we
Have not shared with
You.

The birds still trill their morning abandon
And though as always I am awed by their
Sounds,

I will miss the quiet dignity
With which you faced each
Dawn.

Then that stoicism, facing the sea
And the splendor of your last, glorious
Sunset.

# Desert Stillness

## Rebecca Smith

Constellations drift
Across early morning skies
Low fires nip
High desert chills
Yellow flashes dance
In hot ember blanket
Night's only sound
Junipers snap and pop

Except for the howls
Mother coyote teaching songs
Quiet mind lost track of time
Immersed in the ebb and flow
Silent desert sighs, night sky
Invisible patterns swirl
Perseus chases Cassiopeia
Little Bear seeks the pole

Fire dies at morning's blush
Stars diffuse into violet hue
Morning fingers brush
Night's solitude awake
Dreams are hidden
The quiet's now inside
Where Spirit flows
Be still and you will hear

# *Dream Data*

## Fran Claggett

It is too late to begin the letter, the poem.
It is too late to push back the scrim of sleep,
to let the images through, to recognize
the parts of the dream and know the whole.

The parts, then:
"The way one mourns for a lost love or a dead child"
sounds aloud, a voice from the dream, a voice
reading a poem aloud, pushing the paper over
to the younger voice because a word is smudged
and I cannot read it. Recognizing, now, my voice,
reading the words of another, my own other,
my own words rendered through two voices,
two selves.

Always the two:
the girl, elusive, obsessive;
the woman, knowing again her other, younger self.
And as I know the mind of the other, I am the other
and resent the knowing and pull inward.

I close my eyes,
will my ears to shut out sound,
let my skin grow cold. I recognize
that I am unformed, yearning to be my older self,
and I let the woman draw me back to the sensate world.
For a time, I accept the eyes that read my mind,
the words that express my thoughts,
even before I have formulated them.

I find my solace in color and sound,
not in words or image, but in music and colors
beyond the spectrum until one day I find my dreams, too,
are shared, are open to a knowing I cannot tolerate,
and I break the bond that united me to my self.

Yet still, the girl, I dream,
and sometimes waken with words in my mouth,
but I will not say them. And I, the woman,
mourn for those lost poems
the way one mourns for a lost love
or a dead child.

# *Elixir*

## Juanita J. Martin

Effects of a needle drawing at a soul,
Leave morose thoughts of a tortured life,
Illustrated by tear-stained pillows, slices in skin.
Xeroxed copy of the social scene once emulated.
In a mirror's reflection, is a constant
Reminder that living is purely coincidental.

# Dying Without Her

## Jan Ögren

*"I am NOT going to die,"* she proclaimed.
   - Not going to die?
   Her body is throbbing
   with disease and agony.

*"I am NOT ill,"* she declared.
   - Not ill?
   Her body is shaking
   with anguish and pain.

*"I WILL get better,"* she commanded.
   - Ah, what assurance!
   Knowing her future
   predicting and directing it
   like a general from her hospital bed.

"I am NOT dying," she insisted.
   So finally,
   disheartened,
   ignored,
   her body had to die without her.

   No chance for goodbyes,
   celebrations,
   or love.

"I am NOT dying," echoed off the walls
   at the memorial service.
   Was challenged by the tears
   cascading down her children's cheeks.

   Her body had to die without her,
   it couldn't wait
   for her to remember
   to come home.

# *My Raw Voice*

## Venus Maher

MY RAW VOICE has her way with me in the morning.
Pounding the exposed cliffs of my rigidity
until the uncivilized truth surges
through my pen in the morning.

MY RAW VOICE has her way with me in the morning.
Descending into hidden passages
until a river of secrets pours
through my pen in the morning.

MY RAW VOICE has her way with me in the morning.
Her primal testimony eclipses my ego
Until original words swarm
through my pen in the morning.

MY RAW VOICE
      Has her way with me
            In the morning.

# Recurrent Fugue

## Deborah Taylor-French

Each night, a dream tide swells. Deep in salt water
I wrestle, tangled in bedding. Swimming, I reach for a ladder,
pulled toward consciousness yet sleep morphs into nightmare.
In dreams, they wait. People in known faces shout.
Their nostrils compress in disgust. I swoop by,
gliding over sea after sea, stretched horizon to horizon.

Sharply as a guillotine drops, I fall.
Blinded on impact, skin stinging, I stop breathing.

I thrash and flounder.
Am I dead or have I grown gills?

Resurrected on dry land, I struggle to fly.
At times, haltingly windborne like a wounded goose.
Boulders and pine trees block all escape.
Yet I rise into the air, wings pumping madly.
Air-born, I climb, striving for speed to outdistance
the crowd bellowing like a lynch mob.

My breathing seems to warrant their rage.
Sinking, my feet drag the ground,
weighed by unseen hands. Is it the sky itself?
Or an unnamed God that I've offended?
When I am caught and battered by the horde
I awaken shaking, chilled and lost.

In my fist, I find a shiny butcher's knife.
I brandish it toward a person who holds its twin.
We slice till blood flows over our blades.
I do not see a body. There is no body. Nobody there.

Each night, I do not know myself.
I am a fish, a bird . . . a person holding a knife.

# *Smash the Mirror*

## Pamela Heck

Smash the mirror
and let me out.
I won't be captured
by reflections.

These hard won lines
show where I've been,
not where I'm going.

Mere surface strokes
cannot predict direction.
Forget reflections.
Veracity reversed
invalidates.

What we see is relative
and only sometimes real.
Witnesses recant;
all tell a different story.

"Believe not what you see,"
is an old rule, but right.
The faculty of sight
is frequently faulty.

For mirrors, make no exception.
If you want to hold what's true,
I propose that only flesh
will do.

# *Still*

## Laura McHale Holland

silent as sugar
brash as neon in midnight sky
an aura claims him
from another realm it binds
as he sleeps in his La-Z-Boy

tools that ache for calloused hands
languish locked in dust
farewell to lumber
hewn, sawed, sanded
doors, cabinets finished, hung
kitchens, dens, decks reborn
stairs that sing in memory
of a master craftsman's touch

love twining his heart to mine
is no match for a ruthless grip
gaining ground

he will go sooner than I
the chair will rest empty, frayed

still, I will see him there
watch his chest ease up, down
still, I will long for one last kiss

# *The Snail and the Cactus*

## Simona Carini

A golden barrel cactus sits
At the center of my backyard
Months ago,
I tried to repot it
So it would grow
The cactus' bellicose spines
drew blood from my thumb

The first rays of sun pierce the morning fog,
Making the cactus sparkle like diamonds
A spider spun its thread
From the cactus' spine
Raindrops perched on the spines' tip
Clung to the spider silk

Nestled in the glen,
A small snail sleeps
Its beige head outside a mottled shell

Sensing my nearness
The snail awakens,
Glides downward—stops.

I wonder,
Does it see the sparkling raindrops
As lights overhead?

Midmorning—
The raindrops have dried
The silk has snapped
The snail is gone

Did the snail saunter off the plant,
Accidentally breaking the spider's embroidery,
Or did it tear free
Of the thread's tight embrace?

The silk's breakage
The snail's breakout
May well be discrete

The answer dangles on a silken thread

# This Empty House

## Juanita J. Martin

After two years,
The emptiness seeps into my skin
Leaving a stain
That won't wash away

Wedding photos, his paintings,
Are tangible reminders
Of the imprint
On my heart

Less furniture, less clothes,
Less of our clutter is all there is
After what seemed a lifetime
At this address

Although I packed away my feelings
I can still hear the door whine open
To heavy shuffling
Of a 5'11' figure

Prayers and coffee
Are how my days begin
While sitting and listening
for familiar creaks and groans

# Upheaval

## Laura Blatt

Snowball sun
  melted moon.
Hot wind
  dry rain.
Cheeks burn.
Lips move
  but cannot sing.
Children flee
  as carousel
  turns backwards.
Earth stop,
  Earth stop!

Water hyacinth dies
  dandelion lives.
A rift in the desert
  creates an ocean.
Crevices and flowing magma
  part the Red Sea.
Memory bows to present moment
  as earth stops.

Stand with me
  under snowball sun.
See white-tailed kites
  nest high in digger pines
  this season
  all seasons.
Will love endure
  when earth stops
  earth stops?

# Wasn't that a Time?

## Lilith Rogers

I can't imagine being young at a better time
Than at the cusp of change
But I was there—
The ending of segregation
Rebellion against war,
For the sake of war,
The beginning of feminism

I was there
When signs over water fountains saying
"WHITE" over one,
"COLORED" over another,
Were taken down,
At my hometown movie theater
In Galveston, Texas

I was there
When we marched
Through the streets of Austin, Texas,
Chanting
"Hey, hey, LBJ,
How many kids
Did you KILL today?"

I was there
When we marched
Through the streets of Washington, DC
Chanting
"Bring the troops home NOW!"

I was there
When we marched
Through the streets of San Francisco, California
Chanting
"Our bodies, our choices.
Legalize abortion now."

I was there
At a time
When we thought
We could change the world

When we thought
It was our right
To change the world

No, we didn't change the world.
We did make a good start.

I was there
I'm still here,
making change now.

# Way Too Fat

## Sandy Baker

"Could I join a gym, Mom, I'm way too fat,"
she asked as she exercised by the sliding glass door.
"I need to lose weight, I can't fit in my clothes,
I can't even bend down to touch my toes."

"Could I take ballet, Mom, I'm way too fat,"
she asked as she donned leg and wrist weights.
"I should be a size smaller, I feel really big,
I'd like to model and look like a twig."

"I only want salad, Mom, I'm way too fat,"
she said as she refused high calorie dressing.
"I have to cut out food with croutons or oil
and I'll only eat chicken you broil."

"I don't need any lunch, Mom, I'm way too fat,"
she said as she spooned some plain yogurt.
"I'm down two jean sizes but that's not enough,
I never knew losing weight was so tough."

"I can't eat dinner, Mom, I'm way too fat,"
she said as she looked in the mirror.
"I've lost only forty, gotta lose twenty more,
or I'll never get a boyfriend for sure."

"I'm not a bit hungry, Mom, I'm way too fat,"
she said as they strapped her on the gurney.
As they hooked up her I.V. and oxygen too,
she said, "But Mom, I still need to lose just a few."

# What Child May Come

## Deborah Taylor-French

When did the story child leave?
Was it the moment I wrote the last sentence?
When I typed "The End?"
I washed a window after each moment.

She grew in my cranium, the curse
of second sight. At first, the story child
whispered in my head . . . all day.
One night, an arsonist crept in.

Soon her friends roiled the ashes
as they inhaled the scent of villainy,
they tracked that pyromaniac's burning missives
through the wilds of oak savannah.

Plotting secrets,
driving character arcs,
fleshing out unlived lives.
Bringing crisis, pain and pleasure.

At last, I clicked the *send* icon.
*Dog Leader Mysteries*, my first novel
caused such a tiny sound for 50,000 words.
Whimpering dogs make more fuss.

Thirteen years of story revision on its way.
Today, I painted my office a golden hue.
The computer screen went black,
a bedroom, lacking a child.

# What My Heart Aches For

## David Mechling

My heart aches
for my sailor boy to return home
as it was when he was a child
home, where he should be as an adult

The Eastern Seashore
with all its history and grandeur
is not where a California kid should be

His heart and mine are
where golden hills surround us
where redwoods and vineyards meet

As the sun rises over our shoulders,
it lights the way
shines on our faces
as we look west
towards the sea
towards the day's end

Life here is
where we roam freely
abundant open spaces
not where humanity is
stacked upon each other

His roots are shallow now
3000 miles away
with hopes of
transplanting them one day,
back here where his home is.

# *Writer's Block*

## Wendy Bartlett

Is what I have here writer's block?
It's quite a first, a writer's shock!
My mind's still stuck on last night's show?
Or is it just my hands won't go?

That lady's shoe is clacking loud
I always write; I am so proud
I'm not like them, a pen to lips
Or her, those hands upon her hips

The voices at the table there
Annoy me. Drink and eat, don't stare!
The others write their speedy drafts
And when they read, they'll get the laughs

My mind's a block of solid muck
I try to write. My pen is stuck
It's New Year's Eve and still I know,
I will not have a thing to show

So here I sit, my lip is blue
Listening to that clacking shoe
It's birth again, a moan, a tear
I just want to get out of here!

I'd then let down my writing friends
Who sit here writing verse to send
To agents in New York and France;
I know I'll never get a chance

To publish, but you'd think I'd learn
That writing's hope, but life will burn
At last, a smudge across the page
Displays the heart of writer's rage

A scribble starts the words to flow
Hey writers, LOOK!  A page to show.
The timer says our writing's done
Oh, not quite yet! I'm having fun

# Memoir

*I think most memoirs, though they purport to be about this particular time or this person you met, are really about the effect that person or time had on you.*

—Rosemary Mahoney

# शतं जीव शरदो वर्धमानाः

**May you live a hundred years**

# At the Last Moment

## Leena Prasad

Instinct or habit? I don't know what triggered my response at the last moment.

I was spending a few last minutes with my dad before catching a flight back to San Francisco. He lay in a narrow hospital bed rehabilitating from hip surgery. Too frail and fatigued to sit up, he was in a skilled nursing facility in Kenner, a small town near New Orleans.

"Do you have to leave?" he asked. "You can continue to work from here, can't you?"

"I can. But Josh's exams are coming up so I would like to be home to be supportive," I said.

He sighed and said nothing after that.

My significant other, Josh, was going through a career change, and Dad understood I was needed back home in Northern California. I had used a week of leave for my visit, and I wanted to conserve the remainder of my sick leave and vacation days for future visits.

Feeling as if I were abandoning him in his time of need, I had already extended my stay for a week. For several days, the nursing center became my office; tapping away on my laptop while Dad slumbered.

Dad's greatest pleasures were visits from any of his three children. Before leaving, I told Dad I would fly back for Father's Day in six weeks when he was scheduled to be home and in his own bed. I'm not sure he heard any of what I said. His eyes were shut, and he expressed no sign of acknowledgement.

Growing up, I was very close to my dad. Dad had celebrated my first birthday as extravagantly as a wedding celebration, and as the only daughter at the time, I enjoyed my celebrity status. We were so close that I immediately fell sick for several days when he left India to pursue his master's in the United States.

My parents lived in the greater New Orleans area for over forty years and had many friends, especially within the Indian-American community. Dad was known for his quick mind and witty remarks. However, Dad did not make jokes when friends visited him in the nursing facility. Sporadically, he'd answer questions or smile at others' jokes. Mostly, his only response was to open his eyes intermittently to peek at whoever was in the room.

Dad had one of the nicer rooms with redwood doors that opened into the atrium. He preferred to keep the doors closed and only ventured out when Mom and I insisted. The padded yellow upholstery of two Victorian-style chairs in his room provided ample comfort to the stream of visitors. The remote for the large flat-screen television on the wall was attached to Dad's bed, but he was usually too tired to watch. He'd sleep or lay on the bed with his eyes closed, waking only to request adjustments to the room's temperature, or to be wheeled to physical therapy session, to eat or take care of other personal needs. Occasionally, he sat in a wheelchair after a shower or a meal, but even then he'd soon fall asleep.

During the first week of my visit, Dad was able to focus. His memory was vivid and complete. He had completed a memoir a few years before, that my sister and I had encouraged him to write. After reading and re-reading his life story, I craved more details, and he filled in some of the gaps during this visit. We also spoke about random topics, and he offered advice.

"Be powerful," he said, when I asked him if he had any words of wisdom for Josh.

In the second week, I witnessed Dad's vitality dissolving, despite his physical therapist's opinion that he was getting stronger. He would need to rest after a few minutes of conversation. He needed help to move from his wheelchair to the bed. Increasingly, he was unable to eat meals on his own. Every day, I watched him open his eyes, glance at me and doze off before he could respond.

Given his condition, I weighed the option to stay for a third week or return home. What would be the point of staying, I asked myself. He was too weak to talk and spent most of his time asleep; time I could better spend back in California sustaining the goodwill of my boss who allowed me to work from here. I would need this freedom if I were to spend time with Dad again when he returned home.

I should have paid more attention to Mom's mood. She was usually very talkative, but sat quietly while I studied Dad's condition. Over a year later, I still feel guilty for not realizing it wasn't just Dad who wanted me there; Mom needed me also. A breast cancer survivor, she had lost her natural stamina, and the thrice-daily visits to the nursing home were exhausting her. While I was there, she was getting a chance to rest at home. At the time, however, I was consumed with planning for the future; setting the groundwork to return to New Orleans during the year. I probably noticed Mom's low energy, but I did not give her the attention she deserved.

Dad was asleep when my phone's alarm punctured the silence with a loud "quack" announcing it was time to leave for my flight. I realized I had not thought of what to do or say in this moment of parting. Dad hated saying goodbye. In his weakened state, I sensed his yearning for my continued presence. Mostly, to see him smile, and partly to assuage my own guilt for leaving, I wanted to do something special to mark our parting. What could I say? What could I do to create a joyful moment he would remember later and smile? He would only be happy if I stayed. Anything short of that would be insufficient.

At the last moment, I reached for my father's bare feet, slipping my hands under the cool, white cotton sheets. I touched the top of both his feet with the palms of my hands. Even though we left India decades ago and this ritual may baffle Americans, this silent gesture of respect toward elders fulfilled an Indian tradition.

I enjoy the practice of touching elders' feet when you first see them and when you leave. While many Indians of my generation do not observe this custom, my parents treasure that my siblings and I are not embarrassed by this cultural habit, even at airports and other public places. This tradition, however, does not carry over into a nursing facility where circumstances are different. Typically, people are standing up or sitting when you bend down to make contact with the top of their bare feet or their shoes. They, in turn, reach down with a hand to lightly brush the top of your head and wish you happiness. This response from the elder is considered a blessing.

Two weeks before, Mom picked me up at the airport and took me directly to the care facility. It was past midnight and the center had closed, but after a bit of pleading, the night nurse allowed us to enter with the warning that we only had a few minutes to stay.

Dad was asleep on the narrow hospital bed when I walked into his room. Not wanting to disturb him, I was about to leave when he opened his eyes. His face lit up.

"You came," he said. "Is it lunchtime? Come back after you eat." He held his gaze on me for a while before he closed his eyes. He fell asleep before I could explain it was already past midnight. His normally resonant voice sounded soft and dull. He looked like he had not slept for days. That first night, I was too shocked by his condition to remember to touch his feet.

This time, when I reached for his feet, his tired face blossomed into an immense smile. He motioned with his fingers, asking me to walk over to the side of the bed. I bent down so he could touch the top of my head. He must have summoned all his strength because the feeble voice of the last two weeks was replaced with a booming, "Be happy. Live long." Atypically, however, his blessing didn't end there. He added some lines in Sanskrit; a special Hindu blessing, Mom explained. I didn't know the meaning and neither did she. Dad had already closed his eyes, exhausted from this small interaction. I was sad to be leaving, but thrilled to elicit a joyful response from my father.

A few weeks later, Dad passed away from heart failure. The night he came home from the nursing facility, about two weeks after my visit and one month before Father's Day, his condition worsened. While riding in an ambulance to the hospital, he stopped breathing.

Never again will I be able to touch his feet.

Never again will I see him smile.

I am grateful for that last moment with my father.

# *Awakening*

## Dmitri Rusov-Morningstar

I began my freshman year of high school in September of 1959. Everything was new to me and my generation. We were growing up and the new music of the day, folk music, was about to tell our story. A young man from Minnesota, Robert Zimmerman, changed his last name to Dylan and became the ballad-poet laureate of the 1960s. His music would tell our story. Change was "Blowin' In The Wind."

Soon, an older and more seasoned folk performer named Pete Seeger became known to us. Pete had sung with The Weavers in the 1940s and 1950s. During the 1950s, he was deceitfully blacklisted by the House Un-American Activities Committee as a Communist. Now, after seventeen years of silence, Pete was back. In the 1960s, he wrote and sang topical songs, carrying on the work of his close friend, Woody Guthrie.

Pete was a great believer of folks coming together in a common cause and singing up a storm to make their points. He coined the term *Hootenanny*, which was where my generation entered the picture. These were gatherings in homes and public places where anyone, usually with a guitar, would lead the rest of the folks in songs of the day. Thus, coffeehouses in every town and city became the home of hootenanny countrywide.

Folk Music. The more I listened, the more it defined the truth of my very being. By my senior year, it became the life-blood running through my veins.

Shortly after I graduated in 1963, a series of incidents occurred which, along with the truth of the folk music, changed the direction of my life.

By chance, on a shiny new Pontiac GTO, I saw a bumper sticker that stopped me dead in my tracks. "QUESTION AUTHORITY." In that moment, I had the first independent thought of my life. *Is that legal?* In my New England hometown, most adults would not have dared put those two words together. Once I realized the actual possibility of questioning someone or some unconscionable act or force of power, I never looked back. That single sentence became my battle cry.

Next, in November of 1963, the assassination of President Kennedy stunned me; especially being from the Boston area where the Kennedy's were everyone's family. The moment I heard the news, I fought internal terror that it was a coup, and headed straight for Washington, D.C. to attend his funeral.

The music was my creed, my politics, and my life. The stew in the vessel of those events and emotions propelled me into the midst of the folk movement to help deliver those messages to hundreds of thousands of my peers. I eventually became a producer of folk concerts. I helped bring the power of the music and performers whose ideas were so instrumental in waking up an entire generation from a lethargic daze with a call to action. There was a compelling sense of urgency everywhere. The insidious deeds of the greedy and powerful had to be stopped and there was no one else to do it but us. The music, the demonstrations, and the principles we lived for had to end the evils of war, racism, and poverty. Peace, acceptance, compassion, and love were our reasons for living.

In 1971, I came west to Palo Alto, California and The Institute for the Study of Nonviolence which was founded by Joan Baez and Ira Sandperl. Heeding the words of President Dwight D. Eisenhower to be wary of the Military-Industrial Complex, which was booming not five miles from the Institute, we began protesting with demonstrations, organizing, and educating the community around us. We formed alliances with other peace groups, such as the War Resistors League, to stop the war in Vietnam. We resisted our taxes, resisted the draft, and resisted the false premise that it was "Our Country Right or Wrong." In fact, it was our country and it was going to hell.

Our democracy was not etched in granite and discovered. It was born as an idea; something completely intangible. It was born with hopes, dreams, and ideals to grow and mature wisely. Our democracy was born of the premise we all had certain inalienable rights. These rights were not privileges for a select few.

My generation saw this democracy disappearing. That's why the music and those who made that music were so important, especially today. That we don't have to fall and remain victims to any articular psycho-pathetic set of rules. We can stand up for truth. But we have to do that together and be visible. In my time, the concerts gave all of us that hope, unity, and direction, along with the courage to take the actions that we believed would stop a senseless war and work to change the failings of our own mores.

By 1971, folk music was already embedded in the arenas of most college campuses, as were the demonstrations and political actions that defined the times. I had just spent two years working with Pete Seeger and the Hudson River Sloop Clearwater: a replica of the actual Hudson River Sloops that once transported folks between Manhattan and Albany. It was a political action of monumental ecological proportion to clean up the filthy, dying Hudson River, so badly polluted by industry, barely anything in it was still alive. The Clearwater still sails today and remains a tool of education and litigation as required to keep the Hudson clean. It was the truth of the folk music that the original crew of the Clearwater sang in so many ports of call that awakened the communities into action.

For the eight years that had passed since I left home, I spent every waking hour working for peace, civil rights, and the environment. Through all of these events, I, too, was growing and changing. Outwardly, I appeared to be cool and in charge; inwardly, I was in turbulence much of the time. That turmoil was from fear. What if I was not working hard enough or fast enough to make a difference? What if I wasn't up to the task of making the major events I was responsible for happen or be effective? What if, what if?

But I kept moving forward, even when I shook like an earthquake from fear when facing machine guns or being beaten by police with lead filled billy clubs. I didn't stop. I didn't have an intellectual discussion in my mind as to whether or not I was going to do this thing. I just walked directly into the fear and through it when anything I believed in was on the line.

So many times—then, and even today—when I feel powerless or defeated, it's folk music that picks me up off the floor and gives me the strength to carry on. The lyrics of Bob Dylan's "A Restless Farewell" is a hymn to me:

Oh ev'ry foe that ever I faced
The cause was there before we came
And ev'ry cause that ever I fought
I fought it full without regret or shame . . .

Shortly after I arrived in Palo Alto, David Harris, founder of the Draft Resistance, was released from prison and immediately continued his political work through many channels, including the

Institute. David was married to Joan Baez at that time, so all of us there became a "family" of political activists.

At the Institute, we studied the methods of non-violent civil disobedience used by Mohandas Karamchand Gandhi (Mahatma Gandhi). We organized sit-ins, conducted peaceful demonstrations (picket lines), passed out leaflets, and educated passers-by why we were demonstrating. If Joan was with us, she would sing "We Shall Overcome," and we would all join in—even those walking by. Sometimes, we would join with other peace organizations, making our cause more visible.

Joan Baez had one of the most compelling singing voices of the day. She sang contemporary topical folk songs and those of the past, including ballads, spirituals, and protest songs. On stage, she challenged those in power and inspired those who felt powerless to take action to stop injustice of any kind. Off stage, she walked her talk. She and Pete Seeger were among the first major performers to do benefit concerts in support of these causes.

Eight months after my arrival in Northern California, I worked with the People's Union, a group formed by David as an alternative form of government. We went to San Diego to keep the aircraft carrier, USS Constellation, from returning to Vietnam with its squadrons of bombers and bombs. Instead, we wanted to send it with food, blankets and medicine for the people of Vietnam.

One of the more unusual contingencies of this action was that there would not be a team of lawyers at hand to get us out of jail if we were arrested for any reason. Often, activist organizations provided them. Frankly, I was afraid that if arrested, I would have to stay in jail with no hope of bail, since I had no lawyer or defense team. Regardless, I felt the urgency to be in San Diego with People's Union.

At that time, I worked as a photo-journalist. I was part of a small team who photographed every action we took, every meeting we had, all the people at those meetings, and many photos appropriate to our cause.

The day I arrived in San Diego, I decided to explore Coronado Island on my own. I borrowed a car, grabbed my cameras, and drove over the bridge. Coronado Island was the home of our nation's largest air naval base and the home of the aircraft carrier USS Constellation.

I drove along the main road of the island and could see the Constellation docked. I found a wonderful composition for a photo.

There I was, wrapped in my photo gear, flat on my belly on the sidewalk, trying to focus at just the right angle, when a car pulled up beside me, and a menacing muscular guy suddenly stood practically on top of me.

"Just what in hell do you think you're doing down there?"

Well, I thought, this guy's gotta be a federal agent. I moved the camera away from my face, looked up at him and answered, "I'm bowling. What the hell does it look like I'm doing?"

Believe me, even though in that moment I was down on the ground looking up at this guy and being insolent, my knees started knocking. I was terrified.

As I started to raise myself up, he said, "Do you have an ID? Let me see your ID." Now I could feel myself getting more angry than scared. As I stood up, I felt both my blood pressure and my ire heading off the charts.

"Where are we, in the Soviet Union? I don't have to be carrying an ID. Who are you? Do you have an ID? Let me see it."

"I'm a federal agent, and I don't need to show you my ID. Now get your stuff together and get out of here." He got back in his car, and through the open passenger side window, shouted at me, "Go on now, get out of here."

I was in high gear now. I leaned through the open passenger window holding up my camera and said something like, "Really, you shouldn't get so upset over something as innocuous as this," while I covertly photographed him.

He gave me a stern look of disgust and drove off. As he drove away, I also photographed his car and license plate. Then, feeling proud of myself, I started walking to my car, except I wasn't moving. My knees were still knocking and I couldn't move my legs. All that on my very first day on the job.

Only about fifteen or twenty of us went down to San Diego from Palo Alto, but somehow the group kept growing. In fact, my first-day-agent-buddy turned up at one of our meetings several weeks later. I photographed him, quietly took David aside, and told him we were being infiltrated. I could feel my adrenalin rising again just looking at the man.

David interrupted the meeting and challenged this intruder. "You have been recognized and identified as either FBI or military intelligence. If you're here at our meeting as a concerned citizen of the

United States, you may stay and work with us. If you're here as either one of those police affiliations, leave now." The G-man got up, mumbled something disgraceful, and left.

Many months after we returned from San Diego, we learned, quite by accident that the intelligence community was using our action as a training ground for new recruits.

The turbulence of the 1960s and 1970s became a proving ground of victory for truth and courage over fear and apathy. To a certain extent, there was a level of fear to doing anything that went against the norm or the expected behavior of a good, obedient citizen.

Activists working toward an end that was for the good of all took real courage. Doing that work using the techniques of Gandhian non-violent confrontation disarmed the lies, doubts, or fears that tried to stop us. But, then, even in those moments of trepidation, by keeping my focus on my reasons for living—justice, peace, and ideas as sacred as our freedoms, rights, and liberties—facing the fear was, and is, worth the struggle. I let the fear, right along with the music that shaped my life, fuel my call to action.

Joan Baez is still performing worldwide. I feel Joan is one of the most courageous women of the twentieth century. In her early twenties, while marching with Dr. Martin Luther King, Jr. in Alabama, photos reveal the fear of the confrontation in her eyes. She worked tirelessly as a voice for civil rights and the United Farmworkers. She was an early outspoken critic of the escalating U.S. presence in Vietnam. Her courage deeply inspired me. She inspired all of our generation who heard her sing and speak truth while she looked fear in the eye and propelled ahead in defiance of those in power. Joan courageously tread where very few of us would dare, to stop oppression and inhuman injustice world-wide.

In 1993, during the war in Bosnia, Cellist Vedran Smailovic, courageously played music daily in the streets of Sarajevo while guns fired around him. His gentle courage inspired Joan to go to Sarajevo, to meet him and sing by him in the streets, and to bring the people hope, ease their pain, and share her courage. Joan risked her life, selflessly undertaking countless acts of courage and compassion most people will never know about.

Recently, in an interview for Time Magazine, Joan said, "Speak Truth to Power. It's a Quaker expression. We felt that we could do that, and you know, we still can."

Joan sang. I created pictures and concerts. We all looked for our way to change the world. With folk music, I found mine.

# Bird Watching in Ecuador

## Betty Les

We met on my first day at the lodge. He sat in the breakfast area scanning each member of our birding group as we entered the room. He introduced himself. "Eduardo," he said. "Your field guide."

He was young with jet-black hair and the striking facial features of a native. The fact that he stood barely five feet tall did nothing to lessen his tremendous presence, which seemed to fill the room. There was something familiar about him although I was certain we had never met. Something familiar and intriguing.

There were twelve of us in the group, all serious birders and several life-listers looking to add a couple dozen new birds to their list. Ecuador is known for its species diversity, and our lodge was located in a birding hotspot, a remote cloud forest perched high in the Andes. The tour members were strangers to me except the group leader, John, a former colleague. I relished the idea of sinking into anonymity. As a new retiree, I was in that altered state when big events overtake us and pull us out of the rational world, and I wanted it to last. But now I wasn't so sure. Who was this Eduardo?

We all found a place at the big breakfast table while the smell of bacon and eggs filled the room. I ran my hands over the smooth tropical wood, noting the wide planks, wild grain, and careful polish of the finish. Cocking my head to the side as if reading titles from a bookshelf, I followed the planks the length of the table. My eyes met Eduardo's, his head similarly cocked, resting almost on the table. Caught in curious acts most of my life and often made fun of, I braced for a comment, but I encountered only a good-natured smile. Hmm, interesting.

After breakfast we remained seated while John briefed us on the day. He formally introduced Eduardo and explained that he worked for Bird Watching International and would be our field guide.

"You're in for a real treat working with Eduardo," John said. "He's the real deal."

"We'll have two spotting scopes and a playback recorder," John explained. "And of course, you each have your binoculars. We'll spend mornings on the preserve that surrounds the lodge then venture out in the afternoons to explore. We might even see the elusive

Jocotoco. This preserve is one of the few places on Earth where it still lives in the wild. Wouldn't that be awesome? We'll meet in half an hour on the front porch. Wear your boots and bring your rain gear. We're in the cloud forest you know."

Booted up, gear and bird book stuffed into my field bag, I made my way to the porch. I stepped out into the moist air and breathed in the richness of the tropics. Wet earth, plant growth and decay, and all manner of animal sounds blissfully unorchestrated.

"Ah . . ." I whispered, as deep contentment spread right down to my bones.

The tropics had claimed me years ago when I was a Peace Corps Volunteer in Ecuador. Fresh out of college, I conducted field studies alongside Ecuadorian zoologists, traveling up rivers following fish migrations, sleeping wherever someone would take us in for the night, hiking into the jungle to explore whenever I could. Something deeply satisfying filled me from the beginning.

Now, thirty-five years later, I was back. All that happens in the big middle of one's life had happened to me. Marriage, kids, career, getting cracked open, and taking a stab at deciphering the mysteries of life. But there was no doubt this still felt like home.

The group gathered, and we started up the trail. Eduardo alerted us to bird species we might see and their call.

"Share your sightings," John said, "but quietly. And walk with your lightest footsteps."

The trail was narrow, and I ended up toward the end of the group, which suited me. Plenty of time to look at the plants, I told myself, not to mention the incredible frogs and insects, without bothering the diehards. At one point I guess I got a little too far behind and Eduardo came to retrieve me.

"What are you seeing," he asked, when he found me.

"Oh, plants and things," I mumbled, standing up from the orchid I was crouching over, realizing I had been caught red handed in a non-birding pursuit. "It's an orchid," I said weakly, pointing to it in defense. Eduardo's eyes traveled to the orchid, taking it in, and then back to me.

"We'd better catch up," he said, evenly, his English incredibly good.

I nodded, but lingered for a moment, closing my eyes, taking his measure. What I felt sent a shiver up my spine. I sensed great stillness and enormous power. My eyes popped open, and I caught a flicker of surprise in Eduardo's eyes, as if he knew what I was doing, what I saw. Then I felt his eyes on me and the unmistakable sensation of being stripped naked in front of him. But it wasn't my body Eduardo was disrobing. I realized, with a start, he was looking straight into my heart.

We kept our distance for the next week as our group ranged out into the preserve. Up at 5:30 and out the door by 6:00, we became part of the mountain. Clouds and mist swirled around us, giving everything a tentative mysterious quality, as one by one, the birds revealed themselves to us. Occasionally the sun broke through, illuminating the forest, enveloping everything in a pearlescent steam.

The sight took my breath away.

"Oh my God," I blubbered. "Look at that."

Evenings brought spirited conversation as our group compared notes and debated bird sightings. I couldn't help getting pulled into the talk. But still I watched him, how smoothly he interacted with everyone in the group, how readily he spoke a language not his own. Clutching a beer and telling a joke, Eduardo could have been a college boy anywhere back in the states. I knew there was someone very different inside.

When I had a private moment with John, I asked him about Eduardo.

"Well," John said, "it's a pretty amazing story. Eduardo grew up on the banks of the Amazon River, speaking the local dialect and later, Spanish. His uncle was a tracker and led groups on expeditions into the rain forest. This uncle was an accomplished hunter, as well, and respected in their village for his skills and character."

"He had some sort of special standing," John continued. "A medicine man, or something like that. Eduardo soaked up his uncle's knowledge like a sponge. He could identify all the birds in their area before he was twelve."

"That is amazing," I said. "But how did he get connected with Bird Watching International?"

"That's another incredible story," John said. "BWI had taken a group of birders to the Amazon and got hooked up with Eduardo's uncle. Eduardo came along and the rest is history. They recognized his talent right away and took him under their wing. They sent him to

English language school and gave him the opportunity to work with groups, to see if he had the people skills."

"Well that must have been a quick test," I added. "He has tremendous charisma."

"And you know what?" John continued. "It's one hundred percent real. Eduardo is an amazing person."

The days rolled along and our species list grew longer. One hundred was the first milestone, then 150. Every day was so full and exciting, but at night, when I was alone and lay toasty in my bed under three layers of wool blankets, my thoughts turned to Eduardo. I knew what medicine men were. They were shamans. They advised the people of their village on everything from when and where to hunt and plant, to the rightness or wrongness of their spiritual journey on Earth. Shamans were on intimate terms with nature and drew their power from it. They could travel between worlds.

I became interested in all of this because of my love of nature. It is one of the main reasons why I became a zoologist, and my relationship with the natural world is the closest thing to a religion I have found in life. Through my studies of Shamanism, I found an answer to why the tropics have so much pull for me. Nature is truly alive here. And sacred. In North America, we might appreciate nature, but plants and animals are objects instead of beings. As a result, they are dead to us most of the time.

I had to ask myself, nestled under that pile of blankets enveloped by clouds, what did this encounter with Eduardo mean? Something was opening to me. Perhaps with retirement I was slowing down enough to notice. But what was it? I thought about the hundreds maybe thousands of birds surrounding me at that moment, perched on the mountain together, making our way through the night. I would send up a prayer to them to open the door. Couldn't hurt.

Soon we were near the end of our stay. Everyone knew what this meant. We had only one more day to spot the Jocotoco. For some of the group, viewing this bird was their primary reason for joining the tour.

The next morning, we set out at our usual time but took a new trail. After hiking a couple of hours, stopping every so often to play the Jocotoco's call on the playback recorder, Eduardo suddenly raised his arm and put his index finger to his lips. We froze as he played the call again. Then we heard it. The unmistakable *whoop whoop whoop* of the

Jocotoco. Eduardo tapped three people on the shoulder and motioned for them to follow him off trail, along a little stream into the bush. They came back fifteen minutes later, faces beaming and their thumbs up.

I was in the last group to go in. When we got to where the Jocotoco was feeding on the forest floor, we crouched down low and waited for it to come within range. I knew it was close, but I could not see it. Hiding in plain sight, I reasoned, perfectly camouflaged. The other two birders saw it, then left, leaving me alone with Eduardo. I gave him a pathetic look, shrugged my shoulders, and raised my binoculars, determined not to give up.

Eduardo held up his hand, signaling "wait a minute," and then moved behind me, aligning his sight with mine. When he put his hand on my shoulder, a rush of energy passed through me, and my eyesight became laser-like. The whole forest floor was lit in Technicolor, including the Jocotoco. I turned and mouthed a startled *Oh!* to Eduardo and continued to observe the bird, feeding unperturbed on the forest floor. I didn't understand what had just happened, but I knew it was extraordinary.

We were almost back to the trail but out of earshot of the group when I turned to Eduardo. "Thank you so much," I said. And after a little pause, "How on earth did you do that?"

"Oh, I just gave you a little help," he said, adding, "I thought you might be ready."

On the long hike back to the lodge, only one thought filled my mind. Ready for what?

We got up early the next morning and boarded our microbus, retracing our route down through the mountains then west to the port city of Guayaquil, the end point of our tour. We spent a night on the road at a sister lodge and got in a little birding before dinner. That's where I picked up a bug, and became the last of our group to fall victim. The next day, I had a pretty good fever and dozed through the final leg of the trip.

I was leaning on the check-in counter of our hotel, practically asleep, when John tapped me on the shoulder.

"We have a little problem," he said. "We're shy one room. Would you be willing to double up? The room will be all yours until you leave for the airport at midnight. You have the earliest flight out."

"Sure," I said, too tired and too sick to think much about it. "Whose room is it?" I asked.

"Eduardo's," John said, handing me the key.

I lugged my suitcase up to the room, opened the door and peered inside. It was empty, save Eduardo's backpack stashed in the corner. I brushed my teeth and tumbled into bed, not bothering to change into pajamas. I fell into a feverish sleep, tossing and turning and dreaming vividly.

At some point I awoke with a start, the remnants of a dream reverberating through me. My whole body tingled. I had never felt so alive. I closed my eyes and the dream came floating back. A great white bird, zooming through space, heading straight for my heart, illuminating my body in a burst of light. I mouthed Eduardo's name, and in that moment, I grasped that he was the bird.

Was it the fever, or was it a door opening? All I can say is that after that night, nature opened to me in ways I never imagined. I gained a certainty about myself and my place in the world that anchors me. I never contacted Eduardo and don't expect to see him again, at least not in the flesh. I know he's out there. You might say we are joined at the heart.

# Bullets and Bombs over Bengal

## Inga Aksamit

As I watch images of streaming masses fleeing Syria, it brings back memories. In 1971 in Dacca, East Pakistan, I lay on a thin mattress in a thick-walled, windowless dressing room listening to the rat-a-tat sounds of gunfire. My mother had tucked blankets around me while my father paced restlessly through the house, ducking below the windows when shots rang out. I pretended to sleep and even dozed off now and then. Every time I heard the buzz of a fighter jet overhead or the heavy rumble of an armored tank, however, I awakened on full alert. I was only thirteen, but this was not my first war.

Nothing was conventional about my family, not even the basis for our nomadic lifestyle. Even thirty years later when people ask me where I'm from or where I grew up, I still stutter and mumble something incoherent about growing up overseas. They're usually looking for a quick answer, a way to get a fast read about my values and beliefs. Army? Diplomat? Oil company? World Bank? They never think of irrigation engineering, my father's profession that took us to a lot of hot, dry climates with nearly insurmountable problems moving water around.

Every time my father was transferred to another engineering project our stay ended in the middle of a conflict. It happened so many times, our friends made jokes about who my father really worked for. Did he truly work for a private engineering firm? Or was it something more sinister, covert even? First, the border war broke out between West Pakistan and India when I was a preschooler living in Lahore. Next, it was a military coup in Peru in fifth grade. We waited ten years to return to Pakistan, thinking things had settled down in that region, but we were wrong.

My memories of West Pakistan, our first overseas assignment, are fuzzy at best, photographic images blended with the fantasies of a four-seven-year-old and bolstered by family legend. Click, a smiling me, holding my first fish, caught on a pole in Dal Lake, Kashmir. Click, a tiny me, on a camel with Santa. Click, my stylish, tiny-waisted mother, dressed in all the latest European fashions. Later, there are unphotographed memories of American families banding together in a big house for safety in numbers. The little compound where I had lived with my parents was located near a rail line, and railroads were being targeted for bombing. Inside, kids ran wild as adults fretted over an uncertain future.

Behind the scenes, the U.S. government negotiated with Pakistan to get American citizens out. My mother and I were eventually evacuated with other women and children in a cavernous military C130 airplane, leaving my dad behind—an extraordinary event, even to my seven-year-old brain. The plane didn't have regular seats, just benches along the interior walls lined with netting.

My mother and I hopscotched across the Middle East and Europe, pausing for a time in Beirut, Lebanon, before landing at my grandparents' home in Texas to wait out the war.

Images of East Pakistan, on the Bay of Bengal, separated by the vast expanse of Hindu India between Muslim East and West Pakistan, come into sharper focus. My teenage self was able to absorb and assimilate much more, compared to when we lived in West Pakistan. The cacophony of Dacca was overwhelming, its streets filled with buses, cars, rickshaws, motorcycles and bicycles going in every direction, with no semblance of order. Horns honked, clouds of dust swirled, and nobody got anywhere very fast. Five times a day, mosques blared with the call to prayer. The pungent scent of fried onions and curry filled the heavy, humid air; a pleasant aroma except, when it swirled around with the malodorous open sewer. Women in brilliantly colored saris bought tropical fruits and vegetables from men squatting on their heels at wooden stands in the bazaar.

With no housing for us for the first few months, we were installed in the Intercontinental Hotel (later a Sheraton, now an Intercontinental again) in the up-and-coming Shahbag district, a world away from the strident street scenes. What fun for a budding teen to have her own hotel room next to Mom and Dad's with a connecting door. I had a small desk where I labored over my math and science homework, a big bed, and my own bathroom. Every day I would come from school, where I attended classes with other Americans and ex-pats at the Dacca American School, and swim in the Olympic-sized pool at the hotel. After a relaxing dip, we'd swing through the lobby and I'd peruse the tall, rotating bookstand. I saved my allowance to buy books, soon exhausting the Agatha Christie detective novels. I moved on to Leon Uris, who covered more serious themes and immersed myself in *Exodus, Mila 18,* and *QB VII* to relive the horrors of the

Holocaust. The vivid images of mass migrations of people struggling to find religious freedom deeply impressed my malleable mind.

The tension in Dacca had been building for weeks and the signs of an army buildup were unmistakable, even during the time we lived at the hotel. Tanks rolled through the raucous city and soldiers carrying large firearms stood on street corners. Long-standing conflicts between the dueling sides of Pakistan were finally boiling over. The military-controlled government of West Pakistan was ready to quash the East Pakistani Bengali nationalist movement once and for all.

We noticed an influx of international news reporters gathering stories on the impending crisis, never a good sign. A friend of ours, a fishery expert on assignment, said, "The Intercontinental is like a luxury liner floating in a cesspool of open sewers." An apt description. The country was becoming more unstable.

Nevertheless, our new house was completed, and I reluctantly said goodbye to my beloved hotel room. I'm sure my parents were more than ready to get into a real house before their daughter became just a little too comfortable with highfaluting hotel living. Crowned with large shards of broken glass to discourage intruders, a high concrete wall surrounded the whitewashed house. A garden wrapped around the house on the sides and back, with servants' quarters set apart from the main house. My mom mostly eschewed hired help, not wanting them underfoot all the time, but we did have a cook, maid, gardener, driver, and night watchman. The cook and maid, a newly married couple with an infant, were very much in love. Abdul prepared spicy, fragrant local foods such as dal soup and fish curry, rising early each morning to shop at the market. In the afternoons, when all their chores were done, they would sit on the soft grass under the banana tree while Rina massaged Abdul's feet with perfumed oil.

I was adjusting to the neighborhood, getting to know the servants, and finding new playmates when the military presence around town ramped up even more. Large convoys of soldiers rolled through the streets and jet fighters massed at the airport. Snatches of animated conversation between my parents and their friends caught my attention as they debated the politics between India, the two sides of Pakistan, and the United States. I could barely understand what they were saying but the implications were scary, not the least because they were hazy concepts to me.

"Inga, wake up," my father said, one night, shaking me gently. "Hurry, I think the war has started. Get dressed." Cannons boomed like distant thunder. I sat up quickly and reached for my clothes. My dad left the room to talk to my mother in low tones, but I wasn't able to understand what he was saying. My heart thumped in my chest, matching the rapid pops of gunfire in the distance.

Mom came into my room just as I finished dressing. "False alarm. Your dad realized that it's Pakistan Day. It's a twenty-one-gun salute, done to celebrate independence from India. Go back to bed," said Mom. Relieved, I tried to go back to sleep, but I was too keyed up.

Two nights later, my mother came to wake me in the night. This time, it was no false alarm. The war had started and the shots were random, not like the evenly-spaced twenty-one-gun salute we had heard previously. Operation Searchlight, a military campaign designed by West Pakistan to stamp out East Pakistan opposition forces, had begun. Later, we would learn that dozens of University of Dacca faculty and students were massacred that night, just one block from the Intercontinental Hotel.

We had a diminutive black-and-white TV to watch the one English-language show that aired each night. Dad and I loved the American shows, which rotated through *Big Valley*, *The Wild Wild West*, *Gunsmoke*, and *The Three Stooges*, giving us an hour of respite from the war. But mom was more interested in the news, anxious to learn something real.

We received a few minutes of English-language news each night, a big deal in the days before the twenty-four-hour news cycle and internet. A young man read the news in his Bengali-accented English, eager and bright, reading from his pages with enthusiasm. First, he'd read in Bengali, then English, then Urdu. As time passed and the war heated up, he began to look worse and worse. At first he just seemed tired, then the spark went out of his eyes as the propaganda got more pronounced. The words became monotonous and useless. It bothered me, but I couldn't stop watching. His face appeared puffy to me and then, one day, he had bruises. A couple of days later he appeared with visible cuts. He had two black eyes and his face was so swollen he could barely talk. Replaced the next day with another reader, we never saw him again. My head was so full of books I had read about the holocaust and other tragedies that it was only too easy to fill in the blanks. I was deeply disturbed; his face haunts me to this day. Mom tried to come up with plausible explanations of what had happened, but I knew better. Leon Uris had told me.

As the war dragged on, we adjusted to the chilling activity swirling around us. Days were usually quiet as tanks were re-positioned on the riverbanks, readying for the nighttime assault on villages on the opposite side of the water. At night, the skies lit up with rocket fire and flamethrowers. In the warm evening, when small bats skimmed off swarms of mosquitoes, as the fighting resumed, we would occasionally sit on our rooftop to watch the sinister fireworks. We stared at an enormous stream of people stretching for miles across the horizon. A silent, unending exodus of desperate people—men, women, and children, each carrying small bundles of belongings—slowly snaked their way across the barren land, heading for India and relative safety from their bullet-ridden, torched villages. When they tired, they simply stopped, set their belongings down and rested, napping in brief stretches. When they awoke, they resumed their sad march.

One night, when we were sitting on the deck, I noticed an acrid odor. "What is that dreadful smell?" I asked.

"Burning protein," Dad answered.

I didn't have any context for this, but slowly, as he tried haltingly to explain, the implication became clear. Bodies were being burned in huge pits, one dug near our house. Years later, when curling irons became popular, I'd sometimes singe my hair and that sickening smell would bring me right back to that rooftop. It is estimated that up to three million people were killed in the mass genocide and ten million fled to India in those long lines winding through the land.

A few days later, I was listening to music in my bedroom when I heard a commotion in the front of the house. Opening the door, I was shocked to see an army man towering over my father. Or maybe the effect of holding a .45 to my father's head made the major seem like a menacing giant. My mom raced toward me with a wild look in her eyes. She whispered I should go hide in my bathroom, the next safest place after the dressing room, now blocked by soldiers. I ran to the bathroom and lay on the floor. I couldn't decide whether to crouch under the window so nobody would see me from the outside, or on the opposite side because if a bullet went through the wall it wouldn't hit me as fast. On the other hand, if it went through the window it wouldn't hit me at all, so maybe I should stay as flat to the ground as I could. I tried different positions, considering all the implications. I imagined what a Leon Uris character might do.

Finally, I stretched out in the middle of the floor face down on the cold tile, not daring to look up. Then I heard a terrible wail from Rina, the cook's wife. I cried hysterically, imagining all kinds of horrors in the servant's quarters. I peeked outside, not expecting to see anything. To my horror, a soldier stood under the banana tree where Rina used to rub Abdul's feet, holding a rifle, a pistol at his side. My mom came in to comfort me, and we clung to each other. She said a soldier was positioned at each corner of our compound as others searched for the cook. Abdul was long gone.

Rina was safe; the soldiers sent her and her infant into the main house with us. One of the soldiers pointed a gun to my father's head and said, "If the cook comes back, he's your responsibility. We'll be back at six." They departed, spraying bullets at a bunch of children playing in the street. Miraculously, none were hit. A confusing story emerged, a classic tale of neighbors on opposing sides. The neighbor had turned in our cook to the military police as a traitor. The soldiers were under orders to kill him on the spot. Naturally, the cook never returned, though the soldiers reappeared at midnight, just to make sure.

Shortly thereafter, my mother and I were evacuated—my second military evacuation, this time via Tehran, Iran. My Texas-based grandparents took us in once again, as we waited for my father to get out. He joined us shortly before the East Pakistani forces prevailed, to West Pakistan's great surprise, and Bangladesh was born.

Now, decades later, I see the same forces at work affecting millions of innocent people in Syria. I can only imagine the atrocities repeating themselves in endless cycles of violence and terror. I see pleading faces pressed against fences, enduring another day, hoping for a better life for themselves and their children. I read about it in novels but lived through enough that I know it's real. I had the benefit of being airlifted out of conflict zones, but what of those who aren't so fortunate? I don't think so much about the politics, but rather the Rinas of the world, who simply wanted to be in love and raise a family in peace.

# Conquering Sicily: The quest for mi famiglia

## John Compisi

The sweat was dripping down my back in the mid-September heat as we hustled down the uneven cobblestone streets of Valledolmo, Sicily. My brother Tony and I were maneuvering through the maze of narrow streets toward the city's records office. It was mid-afternoon and everything was closed. We were told that the records office would reopen at 2:30 p.m., and we didn't want to be late.

The office was about six blocks from the small piazza in front of the Chiesa Cristiana Evangelica where we had established our informal rallying point. Linda and Nadine, our wives, would wait while we made the initial contact, and join us later.

Like most hilltop cities, the streets undulated as we moved from the piazza outward toward the fringe. Curtains moved aside as residents furtively peeked out of their apartment windows. Valledolmo is not a tourist town, so our activity was quite unusual. I was uncomfortable being watched. Were they wondering who these strangers were and why we were disrupting their quiet time?

Excitement and anxiety raced through me as we got closer to the office where we hoped to discover information about our grandparents. Was my thirst for knowledge about my family's origins going to be quenched this time?

This was not the first search for my Sicilian roots. I had always wanted to know more about my Italian father and my Polish mother's backstories. Their desire to assimilate and be American seemed to have trumped any interest in teaching the next generation about their histories.

I knew very little of my grandfather and his life in Italy. He died when I was four years old, and my grandmother passed away a couple of years later. I remembered stories told by my father and relatives, but no first person experiences. What was clear, however, was a character of love and humor shared among my father's eight siblings. I yearned to know more. To that end, four years earlier, in 2008, Linda and I made the journey from Northern California to Italy.

The 2008 visit to Valledolmo was nearly a complete bust. After spending a few days in Sicily, driving along the coast, we had discovered how historic, unspoiled, and amazingly haunting this often conquered island is. It had been an agricultural prize for the Greeks, Romans, Phoenicians, Moors, Normans, and Spanish, among others. We made our way north through the center of Sicily to find Valledolmo elegantly situated on the upslope of a hill overlooking miles of rich agricultural land.

It was midday as Linda and I drove slowly through the cobblestone streets. I had butterflies in my stomach and already was regretting my inability to connect with anyone in advance. Feelings of hopeful anticipation and reasonable misapprehension battled for control of my head. I knew my preparations were inadequate, and that we had no solid plan. We had purchased Italian language software months before, but were not fluent nor confident of our skills. Communication would be a big problem.

I remember the first trip like it was yesterday. The sky was brilliant cobalt blue with a smattering of puffy, white chiffon clouds. The streets were narrow and sometimes steep, reminiscent of San Francisco. I was enchanted driving through this medieval city, knowing that my grandparents grew up here and walked these same streets over one hundred years earlier. Linda and I were surprised by the signs on the ancient sun-bleached stone buildings. The street names, Via Alessi, Barone, and Chiavetta were familiar surnames where we grew up outside of Buffalo, New York. We knew these names intimately as friends, neighbors and family. I couldn't wait to tell my three brothers about the name connections that Linda and I thought were so cool. I knew they would be a bit jealous and wish they could have made this discovery with us.

Back then, I thought the richness and rewards of solving the mystery of my roots were just a few blocks away. I remember shaking with excitement and having new confidence with the thought that my search would be successful, and very soon.

To my dismay, no shops or businesses were open, but I wasn't worried. We could just drive to a nearby Polizia office, and they would certainly know everyone in town and point us to la mia famiglia. Our bambino level Italian skills would not be a problem; we were very good at charades.

After driving in circles for nearly an hour and seeing no one, not even a dog or a cat, and no sign of a police department, we discovered a winery on the edge of the city. The familiar smell of freshly harvested and crushed grapes permeated the air and renewed my hopes. We could speak vino.

We parked the car and went inside the winery office. After our unsuccessful attempts to communicate with the woman there, we waited while she went to find the winemaker. He was in his mid-thirties and had recently arrived from mainland Italy. His English was no better than our Italian. Fortunately, Linda's Rosetta Stone® efforts and superior listening skills paid off. She and the winemaker established a baby-talk comprehension and soon we were on a tour of the winery. The president of the vino co-op joined us. He was either a Borzellieri or he knew a Borzellieri, we weren't sure which. That was as close as we got to finding family in 2008. I reluctantly said Ciao to Valledolmo, not knowing if I would be able to return to search for my ancestors.

Fast forward four years, Linda and I were back in Sicily for our second try in 2012. We rendezvoused with Tony and Nadine, their first trip to Sicily, to do some sightseeing in Siracusa, Agrigento, and the mountain-top city of Erice before heading to Valledolmo. All this was a prelude to our main event, discovering our family's ties to this history packed island called Sicily.

Driving from Erice through Palermo, *The Godfather* jokes and references punctuated with our anxious laughter reflected the real excitement that was building. I was thrilled to be sharing this experience with Tony, hoping this search for our Sicilian grandfather would bring us closer. We were never really close. He went to a boarding high school when I was ten years old and he was fifteen years old.

We arrived at our centuries-old agriturismo, a working farm offering lodging, just outside of Valledolmo. The outbuildings dated from the 1700s and the main farmhouse from the 1870s. Its charming combination of stone, probably pulled from the surrounding fields and ancient wood beams, offered a sense of the countryside's history.

I mused that my grandfather had worked these fields as a peasant. I pictured him with a harness and wooden plow as he trudged behind an ox plowing these rows of hard clods. I imagined his sweat and soreness after toiling these fields from dawn to dusk. I reminisced about the story I had been told of my grandfather literally biting a horse out of frustration when it would not cooperate. The distant sound of cowbells from the cattle grazing in the surrounding fields roused me from my reverie.

My anticipation was building and I wanted to get started. I had a fitful night of sleep anxious to get into the city. We had breakfast at the agriturismo and then made the short drive to Valledolmo.

Valledolmo had over 10,000 residents during its heyday. Industrialization eliminated much of the agricultural employment and working class men soon left. The population of Valledolmo dropped precipitously to fewer than 4,000 residents in a few decades. My grandparents were part of this diaspora.

We arrived in a few minutes and parked the car. We found some people in the street this time. Tony began asking, "Buon pomeriggio, conoscete i nomi Compisi o Borzellieri?" (Good morning, do you know the names Compisi or Borzellieri)? He was getting wary looks, which made me a bit nervous. Did my grandfather leave under unpleasant circumstances?

We were directed to the Men's Opera Society just up the street. Several men were sitting on the front steps, which was actually a men's social club. Tony explained why we were in Valledolmo and that we were from Buffalo, New York. To our surprise they invited us inside. My spirits were rising.

We were given a mini-tour. The front room was a bar with tables. The oldest of the men led us through the next space which resembled a game room, and then to the back room—the private inner sanctum where, I imagined, their meetings were held. The signore beamed as he pointed to a picture on the wall. It was the "17th Annual Installation Dinner of the Valledolmo Circolo (Club) and Ladies' Auxiliary of Buffalo" in the ballroom of the Buffalo Hotel, dated February 1953. We were astounded. Who knew that Buffalo had been a magnet for hundreds and hundreds of Valledolmesi for decades? Tears of excitement and wonder welled up in my eyes. My heart filled with joy and expectations of what we would learn next.

The gentleman told us that the records office was closed until 2:30 p.m., so we decided to have lunch. Tony asked the man if he knew the name Chimera. I was incredulous. Where had Tony learned this name? He explained that Nonno Compisi had a stepfather named Chimera. He knew this because Nonno had given him a shotgun with Chimera carved into the stock. Nonno had received this shotgun from his stepfather, Colagera Chimera. Apparently, all the history I was going to learn wasn't just coming from Valledolmo.

The man told us there was a pizzeria named Chimera and how to get there. With this step-family news under my belt, we drove to Pizzeria Chimera. We found it quickly, but just as fast, we hit another roadblock. They were closed. Tony spotted a woman sweeping her balcony above the pizzeria and, using his linguistic magic, soon had Signore Chimera, master pizza maker, welcoming us into his pizzeria. Signore, in his mid-fifties, showed us his "Master Pizza Maker" plaques proudly hung on the wall. He explained that it would take too long to heat up his oven to make us lunch so he led us up the road to a restaurant that was open. He waved goodbye as he drove away.

We entered Il Girasole Di Mule' Rosario and soon made acquaintance with the proprietress who had another familiar last name. We became social media friends on the spot as we ordered lunch.

Then the biggest break-through: the proprietress knew two women who worked in the records office and they were born Borzellieri. She called them and they agreed to meet us around 2:30 p.m. Heart-racing news.

We drove back to the square to wait until 2:30. Linda and Nadine stayed there while Tony and I went ahead on foot. When we arrived, my heart sank. It was a nondescript building with no signage and no one there. Across the piazza, a woman was on her balcony. Tony asked her about the office and she pointed down the street. We saw Sara and Anna Marie, the cousins who ran the office, walking toward us. Were they distant cousins? We greeted them warmly and joyfully, as new cugini (cousins). Both ladies were reserved and appeared a bit curious about these two crazy Americans. They unlocked the door and led us upstairs.

The office was quiet. It appeared that no one else was working there. They led us to a small room, maybe ten by fifteen feet, with wall-to-wall bookcases. The room smelled a bit dusty and musty from the old books. A couple of large, generations-old ledgers were taken from the shelves and placed on a rectangular wooden table. I could feel my heart beating in my chest. One was a book recording all the births in alphabetical order and the other was a chronological recording of all the births in Valledolmo for a specific year.

The books were filled with beautifully handwritten entries. I hurriedly flipped the pages to the Co entries but there were no Compisi. I backed up to the Ca entries. I slowly ran a quivering finger down the alphabetical names: Camizzi, Cammerata, Campisi, Campisi,

Campisi. The entry for my grandfather Antonino was listed, but there could be no mistake, the spelling was Campisi.

This was the answer to a question that had been asked for generations. We had debated this with cousins and uncles who had various spellings like Campise, Compise and Campisi. Apparently, Campisi, had been misspelled when Nonno first entered the U.S. The feelings of connectedness brought a wave of serenity over me. Tony and I looked at each other half laughing and half crying over this minor Ellis Island error. I was giddy to have so many years of wonder satisfied in just these few minutes.

We learned that many Borzellieri remain in Valledolmo but no Campisi. I don't know why we left after only 30-45 minutes. I still kick myself. Why didn't we quiz them, ask them to take us to a cemetery or anything to extend our knowledge? Alas, we did not.

My head was swirling with questions as we silently made our way back to our car. Why did my grandfather leave? Why did the Campisi leave? Was it purely economic? Was there family strife or some social stigma? I know my grandfather had at least one, maybe two brothers who lived in Buffalo, but did he have others? What about cousins who immigrated? The questions just came rolling into my head, making me dizzy.

As Valledolmo disappeared in my rear view mirror, I wondered if I would ever return and how I would get the answers to the new questions that were nagging me.

The years have passed rapidly since the revelations and excitement in Valledolmo. The recollection of meeting the generous and kind Sara and Anna Marie warms me. I continue to experience moments of illumination via the wider network the encounters in Sicily created. Sara continues to provide information from Valledolmo.

I yearn to go back to Valledolmo to get a deeper understanding of what life was like for my grandparents at the turn of the twentieth century. I want to spend more time with any Borzellieri connections and to gain an understanding of why thousands of Valledolmesi left.

My enthusiasm for knowing more has grown with each new revelation. I have become the chronicler for my three brothers, daughter, grandchildren, nieces, and nephews. The richness of traditions, the sense of who and why, adds layers and vitality to my day-to-day life. Contact with the current residents of Valledolmo, whether we are related or not, makes my world closer, richer, and more interwoven.

Is it vital to know who your progenitors were and what their culture was to understand who you are? My answer is *No*. But if you ask me if this knowledge is life enriching, my answer is a resounding *Yes*.

# Crazy Lady

## Pamela Fender

When I was a girl and my family visited my grandparents in San Francisco, I'd climb into bed beside Papa, and he'd tell me story after story, in his British accent, never ceasing to make me laugh until my sides ached.

My brothers and I would take a bus down to Chinatown for Wor Won Ton soup. After filling our bellies, we'd hop on a cable car to Fisherman's Wharf to devour shrimp cocktails while strolling down the wharf to look at all the artists' wares. After a long day of being tourists, we'd bus it back to the Richmond district to Grandma and Papa's for Grandma's beef and cheese noodle casserole—or some other delectable dish she'd be remembered for—some television, listening to old records, and then bedtime.

These visits are still the most joyful memories of my childhood. I felt closer to Grandma and Papa than my own parents—respected and loved in a way that assured me my life and opinions mattered.

I continued to visit Grandma and Papa often when I attended college in northern California. Those were particularly special times because I did not have to compete with my brothers for my grandparents' attention.

After fifty years of living in the same flat, atop two flights of stairs, one outdoors, then indoors, Papa just couldn't climb those stairs anymore. So, they moved into an apartment building with an elevator. And everything changed.

My grandparents would be watching television when someone would knock hard on their front door. Papa would open up to find the police.

"Your neighbor downstairs is complaining about a lot of noise coming from this apartment."

"My wife and I are just watching TV. Would you like to come in?"

"No, that won't be necessary. We see that it's only the television. Sorry for disturbing you, Sir. Have yourself a good evening."

This scene took place on a number of occasions.

Often, the crazy lady would take the end of her broomstick and pound it against her ceiling. When I visited my grandparents, I'd hear the woman banging her broomstick, and then she'd phone the police to complain about her noisy upstairs neighbors.

Papa wished she'd move to a convalescent home where she belonged. Unfortunately, that never happened. He passed away in 1984. Grandma endured the repeated harassment and police calls for another three and a half years. Grandma died on the Fourth of July in 1987.

A week after the funeral, my mother, my twin brother, and I drove up to San Francisco from Los Angeles to empty her apartment. We then spent a couple of weeks cleaning, deciding what would be donated, what we'd keep, and what we'd throw out.

"Hey. Did you just hear that? She's at it again, banging her ceiling."

"I'm ignoring her. She's nuts."

One evening, I left the apartment to return an ice tray to one of Grandma's neighbors. When the elevator door opened, I stepped in. Standing inside was a woman with a sneer across her face. She scrutinized me, scanning me up and down. There she was—the crazy lady. Short in stature, she wore a knee-length skirt with knee-high stockings, and old-fashioned laced shoes. I'd never met the woman, but I'd heard about her so often that I knew it had to be her.

"Are you zee Harris girl?" Her thick Eastern European accent was unmistakable. That's her all right.

"I'm Mrs. Harris' granddaughter."

"Your grandmoder ees wery loud, and she disturbs me een zee middle of zee night. Evwey night."

Naturally, I knew she was insane, especially since she'd always accused Grandma—who'd been asleep in bed—of waking her.

"Well, you don't have to worry about that anymore. Sadly, my grandma passed away last week."

"Vell, dat's a good ting. Finally. Now I don't have to put up wit any more of her racket."

What did she just say? That it was good that Grandma had died?

Instantly, I became enraged, possessed with fierceness, overtaken by an incredible force. Without hesitation, I turned and smacked her across her face with such passion that the woman was knocked back against the hard steel wall of the elevator.

"You bitch! How dare you," I said.

Somehow, I was conscious enough not to strike her with a closed fist. Silence ensued. Fortunately, she didn't fall. Still, we both were shocked by what had just occurred.

The elevator door opened just as I blurted those words at her. The neighbor I was returning the ice tray to must have seen the tail end of our encounter as she stood in front of her apartment door, her mouth agape. I stepped from the elevator, walked over, and handed her the ice tray.

"I can't believe what I did to that woman."

"Don't be sorry. That woman deserved it."

I rode the now-empty elevator back upstairs to Grandma's apartment where my mother and brother waited. I walked in the front door.

"Oh, my God. I can't believe what I just did." I placed my hands on my flushed cheeks. My heart was still racing.

"What happened? You look strange." My mother chomped at the bit for any gossip.

"You're never going to believe what I just did."

"Tell us already. What happened?" My twin was as impatient as a hungry dog.

"I hit her."

"Hit who? What are you talking about?" My mother craved more.

"The crazy lady."

"You what?" My twin was blown away.

"She said that she was glad that Grandma died. I lost control and whacked her. Hard."

"Oh my God? You did not."

"I swear. I did." I took a deep breath. My mind and heart were still racing. To hit an old woman was unconscionable. It was as if I were possessed, and my anger and passion overcame me. "Nobody is ever going to speak about my grandma like that. Nobody."

They couldn't believe I would do something like that; nor could I. It was completely out of character for me.

"Well, good for you. She deserved it—that old bitch. Papa would be so proud of you," my mother snickered.

They applauded me. I was still in shock.

"I bet she phones the cops." My brother certainly knew how to extinguish any fears.

A half hour later, the doorbell rang. Guess who?

My mother ordered me into the back bedroom. "Don't come out, unless I tell you to," she said.

She opened the front door. "Good evening, officers. What can I do for you?" My mother was a fine actress when necessary. It was necessary.

"Well, Ma'am. There was a phone call from a neighbor who claimed that a young woman from this apartment attacked her in the elevator."

"This apartment? It couldn't possibly have come from this apartment, officers. You see, I just lost my mother last week, and my son and daughter are here with me. They've been here all evening." Yes, a lie. Customary for my mother.

"Yes, I'm sorry. I heard the unfortunate news. I knew Mrs. Harris. She was a kind woman. I've been by on a number of occasions."

"The woman downstairs, I'm guessing, phoned you?"

"Yes, Ma'am. We've been up to this apartment several times. The woman has some mental issues, which we're aware of; however, we still need to respond when a caller phones in. She said it was your daughter, I guess. Blonde hair."

"Oh, Officer. My daughter has very bright red hair. She's in the back bedroom. Would you like me to get her?"

"No. No. I don't want to intrude on you any longer. I'm sorry for the disturbance, and please accept my sincere condolences on the loss of your mother."

"Thank you, officers. I'm sorry you had to make another unnecessary call."

She shut the door.

Out from the bedroom I came. "Well, that was a close call. All I needed was to be arrested for assault."

"Boy, would Papa ever be proud of you."

"Really? I don't know how proud he'd be of me knowing that I just hit an old woman. I don't know what came over me, but when she made that comment about Grandma, I just lost it."

When we returned to Los Angeles, my mother went back to the travel agency where she worked. Waiting for her was a statement from the hospital emergency room the crazy lady apparently visited that evening. My mother laughed as she tossed the statement in the trash.

# Dear John

## Carmen Appell

My Dearest John,

Twenty-two years ago, we met in a bar. They say it's a bad idea to meet your future spouse in a bar, but that is where we met. You were sitting a few stools away from me. I could tell you had come straight from work. Hard work. You certainly did not appear to be the banker type. Construction, maybe. I liked what I saw. A slender man, with shoulder length, fine blond hair, and an attractive, though rugged face. Your eyes, as crystal blue and shiny as glacial ice, mesmerized me. I saw honesty and happiness in those eyes.

I was dressed to attract, in a tight pencil skirt and three-inch heels. I had been stood up for a blind date and was slightly pissed off. There was an Oakland A's game on the bar television.

"Who's Jose Canseco?" muttered the rancher who was sitting between us.

"You don't know who Jose Canseco is?" we both replied in unison.

"He's one of the Bash Brothers. He's on track to set the all-time season home run record," you added.

"I guess you don't watch much baseball," I said.

"No, Ma'am," the stranger replied. "I don't have no TV at home."

Everyone was watching the game then. The conversation stalled. The rancher left.

"Can I buy you a drink?" you asked.

"Sure. I guess so."

"Mind if I sit by you?"

"No. Not at all."

Right from the start, our conversation was easy and relaxed. You were funny and smart. You made me laugh and feel pretty. I felt like I had known you for a long time. When you asked if I would like to go out to the lake and look at the moon, I went. Again, not a very smart idea. You could have been a very charming serial killer for all I knew. Still, after stumbling around in the dark, I invited you to follow me home. Another dumb idea. We made love and talked until 4:00 a.m.

In the morning, as you left to go to work, you asked for my phone number. I wasn't sure you even remembered my name, so I wrote it on the slip of paper along with my number.

I didn't care if it turned out to be a one-night stand. I felt like I had broken the chains that had held me down for way too long. Ever since my second divorce, I had been searching for my own identity. Me, just me. Not, me as part of a couple. From that day forward, I knew I would live my life, not just let time pull me along. I felt free.

One year later, we got married in the gazebo out behind that very same bar. On our honeymoon to Calgary, I received a warning from the customs agent that "I was responsible" for you from now on, because I had proper proof of citizenship and you only had a driver's license. It was funny at the time. I was so happy, I wanted to be responsible for you, and you for me.

We moved to Montana and started our great adventure together. Just getting there was an adventure. Remember how we locked the keys in the car at Old Faithful, and when the windshield wipers went out as we drove over Livingston Pass in the snow? You had to stick your head out the window to see where we were going. I was laughing, but you were pretty nervous.

We had a lot to learn about living in the Rocky Mountains. We learned what alpenglow is, and we re-learned how to drive. Remember that day we sat in the backyard in lawn chairs with a bottle of champagne chilling in the snow, watching the cats trying to figure out how to move about in that white stuff? We made some great friends, and we made some great memories.

We worked hard and we played hard. The only constraints we had were that we had to work to pay for the play. We could spontaneously take off for a weekend, or stay in our pajamas all day and watch icicles form on the eaves or snow transform the world outside the window. In the summer, we enjoyed watching tanagers and orioles in the fruit trees, fossil hunting near Fairy Lake, or taking a drive through "The Park" to enjoy the view—the elk and the bison. We also spent a lot of time at the Hub Bar. Too much time. Too much money. Every small town parade or festival was a day full of drinking. Starting with Bloody Marys for breakfast and ending sometime in the afternoon when we had no business driving home to sleep it off.

I used to think it was charming and adorable that you saw the world around you through the eyes of a child. You taught me how to catch a lizard with a lasso made from a blade of grass. You taught me to appreciate the natural beauty of the world around me. You taught me to see with new eyes. Our friends called me a saint for putting up with your antics. Oh, they enjoyed the "show" when you were on a roll, making everyone laugh for hours. How many times have you claimed to be twelve years old as a way of explaining your antics? How many times did the bartender threaten to duct tape your mouth? But there were many times when they were relieved that I was making you take me home. Why do you think they called me Saint Martha?

I did not realize it at first, but after our cat died, you sank into a depression that consumed both of us. You blamed me because I authorized the vet to do a biopsy without consulting you, and the cat died under anesthesia. At first, I understood your pain and grief. I grieved too; so I accepted the guilt you dumped on me. Pets are family members, but I did not realize that you were an exceptionally sensitive and compassionate "cat daddy."

You started spending more and more time at the bar. You seldom did the chores around the house that you had done for years. We started fighting about money, drinking, and responsibility. We never resolved anything. We just went on with whatever the day, or week, or month or fate had in store for us. The laughter and love that had made us so happy was fading fast. We tried marriage counseling, but your heart was never in it. Counseling is a concept you do not really believe in, so it was a waste of time and money.

"So why have you come to see me?" asked the therapist.

He was at least ten years younger than either of us, and I wasn't at all sure he was dry behind the ears. I had been in and out of therapy since this guy was in high school. You had never been to a counselor in your life and weren't happy about being there.

"He has been spending all his time and our money at the bar. We are fighting all the time. Something has to change."

"Is that true?" the counselor asked you.

"No," you replied. Then, after a long and very awkward pause, you added, "Not all the time."

And, so it went. Every session, a battle to get you to participate in the process. No solutions, just tears of heartbreak for me and stubborn anger from you. After five weeks, we quit counseling. Your only complaint had been that I left empty ice trays in the sink instead of filling them and returning them to the freezer immediately.

I desperately sought some solution. After fifteen years of marriage, I realized that your childlike personality was indelible. I think the drugs you started taking as an adolescent stunted your brain and left you permanently unable to grasp adult concepts. You stopped using hard drugs because I asked you. Now I am beginning to understand the extent of the damage, and it is no longer "cute."

You can fake it pretty well, but everything is a struggle for you. Oh, you were great fun at the bar. You kept everyone in stitches, laughing at your antics. I was the only one who knew that you had real difficulty coping with anything that was unfamiliar. Simple things like finding an address for the first time or writing a check at the grocery store. I have been "taking care" of you since the day we met.

Last night, we stayed too long at the bar. For two hours, I asked you to take me home. Finally, I decided to walk home. Apparently, this got your attention. You finally left the bar, got into a small fender bender, and had a panic attack. You were obviously too drunk to drive. We were lucky last night. Right up until we started fighting again. Then, the unthinkable happened. You hit me. I had enough of that when I was married to Tom. I kept tolerating his abuse because I was too scared to be a high school dropout with two kids and no husband. I am a different person now.

All my life people who were supposed to take care of me have abandoned me. I have always been the one to make sacrifices to keep relationships intact. I love you with all my heart, and I have worked desperately to salvage our marriage. But, I am tired of having to be the responsible one. This is the hardest thing I have ever had to do. But I feel like I am living with a stranger. I have struggled for many months about what to do. Sometimes, I'm not sure if I live with Dr. Jekyll or Mr. Hyde. I have pleaded with you, and I have threatened you because I truly believe that you are mentally ill and in desperate need of professional help, which you refuse to consider. I realize that we all have to make our own choices, and I have no right to tell you what to choose. However, I must choose to protect myself from emotional— and now physical—harm, even if that means I have to live without you.

I don't want to do this. I cherish the memories I have written about here. I wish we could go back and recreate that joy. My heart aches. Literally, my chest hurts as I write this, but, you have to leave.

I do not know what will happen next. I need time to come to grips with this. I respect myself too much now to let this happen to me again. You can blame me for saying "the wrong thing" that set you off. Tom used to say that, too. You can say that I am a "man hater," that I drove you to lash out at me physically. Tom used to say that, too. You can say this is my fault, but Tom used to say that, too. I don't buy it anymore. You need to grow up and accept the consequences of your actions. I won't be there to help you up anymore. One thing I do know is that I will survive. I always survive.

Love,

Martha

# Down and Dirty on the Mekong River

## Inga Aksamit

I squeezed my legs together with all the strength I could muster. "I'm not going to fall off. I'm not going to fall off," I muttered to myself. I dug my fingers into the tough, leathery surface attempting to gain more purchase, but the slowly heaving mass beneath me oscillated from side to side throwing me off balance. I rode it out, feeling relatively secure. I had elephant riding down. All I had to do was roll with it. It was simple. The speed picked up, but I maintained my grip and swayed with the rhythm of the exaggerated dance. I had seen my husband Steve slide off his behemoth moments before, falling three feet into the muddy Mekong River with a big splash, and I was determined not to follow. I heard voices calling commands to the elephants in Lao. Oh, good, I thought, maybe the twelve-year-old trainers can get this elephant under control.

Yesterday we had found ourselves with extra time in Luang Prabang, Laos. Strolling along Sisavangvong Road, the main drag in the historic UNESCO World Heritage town, we had searched for something to do. We were in the midst of a five-month trip through Southeast Asia, Australia and New Zealand with only a vague idea of the itinerary. It sounds very spontaneous, but we were planners by nature and had sketched out a rough blueprint. True to form, we had stuck closely to it and the plan had been unfolding nicely. In Luang Prabang the schedule had crumbled. There had been no problem getting a flight from Thailand to Laos, but when we decided it was time to travel on to Cambodia there were no open flights for days. We exhausted every online possibility, then went to a travel agent who confirmed that there were no empty seats. I tried to be philosophical but was vexed to have lost control over our departure.

Killing time admiring colorful gardens tucked into side streets, we debated what to do with ourselves. Though it was early, the daily procession of saffron-robed monks collecting alms from villagers and tourists was long gone. That was a tourist rite of passage I decided to skip. Not only was I loathe to rise at five a.m., but it seemed intrusive to treat the religious ritual of giving alms to the monks as a spiritual photo op.

Ticking off the rest of the activities listed in Lonely Planet, we had already taken a riverboat on the Mekong, seen the Pak Ou Caves with one thousand Buddhas, visited the Big Brother Mouse literacy project, participated in a cooking class, walked to the top of Mount Phousi at sunset and ridden bikes through town. We had even taken a three-day road trip to the Plain of Jars far to the south. We paused in front of a sandwich board advertising an elephant ride. That was something we hadn't done.

The photo showed portly Western tourists in skimpy bathing suits riding elephants. This seemed incongruous because a prominent sign at the airport had cautioned against revealing too much skin in this conservative country. But it looked like fun and we decided to take the plunge, not knowing how literal that would be.

We signed up for the half-day tour from a travel agent who had to shout to be heard over rapper Eminem blaring from a boom box. It was a cross-cultural exchange of sorts. They got our award-winning music in exchange for a ride on their beast of burden.

The next day, a small group of six tourists assembled at the tour operator's office. After a short minibus ride, we disembarked near a pleasant, shady family compound on the bank of the Mekong River. We could look directly across the river to the Pak Ou Caves, now familiar to us since we had visited a few days prior. Three elephants, which comprised their little herd, hoovered their enormous trunks over the ground, searching for edible treats. I tipped my head back and looked way up at the wooden saddle, wondering how we were going to get up there. The guide gestured to the open-air structure. Nervously the six of us clambered up the steep ladder to the platform that allowed us to step off at the height of the elephants' backs. Our elephant, named On, moved into position.

"One of you can sit on the elephant if you wish or you may both sit in the seat," said the young mahout.

I thought sitting on the elephant sounded more exciting than the saddle, but I didn't want to hog the opportunity. Steve declined so I flung my leg over On's back and slipped down to her neck. I tucked my knees behind her gigantic ears that flapped slowly back and forth like a lazy ceiling fan. Following my mahout's instruction, I kept both hands firmly on the two humps at the top of her head. I could feel her solid, bulky muscles working as she picked her way through the woods. Exhilarated to be in such close proximity to the massive beast I giggled and wondered why I hadn't been riding elephants every day in Luong Prabang.

We approached a slight rise as we entered the forest and my smile vanished. Any sense of stability was gone and I thought I was sliding off for sure.

"Uh, is everything ok?" I asked the mahout.

He just nodded, unconcerned. Gradually feeling more comfortable I realized I was secure and got used to the slow, undulating motion. Keeping the elephants focused on the trail was a challenge as they frequently veered off to tear a tasty snack of leaves from low-lying branches. Eventually we made the loop, stopping in a large grassy clearing for photos against a backdrop of sheer cliffs as puffy white clouds drifted across a brilliant blue sky. Beyond the meadow, we descended a gentle incline, which was terrifying. I had just gotten used to the uphill motion, but downhill felt as if I were going to tumble head over, not heels, but head over gigantic head. I pushed firmly on the two knobs of the elephant's neck and crammed my knees behind her ears to hang on. I was happy when the trail leveled out, my legs quivering with the effort to not fall off. This wasn't as easy as it looked.

The morning had been quite cool, so when the mahout asked if we wanted to bathe the elephants I hesitated. "Maybe we could just repeat the walk," I said, knowing we had a long wait while the rest of the group visited the Pak Ou Caves.

"Yes, but I think you will enjoy bathing the elephants. It's fun," he said. Doubtfully, I searched his eyes to see if he was kidding but his expression was most sincere.

"I don't know. I don't think I want to stand around in wet clothes," said Steve. He was even more reluctant than I.

I looked up at the sky, now gray and threatening, and shivered. Finally, I turned to Steve and said, "How many opportunities will we have to bathe elephants in the Mekong?"

"Not too many," said Steve. "Good point." He was game.

"Wonderful. I'm sure you'll enjoy it," said the guide. "You may give your elephants a snack and then we'll take them to the river."

The elephants were rewarded for the forest walk with a good supply of bananas. We each fed our elephant a few, holding the fruit in our outstretched hands. A trunk curled over and plucked the entire thing, skin and all, off our hands and sent them down the hatch. Elephants in the wild have to forage about eighteen hours a day to maintain their considerable bulk. One of the ethical issues with the elephant tourist trade is that if they are forced to work all day trekking or doing demonstrations for tourists, they don't have time to scavenge for food. Similar to many activities that tourists blithely participate in while traveling, elephant riding, a seemingly innocuous activity, is associated with philosophical dilemmas. Many elephants are treated badly during training, even enduring violence and abuse. These long-lived animals form lasting familial relationships, but their social structure is destroyed when they are moved from camp to camp. It's complicated, though. If tourists stop participating, the elephants might be treated worse in agricultural or other work, and tourism dollars support a wide range of economic benefits to the populace.

On was thirty-five years old and had been working in the tourist trade for five years. She was probably enjoying her career change as she had labored in logging camps for many years. She and her two other compatriots appeared to be well cared for, responding to verbal commands from the mahouts, and we never saw a metal prod or whip. Our guide explained that elephants are not native to Luang Prabang and are usually imported from a nearby province in Thailand. I prefer to think that we lucked out, enjoying our elephant ride from a small family-run operation that cares for their animals. Their elephants, who undoubtedly worked very hard in their previous trade, had perhaps been treated more harshly than they were now. I wonder if anyone ever gave them a bath in their previous line of work.

The whine of the boat engine revved up to whisk the other four tourists across the river to see the caves. Steve and I changed into bathing suits and I, wanting to be respectful of the local conservative culture, wore a synthetic T-shirt and sarong over my suit. We each mounted our own elephant this time instead of sharing. As we headed down a very steep slope I mustered my best techniques for staying on, glancing back at Steve. He looked alarmed as he experienced the free-fall sensation of downhill movement on an elephant.

"Just hang on tight and make sure your knees are behind her ears," I said, suddenly the expert in bareback elephant riding.

Not having any idea what bathing an elephant entailed, I envisioned taking the elephant to the bank, getting off and beyond that I could hardly imagine. Didn't they suck up water in their trunk and spray it over their backs, I wondered. I hadn't a clue what our role was going to be.

The mahouts guided our elephants into a shallow eddy where they did, indeed, take a big draw of water and sprayed it over their backs. We got a little wet from the light shower, but it was enjoyable. I loved the sensation of lumbering through the water on the beast and was pleased that we had followed the guide's suggestion. Being above the murky Mekong was vastly preferable to being in it as I imagined that it contained appalling contaminants from its protracted journey from high in the Tibetan Plateau through China and Burma. A gushing waterfall of urine released from Steve's elephant joined the slurry on its way through Laos, Thailand, Cambodia and Viet Nam, to be emptied into the South China Sea many days from now.

The lurching started, mildly at first. I couldn't figure out what was going on. One minute the elephants were just standing around, the next they were rocking and rolling. Luckily it was nothing I couldn't handle. However, I was shocked to see Steve slide off out of the corner of my eye. That's when I started hanging on for dear life. There was no possible way I going in that brown water.

The movements became more extreme and I felt my grip slipping. My toes grazed the chocolate-colored liquid and in an instant it was all over. I was submerged. Laughing uncontrollably, I tried not to swallow any of the river. The two mahouts howled with glee. The air was filled with their shrieks of laughter. The kind of belly laugh that makes you forget you ever had a care in the world. Soon I was splashing around, grabbing onto those huge ears to climb back on, my wet sarong slapping against my legs. Each time I swore I'd hang on tight, only to be dunked again and again. I completely forgot about my concerns and gave in to the pure delight of playing in the water.

The mahouts were shouting and hooting with every plunge. Finally, I caught on. They were hollering commands to the highly intelligent pachyderms and we were part of an amusing show. Like the mechanical bull ride at state fairs across America, there was no staying on. Our guide, bent over laughing from the shore, gasped that we should have a competition to see who could stay on longest. The race was on. The elephants stood still until the mahout yelled a command. Steve fell off immediately. I hung on for a few exhilarating moments, emerging as the clear winner. Advertised as bathing the elephants, it was really bathing the tourists.

When I look back at the trip of a lifetime and replay the blurred images from a half-dozen different countries, bathing the elephants is one that still makes me laugh. How well I remember my determination to stay in control, not knowing that those impish mahouts were in cahoots with their elephants. They delighted in playing a joke on us as we were dumped gleefully back to our carefree childhoods. Frolicking in the Mekong with On showed me that letting go could be a lot of fun after all.

# Finding Myself in California

## Molly Kurland

My body turned to liquid. Everything seemed to be melting as I felt the undulating waves of acid kicking in. Colors poured into each other, whether on walls or on faces. Everything began to be overlaid by its own tapestry of intricate patterns and colorful designs. Sounds were startling, too loud, too sudden. I could feel myself shrinking as I lost the ability to focus. I gave up even trying to make sense of any of it.

My mind stretched to recall how I got here. I had a foggy, dreamlike memory of the plane trip from New Jersey to California, landing in San Francisco just a few hours ago.

The heavy velvet maroon drapes framing the tall bay window of the Victorian house began to dissolve. Cobwebs and dust became rhinestone patterns dancing as I watched, mesmerized.

I slipped deeper into the swirl of faces, sounds, and colors as people entered and left the room, moving around this house that had as many decorative touches as a three-story wedding cake. Every so often, a ripple of anxiety went through me as I wondered if there was something I should be doing other than lying on the floor, curled up among cushions, transfixed.

The large pillows beneath me felt so soft, so comforting—like a cozy nest I wanted to stay in forever. But then I heard my brother's voice and heavy footsteps as he entered the room.

"We've got to get going. There's a show tonight," he said to me. A colorfully painted sign, "Firehouse Theater," dominated the living room. It was my brother's theater company.

My brother had picked me up at the airport earlier that day.

"Welcome to San Francisco," he said as the car moved slowly through traffic in the middle of the city. "Here. Open up." Joel turned around from the front seat and reached toward me with something between his fingers. With his other hand, he popped something into his mouth and gestured for me to open mine. I knew what it was.

I worshipped my brother and the brilliant, creative world of writers and artists who were his friends from his Harvard days when Timothy Leary taught there. I was a bit nervous taking his acid since I was already somewhat disoriented from my flight. Still, I trusted my older brother. He would take care of me.

A moment later, I felt a rush of fear envelope me. What had I gotten myself into? But I knew it was too late. I wanted to fit in so badly. I would have done anything he suggested.

The rest dissolved like a dream as I felt a rhythm pulsing through me, my senses flooded with stimuli as a humming buzzed through my entire being. Members of the theater commune wandered about the large, nineteenth-century house, and the sound of their voices became part of the room, like the flowered wallpaper and the decorative molding. A few of them came over to me to introduce themselves.

"Welcome to California," they greeted me.

"I'm Carolyn," said a tall, smiling woman who had shoulder-length, curly blond hair and wire rimmed glasses. "We have a room for you, up on the third floor, that looks right out onto the roof."

"Hi, name's Ed," said a man with a long dark ponytail that hung down to his waist. His dark brown eyes seemed very intelligent as if he was reading my thoughts. "Your brother says you're a weaver."

Yes. I was. I made my first tapestry loom when I was fifteen and was teaching myself to weave.

The theater was small. The audience encircled the stage.

The company engaged with members of the audience and brought them into the story. For a brief moment, I could still differentiate between the stage, the actors, and the audience. But shortly, one of the actors took my hand and led me into the circle of the stage. At that point, I was truly lost. All the people whom I had just met had different names now, as they played characters in the play.

After the play ended, someone gently took my hand and led me back to the big, three-story Victorian house on Gough Street and brought me up to the third floor, to a room surrounded by windows that indeed looked out onto the roof. There was a mattress on the floor, which served as a bed and was covered with Indian bedspreads, where they had made a place for me. I slipped under the covers and settled into the padding, looking out the windows, watching stars dance as the drug slowly dissipated and eventually left my system and let me sleep. It was my first day in California. I was seventeen.

I lasted three weeks in the theater commune. My brother did not really want to take care of me, and it wasn't long before I realized I had to get out of there.

I rented a tiny one-room studio in Berkeley that I had all to myself. It was near a weaving studio where I began taking classes. My little nest had a two-burner hot plate where I could cook, and I used the bathroom sink to wash my dishes. I loved it. I even had friends over for dinner parties where I made crepes in my makeshift bedroom-living-room-kitchen.

Geraldine, the head weaver of the studio, was a small, wiry woman with short brown hair and a face that easily broke out into smiles. She had operated large weaving studios in New York and in Greece where she designed commercially woven fabrics. She showed me how to set up a four-harness floor loom and taught me to weave complex designs. I became totally absorbed in experimenting with colors and textures. Teach me everything you know, I implored her. Over the next several months, she did her best.

Here I thrived.

Then I met Mark. He was a weaving student, a tall slender man who always had a stocking knit hat perched on his head. He wore loose, blousy shirts—almost like a pirate's costume and Birkenstock sandals. I loved his sincere blue eyes and his soothing, calm demeanor. He was practicing Zen Buddhism and planned to eventually study at Tassajara in Carmel Valley. We became fast friends, taking breaks to explore the many vegetarian restaurants Berkeley had to offer.

"What will you do when I go away?" Mark asked me one day over a bowl of vegetable curry. Days at the weaving studio and evenings with Mark had become my life. It was nearing the time when he would leave to begin his studies.

"I don't know," I confessed. But I told him I couldn't relate very well to the loud political activists who populated much of Berkeley. I liked being part of a food cooperative, inhaling the rich aromas of brie and cheddar as I performed my tasks as Cheese Coordinator. There were two main factions among the counterculture movement of the 1970s. There were the political activists and the "back to the land" farmers. I found the demonstrators a bit too confrontational. I was drawn much more to the organic gardeners who were forming rural communities.

I shared this with Mark.

"I've got to get you out of here," he said.

He sensed my yearning for a place where I could grow a garden and be closer to nature. One spring day, he and I hitchhiked up to

Sonoma County. There I discovered green rolling hills and open space where I could breathe easier. On a bulletin board in a natural foods market, we found a notice for a small cottage in Cotati that I could share with a couple of college students. I rented a room, moved in, and entered Sonoma State University in the fall.

My first class was "Myths, Dreams, and Symbols," a study of Jungian Psychology. As I entered the classroom, the sounds of Cat Stevens' "Where Do the Children Play" filled the room and created a welcoming atmosphere. I was immediately soothed. The teacher had set up an arrangement of photos, books, and objects throughout the room for us to observe and see what sorts of emotions they invoked in us. We walked around the room, silently observing everything for about ten minutes. Then he had us all gather in a circle where we sat, sharing our thoughts and feelings stimulated by the symbolic objects he had carefully placed around us. I took a breath and felt my whole being relax. I did not want to go anywhere. I knew these were my people. I felt completely at home.

# Greyhound to California

## Marcia Hart

The day I had planned for months had finally arrived. On a hot, humid day in 1959, I stepped aboard a Greyhound bus with my ticket to Los Angeles clutched in my sweaty hand. The bus driver had just slammed the door on the cargo bin after casually tossing my battered camp footlocker, packed to the gills with my most important possessions, inside. I was both nervous and excited to finally make my escape.

A year shy of my bachelor's degree and a teaching credential, I had decided another year under the same roof with an angry, alcoholic father, a mother who coped as well as she could but was missing the loving-mother gene, a schizophrenic brother who was in and out of the state mental hospital, and a narcissistic sister was more than I was willing to tolerate. Living in a conservative community as a young closeted lesbian, a word I would learn later, only added to my urge to flee.

After the first hour on the road my good friend, Joanne, who had graduated in June, boarded the bus in Indianapolis. We would be joining two other recent grads in LA, and the four of us planned to share an apartment. The three grads had teaching jobs while I would be scrambling to find something to sustain me until I could return to school. That was the plan, and it was now in motion.

It didn't take long for my initial excitement to wear off. It was a very long trip in so many ways. Cornfields were followed by more cornfields—all well beyond the knee-high stage. Crossing the Mississippi for the first time at St. Louis might have been interesting for a few minutes, but there's not much to see when it's dark. Kansas was mostly wheat fields with only the occasional hint of a gently rolling hill in the distance. Our route through the southeast corner of Colorado bypassed the scenic Rockies, and it was fairly desolate. I don't remember New Mexico. Northern Arizona was flat and arid with the occasional sign informing us of the number of miles to the Grand Canyon turnoff, but there was never a hint of a canyon from where we sat. It was similar to being on an airplane when the pilot feels the need to inform everyone of all the amazing land features below that can't be seen due to cloud cover. Finally, we crossed the California state line and the Mojave Desert through Needles and Barstow——an area that's far from the most interesting the state has to offer.

Some memories stand out of the long hours on the bus. Joanne and I tried playing cards but that got old fairly quickly. My eyes burned with fatigue and soon made reading impossible. And, Joanne did not provide the companionship I had imagined. She was more than a little depressed over a relationship that had not survived the summer, and she slept or kept to herself most of the time.

With a sense of being alone while not alone much of the time, I was vaguely aware of the other bored, tired passengers with glazed eyes and, occasionally, expired deodorant. Some read and others slept or talked quietly while I found myself wrestling with stuck windows trying to get access to fresh air or walking up and down the aisle until the grumpy bus driver told me to sit down. We all spent a fair amount of time staring through the dirty windows at the mind-numbing landscape. When the 24-hour cycle brought darkness each night, I found myself leaning against the same dirty window with my head itching for a shampoo and, after a day or so, my body ached to be horizontal. Too tired and uncomfortable to sleep, with black nothingness on the other side of the glass and the constant drone of the motor in my head, I occasionally checked my watch then counted to 3600 to see how close I could come to nailing an hour. I got pretty good at the mindless game I invented, but it never put me to sleep.

Then there were the usual meal breaks plus pit stops every couple of hours. It was such a relief to get off the bus, breathe fresh air, stretch my body, and have a brief stroll. Those few minutes of exercise were the best part of every pause from the tedium of the bus ride.

Breakfast was usually a greasy, overcooked egg with greasier undercooked bacon and a slab of cold Wonder Bread toast. Burned coffee was inevitably followed by indigestion a short time later. The noon meal was always a juiceless gray burger and limp fries accompanied by a chocolate shake that was the culinary highlight of each day. Dinner was something like a bowl of chili and cornbread that did not bring Mom's cooking to mind. Too bad I had not thought to pack some Tums.

Teeth were brushed over sinks with hair and paper clogging the drains and nicotine burn stains on the ancient, once-white porcelain. Walls were hung with cracked, water-spattered mirrors. Each visit to a toilet stall was a potential misadventure where I might find a toilet seat I wouldn't dare sit on or a toilet bowl that hadn't been cleaned in way too long. Stall doors with broken latches were the norm. Sometimes I hit the trifecta and got all three.

That two-thousand-mile-plus trip from Muncie to Los Angeles felt interminable, and my ability to daydream became my savior. As I stared off into and through the passing landscape during long periods of otherwise unrelieved monotony, I tried to envision what my life was about to become. I pictured finding a job, saving money for school then resuming my studies when I could afford to. I tried to imagine my life in a part of the country I'd only seen in magazines and movies. I wondered what the apartment Amy and Carol had rented looked like. What would it be like living in a place where it never snowed in the winter and rarely rained in the summer? Where there would be an ocean nearby and orange trees growing in people's yards? Would I be able to find a job I could get to by bus? Those daydreams, and many more, were a great escape and made the journey tolerable for hours at a time.

After those four long days on the road, we finally arrived at the Greyhound station in a seedy section of downtown LA. My stomach lurched as the smell of unwashed bodies combined with the noxious odor of diesel exhaust and whatever was being cooked at a nearby greasy-spoon restaurant slammed into my nasal passages.

We slowly made our way through the crowded space between buses. I saw people dressed like anyone might back home: men in suits, ties, and fedoras: women wearing flower print summer dresses and costume jewelry, a couple of girls in poodle skirts and sleeveless blouses with bobby sox and saddle shoes, several guys with pegged Levi's, plain white tee shirts, and the occasional sleeve rolled over a pack of Marlboros. There were also people dressed very unlike folks in the Midwest. I saw my first saris, turbans, and brightly patterned muumuus. There was an old man in Hasidic attire with a full beard and sidelocks. And I should probably mention the good-looking cowboy who was wearing tight dirty jeans and a plaid shirt with snaps instead of buttons. His black felt Stetson was pulled low over his sunglass-covered eyes, and he had a bit of a swagger as he walked along in his well-worn high-heeled pointy-toed western boots. I halfway expected to see him pull a saddle out of the bus storage bin, throw it over his shoulder, then thumb a ride to Hollywood.

In spite of the din of idling bus motors, a crying baby, and a man's voice blaring constantly from the loudspeaker overhead, I was able to hear bits of conversations in many unfamiliar foreign languages. While my visual, auditory, and olfactory senses were dealing with these vaguely unsettling circumstances, the rest of my fatigued body was feeling the pushes and shoves of passengers eager to retrieve their luggage from the bowels of the bus so they could find their way to whatever was next.

We were almost there, but not quite. Amy had mailed details of the buses we would need to catch to take us from point A, the bus station, to point B, the apartment in West LA. Even with a map, a list of the bus numbers, and where to get off each one, we were apprehensive as we set out with our footlockers in tow. Trying to operate in a zombie-like state did not enhance our confidence.

After getting directions at the Traveler's Aid booth, we walked a couple of long trash-littered blocks past sleazy bars—one with an unshaven drunk leaning against the door jamb, an unlit cigarette dangling from his lips while he ogled us through blood-shot eyes—pawn shops with schlock-filled windows, an overflowing trash bin or two, and used clothing stores with racks of well-worn suits, shirts and dresses on the sidewalk. We had hoped to see a decent-looking cafe as we were becoming seriously hungry, but that was not to be, and we would have to wait for food as well as the bus. When we got to our corner, we were relieved to see an empty bench.

With our footlockers at our feet, we sat down to await bus number one. Too weary to talk, we stared off into space, barely noticing the long line of men outside the Union Rescue Mission across the street, apparently waiting for the noon meal service to begin.

We were only there a few minutes when the bus we were looking for pulled up and opened its door. After we climbed aboard—footlockers and all—I asked the driver if he would let us know when we would need to get off. Fortunately, he and each succeeding bus driver made sure we got off at the correct stop to catch the next bus in the series; thus, our fears of becoming lost or stranded did not materialize. In retrospect, it's clear the long-haul Greyhound drivers we encountered who were as bored and disengaged as their passengers, while the city bus drivers who were constantly involved with stops, traffic challenges, new passengers, and problems to solve were alert, fully engaged and helpful. We took it as a good sign.

We had no idea, when we climbed aboard that first bus, our inner city trip would take over three hours. We were grateful to have enough time at one of the many stops to greedily devoured our first-ever tacos—two each—at a nearby Taco-Tia. By far the best meal since Indiana.

We struggled off the last of many buses and for a minute, gloried in the fresh air and perfect weather. We trudged off to finish our journey on foot. We had fifteen or twenty long blocks ahead of us. We somehow found the energy to keep going, trusting with each step we were getting closer to the apartment building with the number we were seeking, and it was awaiting us at the end of a very long rainbow.

On that last leg of our marathon, with our cheap metal footlockers scarring the concrete sidewalk as we dragged them behind us, I got my first close-up look at Los Angeles beyond the less-than-charming downtown area we'd been in earlier. Houses and apartment buildings were made of what I would learn was stucco. Some were modern and unadorned while a few were beautiful examples of art deco architecture. They came in an amazing array of pastel colors that were an exotic contrast to the white clapboard homes of my childhood neighborhood.

Even the yards were exotic. I noticed many landscaped areas had a strange-looking ground cover with tiny flat leaves—*dichondra*, I would later learn—and many other plants I'd never seen such as *bougainvillea* and *ceanothus*, *coreopsis* and cactus, and even a fully loaded orange tree just as I had envisioned in my daydreams. Of course, I had seen palm trees in movies but these were real and close enough to touch—some tall and slender, some short and squatty. The air was different, too; it had a slight smell—almost a taste—to it that turned out to be related to smog. Some of the lawns were even watered by automatic sprinklers. A fine mist from the spray cooled our skin as we continued along. It was a delicious and unexpected treat. It was all alien and a wonderful distraction during the seemingly never-ending hike.

Of course, it did end. When we finally saw the apartment number an overwhelming sense of relief washed over me. We had arrived. The apartment that had begun to feel like a desert oasis mirage did exist and it was about to become my first home independent of my family. My new life was about to begin and I felt a thrill of excitement.

Amy's letter had told us where to find the key; Joanne retrieved it and let us in. As I followed her across the threshold, I looked around at the bright, freshly painted apartment, filled with Scandinavian-style modern furnishings. Even the furniture was different in California.

I gently closed the door behind me and slowly released the grip of my stiff, aching fingers from the leather handle of my footlocker. Reaching into the pocket of my seriously grubby jeans, I felt the crumpled, worn stub of the one-way ticket to LA I had been clutching when I boarded the bus in Muncie four days earlier. My palms were not sweaty this time. I had done it. My escape was complete, and I felt both pride and confidence; my life-long love affair with the state that would prove to be truly golden for me had begun.

# Honoring My Father

## Mary Lynn Archibald

"I'm tired of waiting for your father to put up that kitchen spice shelf I've been wanting," said my mother. "I'm just going to hang it myself."

I watched her spend the better part of a morning struggling with her project. But she was clever. She hung it slightly crooked. When Daddy came home tired from work that night she showed it to him proudly, but he couldn't stand to look at it another minute. Didn't even sit down. Put down his briefcase and took off his coat and called for his toolbox. Hung the shelf properly then and there, right before supper.

It was miraculous.

*She can manipulate him so easily.* I thought. *He's weak. I am ashamed of him.* My real fear was that I was like him. I hated him for that.

I had cultivated a healthy rebelliousness by the time I was six, and as I was an only child and she was the one close by, my mother got the worst of it. To counteract this terrible behavior, she resorted to corporal punishment—but not administered by her. No, she preferred a threat with a delayed payoff that was supposed to act as an inducement for future good conduct.

"Wait till your father gets home." she would pronounce, scowling darkly in my direction, and though I prayed that she would be struck by amnesia before five o'clock, it never happened. Unfailingly, she would find a reason to lurk near the big picture window in the living room just at five, pretending to dust or straighten furniture, but we both knew she was watching and listening for *him.*

As soon as his car pulled into the driveway in front of our modest frame house (identical to all the other houses on the block, except for the bizarre spectacle of a family of white plaster ducks that marched in frozen lockstep across the lawn), she would station herself at the front door, and as my father trickled wearily through it, she would pounce.

With scarcely a hello or a peck on the cheek, she would grab him forcibly by the arm and hiss at him, "She's been insufferable again. I warned her she would get a spanking when you got home, but that didn't even slow her down. She's been *really* naughty."

Ambushed, my father had to perform or appear weak in her eyes. He would glance apologetically at me over her shoulder, pleading for forgiveness in advance for what he was about to do.

Sighing deeply, he would drag himself over to where I was standing. "It seems we have a date in the bedroom," he would say, voice heavy with regret. "Come on. Let's get quit of it and maybe we can enjoy the rest of the day."

Was he nuts? He was the enemy, and he addressed me as a co-conspirator. Once I risked a glance over my shoulder at my mother as we left the room. Her lovely face was screwed into a furious frown: head thrown back, green eyes flashing. She knew he was weak, too.

He always cried as he spanked me. Afterward, he would remain in the bedroom, curled on the bed, tears running unheeded down his tired, sad face. Often, he didn't appear at dinner. Claimed he couldn't eat.

"I hope you understand that this is all your fault," she would say vindictively, and I knew that I was the sole source of his agony.

For my part, I let her know that I shared her contempt for his frailty. "He had a choice," I said.

*Weak as water*, I thought defiantly. No mama's boy was going to make me feel guilty.

It was many years before I understood that his pain in punishing me came from a deep love, and that it was exceedingly difficult for him to punish me when he'd not directly experienced the misdeeds that were the cause of the spanking.

In my early teens I found myself even more profoundly ashamed of his milquetoast approach to human interaction. I fervently prayed that my friends wouldn't notice his spinelessness—the ease with which he could be used. "Oh, I understand perfectly," he would say to angry customers. "I'll take care of it right away." I didn't learn until years later that the customer is always right, especially when one is doing business in a small town like ours.

I turned seventeen and moved out of the house, abandoning my college career after only one year due to lack of funds. I got a job. I got an apartment. I made a few tentative and ill-advised attempts at forming love relationships.

Only once during this time did my father try to interfere in my flight to independence. I had found myself a screwed-up young poet and was threatening to let him move in with me. I even took him home to meet the folks.

I hadn't been back at my apartment for more than a day before Daddy called.

"Listen, sweetie," he said. "I thought I'd come over this weekend and take my little girl out to dinner."

Leaden thoughts and fears I had not acknowledged knocked wildly around the region of my heart. I mumbled assent and named a date and a restaurant where we could meet—neutral territory from which to stage the upcoming battle.

I took longer to get ready for that evening than I had for any previous date. He was there early, looking as sad as he had when he used to spank me on my mother's orders.

"Well," he said, as he held the door for me, "I hope this is a really nice place tonight. It's not often I get to take you out on a date."

Over dessert, he finally got to the point around which we had both been dancing all evening.

"Look, honey," he said tentatively. "You know I don't ever like to interfere in your life." He looked at me hopefully.

"But you're going to anyway," I said, as sarcastically as possible.

My father sighed heavily and began again. "I know you don't want to hear this," he said, "but I could never forgive myself if I didn't say something."

"So say it."

"Okay. I . . . well, I think your new friend has some serious problems. He just doesn't ring true to me; you know?"

"No."

"Well, it's like this." He took off his glasses and rubbed his nose thoughtfully. "I think there's something about him that makes him hate women. I've seen it before. I don't know what it is, but it's there, and I'm afraid he'll hurt you. I was so worried after I met him that I couldn't sleep at all. Call it a hunch, but I've learned to trust them."

"Well, I don't." I said, sullen and annoyed. "I can't believe you're questioning my judgment, Daddy. I'm a grown-up woman, after all."

In my mind, a small voice was screaming, "He knows! He knows I slept with Cornell. How does he know?" I rubbed my forehead, blushing, sure there was a scarlet "A" emblazoned there.

"I understand how you feel—you like this guy a lot. But maybe that's why it's hard to see what I see. I'm outside, looking in. I'm scared. He scares me. I just want you to tread carefully."

Then he said the one thing I dreaded he'd say: "Anyway, I trust you to use the good judgment I know you have, and do the right thing. I know you will."

There it was. The statement I could not ignore. I knew now that as sure as sunrise I would have to face the realization that had been nagging at me for the last several weeks. That this relationship, which I had guarded so carefully, was in some secret way, ultimately destructive.

In the frenzy of my desire to kill the messenger, I hated my father at that point. But I loved him too. For angry as I was, I knew that it had cost him dearly to make his announcement to me, knowing the effect it would have ahead of time.

Assertiveness training was something that never showed up in my family. But I learned from my father that day that when you love someone you must speak even though it's painful to you and to him or her. I was humbled by that knowledge.

"Sure, Daddy. I'll think about it, but I do love Cornell."

At least I thought I did. I had slept with him, after all. "I don't think I'll change my mind."

~*~

I never fully understood my father's quiet power until the death of my second husband. On that sad, horrifying occasion, my father demonstrated true heroism, even as he floundered through his own pain.

My second husband, a college professor I'd dated for three months before I married him, seemed to love my children. I thought I loved him, too. But now, I think it was more likely that he represented security to me, as my first husband, the children's father, had left us rather abruptly. I had been feeling alone, abandoned and scared. More than anything, I wanted a father for my poor, rudderless children.

Only fourteen months after we married, the professor took his own life one night, and we were suddenly left alone once again.

My mother and father traveled two hours to where I was to collect me, take me home, and cradle me in their protective arms.

As the gray morning dawned, I awoke a howling, sniveling mass of mental agony. I could not function; I could only cry.

But arrangements needed to be made. There was a body to be collected, there was a funeral to plan.

And I was unable to think.

It was Daddy, my quiet, sometimes ineffectual, unassuming Daddy, who took care of it all for me. Neither my mother nor I could have done it. She was only holding herself together for my sake. As a mother myself, I now know there is no more difficult experience than sharing the pain of a child.

After that shattering occasion, I began to think of my father with the respect he had always deserved.

And there were other things.

When I found myself suddenly widowed, I was also unemployed. I had taken a year off work to go back to school and earn a teaching credential. My husband had put a gun to his head during the Easter vacation, after which I was scheduled to go into the classroom for the first time to do my student teaching.

There was nothing for it but to finish, so my father decided that the best thing for the children and me was to take the kids into his own home and enroll them in the local school. That way I would have only two things to concentrate on—my student teaching, and my grief.

I would spend each week in the classroom, facing varying degrees of hostility and inattention from my class (mostly attributable to my inexperience, panic and pain). Then, each Friday afternoon I'd drive to my parents' home two hours away to spend the weekend with my children.

It was far from an ideal situation, but my parents embraced it without hesitation, in the same gracious way they had always faced helping anyone who needed them.

And with this new arrangement of our lives, my father soared to new heights of love, sacrifice, and esteem in my view.

He would come home from work in the evenings, never too tired to spend time with my son, instructing him in the ways of men. On weekends, Daddy would take him out into the garage and involve him in his own projects, patiently teaching him how to hammer nails straight, sand wood, and assemble myriad and diverse mechanical parts into coherent wholes.

With my daughter he also labored to take up the daddy slack, spending long hours reading to her, encouraging her, flattering her.

It was as though he knew instinctively what each of the stricken children needed in order to make sense of their severed world. I had never loved him more than I did at that time. Almost overnight, he became a giant to me.

For the rest of his life, I honored him. I still do.

# *How I Fell in Love with an AWOL Paratrooper*

## Pamela Heck

It was the summer after the Summer of Love when I flew from Boston to San Francisco to be in my best friend's wedding. Haight Ashbury was the psychedelic capital of the world. San Francisco State was a hotbed of anti-war activists, and Linda's marriage was taking place at Fort Baker with full military regalia.

After graduation, we traveled in two different directions with one common goal—to get the hell out of Ohio. Now, a year later, I was joining her in San Francisco for the upcoming nuptials. Our friend Lynn was flying in from Cincinnati.

I never would have met Frank if Lynn's plane hadn't dropped an engine over Chicago. During the ensuing emergency, she grabbed the well-muscled arm of her seatmate, who happened to be the current Mr. Cincinnati, and didn't let go until they were safely on the ground. Enjoying the role of protector, Mr. C. invited Lynn on a tour of San Francisco the following day.

Lynn agreed on the condition that he find a date for me. He assured her that he had a number of friends in San Francisco. It would not be a problem.

The following morning, a surly, young Brando look-alike in a torn T-shirt presented himself on Linda's doorstep. Fixing a steely gaze on me, he announced, "I'm not your date." After that curt introduction, he informed us that my date, as well as Lynn's, was waiting at his apartment. Five people could not fit into his dilapidated VW bug, so he had come alone. His name was Richard and he was merely our chauffeur. He made that very clear.

Despite a jaw-dropping ride up and down the hills of San Francisco, we were soon in Haight Ashbury. Political posters and peace signs obliterated shop windows, making it hard to see what they were actually selling. Victorian houses lined the street, some faded and shabby, others awash in color.

Richard's apartment was sparsely furnished. A teabag hung from an old chandelier in the middle of the living room. I found out later, it was an easy, economical way to make tea. One simply had to bring a cup of hot water to the teabag and jiggle it until the water changed color. Ingenious.

90

We stood in uncomfortable silence for a few moments until a figure emerged through a doorway at the back of the room.

"That," said Richard, "is your date."

The young man was small, compact, and perfectly proportioned. He wore John Lennon glasses, bell-bottom pants, and beads. What he was not wearing was a shirt. I liked what I saw.

"Hi, I'm Frank."

"Pam," I said, secretly cursing my pixie haircut and madras plaid windbreaker. I would divest myself of the windbreaker as soon as possible. Growing out my hair would take some time. Frank didn't seem to mind.

He grabbed a shirt and the four of us grabbed a bus. My date was enthusiastic and charming. Mr. C. was cold. He was hungry. He was hungry again. He complained bitterly about the weather and his inability to find a good hamburger. Finally, after disappearing to make a phone call, Mr. C. returned to tell us he had changed his plans. He was leaving tomorrow on the next leg of his trip: Hawaii. It was warm in Hawaii.

Now, Frank and I had a dilemma. I was smitten. So, it seemed, was he. However, Linda was immersed in wedding plans and I wasn't going to leave Lynn on her own. Frank would have to find her a date. I'm not sure how he managed it, but the next day he showed up with Richard in tow. Even more amazing, it was soon evident that Richard really liked Lynn. He was actually smiling. We had coupled up.

Frank was a great listener. He plied me with questions about my past, my job, and my life. Yet he seemed reluctant to discuss himself. Despite diverting many of my questions back to me, I eventually learned that he was also from Cincinnati, had dropped out of college, and was raised by his widowed mother.

Finally, I blurted out, "So, Frank, what is it you do exactly?"

"Well . . . uh . . . actually . . . I'm AWOL from the paratroopers."

I was speechless.

"I was about to be shipped to Vietnam. Since I had a furlough, I thought I'd spend a few days with Richard before I left. He really opened my eyes . . . told me how we were bombing innocent women and children . . . that it's genocide . . . immoral. I see that now. So, Hell, no, I won't go. I simply can't."

"But what's going to happen now, Frank? What will you do?"

"Eventually I'll have to turn myself in. My best bet is to try for an insanity plea and hope for a medical discharge."

The Vietnam War was tearing the country apart. I was solidly against it. I saw Frank not as a deserter, but as a dissident hero. My hero. My Frankie.

Lynn was dating a conscientious objector, I was dating a deserter, and Linda's future husband and all his groomsmen were recently decommissioned air force officers—everyone a Viet Nam vet. Linda divulged the military status of our admirers to her fiancé. As a result, our hippie lovers were in imminent danger of being beaten up. We were forewarned.

That time has taken on a dreamlike quality—some moments blurred, some as sharp as yesterday. We danced at the Fillmore and watched Janis swill bourbon and belt out the blues with Big Brother and the Holding Company. The Who smashed their instruments on stage for our gratification. At night we made love on a mattress in Richard's kitchen. In the daytime we stowed the mattress and Frank made a seemingly endless supply of Infinity Soup—so named because it contained an infinite number of things we had on hand. The one ingredient that never varied was peanut butter. Infinity Soup required peanut butter.

One night when Frank and I were exploring the Haight, I found myself peering into the window of a head shop. A small, beaded, wire contraption intrigued me.

"Frankie, what's that?"

"Why, that's a roach clip."

"A roach clip? Who in the world would want to catch a roach with that?"

"No, honey, not that kind of roach. It's to hold the last little bit of a joint, so you don't burn your fingers. That part of a joint is called the roach."

To his credit, he kept a straight face. I had a lot to learn.

Sometimes we did things with Lynn and Richard. Other times it was just the two of us, like the night we spent hours drawing psychedelic designs on a sketchpad and coloring them in with crayons we bought at the head shop.

"Wow! Far out, honey." Frank always admired my work.

I can still see him poring over the stock market section of the Examiner. In another life, Frank invested in the stock market and had done quite well. I got a lecture on the volatility of pork bellies. At that time, they were up. The irony of getting instructions on how to invest in pork bellies from a vegetarian Jewish peacenik in the heart of the Haight didn't occur to me until much later.

I was addicted to wearing dramatic make-up. Frank wanted my face completely natural.

"You wouldn't paint the rocks at Big Sur. Why are you painting your face?"

I didn't get it until the four of us went to Big Sur. We left San Francisco in the middle of the night. Richard's Volkswagen ran on only three cylinders and there was a huge hole in the floorboard by my feet, but it got us there.

At sunrise, we climbed down a steep hill to our own private beach. I was stoned. We all were. Seconds stretched like minutes before us. Hand-in-hand, Frank and I floated down the beach toward the water, our footsteps and the world around us moving in slow motion. Lazy waves rolled in, slowly swelling to a brief crescendo before drifting down to caress the shore and ultimately, my toes, my knees, my thighs. A molten sun lit up the ocean and the rocks. The rocks themselves were huge monoliths rising up from the ocean floor, drenched in spray. Of course I wouldn't paint those rocks. They were perfect, and Frankie thought I was, too.

Sadly, I had to return to Boston. To my roommate's chagrin, Frank followed me. Within a few weeks we were reunited. Since he had spent all his defense money on me, Frank found a job at a local carwash. We weren't in San Francisco, but we were together. In a month or so, Frank would return to the West Coast to surrender himself. I tried not to think about it. In the meantime, I had an idea. I would take my lover home to meet the folks.

Dad met us at the door. He wore a button-down shirt and dress slacks. Frank wore his usual bell-bottoms and beads. They both opted to wear a necktie though the effect was startlingly different. A manly handshake took place and I hoped for the best. My mother would be a harder nut to crack. She was already upset over the fact that Frank was a vegetarian. I had relayed that information by phone a few days prior to our visit.

"That's ridiculous," she snapped. "What will I cook?"

"He eats fish." I said, trying to put her back in her comfort zone. She knew how to cook fish.

I realize now that my parents were horrified by our visit. What passed for normal in San Francisco was terribly out of context in small-town America. To their credit, they were more than civil. Proper etiquette demanded nothing less.

My mother decked the table with her finest china and crystal. Frank admired the crystal. Picking up his glass, he twirled it under the chandelier.

"Oh, wow, honey, a light show!"

Mom twitched, Dad's jaw tightened. Things were not going as well as I hoped. They took a downturn when my dad asked Frank what he did for a living.

"Well, I'm working in a car wash right now. I'm actually really enjoying it. Great bunch of guys. I can see myself doing that for quite some time."

At that point, I kicked Frank under the table.

"I'm sorry, dear, did I say something wrong?"

After dinner my parents gave Frank the obligatory tour of their almost new dream home followed by a look at the yard. The lot behind our property had not yet been developed. A field of wild grasses rippled softly in the late afternoon breeze.

"Wow, beautiful," exclaimed Frank.

Mom winced. She didn't say anything about it then, but she let me have it later.

"Weeds? Beautiful? That's just crazy."

I'm not sure if it was one more "wow" or the comment about the weeds that incensed her.

Months later, I got a phone call from my parents. They wanted to let me know that money was no object. They would get me a good lawyer.

"What are you talking about?" I asked, totally perplexed.

"Honey, we realize that the only reason you would be with someone like Frank was if he were blackmailing you. Whatever it is, we're behind you. We love you."

I was stunned. What in the world did they think I had done that would merit a blackmail attempt? I didn't have any money anyway. Convincing them I didn't need a lawyer took some time and they hung up with the conviction that they had an idiot for a daughter, at least when it came to matters of the heart.

94

Soon after the ill-fated dinner, Frank flew to San Francisco and turned himself in. He faced two possible outcomes—the brig or the psyche ward at Letterman Hospital. Neither was a great choice, but the latter offered the possibility of a medical discharge. Frank just needed to convince the military he was crazy. That wasn't too difficult since his mental condition had begun to deteriorate the closer he came to surrendering.

Frank presented himself to the officer in charge wearing a blue satin tail. Jumping onto the intake desk he ranted and raved, spouting anti-war gibberish. They put him in the psyche ward.

I'm not sure how he gained access to a telephone, but Frank called me from the hospital one day. It took him a long time to say hello.

"Heh . . . heh, . . . hell . . . oh . . ."

"Frankie? Oh my God, honey, how are you? How are they treating you?"

"I . . . duh-don't . . . know. They're sh-shooting me up . . . with Th-thorizine . . . I was wa-walking down the hall . . . down the hall . . . and a guy was . . . ju-just hanging . . . He hu-hung himself . . . I . . . didn't . . . fuh-feel . . . a thing . . . It's the Th-thorizine.

There was a long pause and then, "I . . . love . . . you."

Click. He was gone.

"I love you, too, Frankie."

Dreams are a funny thing—full of peaks, and holes, and gaps. I recall vividly how our dream started. I can't recall much about how it ended.

Six months later, Frank got his medical discharge. A dutiful son, he went back to Cincinnati. I was teaching school, but as soon as spring break arrived, I booked a flight and went to meet him. Unfortunately, we couldn't stay together. He was living with his mother. There was no mattress on the kitchen floor. I stayed with Lynn.

I had not fallen in love with a nice Jewish boy who lived with his mother in Cincinnati. I had fallen in love with an AWOL paratrooper in San Francisco. I escaped from Ohio once. I wasn't going back—not even for Frankie.

The magic was gone and we both knew it. Strange as it seems, I don't remember what we said during those last few days together. I know we didn't argue. There were no recriminations. Our love belonged to a particular time and place. It didn't travel well. Still, I had loved him if only for a moment. He remains one of my happiest memories.

~*~

Lynn called the other day to tell me Frank had died.

"I thought you'd want to know," she said.

Did I? I wasn't sure. I just felt numb.

"When?"

"Yesterday."

"What happened?"

"Heart attack, I think."

Frank, Frankie—though not really my Frankie for more than forty years. Yet I always took comfort in the fact that he was out there somewhere and that he was well. Now he was gone, and I felt as if a little part of me was gone, too.

I keep the love letter Frank sent me from Letterman Hospital in the recesses of an old bureau drawer. I've never been able to throw it away. Spidery, drugged handwriting drips down the page, but I know he meant what it says:

*"My mind is in a test tube,*
*but my heart belongs to you."*

Rest in peace, Frankie.

# How to Marry a Geezer

## Harker Brautighan

Ingredients:

1 geezer
1 instant family—just add water
1 U.S. state in between you and where your geezer lives, preferably
Oregon
2 weeks a month to yourself
2 households full of stuff
2 mortgages that are or near under water

Directions:

First, befriend the geezer. Next, wait until you become middle-aged
yourself. Add a good measure of death and sorrow. Temper the sorrow
with compassion, an open heart, a good listening ear and tears. Stir
your emotions. Crack yourself open and beat your insides until you
find yourself loving his children. Warm the youngest child with your
love. Never grow tired of talking about his "own mommy" who has
died and gone into the light. Be content to be mama. Know he wishes
it was his new mama—you—who died instead and never doubt his
love anyway. Allow yourself to fall in love with your geezer. Sell your
resentments cheap. Learn to catch your words. Trap them in a net and
release only those that are butterflies. Above all, forget the future.

Notes:

I married a geezer. I'm not exactly young myself. In fact, I'm way too
old to be raising a four-year-old. But if I'm too old, then my husband
is . . . well, let's just say the parenthood window should have been shut
and locked behind him years ago. Yet he has three kids. He's definitely
too old to have a four-year-old; he's even too old to have a seventeen-
year-old. I'm not yet as old as he was when his teenager was born. He
even started late with his first child, his adult son.

So, here we are—a middle-aged bag and a geezer raising two
minor children. His oldest lives a day's drive away. Life is different

now. Marrying in my forties came as a surprise. I had begun to think marriage wouldn't happen for me, despite all the opportunities that were opening up. Wouldn't you know, my geezer came along just as I was turning down other perfectly desirable men my age because they had young children and at a time when I had met someone promising whose only child was grown and independent. When I was seeing one particular guy, I remember my geezer saying over the phone, "If you're willing to date a Chinese guy with children, how about me? I'm Chinese. I have children." He says he was kidding, but look what happened.

You may wonder why I married my geezer. I may have initially deliberated over the decision, weighing imagined pros and cons. But each passing day reinforces my commitment, reinforces my admiration for him. I love him for his loyalty, his caring spirit, his sense of duty to those he loves. He is the one who is always there, who has always been there, in sickness and in health, even before we said our vows. My husband has seen sides of me I am ashamed of and has embraced me anyway. My dad always describes the good guy as "a prince among men." My geezer is a prince, a king, a minor god among men.

He is not the type who sweeps me off my feet and overwhelms me with passion. Rather, he is the rare kind of man who, through sustained, ever-deepening tenderness, makes me see that previous passions have been based on lack. They were attractions, like those of *The Symposium*'s Eros, to what I did not have, and were doomed attempts to fill up an ever-increasing emptiness. When I am with my geezer, I can look to the pit of my being and say, "What emptiness?" With my geezer, there is only a sense of warm, contented fullness. For the first time, satiety.

I have a lot to learn about being married, and about Gary Chapman's love languages. I am learning that my strong sex drive is a burden to my husband. Someone who loves through giving gifts and taking care of people, he doesn't express love through sex. As he ages, he cares less and less about it. For me, sex is the only way I have of expressing love. I have always loved with my body. My words are sharp and dangerous. I used to be decent at giving gifts, but for some reason I can't seem to think of anything to give as I get older. Perhaps because now that we are all older, the people in my life claim to have too many things already. My gifts of experiences go unredeemed (like personalized labyrinth walks or sky diving) and homemade presents are met with indifference. For our paper anniversary, I gave my husband my book-in-progress in what I thought was a beautiful hand-decorated binder, and a clock. He never glanced at the book but he raved about the clock.

For our wedding, I gave him a custom-made bracelet with the Chinese character for love on it. He never even took it out of the box. I guess I'll wear it myself when I am a widow. We were watching an episode of *Friends* the other day in which Joey buys Chandler a flashy gold bracelet that scares away the ladies Chandler is trying to flirt with. He doesn't know how to tell Joey he hates the bracelet. I would have laughed, but the thought of the "love" bracelet in the nightstand, still in its jewelry store box, stopped me. Some things cut a little close to the bone.

I'm beginning to learn my geezer likes getting material objects even though he always says not to buy him anything. Maybe he says that, not because he doesn't want anything, but because he can't stand my taste. Last year I bought him a paper shredder for Christmas—he said he needed one—and he responded with polite but uncomfortable laughter. This year, his middle son suggested a flat-screen TV. That met with my husband's approval. One Christmas, I thought I was getting off easy when my husband hinted he wanted a videogame until I realized the game only played on a game console we didn't have. So, it became a $500 videogame (not exactly in my budget). I love writing cards and poetry for those I love. Unfortunately, so did my husband's late wife, so that avenue is blocked to me. Her cards were only a source of grief to him.

Will I learn a new language of love, or will my husband and I both be bilingual? Perhaps we will have a multi-cultural marriage in more ways than one (I am not Chinese). If he loves me with gifts and actions, and I love him with my kisses, will that work? Or will we drift apart like people who can't speak the same tongue?

When we talk about our love and our marriage, my husband gets scared—of jinxing our relationship, he says. I wonder what else scares him. I know what scares me.

The future is a ghost walking through the rooms of our house. You would think it would be the past, with the velvet-draped box of ashes sitting on the shrine under his late wife's photograph, but her presence resides here serenely. It does not pace the floor. It is the future that lurks, the future that threatens. I try to enjoy every touch, every kiss, every smile that crosses my lover's lips. When the specter of his death haunts me in the night, I turn to watch the gentle rise and fall of his chest. I trace the slope of his buttocks, his hip. He's here now, I tell myself, and so am I. There's no law that says he'll go first; I've lost enough of my young friends to know that. In the daytime, I look at his blood pressure pills and pray he doesn't leave me to be a single parent.

I have to let it go and have faith. Faith that we will celebrate our twentieth anniversary, maybe even our thirtieth. That our little guy will grow up with a father and a mother. My parents marked their fiftieth anniversary this year. For their generation, my mom was an old maid and my dad a confirmed bachelor by the time they got married. Still, they got their fifty years. My geezer and I will never hit that milestone. After all, I'm past it and he's a card-carrying member of the AARP. In my lucid moments, I realize I have traded my future for my present. For these fifteen or even thirty years of togetherness, some of which will be spent nursing him, I have made the bargain to grow old and die alone.

My husband used to say he wanted to die at eighty. Now, he says seventy-five would be a better age. I believe we get what we wish for. My husband's parents are eighty-eight and ninety, but if he only wants to make it to seventy-five, what's going to keep him alive longer? As for myself, I pray to live another fifty years. I don't know if I'll be lucky enough to get those fifty years, but I look at his parents and say to myself how wonderful that they still have time and still have each other. He looks at his parents, and mine, and says aloud, "What a misery their lives must be." Speaking for my own parents, who are frailer than his in some ways, I know they want to live. They haven't had enough, are in no mood to check out, and would never describe life as miserable. Same with my eighty-seven-year-old close friend who got up and danced at our wedding. Apparently she gets up and dances at the neighborhood bars as well. During my last trip to Seattle, she invited me to come dance, too.

I miss Seattle—the cool summers, the evergreens, the misty rain that curls my hair. My little, clean, neat house. For a year or so, I spent two weeks in California where my geezer lives, and two weeks in Washington each month. Being away from my new family while I was in Seattle was a reprieve at first. Then it was a time of loneliness. I gradually moved my stuff to California, began voting here, letting state and local Washington politics roll away. I still go to Seattle from time to time. Now, the Seattle trips are a time of eating, seeing friends, and missing my husband and children.

This Christmas, my parents and brothers came to California. We usually celebrate the holiday in Tucson. I enjoyed the bustle of a house full of people, but my geezer watched my parents closely. Because he has a bad back and a bad knee, Dad has a lot of trouble moving around. And he gets confused. Not quite dementia, but something is different about his brain since his series of mini strokes. Mom tells the same stories repeatedly, and her knees need replacing. They had a really good time while they were here, and we found the perfect assisted and independent living home for them. Mom was ready to sign on the dotted line, but Dad held back. By the time they got back to Tucson, they had decided they would not move.

"Baby," my husband said (I know, how reverse Oedipal complex can you get? A man a generation older than I am calling me Baby). "Your parents need assisted living now. They shouldn't sign up for the independent package, but for the basic care package already, right now."

He's right. By the time one of them dies, which is what they're waiting for, the survivor might not be healthy enough to qualify for this residence. And moving on her own, or his own? Wouldn't it be better for them both to move, make new friends, make memories, together in their new environment? Easy for me to say. I'll probably have to be dragged out of my own home when the time comes, having attached myself to the radiator like a barnacle.

Seeing my parents, and listening to the decisions they are confronting, has probably only steadied my geezer's resolve to die relatively young. I feel insulted that he wants so few years with me. When his late wife died, I urged him to wait on beginning our romance until a decent interval had passed. For the sake of his middle son, I thought it was best. However, I was also selfish and flattered and falling in love and had the sex drive of a teenager. So, when he said that life's too short not to be happy, I capitulated. I lived with him half-time, then full-time. I moved from the guest room into his bed. I accepted the ring, planned the wedding, and wore the gown.

Perhaps marriage to me has not provided him with the happiness he was seeking. Nearly every night, I tell him how glad I am that we are married, how happy I feel with him, how deeply I've fallen in love. Then I stare into the darkness and wait.

# Incomplete Strangers

## Valerie Kelsay

I turn, then stop. I say aloud, "No, I'm not going back."

I'm walking on the old Haul Road toward the trestle bridge at the north end of Fort Bragg. Where the headlands round off at Pudding Creek stands a weather break of four cypress trees. Eighty feet tall, sculpted by Pacific storms, they are an iconic theme in the art galleries of Mendocino.

A young couple a quarter mile ahead of me stroll hand in hand off the road and snuggle together in the grove to watch the sun set into the ocean.

A red-tailed hawk beats through the air to a branch high above their heads. He carries a snake in his talons. At his table in the tree, he proceeds to tear it apart slowly and eat it.

"I always feel so safe in your arms," I hear her say as I pass by.

Will they ever know of the drama overhead? . . . Will they ever look up as they gaze out? . . . If bits of snake body drop, will they land unnoticed behind them? On them? . . . Will they think, "mosquitos?"

In my mind, I see a chunk of snake fall on her shoulder, then another bounce off his head. Later, they decide to date other people.

I imagine instead that they see only bits of snakeskin in freefall through the air above Glass Beach, shimmering in the summer spray. And they marvel, and they take it as a sign. I see them marry and have four children, two mortgages, and deal with her mother's dementia.

I never look back. I may never think about this moment again . . . or I may always wonder what's going on above my head.

# Learning Algebra

## Barbara Toboni

The nightmare began in a college lecture hall. I filed in with the rest of the students, some of them bold enough to take a front row seat facing a massive whiteboard. There were no windows or bookshelves, no art of any kind, only a desk, a podium, and necessary doors with exit signs. The board itself spanned twenty feet with rails that gave it the capacity to grow even larger. Dead center, written in bright red ink, a conspicuous "D" dominated the board. D for dread. D was the final mark—the last letter grade I received in high school algebra. That morning's breakfast of buttered toast and coffee churned in my stomach. I fought the urge to flee as the professor stepped up to the podium.

Dressed in khaki slacks and a white shirt, this faded persona of a man stood frozen, camouflaged by the whiteboard behind him. I strained to hear his barely audible voice. "Blah, blah, blah."

I dropped the class after the first week because, after all, this was college and I knew I had options. Perhaps, I wouldn't need algebra. The formulas were frustrating, and I had little patience for learning them. There would be plenty of time for math later.

Instead, I could choose courses such as literature and psychology. Iambic pentameter and the puzzle of the schizophrenic mind fascinated me, as did my literature professor when he recited poetry.

Granted, with my lack of education, my employment choices were limited. A short stint at McDonalds was my first job. Pressing on, I transitioned from waitress to paste-up artist for the local newspaper. Later, my ambitions changed. I had grown up a bit. I didn't like that I had quit college. I wanted more for myself; more money, a career. Because I had basic math skills, I decided to study bookkeeping at a business college. I felt proud the day I earned my certificate.

For a few years, I worked as a bookkeeper. I was able to support myself during a rocky first marriage that ended in divorce. My first husband had been a musician. It seemed a romantic life at first, but musicians don't make a lot of money unless they are famous. Add to that his drinking problem. Thankfully, there were no children in the four years we were together.

103

My second marriage was different. My husband and I planned a future with children. We had two sons. I didn't mind staying home to raise them, but by the time they were teens, I noticed everyone but me had a life.

By then, David, my husband, had started his computer business. I helped out one day a week with his bookkeeping, but mostly I stayed out of his way. Organizing his home office was beyond my capability. He alone could decipher the piles of paperwork and Post-it notes. The business had been a big challenge for him. I was proud of him, but a part of me was jealous.

We talked one afternoon after I had spent the day running errands and I was tired—so tired, I didn't mind that the kids were microwaving their own dinners. Not the best idea, but easy.

"What do you think about me returning to school?" I asked.

"College? Is that what you want? Now?"

"Look, I know I'm 45, but I saved all my transcripts. I have credits from courses I took over twenty years ago, and I found out I can still use them toward a degree. Isn't it amazing?"

"But what would you do with a degree? If you want to go back to work, fine, but you don't need to. The business is doing well. Do you really need a degree?"

"I do. I need something to stimulate my mind—something other than housework." I went on to explain how the kids could take care of themselves, how there was less for me to do.

"They hate it when I show up to clean their rooms, so let them run the vacuum. And just look at what they're eating for dinner. Do you think they need me to cook them something fancy?"

Dave's cell phone rang. He glanced in my direction and I shrugged, so he picked it up. Our conversation was over. Like most of his calls, this one went on and on. Would he even miss me being gone part of the day?

At the college's guidance center, I felt relieved to meet my counselor—a woman who had undergone a similar back-to-school experience. I should take math and science courses, she suggested, because both subjects were absent from my transcripts. She also suggested I take a math placement exam—a terrifying prospect. Regardless, my test scores proved I earned a spot in pre-algebra.

I assumed that first semester would give me courage to face the next level, beginning algebra. After all, I had earned a sparkling A in pre-algebra, but this was the real deal.

On day one, I stood frozen—a middle-aged woman with a dark-green backpack—outside the classroom staring at room 1046. Finally, someone shuffled behind me.

"Are you going in?" asked a boy about eighteen, the same age as my youngest son.

I nodded solemnly. He opened the door and entered. I followed because I didn't want to take the lead. I took a seat two rows from the front and set my backpack on the floor. The classroom appeared small, a miniature of the classroom I remembered when I was eighteen, and the whiteboard contained no letter D for Dread. Instead, I heard noisy laughter.

The professor was a nerdy-hippy-type for whom I felt immediate compassion because he wore a rumpled flannel shirt that appeared too small for him. He later explained his clothes came from the Salvation Army—all he could afford on his teacher's salary. On and on he joked with the class. I hardly noticed that my hand was taking notes.

All the calculations on the board were written in numbered steps. I copied the steps and practiced solving for X on homework assignments. On weekly exams, I applied the same principles. He used a basic psychological concept I could appreciate, given my past studies: take baby steps. It worked.

The next semester, I was so impressed with my A in algebra, I enrolled in intermediate algebra. I heard from former students the class was tough. I assumed they hadn't been taught to take baby steps. Sure I was anxious, but surrounded by bright, young twenty-somethings, I bravely entered the classroom.

Standing six-foot-four, the instructor was imposing. Based on his height and the advanced nature of the subject he taught, the professor admitted to the class, some students considered him intimidating. Then he did something impressive.

While he kneeled to write on the board, he turned around to face the class. We were eye to eye. All at once, this giant seemed merely human, and his humanity inspired me. He knew psychology, and I knew he could teach me algebra.

# Lost Dreams

## Jing Li

I was fifty-one when my mother told me her life's dream and my role in its loss.

My mother has never smiled at me. Since I was a child, my heart has longed for my mother's smile, but she has bestowed that dream of mine only on my two brothers. She has just looked at me out of the corners of her small, almond-shaped, silent eyes.

Magnolia, my mother, was born in 1935 in the village of Beneath the Cliff nestled in central northern China's pine forest mountains. Her father committed suicide, and her mother was banished from the family when she was five years old. All contact was broken until Magnolia turned twelve and was old enough to walk fifteen li alone. She walked down into the valley where she visited her mother who'd been remarried to a poor old peasant bachelor thirty years her senior. Orphaned, Magnolia and her baby brother lived with their paternal grandmother. The three ate their meals in turns in the homes of Magnolia's four uncles.

"I'll never want to swallow others' charity soup with their resentful eyes," young Magnolia vowed in tears.

A bright child, Magnolia was sent to their village school. She was the all-time top student and especially loved writing. But none of her uncles' families were willing or able to pay the hefty two hundred-kilo sacks of millet tuition to send her beyond their small village school.

For two years in a row, Magnolia walked fifteen li down into the valley to take the boarding school's annual entrance examinations. Both times she scored number one but each time she was turned away. Somebody had to pay for her tuition.

"Whoever sends me back to school, I'll marry their son. No dowry is needed," fourteen-year-old Magnolia told her uncles and aunts and asked them to spread her words.

Was a mere peasant girl dreaming the impossible?

For five thousand years, a Chinese daughter-in-law was a dowry-bought asset to her in-laws. Like a valuable horse, she was to be ridden and bred—just look how the pictographic Chinese language reflects this tradition: the Chinese word for "mother" 媽 "*ma*" is composed of two side-by-side radicals: "female" plus "horse."

Eager to unload Magnolia as a burden of mouth, the wife of her fourth uncle thought of her cousin Jade, who had a son, eighteen-year-old Bright Light, thirty li down the valley in the Red Stone Bridge village.

The only surviving male child, Bright Light was so treasured by his peasant parents that he never toiled a day in the cornfields as did his two younger sisters. His parents toiled from dawn to dusk, scraped and saved to keep him in school to fulfill their great expectations for him to live a leisurely life as an educated man in the city.

At the critical age of eighteen, Bright Light complained and blamed his mother for not having already found him a wife. When Magnolia's word-of-mouth marriage proposal reached Red Stone Bridge, he was fascinated. A pretty girl with a brain? An all-time number-one student? And wanting more education? What a refreshing, beautiful fairy tale.

Bright Light wanted to meet Magnolia right away.

"But how do you suppose we could afford to pay for the second tuition?" His shrewd mother, unlike his good-natured quiet father, detected the underlying trouble. She reasoned with her son. "Can't you see, your weakling father and I—me on my painful three-inch bound feet—are already breaking our backs toiling in the cornfields just to pay for your tuition?"

But Jade raised her son with a lofty sense of entitlement. He couldn't feel his parents' pain.

"A daughter-in-law should be the family's helping hands." Jade further argued with her son. "Whoever heard of a peasant wife as an idling goddess living on the backs of her in-laws?"

But her precious son turned a deaf ear. After all, it was his mother who told his two sisters: "Your brother is the sun, you two girls are the moon and the star. You move around him. His desire is you girls' command."

Bright Light wouldn't wait or trust his mother to arrange for the village's go-between woman to do the match-making, a marriage practice since beginning of time. On his own, he walked the thirty li up the hill to meet Magnolia at her village.

Smart Magnolia had arranged for Bright Light to meet her at the home of her teacher, Mr. Yang Wen Bing, a prominent local figure.

Excited and shy Bright Light walked into the small one-room house. He glanced over to the corner of the room and saw Magnolia for the first time. She demurely sat on the little floor stool. She looked up, gave him a quick shy smile, and again, cast her eyes down.

Teacher Yang jumped up from his seat on the edge of the *Kang* and shook Bright Light's hands, praising him for meeting the "smartest girl ever."

"Now you two have met and liked each other," the witty teacher lost no time. "Magnolia, why don't you go ahead leave us men to talk business?"

With a quiet, happy smile, Magnolia stood up and walked to the door.

Bright Light liked what he snapped in his eyes: her tall slender figure.

"Young man," Teacher Yang assured blushing Bright Light, "your bright future is guaranteed by marrying a brilliant girl like Magnolia. What man wouldn't want an educated wife?"

Half an hour later, elated Bright Light shook hands with Mr. Yang, pledging his hearty promise: Yes, his parents would send Magnolia back to school right after the wedding.

It was 1950 and fifteen-year-old Magnolia, anxious for her dream to come true, married nineteen-year-old Bright Light.

But just days before the entrance examination, Magnolia's mother died. She ignored the ancient tradition of a month-long indoor mourning, walked the fifteen li down the valley to the village of *Shi-Hui-Wan,* resembling a floating ghost out of the tomb in hair-raising Chinese ghost stories, covered from head to toe in her heavy mourning white gown. Magnolia aced the test and was officially accepted into her long-awaited, two-year boarding school.

Meanwhile, trouble brewed. Magnolia's domineering mother-in-law, Jade, packed for Bright Light's return to his boarding school in the town of Ping Yao but had been silent about sending Magnolia back to school. Anxious, Magnolia lay low. She chose the precise moment to stress her point. It was Chinese New Year, a tradition-required time for harmony. No tears, no quarreling, no breaking anything in round shapes to avoid bad luck for the coming year. Chinese Lunar New Year was also a special face-saving time as well-wishing families went around from house to house visiting their relatives, the younger generation paying respect to their elders.

Magnolia stayed in bed, weeping and sobbing, and turned a Happy New Year into a funeral scene.

"Oh, child, what's wrong?" her embarrassed mother-in-law grit her teeth to appear innocent in front of the guests who crowded the floor.

The moment Bright Light bent down to shoulder-pole his two baskets his mother had packed for him—bedding and a sack of millet for tuition—Magnolia charged up and grabbed hold of him.

"Not so fast. What about me? You and your family promised to send me back to school if I married you. Now the wedding is over. What happened to your promise?"

Red-faced, Bright Light turned to his mother who stood erect and calm on her tiny three-inch bound feet, her hands crossed over her aprons.

"Well, why don't you let go of your husband?" mother-in-law told her daughter-in-law. "You and I can sit down and talk about this later."

"No way. You have to make it clear to me right now. Fulfill your promise or I'm walking out for divorce."

"Okay, okay." Jade backed down. "Go ahead; let go of him. We'll send you to school, too." Jade had never been intimidated by anyone; especially, a female beneath her.

Magnolia smiled her way to her dream school life, which would broaden her world and included her discovery of a better man: her handsome young teacher, Mr. Doo.

Rumors of scandal soon spread. Magnolia was flirting with her teacher.

"Magnolia," her classmates asked her. "Who are you knitting those nice socks for?"

"Oh, for my teacher, Mr. Doo." Magnolia answered dreamily and blushed.

Doing needle work for a man was a romantic show of affection from a Chinese maiden.

~*~

Finally, after two years of doubled sweat and blood, Bright Light's parents saw hope of relief. Magnolia graduated. They wanted her to go on to Teachers' College with its free tuition, room, and board to gain an education that would lead to a suitable career for a woman.

"But I want to be a college-degreed journalist." Magnolia wanted to go to high school instead, and then to college.

She didn't return to her in-laws. Unbeknownst to them, Magnolia found another way out with a better prospect. A new national policy was to grant full merit-based scholarships to promising offspring of poor peasants. Magnolia was qualified, except, alas, she was married. A married woman's place was only in her in-laws' home, birthing and raising children.

Magnolia wasn't deterred. With the help of her second uncle, she obtained a reference letter from the mayor in her maiden village. Yes, the mayor wrote, Magnolia was a peasant orphan.

Magnolia sailed into the secondary school in the town of Ping Yao. But more danger loomed to prevent her dream, and she was called into the principal's office. "Someone informed us that you're married."

Her scholarship, the only source of her financial means, was revoked.

Devastated, Magnolia refused to bow down to her defeat.

On that fateful weekend of October 1, 1955, a national holiday for the 6th birthday of Communist China, Magnolia hitched a ride on an open-top truck traveling two hundred li to the city of Taiyuan where her estranged husband worked as a geographical surveyor.

She found him living in a dorm shared with three roommates. Housing, as with almost everything else, was in shambles in brand-new "liberated" China.

"I want a divorce." Magnolia gave him an ultimatum.

"But the court's closed," he told her and talked her into staying with him for the weekend.

They slept in the vacant kitchen on the cook's bed and made a deal to stay married, with him keeping her in school. I was conceived that night, seven years after their marriage, and the fatal blow was struck to my mother's long and hard-fought dream, too powerful even for her iron-strong will.

Abortion was illegal in 1950s China. Desperate, twenty-year-old Magnolia jumped violently in her physical education class. And, secretly, in her dorm room when no one was around, she pushed a thick pinewood washboard hard, and repeatedly, against her pregnant belly, all in an effort to abort.

110

~*~

Mother Jade never forgave Mr. Yang for having manipulated her naïve-like-an-idiot son into the marriage. Years later, during the Cultural Revolution (1966-1976), when Mr. Yang was a school principal, he was beaten to death—his head split open, his tattered body thrown into a well—by his Red Guard students. Jade uttered under her breath, "Served the SOB just right."

The marriage between Magnolia and Bright Light was a stormy, miserable marriage.

"But I never got a good look at her," Bright Light complained years later. "I'd never have agreed to marry that ugly, bad omen."

When he heard the rumor of Magnolia's flirtation with Mr. Doo, Bright Light was quoted as saying, "No way Mr. Doo would want anything to do with that ugly, bad omen. Mr. Doo is a principled man with integrity."

~*~

I wept, writing to my mother, Magnolia, in China. I am sorry, Mother, but please see how I've fulfilled your dream—I've become, not only an author in Chinese language, but an American college-degreed writer in English, the world's most prestigious language.

At age eighty today, my mother's heart has yet to smile at me. Our dreams, as of yet, unfulfilled.

# Mint Tea

## Simona Carini

In the spring of 1989, I stepped into the office of Club Med in Milan and, on the strength of my professional credentials, I applied for a job as a nurse. I imagined dispensing aspirin and sunburn cream to vacationers while leisurely mapping my next moves as a twenty-something European woman. I was hired on the spot and, at the beginning of June, I was sent to the Malabata Club Med in Tangier, Morocco.

Housed in the vast garden around the Hispano-Moresque Villa Harris (named after the original owner, The Times correspondent Walter Burton Harris, 1866-1933), Malabata, like all the Club Meds, was a small world unto itself. European staff, with the *chef du village* at the top of the organizational chart, ran the operation, while local workers served as waiters, gardeners, and janitors. As skilled professionals, the other nurse and I commanded respect in the hierarchy. We ran the Club's clinic and were on call for emergencies. We also participated in some of the Club's activities, welcoming the guests and taking our meals with them, and dancing in the evening performances of choreographed musicals.

The guests, mostly from France and Italy, ran the gamut, from young and single, to married couples with children, to retirees. They all knew who I was, respected my expertise and were kind to me—even if only for fear they might need my assistance.

Outside the gates of the Club, it was another story.

In Tangier, which I visited to run job-related errands, my European summer clothing and the fact that I was a single woman unaccompanied by a man got me unwanted attention. Men dressed in djellabah sat outside cafes talking animatedly while nursing tall glasses of mint tea. Their eyes pierced me when I passed, and scorn grated in their voices. The language barrier thankfully hid from me what sounded like a damning verdict.

Women were not allowed in those cafes, but I saw them walking on the city streets. Young girls wore frilly dresses that left their arms and legs free. As they neared puberty, their dresses became sleeved, hems got longer, the colors of their clothing darkened. The additions were progressive. By the time they reached adulthood, women were a pair of eyes peering out from amorphous layers of fabric. As they became of an age when I had been able to express my individuality in the choice not only of haircut, clothes, and shoes, but also of job and place to live, they turned into featureless shapes, gliding along the streets under the close watch of at least one man.

One day, on a guided tour of small villages in the hinterland of Tangier, I saw an old woman on the road, hunched under the weight of a sack of stones. She was almost crawling. Her head was covered with a piece of cloth tied into a knot under her chin, but her face was mostly visible: her skin was sunbaked and deeply furrowed, her eyes expressionless. A man rode a donkey next to her, unencumbered. Searing anger etched that image in my memory and burnt to ashes all other images from that outing.

That day and every time I went outside, I was relieved to get back to Club Med, to the caressing shade of the many trees in its garden, and to my established position as a nurse inside its gate. My tiny bedroom was close to that gate. If I got up early to go for a swim in the pool, chances were the light morning breeze would waft a nose-tickling mint aroma, and I would see a man wearing a white or blue djellabah carrying a large bunch of the herb to the kitchen. It would be used mainly to make mint tea.

I usually don't like mint-flavored foods, yet I relished the mint tea I drank at the Club. Eyes closed, I picked up the clear glass through which I could see the leaves steeped in the amber liquid. I brought it to my lips, inhaling deeply to fill my nose and lungs with the aromatic steam. The first sip was pleasantly scorching, waking up my mouth to the refreshing hotness of the beverage. Light sweetness and mint's bold flavor waltzed in every sip that followed.

Moroccan mint, a variety of spearmint, has bright green, lightly textured leaves on longish, slender stems. Its perfume is expansive, like the vast blue sky over the North-African desert. I wanted to bury my nose into that green cloud before it disappeared into the kitchen, but I did not feel comfortable addressing the man carrying it. I breathed deeply and the smell of mint stayed with me as I walked to the swimming pool.

Swimming early in the morning, when the Club was still asleep, was a luxury: I had the whole pool to myself. I wasn't totally alone, though. A small group of Moroccan men dressed in long-sleeved, blue-gray tunics and matching pants were busy cleaning the area around the pool. As they swept and mopped the floor, and rearranged tables, chairs and deck chairs left in disarray after the previous evening's revels, they whispered among themselves, so as not to disturb the sleeping guests.

When I arrived, wearing my one-piece swimsuit and carrying a towel under my arm, they smiled a sheepish greeting, and I smiled back. They knew who I was. I was aware that my attire was unacceptable in their culture, though it was rather austere compared with the guests' bikinis. I interpreted the smile we exchanged to mean that underneath the different layers of fabric on our bodies, we recognized our shared humanity. Although shaking hands was not part of the program, I was confident that they would have lent me those hands in case of need. In time, I felt that they watched over me, making sure I could enjoy my solitary swim undisturbed.

The antics of some guests—who ate or drank too much, forgot the medicines for their chronic conditions, and hurt themselves in various ways—kept me busy. I rarely had time to dwell on the misogyny of the world outside. The Moroccan men with whom I interacted daily, people working at the Club, and the doctors I talked to on behalf of the guests, were all impeccably kind.

The Club had horses and offered riding lessons to guests. There were a few accidental falls from the saddle, but they were nothing compared to a freak accident that happened late in my tenure: A horse kicked an experienced rider on the shin. The wound was highly suggestive of an open fracture that required immediate surgery to prevent a dangerous bone infection.

While the other nurse held the fort, I took one of the taxis always on standby outside the Club's gate, the fastest way to get to the emergency room with the wounded young man. During the short drive, I practiced the words I would rattle off upon arrival. I rushed into a room wherein details remained blurred at the periphery of my priority: getting my patient attended to without delay.

"Excuse me . . ." I addressed the first person I saw that looked like a member of the staff. He looked right past me and continued on his trajectory. Carried by the flow of adrenaline, I reached the front desk and tried again my opening with a man sitting behind it. In his unfocused gaze, I read the bad news: I was invisible.

I moved away and stood in the middle of the busy room, people flowing past me as if I did not exist.

I wanted to scream, but understood it would be futile, as the resolution to ignore me was not related to the loudness of my voice. I bridled my anger and concentrated on what to do next. The only solution I could think of was to go back to the Club and get the *chef du village* or another man to accompany me: they would see him and listen to him. That meant losing precious time but what choice did I have?

And then the God of European Women intervened. A soft-spoken "Can I help you?" startled me. "Can I help you?" I recognized the local doctor who had stopped at the Club a few days earlier, wishing to become part of the roster we used for referrals.

"Open fracture," was all I needed to say. He barked an order and the wounded rider was wheeled inside the surgery.

I sank on a chair—but only for a moment. The doctor came out to tell me that they would operate right away.

I took a cab back to the Club, anger rising in waves up to my mouth, leaving a bitter taste not even mint tea could have eased.

Later on, I asked a guest who was an orthopedic surgeon to visit the wounded man. He reported that all that was necessary had been done, and done well.

That evening I collapsed on my bed, weighted down by the punctured dream of shared humanity.

A couple of days later, the young man was discharged. After a day of observation at the Club, he flew back to France. I never told him that he owed his life to the God of European Women.

Years later, at a farmers' market on the California North Coast where I now live, a seedling of Moroccan mint sparked a desire to taste again refreshing mint tea. I brought it home and transferred it to a larger pot. The plant did well initially, but then slowly wilted before I could harvest leaves in sufficient amount to quench my thirst.

# My Life as a Zombie

## Sue Kessler

I lay still, afraid to move, more afraid I wouldn't be able to. The last thing I remembered was hearing a loud explosion. Now, hemmed in by white fabric, disoriented, and unaware of where I was, I stared at the white stippled stuff covering the space where my driver's side window ought to have been. A small movement caught my eye, and I coaxed my head to turn. I watched a hand inch forward. Mine? I had no idea what happened—or why—until a small man ran up to the passenger window and said, "Are you okay, Ma'am?"

"I guess," I answered.

I ran my fingers across my shoulder closest to the impact to see if I was bleeding. No blood and I felt no pain. I ached, but not a major ache. The realization I'd been in a serious accident percolated snail-slow through my brain. My world seemed to move in slow motion. The man beckoned and held his hand out to me. As I tried to move in his direction, my joints protested, resisting my commands. I forced myself up and over the console, crawling to the open passenger door. I moved stiff and sluggish like a paper doll made of heavy cardboard.

As soon as my feet hit the pavement, everything I had on was sodden, saturated by the heavy rain. I sloshed through water high enough to cover my shoes until I reached the side of the road where three men and one woman huddled under the shelter of a tree. I stood with the group, feeling detached from all. The woman —a witness I found out later—offered me an umbrella. The others ignored me. The driver who'd center punched me with his F150 truck, collapsing the driver's side, said, "I saw you and thought you'd stop, but you didn't. I slammed on my brakes, but I lost control and hydroplaned right into you. I'm so sorry."

I stared, didn't say a word, too dazed to react. The driver's phone rang and I heard him saying, "Nah, not much damage to the truck. Ding or two on the bumper, scratch on the front fender…" before he walked out of my hearing range.

A parking control officer drove up, "Did anyone call the police?"

I gave her a blank stare.

"I'll call it in," she said.

We all stood, dripping under the tree until a patrolman arrived. He took my statement and interviewed the witnesses. When he finished, he said, "Seeing as you seem to be walking around just fine, I'll not be filing a report. We only do that with injury accidents."

My husband arrived and contacted AAA to send a tow-truck. We watched as paramedics jumped out of a fire engine to check for any injured in my car. "Gotta be someone in there, a wreck this bad."

As my car was towed away, my husband said, "To be safe, I think I need to take you to get checked out."

The next eight and a half hours we spent at the ER—x-ray, CT Scan. The tests confirmed I'd walked away almost unscathed, except for some loose screws on my cervical fusion—but all my friends always said I had a loose screw, making this old news.

For the next few days, everyone told me, "I can't believe you walked away from that."

And I'd respond, "Yes, I'm one lucky puppy."

After a while, though, after so many "I can't believe you lived through that's," I began to think, "Maybe they're right. Maybe I didn't live through it."

The more I thought about this, the more sensible the idea of my being dead became. The fact no one seemed to look through me and walk on by meant, at least, I wasn't a ghost. So, if I were dead, then what might I be?

A zombie, I thought. Zombies are all the rage these days. I'd be part of the in crowd, up on the latest fads.

I spent the following week reading up on zombies. Although I suffered from sore fingers from so much intense web surfing, I was relieved to be able to eliminate that particular form of the undead. I conducted a number of tests to verify my hypothesis. I walked through the meat department at several of my favorite supermarkets. I didn't twitch nor bend over to sniff the steaks, not even once. I didn't crave human brains, and I wasn't any clumsier than I am normally. Not a single neighborhood dog trailed at my heels howling and drooling, despite my stopping to let them get closer. All they did was wag their tails and beg for treats. Best of all, not a single body part fell off. I must admit I set up a regimen I still follow—checking between my toes and under my arms for any spots of black putrid flesh. So far, only toe jam. Chalk up one for the good guys on the zombie front.

Not a ghost, not a zombie; back to the web.

I ditched banshee because my name doesn't start with a C and no one has died around me since the accident. I'm not a ghoul. Cannibalism is not my thing. Being a vampire and living off someone's blood didn't excite me much. I admit I checked the mirror to see if my canines had grown. Good thing they didn't. I'd starve rather than spend years alternating sips of warm blood and barfing. To say nothing of the major case of bad breath I'd need to deal with. I could go for a chilled Chardonnay maybe, but not body temperature blood, type A or not.

My friends would've noticed if I were a shadow person with all my facial features and various lumps and curves obscured in the dark silhouette. A wraith seemed promising, but turned out to be nothing more than another name for ghost—a category I'd already eliminated. I started seeing sites in my sleep—browsers, twitter tweets, Facebook posts, snapchat pics, looking, looking.

I decided to make one more effort and, if nothing credible showed up, bag the whole thing. After half an hour, I realized the prof from my Econ 101 class who claimed "last in, first out" was right. My last possibility turned out to be—a draug.

According to an obscure web guru, these Scandinavian natives had animated bodies, strong wills, and retained similar physical abilities as they had when they were alive. Check, check, and check.

My friends could see me. I'd still walk funny and dislike classical country. So close, but no cigar. I wasn't a Swede or a Norwegian, Dane, or Finn, and I lacked the draug's prerequisite grave in which to hide its treasure—or any treasure, for that matter.

Bottom line, my research convinced me. I'm not dead. Against all odds, I really had walked away alive, and, considering the alternative, alive is a good thing.

Alive means I have a second chance to learn Russian, lie on a beach at Phuket, ride the Orient Express, or, better yet, use my second life to actually stick to my diet.

# New Year's Eve 2014

## Roger DeBeers, Sr.

The text message from the dispatcher read, "I sent you one."

"What the hell is this?" I asked. It was three in the afternoon, New Year's Eve, 2014. Of course, I knew what it was because I had volunteered. It was a pickup at Infosourse at 4:00 p.m.

I was angry with myself for being on call, and now, the reality that I would have to drive with all the crazy drunks out on the road on New Year's Eve. No question, I was a registered and certified fool.

"Dipstick," I said.

I had planned to stay in and watch eight hours of Cadfael with Sir Derek Jacobi as the former crusader, now a monk in medieval England. It annoyed me that my well laid plans to spend a quiet night ignoring the coming New Year were dashed by stupidly volunteering to be on call. With ten years of sobriety, I did not want to venture out into what I and many other former heavy drinkers referred to as Amateur Night.

I checked the five deliveries I would have to make, and then spoke each city out loud. San Leandro, Hayward, Livermore, San Jose, and Santa Cruz. I berated myself for my foolishness in volunteering to be on call. I was way too clever for my own good. I figured that no one would have any nighttime deliveries, so it would be safe to assume I would celebrate the New Year watching Brother Cadfael.

I was dead wrong. Infusion medication for the chronically ill had to be delivered. For the next half hour, I messed around with Google Maps and laid out my route. If I finished up in Santa Cruz around ten p.m., I'd still be two and a half hours from home. And New Year's Eve 2015 would be spent on U.S. Highway 101.

I picked up the five boxes of meds in Rohnert Park at four in the afternoon. Loading the addresses into my GPS, I inserted a Mario Lanza CD in the player, opened a bottle of lime mineral water, and set out on my adventure.

Traffic was remarkably light as I headed south on 101 to Interstate 580 in San Rafael. Passing Novato, I fished out my company badge and slipped it around my neck. I figured the Highway Patrol and every local police department would have all available officers on patrol looking for the inebriated stupid enough to be behind the wheel of a vehicle. I wondered how many driving check points I would encounter.

In San Leandro. A tall black man about thirty answered the door.

"What's up, man?" he said.

"I'm the courier delivering the meds for Barbara Ann Wright."

"They're for my mom."

I handed him the box with the label stating that the contents should be refrigerated upon delivery. There were tears rolling down his tawny face.

"You don't have to sign for them, so I'll be on my way."

The man put down the box and held out his right hand. I took his hand to shake, but he pulled me into a fierce bear hug. He seemed to be trembling all over when he released me.

"Bless you," he said.

"You, too."

I was hesitant to wish him a Happy New Year with his mom being ill.

"Happy New Year," he called. "and thanks for coming out to deliver this stuff on New Year's Eve."

Saying nothing, I waved.

In my car, I, too, wiped away tears. I was profoundly touched by the man blessing me for doing my job; a job I was getting paid to do, and didn't want to do on New Year's Eve.

Hayward was next. The delivery was quick. The woman who accepted the meds hardly acknowledged me. It was a mild night with no hint of rain. The roads were perfect when I encountered my first road check. A decade earlier I got a ticket on Lake Herman Road in Vallejo for driving under the influence. This night, I had no fear of the flashing blue lights on the patrol cars.

In Livermore, per my instructions, I called the recipient. The woman who answered gave me the gate code. It was a gated community and there were about a dozen upscale cars, many of them sporting old Romney bumper stickers. And here I was with my Nissan, emblazoned with an Obama 2012 sticker, delivering medication.

At the door, a medium-sized man accepted the box and offered me eggnog. "Ya need one for the road, don't you?"

"Not tonight, sir."

"Drive safe," he said.

"Thank you."

I didn't think spiked eggnog would have helped in any way for me to drive safe. I cracked another mineral water. Driving out, I concocted verbal jousts with the gated conservatives. Of course, I was victor in our verbal jousts. Trounced them I did.

Next up was San Jose. I called the number and a young woman answered. She told me to meet her in the parking lot of her apartment complex.

Driving into the designated area, my headlights shone on a young Hispanic woman dancing alone in a shimmering party dress. I stopped as she waltzed between two rows of cars.

"Are you the courier?" she asked.

"Yes."

"Please put the box on the trunk of that car," she said, pointing to a Honda Civic.

As I turned to leave she ran up to me like a ballerina catching up to her partner for a pas de chat.

"Dance with me, please."

"I . . . uh," I stammered glancing at my watch.

"One dance. I can't go out tonight to a party or dance, and if my mom sees me dancing she will yell at me for getting too tired."

She tugged on my arm. I could not deny her request.

For a few minutes, we waltzed among the rows of parked cars. She held me for support when we stopped and she appeared exhausted. When she released me, she leaned against an old Mercedes.

"The medication is for the pain," she said.

"Oh."

"You might be my last dance partner because the Heavenly Father is calling me to heaven very soon."

"Yolanda."

"That's my mom. I have to go. You have been sweet, dear sir."

My throat constricted and I was unable to speak.

She kissed me lightly on the cheek and walked slowly to her apartment. When she was gone, I thought about how blessed I was to be going home later tonight to a very healthy son.

Following my GPS to Highway 17, I drove to my last delivery. I wasn't tired, but I felt drained. Without difficulty, I found the Seaview Estates, but not unit 215. Most of the manufactured homes were the double-wide variety. The numbers ran consecutively; not odd on one side and even on the other. Creeping along at five miles per hour, I came up to 215. The lights were on and an elderly woman was standing on the porch like a Marine on guard duty.

The package I carried was small and light and I knew from experience that the contents must be pain medication. I suspected that the medication was for someone terminally ill. The lump and constriction of my throat had returned. I fought back the tears that were on the verge of pouring.

"Hello, I'm the courier with the medications for Rolf Mattson."

"Thank you. I'm his mother."

She put the box on a small table beside a swinging outdoor couch, and immediately held out her right hand.

I took her hand and she pulled it to her cheek. I resisted briefly, and thought, *Get back. Let go. Don't. Not again. Please, don't. I just want to go home.* But it was too late. She held my hand firmly to her cheek. I could feel her pulse under her soft skin, and then her tears struck my hand and found a way under the cuff of my jacket to roll down my arm. Her warm tears turned cold and were like a low voltage electric shock that intensified as they continued to flow from her eyes to my forearm.

"Stay with me for a few minutes."

"Okay," I stammered.

We stood there immobile for what seemed a lifetime. I thought about my son at home safely playing a video game, and how fortunate I was in my life. Soon, I would drive home and have a hamburger and a milkshake with my son Roger. This woman whom I did not know, but had, in a few moments, become eternally bonded with, would administer powerful pain killing drugs to her son.

"Thank you for coming out on New Year's Eve. Do you have a long drive?"

"Santa Rosa,"

"I'm sorry you had to spend your New Year's Eve with a sentimental old lady."

"It's fine. It's okay."

"God bless you," she said, as she released my hand.

"Thank you, I think he already has blessed me."

# The Believer

## Elspeth Benton

Mib was petite, slender, and well proportioned. She was smart and witty, and I felt cheerful around her. I liked her and she seemed to reciprocate. During our freshman year at Mt. Holyoke College in South Hadley, Massachusetts, I got somewhat acquainted with Mary Isabel Brown, "Mib." We both wanted to be fluent in at least one other language, and we both loved and were majoring in English Lit.

Each of us had attended a (different) Quaker boarding school before coming to Mt. Holyoke in the fall of 1950, which helped connect us. Three out of three hundred at my Quaker high school had been African-American, and a similar percentage at hers. Our high schools were considered liberal—or crazy, by many—for their policy of including black students. And in those high schools the whites assumed without even considering it that they were above racism.

What Mib and I didn't have in common was that she was black—*negro* was the accepted, supposedly non-racist word at the time—and I was white. Or pink, as I prefer to call it. I've always thought if we referred to browns and pinks, it would do a lot right there to reduce racism.

To my delight, Mib agreed in the spring of our freshman year to room with me the next fall. As sophomores, we would live at Le Foyer, on the edge of campus. This French-speaking dorm housed just seventeen young women, compared to the two hundred in our freshman hall. A reconverted, three-story former home, charming and informal. Le Foyer also boasted a French housemother, Ginette, who wasn't like the elderly dowagers watching over most of the other college dorms. Ginette resembled the idol of my teen years, Ingrid Bergman.

As a Midwesterner and scholarship student at this women's college in New England, I often felt like a fish out of water. I was gaining weight, always a sign of insecurity for me. Some might say Mib's and my "differentness" was a trait we both shared—I was getting fat, I was usually broke, a stranger to Eastern ways, and didn't have a decent haircut, and she was black. Of course in 2016 everyone knows that race difference stands alone, not even slightly comparable with any other differences, such as fatness or looking dowdy.

Mount Holyoke's evening curfew for dorms was at 10:00 p.m. Sunday through Thursday, 11:00 p.m. on Friday, and midnight on Saturday. We were required to dress up for dinner Wednesday evenings and for the midday meal on Sundays. Every dorm had a housemother who dined with and tended us. Chapel was required twice a week. In class, Mib and I were addressed as "Miss Brown" and "Miss James." We were of one mind about the over-protective ways of our college.

"Here comes the old battle axe," she'd warn me as the housemother of our freshman dorm approached. We'd hide behind one of the ancient campus trees, gasping and wiping away tears of laughter.

Before I went home to Wisconsin at the end of freshman year, Mib and I met my dad for lunch in New York City. He was there for a few days, living on a shoestring but always looking dapper and successful, raising money from the Ford Foundation for the Columbia University edition of the *Milton Variorum*. An English professor and scholarly editor, he could be formidable with his piercing look, long words, and probing questions. But unlike most of my friends, Mib was his conversational equal. She laughed often as she chatted away with him, and I thought our time together went well. Afterward, though, he expressed to me his doubts about our compatibility.

"She's hard, Janet," he told me. His eyes were tender, looking into mine. It was one of the rare moments when I felt his concern and even a dash of protectiveness.

"She has an iron surface, and you . . ." he paused, for once searching his words. "You're always striving to be open, sincere, genuine. You're vulnerable."

Dad remained in New York while I continued south. Mib's mom had invited me to spend a week with their family in her hometown, Washington, D.C. "You girls can get to know each other a little more before you become roommates next fall," she'd written me, "and it will be so nice for Mib's dad and me to get to know you a little, too."

Once there, I was amazed to see at least thirty photos of Mib, an only child, on the walls of her parents' dining and living rooms—as a baby, a toddler, a preschooler, and on up to her then current age of eighteen. It was the opposite of my home in this regard: my mother had one photo of me at age four on her upstairs bureau, period. Downstairs at my house, there were etchings of European villages and a reproduction of one of the sibyls from the Sistine Chapel. Coming from poverty, my parents had found their way, through education, to a cultured life. I see now how their small steady economies enabled them to keep an interesting home and to travel widely. They learned foreign languages, worked together at Dad's scholarly endeavors, and were jubilant in their adventures together.

Mib's parents were welcoming and friendly to me and I felt at home with both of them right away. Her mom was an elementary school teacher, her dad a school custodian. At the time, I barely took in these facts. I'd been raised to see value in every human being, and the discrepancy between a professor and a custodian didn't register with me. Their D.C. home, though no more luxurious than mine in Wisconsin, was comfortable and pleasant.

And, they had a summer cottage on the Chesapeake. Mib's mother told me we'd be spending a few days there, later in the week, and I was thrilled. I'd always envied some of my Wisconsin friends whose families had summer cottages. It sounded so great to go to a cozy, comfortable place and just swim, hike, row a boat, and read on a raft. My family either stayed home during the summers while Dad taught, or went off to a university in some other state where Dad would teach and we would see "Interesting Things," like Yosemite or Yellowstone or Arizona pueblos. I could see the beauty in national parks, but much of it was lost on me because I mainly wanted to be "normal," staying close to home in Wisconsin like all my teenage friends there.

Before we left for the Browns' summer cottage, Mib's parents invited a small gathering of friends and family to their D.C. home, where I was introduced as Mib's future roommate. A black man in his thirties commented privately to me during the evening, "Mib's lucky she's so light-skinned—lighter than her parents. But it makes for quarrels in her extended family."

Was I hearing him right? I'd read that some southerners actually still judged people by their degree of color, but I was sure it couldn't really be true. My mind boggled. This was just like Hitler and the degree of Jewishness. Unbelievable. Not in America, not possible. Hey, we'd just finished a war about this. No way.

On the Chesapeake, Mib's snug family cottage was right on the water, so we could swim pretty much anytime we desired. It had a creaking porch swing that seated two, where we sat evenings, telling jokes and laughing as we rocked. Mib's mom made sure we had plenty of easy food whenever we wanted. It was perfect, everything I'd dreamed of.

One night while we were at the Chesapeake, the Browns took me to a nearby cottage where Mib's uncle was vacationing. Unlike Mib's parents and my own, he had TV, and had turned it up loud, to a boxing match between Joe Louis and a white man. When I was introduced to the uncle, he kept his gaze on the screen and said nothing. I hated watching violence and sat quietly in a corner.

"Get him. Hit him. Knock Whitey down." Mib's uncle kept shouting. "Kill him."

I mostly just kept my polite mask on and looked at the floor. Mib's mom seemed embarrassed at her brother-in-law's rudeness and we left before the match was over. Mr. Brown drove, with Mib in the front seat. Sitting in back with me on our return to their cottage, Mrs. Brown apologized for what had happened. I tried to reassure her I'd not been bothered and everything was okay.

Of course I did feel the uncle's hostility and even realized it might be possible that he kept yelling about whitey because *I* was white. But it all seemed so strange. I reasoned that since *I* didn't feel discomfort with him because he was black, why would he feel unhappy with my whiteness? *I* wasn't angry or threatened, just puzzled, as only a young white girl raised in a world of good intentions could feel.

Mib kept quiet. She never referred to what happened, and since I was embarrassed by the incident, I kept silent about it, too.

I look back now and pound my head at my puzzlement. It was 1951, right? In the D.C. area, right? The unspoken, unbreakable barrier between blacks and whites then had barbed wire and broken glass on top. Mib's mom and dad were doing everything they could to help her get ahead, to find her way in America as it was then. Her uncle probably thought the parents were idiots, setting up their daughter for misery and rejection by sending her to a white college and welcoming her white roommate.

After a few weeks back at Mount Holyoke in the fall, Mib confided in me one night, after lights-out, about how hard it was to be one of only two black women (*negro girls*, we said then, of course) out of twelve hundred women at our college. She shared how the senior black woman ("*girl*," we said then) had told her she must always remember to be a model of good behavior, in order to give a positive

126

impression to the whites, most of whom had never been around blacks-as-equals before. Mib told me how painful and difficult this was for her. She said she felt she could never feel her own feelings, be who she really was. It was the one time she ever opened up to me.

"Mib, that is so terrible," I told her, "so wrong. How do you stand it?" I felt such shame and outrage that she didn't feel she could be herself here at our college. But I didn't feel she heard me.

Perhaps, with great tact, she was preparing me for what happened shortly after. Or maybe she truly did need to unburden herself, as in a friendship between equals, to the point that she actually shared a real feeling with me. Her need, then, would have been to be heard but not necessarily to receive my response. That was how I heard what she said that night. But empathy from a white girl, no matter how genuine it might be, must not have seemed possible to her.

A week or two later Mib told me that a single room had come empty in our dorm and she'd opted to take it. "It's not about you," she told me. "I just need space to be me."

This left me to room the rest of the year with a girl who didn't share my interests. I smarted as I felt my friendship with Mib dwindling to nothing. I noticed she seemed to be really close with another white girl (not in Le Foyer) and this added to my sense of loss.

I didn't see Mib in the intervening sixty years, but the college sends a quarterly publication with class notes, so I knew she'd married a nationally known, politically active black man and had children. I knew she was divorced, had a Ph.D., and taught English Lit at an Ivy League college until she retired. To become a full professor at a respected college is a huge achievement for anyone, especially a woman and an African American.

Today, the Mt. Holyoke campus is racially integrated. "Thirty-four percent of MHC students identify as African American, Asian American, Latina, Native American, or multiracial," the MHC website tells me. I didn't return for our sixtieth reunion in June 2014, but a classmate suggested I write Mib. "I think she'd love to hear from you."

Expecting little or nothing, I wrote her a friendly catch-up letter. I asked how the current MHC integration felt to her, as a professor emerita. I mentioned my granddaughter, who was a nurse in Chad, and shared that in the sixties, my husband John and I had sued the Pasadena Board of Education for integrated schools. Mib had known John in 1951-52, the year John and I fell in love and got engaged. She would have known from the *Quarterly* that he died in 1988.

Weeks went by. No reply. No surprise, I thought, but I kept hoping. One afternoon I sat reading on my back deck, cat on my lap. The phone rang and Mib's name appeared on the tiny phone window. I picked up and heard her voice, strong and warm as I remembered it. We chatted a few minutes. Then she told me, "I've been away on a trip but now I'm home again. I just got your letter and was so happy to have it. I wanted to hear your voice before writing you. Expect a long email from me."

How would this turn out? It seemed pretty hopeful.

But there's been no word from Mib since.

I like to think I've grown at least a little out of my old blind naiveté. I like to think that when she said she'd write, she meant it.

I've been called naïve, always hoping racial relations would improve, always thinking this possible. I've continued to allow myself to be vulnerable, just as Dad told me sixty-plus years ago, in effort to bridge the gap. Maybe racial relations can improve and maybe not, but I still believe they can, even if this might be a need of mine rather than a reality-based expectation.

I guess this must be what people call faith.

# The Envelope

## Taryn Young

I knew before he spoke. I could read it in his face. I could see him composing himself. His earlier assurances had been wrong. The exam table was cold, a glance at the window confirmed the afternoon had not shrugged off the gray. Fitting, I would not want it to be sunny.

Did my bronchial cough cause this? I asked.

He rushed with his answer. "It's not your fault. Sometimes it just happens in later term pregnancies. The umbilical cord gets tangled around the baby's neck. Nobody knows why."

I nodded that I understood through the tears. I knew that he was probably right, but I was not as sure. I remembered crouching over the bathtub running hot water hoping the steam would stop my coughing. My daughter exhausted from the friendly, but constant, onslaught of the happiest place on earth, Disneyland, was asleep in the hotel bed. My husband Lee asked me if I really wanted to take our two-year old to the Emergency Room. *Yes. Yes, I did,* I thought as I imagined the baby somersaulting and trying to find his thumb during the turmoil of the day. I should have gone, but I turned away and focused on the running water.

"Do you have someone to drive you home?" the doctor asked.

"I do," I lied, clutching the appointment card for the procedure to remove the fetus. Lee had not accompanied me to the appointment. He was unable to confront the possibility the baby had died while we were on vacation.

Sitting alone in the parking lot, I couldn't control the tears. I tried to think of what to do next. I would need to call work. I would need to call my mom and sisters, and tell Lee.

It was two weeks before I returned to work. Days had a fuzzy hue. At night I was plagued by the same dream of falling, jolting awake breathless. I returned to daily routines hoping to find comfort in order. I packed up all the baby clothes, releasing them from the drawers where they had been so carefully tucked. I kept the pumpkin costume the longest. Finally, I placed it in the Goodwill box.

My first day back at work was the day of Evangelina's long awaited baby shower. At first, I thought I would not go, not sure I could control the tears. This was Evangelina's first baby. She knew it was a girl. I decided to go and leave the gift I had purchased. I loved buying gifts for babies—usually making multiple trips to get the gift just right.

Martha, one of the more senior employees, approached me right before lunch. "I think you will be uncomfortable at the shower," she said. "It will be okay if you don't go."

I told her I would be okay, explaining I had a gift. She responded more firmly, saying I should not go. It took me a few seconds to understand that Evangelina would be uncomfortable and Martha was telling me not to go.

"Yes, of course," I said. "I'll just leave the gift on her chair."

My boss, Karen, found me in the hallway a short time later. "You are so much stronger than you know," she said. I liked my boss. She was genuine, and very earthy Berkeley. She represented the University well in dark-blue suit jackets and Birkenstocks. As she turned away, I wanted to scream, "I am not strong."

Getting through the day was proving harder than I imagined. I kept looking at my wristwatch willing the time to go by faster. Walking back from the copier I saw Janine, the department secretary. Janine had strict social protocols. She spoke only with the girls from the clerical pool, or the students. She and I had never chatted or had what I would have called a friendly conversation. I smiled preparing to walk by.

Janine stopped me, planting herself in my way.

"I can't imagine what you are feeling," she said.

I thanked her, the tears I had kept at bay all day threatening to flow over the guarded banks.

"I have five hundred dollars that I could lend you, you know, if you need it."

I was surprised, and taken aback. In my family, talking about money, and the need for money, was a formal exercise. I told her I was okay. She was insistent, extending an envelope.

"Only for a little while," she said, "until you are on your feet."

I realized she was worried about the weeks of work that I had missed. "Thanks, but I have my mom if I need help. I am okay."

She extended the envelope again, "You can pay me back in a few weeks."

I reached for her hands, and guided the envelope back. "My husband has a good job, my mom is well off, and my sisters will help," I explained.

Janine seemed satisfied. In that moment, I realized that I would be okay. I had more resources than many. I had the strength of a very tight family.

Janine and I did not speak again. But we smiled at each other more often. Now, as I await my first grandchild, I wish I could tell her how much it meant to me, not the generosity, but the bravery. So many good friends thought they were being kind saying "it's for the best," or worse, saying nothing at all. Janine was the first to acknowledge that I was hurting, and that it was okay to hurt.

# The Govement

## Don Dussault

Folks talk about the govement like it is real, like our house. Grandpa says it is paper. I asked him how he knows when nobody can see the govement. He says look next time I go to the post office. One day I figured out what it is made of.

We live a little ways outside the village. Mommy and I walked to the post office on the tar road everybody says is black except it looks dark gray to me except when it rains. I saw some new yellow flowers in the skinny grass by the road. We walked by the field with the high grass and no flowers and it got boring to see, so I thought about the govement and what it is.

The post office has a flagpole in front with a limp flag on top and a wide window made of one big piece of glass like the grocery store. Inside, two of the walls are made of little square metal boxes with little glass windows in each one so you can see if any mail is in them.

We never stay long enough for me to see everything in the glass showcases with glass shelves full of stuff you can buy, like scarves and baseball caps and colored hats. My favorite is the one with candy and cookies except Mommy never bought any. On top of the showcases perch huge glass candy jars with wrapped hard candies in one, gumballs in another, sticks of lickrish in another. My favorite glass jar is the fourth one. It holds striped red and white canes.

Mr. Smith is always behind the glass showcases and he smiles when he looks at me through his thick glasses.

That's how I got it. The govement is made of glass.

# The Gradual Instant

## Fran Claggett

At what moment does wood become stone, peat become coal,
limestone become marble? The gradual instant.

—Anne Michaels: *Fugitive Pieces*

There's no telling when it began. Was it when she was four, sitting on
a folding chair at the family reunion, forgotten, but obedient? And so
she sat, golden-haired, dressed in a yellow polka-dot dress with
matching socks and a big yellow ribbon in her hair. What was she
thinking, sitting under that big chestnut tree (because there were still
chestnut trees then, spreading their branches as in the famous poem),
while aunts and uncles, cousins of all ages, babies, grandmothers,
including the one who could cure warts by saying magic words and
rubbing them, sitting there while all the family wandered about with
paper plates, eating, by now, cakes and pies, and still, she sat there,
unnoticed, the mother distracted, having forgotten she had told the
daughter to just sit there like a good girl and she would be right back.
What did she hear? What did she notice? Did it begin then?

Or was it in the afternoon when she climbed up the dark stairs
to the attic and found her mother's old cedar chest, the one that had
survived the wedding day fire, falling from the second floor bedroom
to the first floor, filled then with the wedding dress and everything she
owned, now one side charred, the legs uneven, but inside, everything
pristine. The folded pillowcases, each embroidered with fine stitchery,
flowers and birds in threads. Had anyone ever laid her head on these
pillowcases? Did she wonder that? And the quilt, the wedding ring
quilt, did she wonder about that? Did she wonder who made it? Was it
her Scottish grandmother's mother, the one who told her the stories at
night when she slept in her bed? Were there books in the cedar chest,
books that had stories about the boy who told a lie and the word
L I A R appeared on his forehead so everyone would see and know?
No, that was her father's book. The cedar chest was her mother's
things. Did it begin then?

Perhaps it didn't begin in the attic. Perhaps it began when she
took her book *Arlo*, well, it wasn't really her book, it belonged to the
library, but she took it up into the black cherry tree that leafed out in

the summer and hid her for hours. She kept *Arlo* hidden in a small recess built into her closet as a backup for bathroom pipes. So it was safe there and when she walked right into the library and told the librarian she had lost the book and how much did she owe, she felt the hot flush of lying, which she wasn't very good at. But knowing as she did that only one copy of a book existed in a library, she had to save all her allowances for weeks, then tell a lie to keep the book. And she really couldn't give this book back.

Yes, perhaps it did begin there, with *Arlo*. Some details have faded with the years, but there was the boy Arlo, whose real name was Orlando, son of royalty, suddenly uprooted and living in the forest where his old violin master Comrade found him. And they lived in the forest and the boy studied with Comrade and composed a sweetly haunting piece, and later, proclaimed a prodigy, played before the newly-restored king and queen, and yes, the melody was the lullaby the queen had sung to her infant son those years ago in the palace, and, such joy to the nine-year-old girl, they were reunited, all because of the power of memory and music.

The year that brought *Arlo* also brought other beginnings, beginnings which wove themselves in and out of her life until she thought sometimes that everything meaningful in her life began that year, the year she was nine, the year her fourth-grade teacher Mrs. Patterson made all the difference and set her passions aflame. Birds (she still had the big beautifully illustrated *Birds of America* that Mrs. Patterson had given her), Greek gods that were to be with her forever, small animals (she took home the mice she had named Odysseus and Penelope over summer vacation), music (Mrs. Patterson came to her recital when she played Beethoven's *Sonata Pathetique)*, foreign lands (Mrs. Patterson brought her a small Norwegian doll from a trip she took with her sister and she learned about fjords), and the Native Americans: she never knew why Mrs. Patterson took her on the trip to the Indian Mounds of Ohio and then to visit her niece who was the same age and ended up going to the same college much later, but it was her first experience with Indian artifacts and stories.

She couldn't believe her good fortune when her family moved during the sixth grade and she found that their new house was just behind the house that Mrs. Patterson and her sister lived in, with just an alley between them. All that knowledge, right there. And they had a dog, which she wasn't allowed to have because her father said the city was no place for a dog, but it was and she became the dog whisperer (she learned that phrase later) of the whole neighborhood. Just a whistle, a secret whistle, and Tiny, the Saint Bernard, and Cutie, the little mix with a laughing mouth, and Brownie, the Chow that nobody else could pet, all came to her. And later, her very own Skipper, who followed her home and her father didn't say no or yes, but Skipper stayed.

In that beginning time she gathered words to her, words like "manifest destiny," which she never truly understood, even as an adult, but she liked the sound of the phrase and let those two words embody all of her new obsessions. Later, when she discovered Einstein, although she never understood his theories either, she morphed her curiosities about her manifest destiny into what was to become a lifelong quest, creating a work that embodied not just the "unified field theory" but what the physicists came to call "a theory of everything." So perhaps it was Mrs. Patterson, along with Arlo, that was, then, the beginning. Of everything.

# The Serendipitous Journey

## Pamela Fender

### Spring 1929 San Francisco

Joe Harris was excited to be on his way to visit his sister Annie. It was a typical brisk, sunny day in San Francisco. Everyone in the city dressed impeccably, especially when shopping or doing business downtown. Joe wore dark brown pleated trousers, a white cotton shirt, brown tie, and matching jacket. His dark brown brogue shoes complemented his dark brown Fedora hat. He splurged for brand new attire; it was worth it for the special occasion of seeing his sister. A bouquet of pale pink tulips he bought from a vendor on Market Street were clutched in his hand.

He ran down Market Street to catch the streetcar, its bell clanging loudly before coming to a stop halfway up the block. If he sprinted the thirty or so yards to it, he could catch it.

Joe patiently waited for the passengers to step off. It was midmorning as a crowd of busy shoppers and businessmen moved toward the streetcar doors to scramble aboard. The streetcar was always crowded at this time of day. He was getting ready to climb on when he noticed a newer streetcar pulling in behind the older one. Joe turned and rushed toward the shiny, new mint-green and cream-colored trolley. He managed to board just as the doors closed behind him. Walking slowly toward the rear of the car, there were no vacant seats. He grabbed onto the strap hanger. With a jolt, the electric streetcar surged along Market Street toward Powell. *Ah, yes. An empty seat.*

"May I?" Joe eyed the seat beside a young man already seated.

"Yes, of course," the young man replied.

"Can't believe I managed to catch one of the new ones," Joe said. "It's much smoother than the older cars I've been on."

"It sure is smooth." In the man's lap lay a colorful assortment of peonies, dahlias, and roses.

Joe recognized an accent. "You sound like a Brit. May I ask where you're from?"

The young man turned in his seat to face Joe.

"I'm from England but I live in Texas now. You sound like you're English as well."

"Yes, I'm from England, too."

"If I may ask, what part of England are you from?"

"London," Joe said.

"Me, too."

"What part of London?"

"Notting Hill."

"Really?" Joe raised his eyebrows.

"Yep. Portobello Road."

"No kidding? I grew up on Portobello Road, too. What a coincidence. What house number was it?"

"Oh, I don't remember. I moved away from there when I was about two."

Judah had little memory of that time. He was the youngest boy of a dozen children. He despised that he grew up in an orphanage, not having the privilege of living with his older siblings. He wondered where his other siblings were and if they had families of their own. His heart ached from the pain of his loss, of not knowing all of his siblings.

A tall woman neatly dressed in a suit jacket, jersey blouse and pleated skirt, stood from the bench across and reached her arm up to yank the pull cord. Judah took notice of her soft gray felt cloche hat and matching gloves as she moved toward the rear doors.

"So, when did you come to America?" Judah asked.

"Well, I was born in Russia. After my older sister and I moved with our parents from Russia to England, my mother had ten more children. She died when I was nineteen so I decided to leave England and come to America in '04. I've been living here for twenty-four years."

"My mother died, too. Very suddenly and mysteriously. That's why I left Portobello Road. I had to. I had no choice. My father's new wife didn't want us and I ended up in an orphanage like so many other kids in those days." Judah exhaled an audible sigh. "Turns out she couldn't bear children herself and raising his kids would be an inconvenience to her." Judah revealed more than he normally would to someone he just met, but somehow he felt relaxed sharing his stories with this stranger who seemed familiar.

"I understand. It's shameful, some people . . ." Joe trailed off.

Joe missed his younger brothers and sisters, some he hardly knew, they were so young. He often thought about what it'd be like to meet them someday, if fate allowed.

Both sat quietly. Moments turned to several minutes of silence.

"So, what line of work are you in?" Joe asked.

"I work with my brother-in-law in his department store. Battelstein's, Menswear Department," Judah said. "And you?"

"I've traveled back and forth from Oregon to San Francisco for work. Next month, I'm permanently moving to Oregon to be closer to my wife's family. I'm starting a small business there. Produce. Fruits and vegetables."

Their conversation flowed as if they'd known each other forever.

"What did you say brought you to San Francisco?" Judah asked.

"I didn't mention it. I'm here to see my sister again before returning to Oregon."

"How curious," Judah said.

"How is that?" Joe asked.

"Just odd that I've traveled to San Francisco to meet up with my sister, too. I won't be staying long, though. I'll be leaving in a couple of weeks to return to Houston. Gotta get back to the old grind."

"How long's it been since you've seen your sister?" Joe asked.

"I haven't seen her in thirteen years. We've exchanged letters and she knows I'm coming to San Francisco to see her, but not exactly *when* I'm coming to see her. I certainly hope she's home. I can't wait to sit down and have a fine cuppa tea."

"Thirteen years? Blimey, you've got some catching up to do."

"Yessir, you can say that again."

Judah recalled the last time he saw Annie, his older sister. It was at the orphanage. He longed for his sister; his heart fluttered with the image of seeing her again.

"My stop's the next one, mate. It's been real pleasant chatting," Joe said as he began to rise from his seat, reaching for the pull cord.

"Hold on. I'm right behind you. I believe it's my stop, too. Fella at the ferry terminal said to get off on Balboa at Nineteenth Avenue," Judah said as he rose from his seat.

Joe moved toward the rear of the car. He looked back as Judah followed him. Judah appeared taller than his short stature, dressed in a fine midnight blue wool suit with neat silver pin stripes, double-breasted vest, dark tie and steel gray Fedora. He wore gray and white two-toned shoes. The car slowed, then came to an abrupt stop. Both men lurched forward, catching their balance. Stepping down to the sidewalk, they stood for a moment watching the streetcar continue its journey.

"Well, like I said, it's been a pleasure to meet you." Joe extended his hand.

With a firm shake Judah said, "My pleasure as well."

"Which way you headed, mate?"

"That way," Judah pointed up the street.

"Looks like I'm going your way, too," Joe smiled.

"Talk about coincidences."

Joe and Judah crossed the street and continued to walk and talk as they approached the corner.

Judah pulled out a crumpled envelope from inside his jacket, then looked down at it to confirm the address. "She lives on Twentieth Avenue, right around the next corner, I think."

They continued walking together, turned the corner and walked a half block down the street. Judah looked up at the house address in front of them.

"This is the place. Five-forty-eight Twentieth Avenue."

Joe stopped so suddenly that he nearly lost his balance. "Are you bloody kidding me? This is where Annie lives." Joe's heart began beating faster than normal.

"Annie? Are you *kidding* me? That's *my* sister's name."

Adrenaline rushed so rapidly through Joe, he could hardly breathe. He shook his head, speechless.

"What's wrong? Are you okay?" Judah asked.

Joe stepped back with a look of utter disbelief upon his face. He gasped, cupping his hands over his mouth. He dropped his hands by his sides and exhaled a long breath. His mouth hung wide open.

"*What's* your name, again?"

"I never did say my name. I'm Judah. Judah Harris."

Joe looked straight at Judah with tear-filled eyes. "I have a little brother named Judah." Joe outstretched his arms, hopeful for an embrace. "I'm Joe Harris. I'm your big brother."

They fell into each other's arms, the older brother enveloping his younger brother as Annie opened her front door.

# The Sound of Coat Hangers[1]

## Michael Welch

I'm sitting on my deck in Noe Valley early Saturday morning talking to Dan back in Ohio.

I woke up in the middle of the night, I tell him. A week ago Friday. At first I thought I heard metal coat hangers. You know, the sound they make jingling on the rod? Weird, huh? Then, I realized it was Sandra crying. I turned to wake her up but she wasn't there. I got up and followed the sound. She was lying across the bed in the guest room. What's wrong? I asked. I thought someone had died.

She said she was in love with another man and dreamed of having a family with him.

Dan clears his throat. What the hell?

I know. I felt like someone had come up behind me and slit my throat. It was terrible. Completely out of nowhere. I mean, we were everyone's perfect couple. That's what I thought, anyway. I just stood there like an idiot.

Dan says nothing. His silence underscores the futility of it all. I blow my nose. All my hopes and plans have turned to snot. The irony of the situation is so prosaic; it feels as if I'm trapped in the pages of a bad novel. When I thumb through my grievances, I can't believe what I see there. My wife, whom I've loved so loyally for fifteen years and never doubted, is in love with someone else. Unbelievable and, in a perverse kind of way, thrilling.

The worst part is the humiliation, I tell Dan. She knows I wouldn't do anything to hurt her or what's-his-name. God, what is his name? So, she pretends nothing's happening and talks about going camping with this guy, in front of the kids, as if I were part of the fucking woodwork. Can you imagine?

No. Why would she do that?

I told her I'd go along with whatever she decided to do and she took me at my word. Last night she was on the phone with her sister talking about how it was all working out so well. That really pissed me off. I tried to pull the phone out of the wall and pulled her off her chair instead. She hit her head against the edge of the desk and started

---

[1] This story is written without dialogue quotes.

bleeding. I actually smelled blood. Christ. Just because I'm a decent guy doesn't mean I don't have any feelings.

Maybe you oughta fight for her.

Wouldn't do any good. Turns out she's had a couple of flings that didn't amount to anything. That's how she knows this one's serious. She says she wants a new life. Says the whole thing's her fault. I say it's fifty-fifty, right down the middle. That's where it stands.

Come on, Mike. None of this is your fault.

It is, Dan, in a way. Remember, she's only thirty-five. I'm fifty for Christ's sake. I don't care about going to raves or talking to my co-workers 24/7 on the fucking computer. I can't tell you how many times I've left this house in the morning thinking she deserves somebody younger. Without wanting to, I've been trying to find the courage to tell her she should leave.

Bullshit.

Here's what really gets me. It's one thing for this guy to waltz into her life, but suddenly there's another guy in my daughters' lives. It seems like I should have some kind of say in that. He may be the greatest guy in the world, but my time with my kids is going to be cut in half. Talk about the law of unintended consequences. Ruthless.

I glance back through the window. Sandra rushes into the kitchen wearing a T-shirt, and nothing else. She hides behind the door. She's just gotten up. Even with her Coke-bottle glasses and her hair sticking out every goddamned way, she looks beautiful to me. Just like she's looked every morning the past fifteen years. Her legs are long and elegant. Nothing about her has aged since I first met her.

Our nine-year-old daughter, Darin, runs into the room, finds Sandra immediately, and starts tickling her. They laugh and carry on as if they don't have a care in the world. I consider ramming my fist through the window, but I slump down on the deck and lean against the side of the house where they can't see me.

Mike? You still there?

What else I can do, Dan. It's not a rhetorical question. I'm desperate for an answer.

He sighs. Well, you could tell her to shape up or ship out. But she can't move in with someone and take the kids along 'til she's got a divorce. What do you know about this guy?

Not much. When I asked her and she started talking about him, it made me sick.

What did she say?

She said he'd worked on himself every day of his life. I wanted to throw up. I expected her to say he was younger, more energetic, more fun . . . that kind of thing. I didn't want to hear he's a better human being than I am.

That's hogwash.

The other day I walked into our den and found her talking to him on the phone. I asked if I could talk with him for a second. She handed over the phone, and I said, "Look. I'm gonna make it easy for you because I love her, not because I don't love her."

That was too complicated for him, I suppose. He said something, I forget what, and I gave the phone back to Sandra. She laughed and told him, Welcome to divorce in California.

Well, Dan says, look at it this way. You're gonna be single in San Francisco. You're gonna have women lined up around the block. Call me back next week. Okay?

I don't want other women. Just her.

It's not the end of the world. It's the beginning.

Yeh, yeh. Okay, buddy. Love ya.

Ditto to that. Talk to ya later.

After Dan hangs up, I find myself listening to the dial tone. The life line to my self-respect has gone dead. Nothing I say and no one I know is going to reconnect me.

Directly above my head, the kitchen window flies open.

Sandra sticks her head outside saying, I wonder where Daddy is?

I could walk down through the garden, out into the alley and off into the sunrise never to return while my wife watches in wonder, but I know she'd merely think I went to get a newspaper. She's sure I'll do the right thing. I'm the rock. She's the river that flows around me. She's moving on. I'm stuck.

I try to console myself. This is just an affair of the heart. She's not trying to destroy me. She's simply trying to leave. I should be able to handle this. And yet every negative thought that comes my way is guided like radiation to the magnet she left in my heart. I've loved her more than anything and everything. Now, I own a warehouse full of love that's worthless.

How did I get in this position?

I was raised on a farm in the Ohio River Valley, an only child, self-reliant, fully capable of keeping myself entertained. I grew up during the McCarthy Era and the Cold War, skeptical of any allegiances beyond my native soil. I went to college when existentialism was all the rage.

How did I become a fatuous, fainthearted romantic?

I enter the house and walk by the den where Sandra's chatting happily again with what's-his-name, the phone tucked under her chin, braiding Darin's hair. My wife, the great multitasker. Darin's reading *One Morning in Maine*. She glances up at me and returns to her book.

I catch Sandra's eye. When you wrap that up, I'd like to have a word, I say. I want to be firm, but I sound like a man who's gotten used to groveling.

Sandra looks up, smiles without the least tinge of embarrassment and says into the phone, gotta go now. Call you later. She whispers something else. Then, she joins me in the study.

What's up? She sits on the couch.

I turn around in my swivel chair. Any pretense of a normal life is a colossal affront to my dignity, I say. I sound pompous. These days, try as I may to be cool, I sound like a jackass.

She folds her legs sideways beneath her, pulling her T-shirt down around her knees.

I watch the ceiling fan going around and begin to get dizzy. All I can think of is how much I want to lift up her shirt and make love to her. This is humiliating, I say, beyond belief.

I'm sorry.

Remember when we were on our honeymoon, and I told you I'd never want to keep you in a pumpkin shell?

Of course.

All these years, you knew you could have your freedom whenever you asked for it, but you still didn't have the decency to tell me you were having an affair. You deceived me and made me feel like an idiot.

I'm telling you now. And I haven't had an affair. Her lower lip quivers.

I regret the tack I've taken but I sail on anyway.

You handed me some horseshit about going to meetings and who knows what else when you were really just sneaking off to be with him. You should have trusted me—trusted that I could handle it. Why didn't you tell me you'd found someone else? I can't believe you just took what you wanted and threw my feelings away like so much wrapping paper.

That's gets her crying.

I know you didn't want to hurt me, but you've always been great at confronting things. Why didn't you just come clean? I would've given you anything you wanted. All you had to do was ask. That's all. You could've done that. You're the great you. What were you thinking? I clear my throat quickly and go on before she can interrupt.

I suppose you wanted to be certain he was worth all the trouble and he was good with the kids. You wanted it to be a done deal. Well, you pulled it off. Is that one of the things they taught you in business school? It feels like I got bought out and laid off in one fell swoop.

Sandra sits forward. It kills me to hurt you, she says. I didn't think you'd take it so hard. You've been so supportive of everything I do. I'm really sorry. I think it'd be better if I moved out. Into a transitional apartment. I've already found one actually.

With all the detachment I can summon I say, go ahead then and do it.

I'll leave tomorrow, she says. She seems relieved.

I'm floored. There's something else I was going to say, but I've lost it. My big speech is finished. The battle is over before it began.

We've made love almost every night since I discovered her crying in the guest room. She swears she hasn't gone to bed with what's-his-name. No matter how many times I hear it, I can't remember his fucking name.

She looks thin. I sit down beside her and wrap my arms around her shoulders. She feels thin. We've both lost weight. Maybe it isn't as easy for her as I think. I hear Darin and Karin chasing each other through the bedrooms upstairs, shouting, giggling.

Tonight, during a candlelit memorial service for AIDS victims at a local synagogue, we hold hands. I want to pray our marriage will be saved, but that's asking too much. Sandra, I know, is praying it'll soon be over. Later, after the kids are asleep, she lights her own candle by the bed, turns out the overhead light and says not to worry. We don't have to be careful tonight.

Don't worry. Those words were always my rallying cry. Now they sound like a death knell. Don't ask for whom the bell tolls. It tolls for me.

I wonder if condemned men enjoy their last meals like I'm enjoying this. When the sorrow becomes too much, I let it carry me. I love you, I say.

Me too, she says, patting my chest.

She rolls over, tucks her head into my shoulder and falls asleep. My happiness is spent. I feel the naked length of her, her thigh thrown over my inconsolable cock.

How I admire her. I try to imagine having the courage to hurt someone like she's hurting me but I can't. The truth is too painful to be borne. I believe in her more than I believe in myself.

As for what's-his-name, who's worked on himself every day of his life, I wonder if he's gotten it right by now. What a joke. Sadly, this one is on me. Like a man falling on a banana peel. It'd be funny if it didn't hurt so much.

# The Thermometer

## Venus Maher

### September 19th, 1973

At fourteen I'm considered weird for still being a virgin. In my circle that is stranger than my mom living in a hippie commune, or me living here with another family to go to school. There are no kids my age in that crazy commune in the mountains, so my mama left me here last year.

Mom's visiting me this weekend. When she hugs me she gives me a present in a velvet bag. Inside there's a thermometer, and a calendar filled with funny little graphs.

"What's this for?" I ask.

"You take your temperature every morning before you get up," Mom says. "Write the results on the graph and draw a line between the numbers. When you ovulate, your temperature will drop for three days. That's when you're most fertile and should avoid intercourse. A week is best, but that leaves three weeks a month as a safe zone. Knowing when you could conceive, and how to avoid making babies, allows you to enjoy being a woman," she says with a grand flourish of the thermometer.

I don't even have a boyfriend yet.

"Isn't there more to it?"

"Knowledge is power, Honey. This way you don't have to take harmful chemicals like birth control pills. Just keep track and avoid sex during that week of ovulation." She sounded like an advertisement for the rhythm method.

Tomorrow she's going back to the commune and I'm staying here for school. I'm lonely. I want to be kissed, and to have someone's arms around me. I want love. If it helps, I'll take my temperature every morning for the entire year.

### October 25th, 1973

We're on a camping trip to the Eel River, and everything's changed. Tom has noticed me. He's seventeen, granite-strong, with a warm laugh, and eyes that follow me everywhere. I'm uncomfortable when

146

most boys watch me, but under Tom's caressing gaze I feel like a woman. I move with fluid grace.

It's late on the first night. Our tents are pitched, dinner's over, and we've finished our big campfire sing-a-long. Tom and I have been passing looks back and forth all day. My breath comes in shallow waves of excitement. I go to my tent after telegraphing an invitation to Tom. My sleeping bag is cold, but I lie there dressed in nothing but goosebumps, listening for footsteps. Tom waits until the camp is quiet, then he sneaks into my tent.

It's awkward fitting our bodies together, but kisses bridge the tension. I like Tom and he likes me. I've kept my chart up, and I'm in the safe zone.

It's so good to be in his arms. Then, he starts to enter me and pain stabs my legs shut. Tears color my voice as I stammer an apology.

We try again. Oh my god it's painful!

"Stop. It hurts too much," I whisper urgently. Thank God Tom listens, and rolls off, breathing hard. He's silent. I don't speak again until dawn.

I'm curled up against him, my face resting on his chest. His heartbeat has slowed. I move as close as skin will allow.

"I'm sorry," I say. "Forgive me?"

There's no answer.

When gray edges out the black inside my tent, Tom gets up and leaves. There are no arms around me now. I huddle alone in my sleeping bag.

## March 16th, 1974

It's spring, and I'm trying to connect again. Tom stopped looking, but Jeff's eyes are brown pools of invitation. Jeff's sixteen, creative, witty, and kind.

We're on another field trip, this time to Black Stone Ranch. He and I got the upstairs loft in the main cabin tonight. We have the upper level all to ourselves, and we're cuddling under the blankets in this single bed. It's cold outside. They build a fire in the wood-stove downstairs.

Oh, my God, it's hot in here.

We're kissing. I'm melting. Jeff's breathing fast. I can't catch my breath. He flings the covers off. We're wrestling, sweating, and panting. It's so intense. Suddenly I roll over and fall right off the bed. The sound of my naked body hitting the wooden floor echoes throughout the house. I'm so embarrassed. My right shoulder and hip hurt. I want to die.

"Are you okay up there?" our teacher, Lori, calls out.

"Oh, gosh, everything's fine. I just . . . tripped," I yell.

Jeff helps me up, and we resume, but I'm flustered and confused. We begin to kiss again. He moans into my mouth. He's poking me in the stomach. Now my belly is wet and sticky. He's turns over and fades into sleep before I know what's happened.

I'm still a virgin.

I feel so alone. I don't think the damned basal thermometer is helping. I don't know what all the books, movies and love songs are about. This is just awkward as hell. I don't sleep.

Jeff stops looking at me.

## December 24th, 1974

It's Christmas Eve at the women's commune in Mendocino where Mom now lives. Tom and Jeff are ancient history. I went to three women's festivals during the summer. I've discovered I'm a lesbian. I haven't made love with a woman yet, but I think I'm in love. Her name is Rachel. She's older than me and more experienced.

We're having a party. This could be the night. Our night. We're playing Lavender Jane, our first album of woman's music, and everyone's been dancing to it for hours. Rachel's looking at me, and I'm looking back. We've been flirting for days. She amazing. I want her to touch me more than I want food or air. We dance and dance and dance.

When the music stops at midnight, I reach for her. She takes my hand and we go to her room. She strikes a match and touches it to the candlewicks and to the firewood laid in the wood stove. This time, there will be light, and words, and grace.

Rachel is in my arms, and I am in hers. We're undressing each other kiss by kiss, leaving wet trails across soft terrain. When we're entwined together under her down quilt, Rachel asks "How often have you made love?"

"This is my first time with a woman," I answer. "My first real time in a way that counts in my heart."

Her body goes rigid.

"This is your first time?" Rachel asks, pulling away. She leans on one elbow and looks down at me. Her forehead is creased. She isn't smiling now.

"Yes, and I'm so happy it's with you Rachel," I say, my stomach twisting. I try to pull her into a kiss. She resists.

"Are you sure you're ready?" Rachel asks.

"I've never been more sure of anything. I want to make love with you Rachel." I let the passion inside of me rise into my eyes, my fingertips, my breath, my undulating body. I'm on fire.

Rachel looks down at me, and I can see desire warring with hesitation.

I reach for her with a kiss, a long extravagant kiss that contains everything in me, offers everything in me. She holds back for an unbearable minute, then she unites with me, as fire consumes us in a flurry of desire.

## December 28th, 1974

We stay in her room for three glorious days, only leaving her bed to play guitar, drink tea, and, dressed in velvet robes, run to the bathroom in the main house. Now, my world is fiery music, and liquid passion. It is primal smells and feather touches. All I care about are her arms around me, and my arms around her. My world is our lips and hands exploring the edges of sensuality.

After three days, we decide to join the others for a party next door. I visit my abandoned guest room for clothes and catch my reflection in the mirror. I see a woman. I look older, and so happy.

Turning, I reach into my bag for my favorite shirt, and my fingers touch the velvet bag. I take the thermometer out and look at it. I hold it directly over the trashcan and let go, before grabbing my shirt and running back to Rachel.

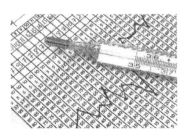

# *Wake*

## Harker Brautighan

Every time I turn around, you are there, dead. You have taken my memory hostage. I look at the water in my tub and I see you, Don, my college friend, lying there dead, on a massage table, on ice, in your brother's garage. How like you to choose a green funeral, no casket save for a cardboard box we all decorated. How like you to be ushered out of this life by someone calling herself the Death Midwife and specializing in traditional, at-home funerals. Your body is surrounded by photographs of you and your artwork, the smell of stargazers fills the room like your presence—your beautiful, immutable, ethereal, impermanent presence.

I remember your voice calling my name as I walked down the strange, San Francisco streets. You'd seen me from the back of a moving motorcycle. If relocating from Chicago to San Francisco was a rebirth, you were my midwife. I hear your laughter sweeping the cobwebs of my brain and shining like a beacon, like a buoy in a troubled current.

There's no getting away from it; there you are, Curt, my cousin, dead in a casket at the funeral home. The lid is closed with your high school yearbook picture on top because you spent five months under water after the river froze. After you threw yourself from a bridge and the winter came and you traveled downstream under the ice and your mom and dad and sisters and brothers all knew you were alive, knew that your car on the bridge and the suicide note they found meant something else, could not possibly mean that you were dead. You floated and drifted and froze while they floated and drifted and froze because you were not dead, could not be dead, because, after all, there was no body.

And you, Mrs. L., you float into my day; your memory floats as if on gas, your ridiculous yet fascinating bun always exactly the same, on top of your head, how did you get it so wide? I try and try to replicate your hairstyle, but my hair will not cooperate. I remember seeing you every day from my classroom. I could see you almost as well as I could see my own teacher, Mrs. H., because I sat in the front row and at an angle. Did you know I had a crush on Mrs. H.? How I wanted that woman. What longing for a second-grade body.

I remember you, Mrs. L., at parent-teacher conferences and happenings about the school, and I remember your name always on the tip of Mrs. Wright's tongue. Also a second-grade teacher, Mrs. Wright was your friend, and the mother of my best friend. I wonder if you know that when you turned your ignition over that night in your garage there was a ventilation problem in your house. I wonder if you know that when you died, you took your daughter with you. And you weren't even sick. Did anyone ever tell you that, wherever you are now? The test results came back; you didn't have cancer. You were going to be just fine. You floated away.

What floated in the little rivulets of blood, drying in the far corners of the bathroom? You bled out, Uncle, on your bathroom floor, alone, after you hemorrhaged. How many days had you lain there? What happened to your cat? I think he bolted when the police broke down your door, after your sister, my aunt, had missed you for days. My family and I were in Europe, tripping through the cathedrals of rural France and eating delightful cream puff pastries with a new surprise in every bite: cherries, custard, cream, chocolate. With my father overseas, Auntie felt all alone. Do you know that the police don't clean up after a death? Do you know the family does? You bled to death, and my cousins, down from their home up North, cleaned it up, scrubbing your blood from the bathroom floor, from the tile and the grout. What as-seen-on-TV infomercial product will they buy to bleach the scene from their hearts?

I forgot this was a list of suicides. If I meander into the deaths of all the loved ones I have lost, they will come to more than the number of years I have been alive. Can you believe it? I must be like that dog, Pard, in *High Sierra*, who brings death on everyone he takes a fancy to. This isn't a list of all the dead—grandparents, aunts, uncles, childhood friends and neighbors, the stillborn babies of my friends.

Even among the neighbors, suicide lurks. Mr. W., I rode the bus home with your kids every day. More popular than I was at a time when that mattered, your son was still a friend. I liked walking home from the bus stop with him, saying, "So long," and turning our separate ways, and maybe talking together when I passed your house on my relentless tramping through the neighborhood. Your son who, barely a teenager, got off the bus one day with his nine-year-old sister to see you in flames, burning to death on the front lawn where you had doused yourself with gasoline before lighting the match. How do two children survive watching their father die? How do they survive knowing you did it on purpose? I can barely believe it's true, and perhaps it's not, because in the first version I heard of the story you had hung yourself.

And Beth, my neighbor, for God's sake, your brothers had already lost both of your parents. Beth, beautiful Beth, after making it through losing your parents, making it through helping to raise the child they left behind, after marrying, becoming a lawyer, and all you achieved, you still decided to die. I don't know who I grieve more—you or your brothers, part of a dwindling family, exactly half of whom are now dead.

It's all too much. I walk the streets of the old neighborhood in my mind, remembering those middle-of-the-night walks of my adolescence with Tory, my dog. I would go down to the pond in the new subdivision to get stoned and think. No sounds but the whoosh of traffic and the moaning of the trains. The only way I got any sleep was to sit there and smoke dope till my brain was so addled that by the time I walked the ten blocks home in the pitch dark I would be too stupefied and too tired for anything but sleep. I always thought Tory would keep me safe.

My therapist's eyes almost bugged out of her head when I told her my father, a wanderer and an insomniac himself, knew I took these walks and didn't stop me. I never even told the therapist that these walks took me past your house, Alice, the house where you were murdered on the front lawn while your parents and sister slept inside. You drove up to Wisconsin, where the drinking age was eighteen, and a man followed you home from the bar. When you got out of your car, he raped you and strangled you with your own bra. I see your face in grainy black-and-white newsprint. I see your sister's picture next to yours. Did you know I had a huge crush on her? And also on her boyfriend, who was my beloved relative's best friend. The relative who has tried to kill himself four times that I know of. He's hung himself and broken the beam—or was it the belt that broke? He's slit his wrists. "Did you know," he says matter-of-factly, "that blood coagulates far faster than you would think? That's why you've got to slit your wrists in the bath." I want to puke just thinking about it. My flesh, my best friend, the best part of my life. If he died, what would be left of me?

Another relative has tried it too, with pills I think. And I've done the slow cook suicide method for years and years. I've pickled my liver or smoked out my lungs, let pills steal little pieces of my brain, driven through stop signs in storms, woken up in neat little deposits of my own vomit after drugging till I passed out, then woke in the middle of the night to an eating binge, then passed out again.

It's all just chasing little bits of death, isn't it?

The death you chased until you caught it. I'll carry your face, Don, with your dreamy eyes, sad and peaceful, with me forever. Looking the way, I imagine you felt when you stepped off the Golden Gate Bridge three months ago. Your left eyelid slightly drooping. I said I don't ever want to forget. I'll carry the feel of your arm as I rubbed it while I was looking into your eyes and talking to your body that icy cold but very real feel because you were not embalmed but simply lying on ice. I'll carry the way your hand felt as I held it. In massage school, the teacher talked about honoring, appreciating, and loving the hands as a student was massaging mine. I had come from your visitation days before and the last time I had held a hand in mine, that hand had been dead. That hand had been yours. I said I don't ever want to forget. The way your body looked somehow stuffed under your clothes. And so much smaller, so much thinner than when you were alive. (How is that even possible? You were always so skinny.) The haunted look in your eyes. The way the makeup they put on you didn't quite cover the bruise at the bridge of your nose where you had broken it. The way the crack in your skull was so visible, so there, despite the little halo of fabric they had artfully arranged around the top of your head. They didn't cover your face and, though the skin was unbroken, the bone in your forehead was not. I should know the name of that bone, but you see, I didn't study anatomy when I was at massage school; I held hands with strangers who listened to my stories of you and held my love for you in their hearts. Your bones were crushed and splintered when you broke apart your body when you tumbled off that bridge. That fucking red monstrosity of a bridge. I hate that bridge and I can't go anywhere in the Bay Area without seeing pictures of it. And then I see you, on ice in a garage that's now a temple, softly muted by fabrics, lights, candles, the scent of stargazers; ever they will carry me back to this two-car funeral parlor where we all came to visit you, to love you, to get angry with you, or to say we understand. Even if we do understand, we want you back; we want you here. I would forgive you for murdering yourself and I would take you back. Would you take me back even though I helped murder you, by omission and commission?

153

You told me what you needed from me. Could I deliver? Could I see it was a matter of life and death?

I also see you smiling and making that gape-mouthed, goggle-eyed, goofy expression you liked to make. I'm so glad I have a picture of you doing that. It's a little out of focus. I guess that's what your life is now.

Maybe death is just life a little out of focus.

In my mind, you are still in focus, lying dead in that garage. I said I never want to forget. Curt jumped off his bridge twenty years ago. I almost forgot. I almost forgot his mother, my aunt, collapsing as she walked into the funeral home. I forgot I have no right to tell my parents that when the pain is too great, and the medical interventions stop working, I'll put myself out of my misery. I forgot such a choice isn't mine to make. For twenty years, the aftermath of Curt's suicide was the one thread I could hold onto in the blizzard. It might not be thick enough to lead me back from the barn to the house, but I could just stand there and hold the thread till the sky cleared. My relatives who've tried suicide didn't go to Curt's funeral. They didn't see. I don't ever want to forget.

I judge you, judge where perhaps it's not my place, because I see a reflection of myself, because your suicide is too horrible to be real, because I have to distance myself from you because I can't be you. One day, I'll accept your choice and love you and empathize unconditionally. Not yet. For now, it can't be you that acted. It has to be depression. The demons in your mind. Something I can grab hold of. I love you, Don, and I accept your decision, but only because I have to believe it wasn't you who made it. Because I think the thirst for death is like a possession. When it descends on me, another occupies my soul; I disappear. When it lifts, the other evaporates as if she were never there at all. It's like waking from a trying, troubling sleep. If I could awaken from mine, why the fuck couldn't you?

# Fiction

*What's in a name? That which we call a rose,*
*By any other name would smell as sweet.*
  —William Shakespeare from *Romeo and Juliet*

# 30,000 Feet

## Renelaine Pfister

30,000 feet

The clouds, bundles of beauty against azure sky. The wind rushes, caresses her face, tousles her hair. Orange and pink streaks against blue; she's never seen colors this vivid. The world below is unwelcoming.

*Omigod!*

She is swimming in the air, her limbs parting the wind as graceful as ribbons in Rhythmic Olympics. For the first time, she doesn't feel self-conscious; she even feels beautiful. Gravity pulls at her. She doesn't resist.

*Release the . . .*

28,773 feet

Her head is throbbing from work. A day filled with customers who disliked the amount of icing on their cupcakes, the temperature of their beverage, or the lack of parking stalls in their lot. She opens the refrigerator. It is half empty. The veggie burgers are gone along with yogurt and the sliced fruit. Kevin's vegan food is gone. Did she forget that he was going away on a trip?

The cupboards and drawers are open. Random things are missing. A burglary? She should call Kevin.

Instead she walks around to investigate.

The CD tower only has five CDs left. Kevin's shoes are gone from the cabinets and shelves. His Bose speaker, his laptop, his toiletries in the bathroom have disappeared. His clothes are all missing. Their bed is ruffled as if someone had placed things there and then moved them again. Pillows on his side of the bed; even his pet fish is gone.

There is no letter, note, or even a Post-it. Kevin was acting odd in the morning, barely speaking and not rushing her in the bathroom. Where did he go? What corner of the world didn't belong to the two of them?

25,545 feet

She's home for the day, curled up in bed. Kevin comes home early to comfort her. He slips in next to her. Her back is turned toward him, and she pretends to be asleep. He touches her shoulder, probing. She doesn't stir.

He suggests that she ought to see the lady psychiatrist referred by her primary doctor.

She snarls at him. I don't believe in doctors. Charlatans, the whole lot of them. They have never helped me before; no one will. Not you, Kevin, even though I know how much you want to be the hero.

She stomps away like a child. He's hurt and she knows it, but she can't help herself. She is as self-destructive as a landmine.

23,552 feet

It is their first wedding anniversary. Kevin has planned a whole day of activities. They rent kayaks and paddle to Strawberry Island. It is eight in the morning when they arrive on the beach. No one else is around. They lay on the beach for an hour, holding hands and baking under the sun.

People start trickling in—walking from the opposite beach with beer cans in their hands. It is low tide. She and Kevin rise and start hiking to the top of the island. There are narrow paths all around, with sharp dry sticks poking their bare skin as they ascend. Some areas along the path cut off and they have to climb up sharp rocks. She slips in her cheap water shoes but balances herself with her hands. As she looks down at jagged rocks she thinks, if I fall and hit my head, it will crack open like a coconut.

She makes it to the top first. The wind is blowing her hair, cooling her neck. The ocean is sleeping. She takes in a deep breath and lifts her hair off her neck. The familiar snaps of a phone's camera go off, and Kevin walks over with a grin. The black and white pictures are beautiful.

It's tempting not to go back down, but Kevin entices her with talk of getting *Panang* curry and Thai iced tea at their favorite food truck. She consents.

As they sit on a wooden bench next to the food truck, she thinks of the perfect day they're having and how happy she feels. In the next second it hits her: it's gone. She sets down her chopsticks and pushes away the curry.

18,908 feet

The psychiatrist scribbles in his notepad. Does he even remember her name? She's so tired. Why isn't she happy?

Cupcakery is on the top ten list of best dessert shops in the city. Kevin is a perfect husband. Everyone says he is, and she has to agree.

18,133 feet

Let's go skydiving, Kevin says. Let's get certified. It's not too expensive; there's a special on Groupon.

He knows how much she enjoys the speed afforded by rollercoasters, zip lines and skiing. She loves the freedom, letting go, having no control, conceding to gravity . . . gravity the master.

*Okay.*

17,376 feet

She meets Kevin at a pet store. She is picking up kibble for Raven, her black Yorkie. He is buying a fish for himself.

"What should I name it?" he asks, standing behind her at the cash register. He isn't very tall, but she likes his face—familiar and comfortable, like he's someone she's always known and trusted.

She replies, "Ernest."

He laughs. "Why Ernest?"

"It's a nice name."

"Ernest it is. What about you? What's your name?"

She marries for the second time.

15,992 feet

She has her maiden name back. A name she was happy to replace—a name she despised for a long time because it twisted her insides and disclosed unbearable memories.

But right now she's happier to be liberated of her husband's name. She swears she will never marry again.

15,185 feet

Tristan appears on the night of her mother's funeral. She was planning to have a solo party with a bottle of vodka and her mother's leftover water pills, narcotics and anti-coagulants. Since there is no need to watch her figure anymore, she buys a bacon cheeseburger at her favorite fast food place.

She sees him while waiting in line. Her brother's friend, Tristan. He says he's sorry about her mother. He asks for her number. When she gets home, she pours laundry detergent all over the pills and the cheeseburger.

She is 23 and he is 33 when they marry. They make love, they fight, they make love again. He is her savior and her slayer. The heat of his temper is breathtaking. Soon the lovemaking ceases, and only the fights remain.

You frigid bitch, he lashes out. His insults feel like being grazed with a lit cigarette; the pain is searing and swift.

She is back in her hole, seized by a panic upon realizing that she is trapped.

12,402 feet

Her mother is diagnosed with early-onset Alzheimer's disease. One night she goes to the bathroom and trips over the rug. She breaks a hip and isn't discovered for another twenty-four hours.

She flies to her mother in a swirl of panic. After four months, the bones heal, but her mother is no longer the same in her head.

She demands to know why.

The doctors say it's medications, the aging process, early dementia . . . the whole brew. Her mother is going away, somewhere she can't reach her. They place her in a nursing home for several months, but her mother is raising hell and wants to go home. She terrorizes the staff and other patients.

She falls again and breaks her other hip. Against the doctor's advice, she takes her mother home.

She sits at her mother's side. They don't know how long they have left together. So she leans in, with a thundering heart, to tell her mother a secret so old and buried, it is almost not real anymore. Except that it is.

First, thank you for bringing me home, says her mother, taking deep breaths. Second, please forgive me. I didn't know. I wish . . . she breaks off and sobs.

She too, weeps.

9,009 feet

She is seventeen years old. Her room in the attic is her sanctuary; she never leaves it. The only thing that lures her from it is the smell of her mother's baking. Weekends are special; her mother always makes something different every week. Her favorite is the lemon-strawberry cupcakes.

One day, she asks her mother for the recipe. They make it together. Sugar, butter, flour, eggs, a pinch of salt . . . she knows just the right amount to use.

Her brother says her cupcakes are better than her mother's. "Cupcakes are your calling," her brother says with his mouth full. Her mother smiles.

It becomes their weekly engagement: baking and flooding the house with sweet smells.

7,115 feet

She is in junior high. Alanis Morrissette is her world. She plays the entire *Jagged Little Pill* album, over and over. She doesn't go out with her friends. She's not interested in boys. Her mother spots thin scars on her arms, just above her shirtsleeves.

Her mother frets; wonders what is wrong. She sends her husband to investigate, but he comes back empty. He shrugs and says if she's not talking to you, she's not talking to me.

5,863 feet

Her grandfather gives her older brother an ATV for his birthday, however, she becomes addicted to it. She loves the hum and roar of the machine beneath her body. She goes on excursions to the ranch close to her house. Mr. Moore says she and her brother are welcome to use the ATV on his land if they mind the animals. She disappears for hours and returns with numb hands, wild hair, and happy heart. Or, as happy as she can let herself be. Her brother is livid.

"Where have you been with my ATV," he demands.

4,299 feet

Thirteen years old. She cries to sleep every night. There are no answers to her questions; there is no one she can talk to. Why did he do it? Instead of protecting her, he hurt her. She's so tired of thinking.

3,623 feet

She is eight. Her father comes into her room while she is on her hands and knees, designing a poster for school. He is wearing a white sleeveless shirt and white shorts. He goes down on his knees behind her, and pushes himself against her. She collapses on the floor, confused.

2,783 feet

There are leaves in her hair. She wrestles in the yard with her yellow Labrador Ernest, who whips his tail so hard she thinks it might snap. She is six.

2,289 feet

She is crying because she doesn't want to go to school. She wants to stay home with Granny and make fish origami. Walk to the park and swing from the monkey bars. She is still a little lamb that has not encountered wolves; she is unaware that wolves live inside her house.

*Mommy. What's that up there?*

1, 351 feet

She's not tired anymore.

She feels exhilarated.

She is free.

1,186 feet

She is crawling on top of a table, reaching for a vase full of pink roses. Does she truly remember, or does she remember looking at a picture of herself crawling on top of a table, reaching for a vase full of pink roses? She is wearing a light blue tube top and a cotton diaper. Chubby, curly-haired, wide-eyed. She is made of dust and water. She wants to . . .

# A Theory of Relativity

## Jane Wilder

Petra was banging file drawers open and shut. "Mom," she cried from the study, "you gotta help with this financial aid thing."

"Okay," Eleanor said, calmly from the kitchen table, where she was sipping coffee and planning the coming week's menus. "What do you need?"

Petra came in and flung herself on a kitchen chair. "I've got the Social Security stuff, and your income tax returns. And what about life insurance?"

Eleanor put her cup down on its matching saucer, the last of a set that had been a wedding present. "Where's Rand?"

"Out playing basketball," Petra said. "He expects me to do everything. Even though this application applies to both of us." Petra's twin was also named after their father, but he had always been called by his middle name.

Stirring her coffee, Eleanor thought about Peter who, from the day after their wedding, had assumed Eleanor would be responsible for household cleaning, shopping, cooking, bill paying, earning a living, obtaining his marijuana and even helping him quit tobacco, since she was the one who was allergic to it.

"Earth to Mom," Petra was saying. "I still need the information. Dad's date of death. Assets. Life insurance. Is there any left?"

"Uh, no," Eleanor said.

"Is it all spent?"

"There wasn't any."

"No insurance? But you're actually so responsible and organized and all."

"Well, maybe things were different fourteen years ago." Eleanor ducked her head over her menus.

Rand came in, letting the kitchen door bang behind him. "Hey." He bounced a basketball on the floor. Petra made a face at him and a "stop it" gesture. Rand caught the ball and put it out the back door. "How's it going?" he asked.

"I'm almost finished getting the information," Petra told him. "We should qualify for financial aid."

"Cool. Is it lunchtime yet?"

"It's only eleven," Eleanor said. She picked up her cup and saucer and carried them to the sink to rinse them, looking out the kitchen window at the back yard. The grass was tall. "Rand, please mow the grass today."

"Me and my buddies—"

"My buddies and I," Eleanor said.

"Are you comin' along?" Rand laughed at his own joke. "I'm goin' to go hang with a couple of other guys. Shoot baskets."

Eleanor put her cup and saucer in the dishrack. "You can mow later this afternoon. Go shoot baskets now. I'll call you for lunch."

Rand looked down at his pockets where his cell phone usually was.

"Right. Just come back in a little while," Eleanor said. She had taken his phone away for a week as an attempt at discipline.

"Okay." Rand's face went blank for a second, and then he went out the back door.

"Stoned," Eleanor said, under her breath. It was evident, though, now that he vaped it, and he no longer smelled of pot.

Petra stood to leave. "I've got to finish this application so I can work on the paper on *Sophie's Choice* for my cinema course." She turned back to Eleanor. "I'm surprised you got so upset when we saw it last week."

Eleanor waved vaguely at her daughter. "Heavy. It was heavy."

"Right." Petra left the room.

Sitting down again, Eleanor resumed planning the week's menus and shopping list, small efforts to create order over chaos. She liked coming home from work knowing what dinner would be and what help, if any, she would request. She asked little of Petra, a good student who spent a lot of time doing homework and reports. Rand was so scattered that having him help prepare food was almost counterproductive. At least he did the dishes after the meal, along with Petra. And he took out the trash.

But despite discipline, Rand persisted in smoking pot. Eleanor had already taken away privileges, such as a week off cell phone. She didn't want to take basketball away—the physical activity was, she hoped, a deterrent to smoking pot.

Eleanor thought again about how—though Petra looked a little like Peter, mostly in the shape of her nose and cheekbones— Rand looked so much like him, sometimes it took her breath away. Rand looked like Peter in a time warp. He looked like him, moved like him, sounded like him and now had the same stoned expression that Peter once had.

A year or so after they married, Peter's vacant, pot-smoking look changed into a demeanor of intense wariness. Hypervigilant, Eleanor thought, remembering his piercing gaze and overactive startle reflex, his fears, and his belief in conspiracies.

Eleanor wondered whether Petra would ask more questions. The children had only been three years old when he died. She had hidden the most important papers in a drawer in her nightstand, where she mainly kept a few folders related to work, with a misleading title on the manila folder. Someday, when they were older, she would tell them what really happened to their father.

"Mom," Petra said, coming back in, "you're gazing into space."

"Right. How's it coming?"

"Almost done." Petra pulled out a chair and sat. "We'll qualify, especially with the Social Security ending as we turn eighteen. Why was it so little anyway?"

"It's based on the deceased parent's earnings."

"Oh."

"Didn't he work after college? After you were married?"

"A little. He dropped out of college."

"But you didn't."

"We married after I graduated. And he eventually worked . . . some."

"Did you stay home after you had us?"

"For a year."

"Did he work?"

Actually, they had been on welfare that year. "Why all the questions?" Eleanor asked. "You've probably heard this before."

"Well, I must have, but it was in bits and pieces. You really never talk about your life together."

"Well," Eleanor said. She shook herself a little and looked at her beautiful daughter sitting here with her in a sunlit kitchen.

Petra drummed her fingers on the table. "And we were only three, so I don't remember him."

Peter used to do that. Eleanor's teeth clenched.

Mercifully, Petra stopped drumming. "What about when you went back to work, did Dad babysit us?"

"It's not babysitting if it's your own child," Eleanor said.

Petra looked at her. "Mom."

"I put you two in day care."

Petra smiled back and took her hand. "We must've been a handful. Did he work then?"

"Sometimes. A little. I couldn't depend on him. Even when he was home, he was—well, opinionated and unpredictable. And when he smoked pot he got paranoid."

"Most people do," Petra said.

"Do you know that from personal experience?" Eleanor asked. *Oh God, no, please not her too*, she thought.

"Observation." Petra let go of her mother's hand. "I need to get back. Do I have all the financial records?"

"Yes." Thank God Petra hadn't started smoking. Eleanor wanted to stand up and cheer.

"And his date of death?"

"December 31, 1999."

"Y2K," Petra said. Turning back as she was about to leave, "Did you ever smoke pot?"

"Maybe twice. I didn't like it or the effect it had on your father. He smoked far too much."

"Why did you stay married then?" She stood in the doorway, not leaving yet.

"We were young and in love at first." Eleanor drew aimless circles on the tablecloth with one fingertip. "He was charming and artistic." She paused. "Things changed gradually. Sometimes you wake up and things are bad, and you can't put your finger on when it got that way."

"Oh," Petra said. "Bummer."

"Well, Petra, a lot of life is what you make of it," Eleanor said.

"Back to the paperwork for me."

Eleanor picked up her pen again. At least, she reflected, she had begun to talk to Petra about the whole story. Really, it was time to begin telling them. To try to tell them.

When Peter was at his most paranoid, the last couple of years of his life, Eleanor had been reduced to whispering to the children and saying as little as possible at home to Peter because he twisted her words, finding a threat in everything, turning words back on her. He woke her repeatedly in the night to interrogate her about imaginary enemies and phantom conspiracies. When the Y2K hype began and then persisted month after month, he went off the proverbial deep end. Eventually, he began to ask her to stop him from killing himself. Then he began making veiled threats against Eleanor.

On the last day of the old century, Peter ran their car over a cliff at the ocean's edge. His shirt pocket contained his handwritten suicide note.

In her sudden widowhood, Eleanor had to adapt, cope, keep her job, act as though life made sense, and care for two three-year-olds, utterly alone. Now there had been fourteen years of relative peace in which she could speak freely, sleep the night through without the interruption of nighttime interrogations, and reflect that she had survived the long, dark night of his madness while he had not.

Petra was back in the room, holding up the folder titled "Theory of Relativity," from the nightstand drawer. "What's this about? You said there wasn't any insurance."

Eleanor sat very still. "Why do you have that?"

"I thought I'd check the rest of your files."

Eleanor waited.

"It says the life insurance policy was invalid because he committed suicide."

"Yes."

"Why?" Petra cried.

"Nobody really knows why another person does that."

"But—what happened?"

Eleanor's fingers, acting on their own, twirled her pen. She set the pen down, clasped her hands together, and put them in her lap. "Why don't you come and sit down, Petra?"

Petra came back and sat, looking intently at her mother.

"Petra," Eleanor began.

Rand was at the back door. He dropped his basketball, caught it, and set it quietly on the floor in the corner.

"How long until lunch?" he asked.

Eleanor looked at her watch without seeing it. "I'll start it in a few minutes. Go shoot some more baskets."

"Okay." Rand disappeared. The door slammed.

"There're some things I've been meaning—"

Rand was back. "Forgot my ball," he said, picking up the ball and looking intently at the women as he disappeared behind the closing door.

Petra was watching her mother, her gaze like Peter's, but less intense.

"It's a long story," Eleanor said. "Your father started smoking pot about a year after we met, and he stopped doing things he used to do, like work and study and read poetry and paint pictures. Once we got married, I had to do everything for both of us, and he did nothing. He dropped out of college and after that, when he'd get a job, he'd quit it. There was always something wrong—they didn't appreciate him, or it was too hard, or he didn't want to get up that early."

"Maybe they weren't good jobs," Petra said.

Eleanor ignored the interruption.

"After a while he started saying the reason he quit was because everyone was plotting against him."

"What did you do? Did you talk to Grandma and Grandpa?"

"No. I covered for him, said he was working when I was the one who was working steadily while he kept quitting. I couldn't tell them—either set of parents—nobody'd wanted us to get married. I just kept going, doing my best to keep a job to make money so we could eat and pay rent."

"Why didn't you ask anybody to help?"

"He'd made us move away from everybody. He said it was to assert our independence. But he kept me more and more isolated. Nobody could come to our house."

"So why did you stay?"

"I had to take care of him. I still loved him." She paused. "He was charming, like Nathan in *Sophie's Choice*. In the beginning. Before his delusions really set in."

Petra thought about Nathan, witty and charismatic, lean and dark. Her father had looked like that in the wedding pictures. Nathan, who had killed himself and Sophie in the end. "Why didn't you tell somebody if you were afraid?" she asked.

"There was no one to tell. He wouldn't let anyone near our house, near me. He got worse than just being a pothead and sitting around saying "far out" and eating. Petra, he had delusions, stuff I knew couldn't be true, that he'd talk about all the time. Including all night when I needed to sleep. He went way beyond just being stoned all the time. He was watchful and wary and suspicious, vigilant, always on, accusing. Accusing, with veiled threats. It got unbearable."

"Why did you stay?" Petra asked again, this time more softly, compassionately.

"I was ready to leave. I'd had enough. I made plans—and then I found out I was pregnant. So I stayed."

Petra nodded and listened.

"He was entranced by you two babies for a month or two. But after that he got really, really worse."

"Couldn't you get help for him?"

Inside Eleanor, the last of the dam that had held for fourteen years broke, and words she had kept within for so long came rushing out. "I tried. You can't force treatment on someone who read *One Flew Over the Cuckoo's Nest* and believed every word. Who thinks the television set is wired to an invisible network? Who is convinced that his wife is part of the conspiracy so he keeps her up all night asking questions and not believing anything she says. Who thinks if the psychiatrists get hold of him they'll force a lobotomy on him. Who calls his wife at work to tell her he's terrified, and then has the home phone disconnected because it's transmitting information to the network that's after him. Who thinks the world is about to end, and maybe there's only one way out?"

"God, Mom, what—"

"You can't get help until the person harms someone. Or himself. That's what they told me at the drug rehab place. And the mental-health emergency place. I know because I called from work."

"Why—it shouldn't be that way."

"But it was," Eleanor said.

"Oh, Mom." Petra had tears in her eyes. She sat looking at her mother, her mouth hanging slightly open.

"The hype about Y2K was the last straw." Eleanor looked toward the light from the window, then back at her daughter. "He fixated on it, talked about it all the time. Said—with significant stares at me—that both of us might die. Along with you children." She took a deep breath. "But when he drove away that day, he put in his pocket a note saying that the end of the world was coming and he couldn't go on."

"Did you know he was going to . . . kill himself?"

Eleanor put her hands over her mouth. "He had asked me to stop him. But I couldn't. You can't reason with someone who's out of his mind." She put her hands down. "I've tried for fourteen years not to feel that I failed. Seeing *Sophie's Choice* showed me how guilty I felt that I couldn't change him. And how close we came to going with him."

"Oh, my God. Is that why you got hysterical after we saw it? Because of Dad?"

Eleanor put her face into her hands and nodded. "I hadn't realized until then how relieved I felt for us—and how guilty because I survived his madness and he didn't."

After a moment, Petra said, "Mom, why'd you never tell us? This is so . . . huge." She spread her arms, then dropped them again.

Eleanor said. "I meant to. When you were old enough." She walked to the far side of the dining room without seeing anything, then into the kitchen, looking out the window at the ragged lawn that Rand should mow, that she would end up mowing herself.

She thought about the title she'd given the secret folder and put in her nightstand drawer.

"I think," she said, "I wanted to protect you from the truth, that your father was a mentally ill pot head who killed himself." She was wringing her hands. "I didn't want you or Rand to be like him. I never wanted to say, or even think, 'You're just like your father.'"

"I am?"

Eleanor turned to see Rand standing in the kitchen doorway, holding his basketball.

"Just like our father?" The vacant, stoned expression on his face had given way to a newly wary one.

Eleanor looked back and forth between the twins, not noticing the tears on her face.

"I'm really so very sorry," she said.

# *Blast*

## Patsy Ann Taylor

Dean Blankenship sneered as he watched his wife, Karen, say goodnight to the last of their guests. She paused, holding the hand of a dark-haired man a tad too long for friendship alone. Dean shrugged. *Won't be long now. Tomorrow, in fact.* Karen had packed, had gassed up the car, and she had a ticket for Maui tucked in her purse. His own destination to anywhere in the opposite direction still unplanned. He only knew Karen would not be part of it. *Aloha, baby.*

The sold sign in their front yard leaned at an awkward angle, but the message was clear. The Blankenship's were leaving the neighborhood. Their real estate agent would deal with the final packing and movers. And tomorrow, Dean and his soon-to-be ex would be on their way to a new life in a new town. At least that is what he hoped the neighbors would think. Neither of the couple wanted the gossipy questions that accompanied news of a breakup. To their friends and neighbors, Dean and Karen were the perfect couple.

"Let them think we're off to new pastures," Karen said. She had bought the ticket to Maui in anticipation of selling their home. "I don't want any reminders of this place, or of you. Sorry, honey, but I'm sure you feel the same."

He did. Nothing in this house or neighborhood meant a thing to Dean. Almost from the fatal words, *I do,* he'd set his heart on single life. Not that marriage to Karen hadn't had its perks. She came with a full set of accessories: stocks and bonds, a real estate fortune passed down from her parents, and she looked good stepping out of the shower. He tried not to think about that. All he wanted now was freedom. And Karen's estate.

"Ready for bed?" Karen's voice sawed into his thoughts. "We can finish the rest in the morning."

"Doesn't your plane leave at nine?" Dean wanted some time alone before this last night with Karen. "I'll take care of the dishes. You go on to bed."

"Gee, thanks, Sweetie." She gave him a peck on the cheek. "Maybe I'll come down for a nightcap after I slip into my jammies." She headed for the stairs before Dean could object.

*Hell fire.* Dean scraped leftover lasagna from dinner plates then set the kitchen straight and poured himself another brandy. He was on his third when Karen joined him at the table.

"Will you miss me?" She breathed into his ear. "We could change our minds, you know."

"I hate when you do that." Dean jerked away from her. "We're done, babe. You said it yourself." He downed his drink and went to the sink to rinse the glass.

"Just checking." She pulled another glass from the cupboard. "Want one for upstairs?" She poured brandy into the fresh glass, topped off her own.

"Thanks," Dean said to her back. *Just like her. Just goes ahead and does what she wants. Makes it look like a favor.* "Set mine next to the bed, will you? I want to check on something in the garage."

When he finally went upstairs, Karen was sound asleep in the master bedroom. Dean had taken to the guest room months ago. Set deep in the heart of the house, the room's solitary feeling swept over him when he entered. *This is what it will be like once she's gone.* He could sing, or shout; no one would blink an eye.

It had been Karen's idea to sound proof the space. She was a light sleeper, and even the most soothing music kept her awake. Yes, he would miss only one thing. This room. Sipping the brandy, he smiled at the mess: socks and underwear strewn across the floor, shirt, tie, jacket spread over the chair. His mess. Draining the glass, Dean fell into bed and closed his eyes.

He woke to silence. The room was dark except for the glow from the clock radio on the nightstand. The dial read seven o'clock. His alarm had not gone off. He'd planned to be downstairs cooking Karen's breakfast by now. One last kind gesture before the little surprise he'd planned.

He reached to turn on the bedside lamp. *What the hell?* He couldn't move his arms. He couldn't even roll over. "Karen." Then he remembered. Sound proofing. No way she would hear him. *Now what?* He struggled for a few minutes, trying to free himself. *Damn.* He tried again, this time putting all he had into it. No luck. "Karen." He screamed this time.

The door opened, and Karen stood in the doorway, a silhouette. "Awake, darling?"

"Cut me loose." Dean didn't even try using his pleasant voice.

"Can't do that, Sweetie. You'll spoil my plans." She flicked the light switch and came into the room. "Sleep well?" She looked at his empty glass. "Lucky for me you can't resist a goodnight toddy." She patted his head. "I'm off now."

"You can't just leave me like this." Dean jerked at the duct tape that held his arms. He tried to kick his feet loose from the tape that bound him to the bed.

"Oh, but I can. I have." She reached into her purse and pulled out her car keys. "But don't worry, Dean. You won't be alone for long." She smiled. "The fumigators are due . . .," she looked at her watch, "just about now." She closed the door behind her.

"Karen." Dean screamed though he knew it would do no good.

It seemed forever until the house was tented and the chemicals pumped inside. Dean's throat rasped from screaming. He had given up hope the men would hear him. Instead, he thought about the device he'd installed in Karen's car, the device set to go off just before she reached the highway. *You'll never see Maui, babe.* As he breathed in the poison, he sighed. *Too bad I won't hear the blast.*

# Breathing Fear

## P. H. Garrett

Teresa remembered her first brush with terror. Seventeen, newly independent, giddy with freedom, she was fearless. Though her watch showed well past midnight, she struck out alone for her East Village apartment, several blocks away. Her older sister scowled, chided her "wilding ways," and called her foolish. Undeterred, Teresa waved goodbye and clattered down the stairs onto the sidewalk. The balmy Manhattan night seemed perfect for walking home.

Around her the city slept, quiet as death. She strode forward in its soft warmth, her blue-jeaned, dancer's legs eating up the pavement. Her only company, the dim light of wide-spaced street lamps, fumes on oily pavement, and the reek of uncollected trash. Not even a car at this hour.

Whispers of a second stride began when she was about a block from her brownstone. Her spine stiffened. The cadence of unwelcome steps matched her own. Her sister's warning rattled, tinny in her head. Her body held its breath, preparing to flee.

Then, from a place so deep inside its location still remains a mystery—a message reached her brain. *Careful*, it cautioned. *Walk. Do not run. You are the hunted.* Teresa obeyed. Fright chilled her neck and climbed her arms.

Behind her the tick-tock of footsteps sped up. She fought the shriek that bubbled in her throat. She didn't dare turn around. Instead, she moved toward the brownstone's stairs, only yards from the building's entrance. Her secret angel commanded again. *Walk.*

Teresa prayed someone would appear, come toward her, jog down the front steps. Anyone. But no. Not a soul in sight. Her tormentor's footfalls edged closer.

Mouth fear-dry, she forced measured steps as she started up the stairs. At the top of the concrete stoop, her body screamed, "Run." And she did. Feet flying to the tune of terror, she shoved through the building's entryway with its broken latch, her shoes chattering down the backstairs to her basement apartment. Above, the entry door opened and closed. Then sudden stillness—she felt her stalker's presence in the small quiet—the predator ready to pounce.

A panicky whimper fought to escape her clamped lips. Adrenaline zinged from her toes to the roots of her hair. Hands shaking, fingers somehow steady, she turned her key in the flimsy lock and slipped into her three-room railroad flat. Pushing the door shut, she slid the double safety bolt home. It was dark as a cave. She'd left no welcoming lights on.

Terrified, Teresa crawled from her barricade. Carefully monitoring the sound of her breathing—fear in, fear out—she crouched in the middle room. She heard him coming down the stairs, click, scuff, click. He tried the doorknob. Once. Twice. Her heart pounded so hard in her chest, she thought the man might hear it.

In the hollow silence that followed, she held her breath. Had he moved from the door? Minutes later his feet scraped in the gravel of a tiny courtyard adjacent to her living room. She prayed silent thanks for the iron bars that spanned her two windows. The bars she'd insisted held her prisoner. That she'd hated just yesterday.

She curled, rigid, against the bathtub in her cold-water flat's old-time kitchen for next-to-forever, hoping the man would give up and seek his evil elsewhere. At last, he retraced his steps. She heard his footfalls grow faint, and fainter, then the entry door slam. He was gone.

*Or was he?* The thought unleashed a nightmare so frightful, it engulfed her to the bone. Stampeded by horrific imaginings, her flesh shivered. Ice crystals traveled her bloodstream, coated her lungs with dread. Huddled on the floor beside the big, cast iron tub, she trembled, eyes wide open until the sun came up.

Peering into the morning shine, cautious, still afraid, Teresa unwound her aching limbs and straightened her torso. She knew she'd reached a fork in her road. She understood. Survival was a gift. Threats were alive in the shadows. Sobbing with relief and the suffocating burden of never feeling safe again, she crept to the phone and dialed her sister. Her "wilding" had ended.

# Cold Space

## Mara Johnstone

A painful crash, but not the worst I'd been through. And just light turbulence for the other passengers who had exoskeletons that would make a boulder jealous. Since the shipmakers had them in mind rather than a stray human female looking for a cheap flight, I'd braced myself in a tight corner when we started going down.

I unfolded my limbs with a wince and found most of the lights in the passageways dimmed. Anxious keening drifted down the hall at just the right tone to make my eardrums itch—the same sound an alien crew member had made when he'd gotten caught in a hydraulic lift last week.

I grimaced and started toward it. *Here's hoping that's not as bad as it sounds.* I entered an open door to private quarters where two of the Hard Skin passengers were scraping ice off a table and making a symphony of whines that sounded like anxious hoverbikes.

"What happened?" I asked.

The small one with the markings of a juvenile male whirled, his back plates rattling in distress. "Precious creature cold air," he exclaimed. "Cold air." He rattled harder, visibly frustrated with his imperfect AllSpeak.

The tall one spoke up. "Vessel is having breach of hull," she explained over her armored shoulder. I realized I'd met her before; this was Grandma Mandibles, the matriarch of a small clan. Her AllSpeak was better. "Micrometeorite. The systems of emergency have sealed the hole, but tube of coolant runs through wall. Is burst."

I joined her at the table and found what looked like a frozen-over hamster cage. The thing inside, ice-covered and immobile, could have been a Thorkian Fur Piranha for all I knew. My vet training was strictly Earth-based. All I could say was that its stillness was a bad sign.

Junior ignored me while he clawed ice off the latch and pried open the cage. He clamped down on his rattling plates, but I felt the vibration through the floor as he lifted out the limp creature. I watched with growing concern while the alien tried to wake his pet to no avail.

"Is it breathing?" I asked, wondering if it was supposed to.

"No knowledge." Junior bobbed his head in uncertainty. "Need heat." He looked frantically around the room, finding only weak emergency lights. "Power being gone. What has heat?"

I tilted my head. "Can't you just hold him close?" I gestured. "Isn't your body heat enough?"

"What?" His pupils spiraled open and shut in confusion as he freed a talon to touch my arm. A talon still covered in ice. Oh.

"Give him to me," I demanded, taking off my gloves and unzipping my flight suit. "Hurry."

With his eyes wide, the alien deposited the bundle of icy fur in my hands. Grandma Mandibles stopped searching when Junior exclaimed at the ice starting to melt.

I held the beastie against my neck with my hands cupped around it, hoping it wasn't the biting sort. Rubbing its fur and brushing the ice off—trying not to shiver as it dripped down my shirt—I spoke the traditional soothing words of my people.

"Hey, Little Guy. You'll be fine. You gonna wake up for us? Please don't pee on me."

After a few moments, I felt a wiggle. I held it up and witnessed a tiny sneeze.

The alien uttered a joyful-sounding mishmash that could have been the creature's name. He reached out hesitant talons to stroke its fur, obviously wanting to hold it but unwilling to remove it from my life-giving warmth.

"He's shivering," I said. "That's a good sign. I think he'll be okay." The furball was starting to make faint rattling sounds of its own, which seemed oddly like purring. I was trying to figure out how it rattled without plates when a group of other Hard Skins arrived. Junior treated them to a dramatic retelling of how the human could bring animals back to life from icy death.

I made a few modest interjections to keep the tale grounded in reality, but only a few. I'm not one to say no to some well-earned gratitude. Makes my day every time.

In the lengthy repair that followed, my days continued to be made, when the aliens showed their fascination with my exotic ability to create heat by moving. Hard Skins popped up left and right, asking me to warm things for them. I didn't mind. It was easy enough to soften somebody's energy bar or a block of fix-it putty by sticking it in my shirt for a few minutes. I was glad the heating system was fixed right away though; otherwise, I might have ended up doing jumping jacks in a small room for the common good. The Hard Skins reminded me of a lizard I'd had as a pet: never more than room temperature, but oh so fond of outside heat sources.

Their interest in my warm-blooded nature eventually gave way to an invitation to join the crew on complicated external repairs. I'd proven useful.

*Why, yes. I do have slender fingers, perfect for manipulating wires.* I smiled as I followed the hulking forms of the repair crew toward the airlock. *Now let me show you what kind of climbing monkey my species is descended from.*

# Deliberate Defiance

## Belinda Riehl

"Now I lay me down to sleep," Matt said, facing the underside of the top bunk. "I pray the Lord my soul to keep. If I should die . . ."

"I don't want to think about dying," Trevor interrupted from the top bunk.

"Mom says we have to . . ."

"Mom also says, everything we need to know we learned in kindergarten, so why do we have to go to second grade?"

"Yeah," Matt said, joining the complaint-fest. "And it's stupid they won't let twins be in the same class."

"I know." Trevor stared up at the ceiling into the dark, remembering how much he liked his old backyard. He missed playing army men with Matt in their fort.

*Our new house is in a perfect neighborhood for our boys*, he had heard Mom tell Grandma over the phone. *Twelve houses with thirty-two kids in our cul-de-sac.*

But the new neighborhood wasn't as perfect as Mom thought.

First of all, her warning, *Follow the rules and no harm will come* was getting in the way. They were not allowed to leave the cul-de-sac, not even to go to the playground with older kids. They couldn't swim in the neighbor's pool without Mom or Dad. Sometimes the families filled their twelve-passenger vans to go to McDonald's for sundaes, but Matt and Trevor couldn't go because there weren't enough seatbelts.

Trevor never felt comfortable playing up the street with the other kids like Matt did. Some of the neighborhood kids teased and called Trevor names. The first time he got in a fight, both boys were punished—Trevor for fighting and Matt for running home to get help.

"Any trouble that comes along, comes to both of you," Dad had said. "Never leave your brother behind."

Dad said it was about looking after each other, but Trevor thought Dad had no confidence in him. He thought he let down Dad if he didn't score at every game. He liked soccer better before Dad decided to be the coach.

Leaning upside down from the top bunk, Trevor whispered to Matt, "I got a plan."

The next Saturday morning, knowing Mom and Dad would sleep in, the boys tiptoed through the house and made a clean escape, like jewel thieves with peanut butter sandwiches and Oreo cookies.

They weren't running away. They were two best friends off on an adventure. Their first stop was the park. With no one there to enforce the height requirement, they raced to the wooden bridge with the sagging middle and braided ropes.

Matt climbed the ladder first, but Trevor pushed passed him, running across the splintered slats to the covered slide on the far side.

"You're making us off-balance," said Matt. "We have to stay in a straight line."

Trevor tagged the end and headed back toward his brother, yanking the ropes, making the bridge wobble.

"You jerk," Matt said. "Just because Dad says you're sure-footed doesn't mean you won't fall."

"Oooo, scaredy-cat!"

Before Matt could cite more rules, a gust of wind swayed the bridge and dropped them to their knees. Lightning brightened the sky while dark, hovering clouds held the sound of thunder like a pillow containing a scream. Raindrops splattered on the wooden planks.

"Uh-oh. What if it starts to rain?" Matt said, squinting, as he looked up.

"So what," Trevor said. "Don't be a sissy."

The boys slid down the spiral chute. At the bottom, they adjusted their lunch sacks stashed inside their zipped jackets.

Trevor pointed to the park bathroom. "Ever peed in there?"

Matt hesitated.

"On your mark, get set, go." Trevor raced ahead. He pulled open the door and skidded to the urinals. He was aiming his stream when he heard guttural groans like Dad with the stomach flu.

"Matt, somebody's in here," Trevor whispered.

"So?" Matt was just beginning to pee. Their heads turned when they heard the man gather his phlegm with a snort and gag, then spit in the toilet.

"Hey, mister," Matt said. "You okay?"

The stall door flew open, filling the room with the smell of an outhouse. A man in a filthy coat and cockeyed, knit cap held the doorjamb with both hands.

"Hey, boys." His voice was deep and gravelly. "What are you doing out on a day like this?" His smile showed stubby, brown teeth.

As the man stepped forward, Trevor yelled, "Stranger danger. Run." He blasted out the door.

Matt turned to leave, but not before the man grabbed his sleeve. "What's your hurry?"

Trevor paused outside only a second before he heard Dad in his head saying, *Trouble comes to both of you.* He rushed back and pulled open the door.

The man looked taller hovering over Matt. "Where do you boys go to school?"

"Meadowview just around the . . ." Matt started.

"Matt." Trevor shoved the man hard in the ribs, knocking him off balance. He yanked Matt's arm. "Come on."

The boys ran as fast as they could through the park. At the far corner, they looked back to see if anyone was following, but saw only heavy rain.

"That was close," Matt said, both boys laughing with relief.

Trevor felt proud of himself. He wished he could tell Dad that this time he had helped Matt out of trouble.

"I told you we were going to have fun." Trevor stomped his feet in a large puddle, soaking his pants. "Let's go to the wash. Maybe something cool will float by."

"We'll get in trouble," said Matt.

"Who's going to see us?"

The V-shaped concrete wash collected runoff as it snaked through the neighborhood. It was off-limits even to the big kids, except when it was completely dry in the summer. The boys ran down the ramp that leveled off to the path that was barely wide enough for two bicycles.

"Whoa, it's a river," Trevor said.

They ran side-by-side trying to keep pace with the leaves and fast-food wrappers floating on the churning waves, squealing in delight as the rain pelted their faces. They raced each other until they were out of breath, stopping under the bridge. Trevor pulled out his sack lunch, but Matt had lost his.

"Bet that creep got it." Trevor handed Matt half his sandwich. They giggled, remembering their escape.

The sound of sirens echoed off the walls, and the boys felt the rumble of a fire truck passing overhead.

"What could be on fire in the rain?" Matt asked.

"Who cares?" Trevor licked the creamy center from the last Oreo.

After the next lightning flash, the boys counted together, "One one-thousand, two one-thousand . . ." Boom. They jumped when the thunder arrived sooner than they expected.

"I'm cold just sitting here," Trevor said.

"What do you want to do next?" asked Matt.

Trevor looked at the milky river that had risen several inches while they had been eating their lunches. He looked up at the backyard fences, but knew no one would hear him yell over the storm. Still, he didn't want to call it quits.

"The arcade," Matt remembered. "Bet there's a ladder on the next bridge."

"I get first pinball game," Trevor said, taking off running.

The wind blew waves onto the bike path, making puddles that soaked their shoes. Their feet slipped inside their soggy socks.

When they got to the bridge, they saw steps in the concrete wall, but the rails were gone. There was no way to climb straight up.

"Should we wait here until it stops raining?" Trevor asked.

Matt shook his head. "No way. Look how high the water's getting. We have to find another ramp."

"Remember when Dad yelled at us for playing on the stairs at Oak Park?" Trevor said. "I think we're almost there."

They sloshed in water above their ankles. Trevor could tell Matt was slipping more than he was. He took the side closest to the water so Matt could be next to the wall where the water was shallower.

Matt pointed ahead to flashing red lights on the bridge. "I wonder if there was a car accident." When they took their focus from trying not to fall, a wave hit them behind their knees, nearly knocking them down.

A man's voice filled the concrete canyon. "Matt and Trevor, stay close to the wall. Move as quickly as you can toward the stairs."

Now in single file, Trevor couldn't see Matt's face but saw him quicken his step. Trevor was nervous about getting caught. He could hear Dad scolding him already, but at least they were going to be safe.

"We're almost there," Trevor yelled to Matt. He could see the stairs and people in yellow slickers at the bottom.

With only twenty feet to go, a swell lifted them off their feet and dragged them into the swift-moving water.

"Reach for the poles," someone yelled. Trevor tried to swim to the side but was powerless against the current. He knew he was the stronger swimmer so he pushed his brother toward the pole and saw him grab hold.

Matt reached out his other hand for Trevor, but the river had already grabbed him. "Trevor," Matt screamed.

"Don't let go," the fireman said. "We'll get him." That's all Trevor could hear as he was pulled underwater.

From somewhere deep in his brain, Trevor remembered when they were playing in the ocean Mom had said, "If you get tossed by a wave, hold your breath, and you'll float to the top."

*Hold your breath . . . float to the top*, Trevor repeated. He bobbed up and took a breath, seeing backyard fences zooming by. Ahead, he saw flashing red lights and people in yellow slickers hanging a soccer net from the bridge.

Someone yelled, "Grab the net. Grab the net." But when Trevor put his hands up, he went underwater and spun around. When he bobbed up, he felt the net brush the back of his head. The river was pulling him toward the fast-moving center. He felt like he was in a washing machine.

*Hold your breath . . . float to the top.* The next time he resurfaced, a log thumped him in the chest. He pulled himself up and hung his tired arms over the top. The log didn't seem to be moving, so the water was rushing up his back, over the top of his head. So much water was getting in his mouth, he wondered if it wouldn't be better to let go and try for the next net. *Matt's smart. What would he do?*

Trevor wished it was a regular school day—boring, predictable, and warm. And he wished he hadn't complained so much. *Mom and Dad are probably worried, but I'll make it up to them by practicing really hard at soccer.* Even though he hated prayers at night, in his head he said, *God, I promise never to break the rules again. Please help me. I'm really cold.*

Suddenly it got windy and the water started to vibrate all around him. When Trevor didn't think he could hold on any longer, he heard the loud speaker again. "We're coming down to get you. Hang tight."

183

Trevor looked up to see a man in a wet suit with a florescent vest, slide down a rope, and position himself on the same side of the log.

"Hey, Trevor. I'll bet you're tired."

"I am." Trevor's voice was shaking hard like the rest of his body. He started to cry, but not because he was scared. He didn't exactly know why, but he made himself stop because he didn't want to look like a baby.

"Okay, you did the hard part—we'll do the rest." While he tied ropes around Trevor and attached them to rings on his belt, the man said, "Maybe you'll want to join the fire department and train to be a first responder one day. We go where the danger is to help people." Trevor thought it was funny that a fireman was pulling him out of water and not pouring water on a fire.

"Here we go. Hold on." Even though Trevor didn't know him, he held onto his neck as tight as he could. The fireman signaled the helicopter to lift them out of the water. Trevor felt like he was on a scary ride at the county fair, hanging from a rope over a river. He could feel the man hug him like Dad did when he scored a goal.

At the helicopter door, two pairs of hands pulled them inside, unfastened the ropes, and wrapped Trevor in blankets. They hadn't flown far when the helicopter touched down in the middle of Oak Park. A fireman in a regular uniform carried him to the back door of the rescue truck and handed him to Dad. Matt joined the hug and spread his arms around them both.

"They're probably fine," said the fireman, "but as a precaution, we're headed to the ER." He closed the door, but before they could drive away, they heard pounding on the back.

"Hold up," the fireman yelled to the driver. The door was barely open when Mom started to climb in, even before the fireman could help. She hugged Matt and Trevor separately and then squished them together. "I'm glad you're okay," she said, crying happy tears, "and I'm so mad at you." Mom's voice was as shaky as Trevor's had been in the river.

Dad looked at the boys with an expression that said, "We have a lot to talk about, but not now."

Trevor knew Dad would be proud of how he'd taken care of Matt that day. But for now, exchanging glances, he and Matt knew they were going to have to be on their best behavior for a long, long time.

# Head Banger in Paradise

## Kathleen Thomas

Visitors are rare here. On admittance, our patients generally see that their friends and relatives have a way of moving on.

Three-dozen men, twenty-two to sixty-three years of age, live on my unit, a drop in the bucket of over a thousand patients, hospital-wide. They share bedrooms, bathrooms, and just about everything else. They struggle with schizophrenia, depression, and psychosis. Delusions, hallucinations, fear, and paranoia routinely show up.

Our patients often have little or no self-control. When paired with anxiety and anger issues, they act out on a regular basis, assaulting staff or one another. Often confused, they lack motivation to do much to help themselves.

Behind our backs, patients cut themselves with sharpened plastic utensils, broken CDs, pencils, or worse. It's a tough place to be a patient. It's a rough place to work.

Breakfast was over and done with. It was quiet on the unit, and I was glad of it.

I heard keys jangling from the other side of the door. *Right on time, here he comes.*

He walked into the unit, escorted by one of the psych techs from the admission unit.

Frank's arms hung like flabby sausages. Thirty-three years old, he shuffled like an old man, a side effect of medication to reduce aggressive behavior.

His man-sweat, accompanied by a robust urine aroma, percolated the air as he approached me. Frank had been next door for thirty days now. He'd refused to shower every one of them.

"Morning, Shea," the escort said.

"Good morning," I answered. "How is everyone?"

"Not bad. He was at it again last night. Fine this morning, though."

I noticed the bruises on Frank's swollen forehead where he'd smashed his head against the wall.

"How do you feel, Frank?"

Silence.

Head banging was Frank's unique trademark. One minute, he'd be standing quiet as a doorknob. Next minute, he'd be methodically slamming his forehead against the wall. No wailing, no crying. Just the thud of boney skull on plaster.

I started ransacking through the black trash bag, AKA patient's luggage, which Frank handed to me. I latched onto a pair of hospital-issue sneakers, a denim jacket, a pair of sweat pants, and a San Francisco Giants T-shirt.

"Is this all you've got, Frank?"

He didn't answer.

His escort did.

"That's it, Shea. Here's his chart. Have fun now."

He fist-tapped Frank's shoulder as he turned back to the admission unit.

I'd met Frank a week earlier on a help call to his unit. One patient had cornered another in a bedroom. They were pounding each other with fists, their obscenities scouring the room. They each weighed close to a couple hundred pounds. It was all we could do to separate them. The hospital police arrived in time to catch a young nurse being thrown to the wall.

Frank watched the action from across the hall. Leaving the room, I didn't realize he'd quickened his step behind me until I felt him punching the back of my head.

He was sedated then, but my neck was stiff for a week. The real injury was to my psyche; a potent reminder to keep those eyes in the back of my head wide open.

He couldn't help it, really. The voices crawling in his head screamed danger. It sent him straight into attack mode. A variety of meds helped only sometimes.

"Come on, Frank. Your bedroom is up the hall," I said. He flinched when I placed my hand behind his elbow.

"Okay," I said, pulling back. "It's okay."

I carried his meager belongings to his room.

"Do I know you?" he asked.

"Yes, I'm an RN. My name is Shea. We met next door. I work this unit most of the time."

He slowly nodded yes. "I hit you, didn't I?"

"Yep," I said, smiling. "It's okay, Frank, I'm fine."

We arrived at his bedroom.

"This is your bed," I said. "You've got three fairly quiet roommates. You'll be fine here."

He looked at his roomie who was lying with his back to us on his own bed six feet away. He checked out his closet, the grimy steel reinforced window, and finally slid his hand across the thin cotton sheet. Sitting on the edge of the bed, he was hunched over, elbows on his legs, looking down.

"ECT will help, right?" He looked up at me.

Electroconvulsive therapy. It was a technique we used on severely depressed patients like Frank who presented a danger to themselves and others. It was also as controversial as it was misunderstood.

I nodded. "We hope so. Your first treatment will be next week. Let's take it easy until then, okay?"

"Does it hurt?"

"No, you'll be asleep. You won't feel a thing. It just shocks a bit, relieving the depression and voices in your head. I think it'll be good for you."

A week later, after three episodes of head banging and one incident of assault, I woke Frank early to prepare him for his initial ECT therapy.

The surgical suite where ECT takes place was a five-minute walk from the unit. Cardinal rule in the hospital: never escort a patient out of the unit by yourself. So Jerry, my psych tech friend, pushed Frank along in a wheelchair. Frank was more quiet than usual. I attributed it to the sedative we'd given him. Jerry and I carried on, talking about our kids.

"Is your son in the hospital, too?" Frank interrupted, tilting his head up toward me.

"No, my son's in college."

"Did he have ECT?"

"Nope. He was never a patient here."

We moved our way through a maze of bleak corridors into a shiny, brightly lit surgical suite.

Frank's gaze landed on an old scuffed rectangular black metal box with red and silver knobs jutting from one side. Dr. Afzal, Frank's psychiatrist who would administer the ECT, was adjusting the equipment.

"Why am I here?" Frank asked.

The anesthesiologist greeted him with an outstretched hand that Frank ignored.

"Morning, Frank. I'm Dr. Umbar. We met on the unit. Good to see you."

Frank stared at him.

Dr. Umbar continued. "Your first ECT treatment is today. We're hoping to get you back home soon."

Frank's eyes skirted back to the black box.

"Is that the electricity? For my brain?"

"Well, yes," I answered. "The box helps the doctor calculate just enough energy to help your brain heal itself."

Frank seemed fixated on the black box.

Jerry helped Frank over to the 1950s chic avocado-green vinyl bed wrapped in a ribbon of stainless steel. Frank's tongue darted across his lips as he scanned the room.

And then, halfway onto a bed barely wide enough to hold him, Frank began thrashing about with a wildness that surprised even me. His left foot kicked my right flank. His arms whipped about. His clammy hands latched onto me, nearly knocking me off my feet.

"Frank, please, stop," urged Dr. Umbar.

"Stop." I heard my own voice echo the doctor's.

A triplet of stainless steel tables clanged onto the floor.

"Frank, relax," Jerry yelled.

Dr. Umbar pressed Frank's shoulders onto the bed while Jerry and Dr. Afzal each grabbed an arm. I moved quickly, tripping over Jerry's feet while I secured Frank's body and limbs to the bed with red, white, and blue Velcro straps.

Mute, Frank blinked rapidly.

"Okay, now," Dr. Umbar said. "You're fine, Frank. You'll feel a little poke now—a mild sedative to help you relax."

Calm again, Frank watched the tip of the needle disappear into his right shoulder.

I applied electrical leads to the pulse points on Frank's head, chest, and feet while the docs reorganized the scattered equipment. Dr. Afzal added blood pressure cuffs, one on Frank's left arm and another on his right, lower leg to monitor the immediate ECT effects.

Frank's chest swelled up and down, slow and steady.

Dr. Umbar methodically cleaned Frank's right arm around and inside the elbow. "You'll feel another pinch now."

Frank flinched as the anesthesiologist slid the needle tip into his vein. The IV drip assured good fluid intake while providing a line to piggyback Frank's treatment meds.

"You'll be getting sleepy now," Dr. Umbar said, opening the valve to adjust the flow.

Frank eyed the milky white liquid slithering down the thin tube from the tiny valve below the IV bag. A snowy river streamed toward him. His lips stirred, occupied by his inner self-talk.

*Three, six, nine, twelve. One, two, three. Three, six, nine twelve. One, two, three. Three, six, nine, twelve. One, two, three.*

Frank looked at me. I took his hand in mine as his eyes glazed over. His eyelids fluttered in rhythm to his heartbeat until both eyes closed.

Dr. Umbar told us Frank was receiving IV Propofol, the same medication Michael Jackson received shortly before he died. It gave me the chills. I wasn't concerned Frank would die, merely aware of a brief pall of sorrow paying me a visit from the King of Pop.

Within three minutes, Frank was deep in sleep.

"Dr. Umbar? Are we ready?" the psychiatrist asked.

Dr. Umbar nodded in agreement. "Good to go."

Dr. Afzal looked to the black metal box. A paper strip spooled out like a receipt at a checkout stand.

He pressed the red button, holding it for a count of three seconds by the machine's digital readout. Frank's body twitched, just enough so you couldn't miss it. His upper body and head spasms lasted six seconds. His fingers and toes continued their tiny dance for another dozen beats on the monitoring strip.

We were all quiet.

Soon enough, Dr. Umbar loaded Frank's IV with a massive dose of caffeine.

While we waited for the caffeine to kick in, I asked about Frank's unexpected pre-ECT behavior.

"That was an unforeseen experience," Dr. Afzal said. "I believe the anti-anxiety medication given on the unit beforehand induced an abnormal response."

"Surely, that wasn't all of it?" I asked.

"Frank talked to me last Friday," said Dr. Afzal, "before my weekend off. He told me about a dream he'd had recently. It involved him rolling in a wagon through a dark cave, eventually landing in a sunny arena filled with children at attention, all outfitted in white playsuits. I think, this morning, our patient confused reality with his dream."

"So," Jerry said, "next time he walks here. No rolling."

*My goodness. It would have been nice to know about the damn dream.*

Thirty minutes later, Frank was up, still groggy from the ECT and the assorted meds swirling around in his body.

Jerry helped him to the wheelchair.

The return trip seemed much longer than the previous one. I was still shaken by Frank's outburst.

Hospital policy dictates one RN accompany patients to and from ECT and continually monitor health status two hours post-treatment. I charted Frank's vital signs every fifteen minutes, relieved to see no blood pressure spikes, paranoia, fear, or loss of consciousness.

Short-term memory loss is a common side effect of ECT. The extent of memory loss after additional treatments would determine whether or not to continue the therapy. The positive aspects of ECT would be weighed against any detrimental memory loss.

It was warm where we sat in the day hall, sunlight streaming through the windows onto my assessment sheet.

"What's your name?" I asked.

"Frank."

"Where are you?"

He looked out the bank of steel-framed windows holding the world outside in a giant picture frame.

"Valley State Hospital."

"What day is it?" I asked.

"Wednesday?"

"Right. What's my name?"

"Shea."

I smiled, nodding in agreement. "How are you feeling?"

No answer. His forearms rested atop the wheelchair armrests, fingers dangling. He seemed taken in by the giant tulip tree blooms drifting in the courtyard.

I chatted with Frank, other patients, and staff as they drifted into the day hall. Judge Judy ruled the TV in the far corner.

After a while, Frank said he was cold and sleepy, a common ECT reaction. I wheeled him to his room. He was a little shaky but

190

able to get himself into bed. I covered him with an extra blanket and watched him roll over to face the wall.

"Thank you," he muttered.

"You're welcome, Frank."

This routine went on for a few weeks, one treatment each week, increasing to two treatments, then to three. After four months, Frank was having far fewer instances of violent behavior with only rare episodes of head banging. He slept better. His attitude was much improved. The treatments seemed to be working, with only minor, temporary, memory loss. Some days he would forget having breakfast. A few times, he didn't remember the ECT treatment at all.

Frank's parents, far from the norm, came to visit him often. They were amazed at the positive changes in their son's demeanor. They'd delivered him to us from their foothills home less than six months earlier, after watching his long decline. They were hopeful. I'd seen life changing results in other patients after ECT. It was looking as if Frank really would have a new start in life.

After returning to the unit one day, we were again sitting in the day hall.

"Shea, can I tell you a secret?"

"Sure. Tell me a secret. I may not be able to keep it, though. What is it?"

"During ECT sometimes, I feel really high, like over-the-top stoned. I try to stay there to keep it, but it runs away. I keep trying to get back to it, but I can't."

"I haven't heard that before," I chuckled.

"Do you think you can get my doctor to give me more drugs to keep it going?"

"Ha, ha. I don't think so, Frank. It's just one way you're responding to the treatment. Do you think, besides the unusual high, you're improving?"

"When's the last time I hit someone?"

"A few weeks now."

"Good," he said, his blue eyes glistening.

After several more treatments, Frank was showing great progress. No violent outbreaks and no head banging. His depression lifted, he laughed often, and he enjoyed the company of others. His memory loss, though, was becoming serious. In consultation with his doctors and parents, he decided to discontinue ECT.

Just before Christmas, Frank was discharged home. It was a grand gift for him and for all of us who had been part of his success.

He was happy, and I was happy for him.

On a road trip the following summer, I braked for a stoplight while driving through the tiny foothill town of Paradise. I spotted Frank walking in the crosswalk. He was holding hands and laughing with a nice looking woman about his age. He turned his head my way, squinting into the sun behind me.

He couldn't see through the glare. I'm quite certain he couldn't make out the big smile on my face.

# Hide and Seek

## Joelle B. Burnette

"How is she doing? Is she still seeing that doctor?" Beth asked.

"Yes, but—"

"Maybe he's making her worse. I read this story in the *Times* that said—"

"He is helping her," Karen insisted.

"You do realize, I'm standing right here," Grace began.

"Why does she still need a doctor?" Beth asked. It was futile to expect even a modicum of polite restraint from the family's matriarch.

"Why don't you ask *her*," Karen suggested to her cousin. The two women stared at Grace.

"I want . . . I'm trying to . . ." Grace felt her cheeks warm. "I have to find a bathroom." She crossed the crowded room and neared a narrow door.

"Beat it, Freak. Beth has three other bathrooms. Go find one. This is gonna take a while." Gary closed the door. Normally, Grace would have glanced over her shoulder to see if anyone noticed her brother's tease, but not today. Already dancing in place, Grace sensed she had little time to waste.

Fleeing the crowded living room, she trotted down the long hallway toward the back of the house. Her shy knock on a door was offered by habit, but her quest for a toilet eliminated courteous hesitation. She turned the knob and burst into the room to find several women sitting across from each other on parallel twin beds. Their conversation wasn't broken by her sudden arrival, and the women continued chatting, oblivious to the girl's search.

Grace let out a groan as she backed out of the room and closed the door. She continued down the darkening hall that absorbed her stretching shadow. With each step, single conversations melted into the party's overall muffled roar. The living room's glow faded, and the girl's gaze tracked the shadow down the wall as the darkness blurred the oversized print of the wallpaper. The soothing sound of her fingers searching for a doorknob halted when she gripped a handle's cool metal and twisted her way into the silence of a spacious bedroom. Sunlight beamed down through a skylight, stunning her with blindness. Red orbs and orange streaks corrupted her sight.

She felt her way around the corner and into the bathroom's darkness, but a haze of pulsing hues impaired her vision. The warped door required her to lean against the old wood that squawked a complaint when she shoved the oak into its frame.

*Someone must have heard that,* she fretted. After fumbling with the door's lock to secure her privacy, she backed up to the toilet as she struggled with her belt, a button, and the zipper. Grace slid her pants down around her thighs and sat on the commode. Her eyes closed as her head tilted back with relief. Her features softened, and she breathed a timid sigh. Her shoulders dropped, and her body settled as her mind drifted to a calm scene that carried her away from the boisterous throng amassed elsewhere in the home.

Feeling at peace, Grace opened her eyes and scanned her dreary surroundings, studying the room's contents. The odd mix of knickknacks strewn about reflected her cousin's obsession with discovering cheap discards at local garage sales. The one elegant item in the garishly wallpapered room was a smal antique cabinet diagonally angled in front of her.

Looking more like an ostrich, the top-heavy tower stood a few feet tall atop spindly, metal legs. An intricate design of dark, inlaid woods were crowned by a square slab of polished stone displaying meandering blood-red lines marbled throughout. A short border of scalloped copper guarded the edge of the stone and reminded her of the haunted tower of an old mansion sitting beneath stormy skies. The soft metal was slightly bent in spots and gave the same flimsy impression of the haunted mansion's weather-worn wood; a weak barrier that breaks away when a bystander is shoved into terror as they fall from their lofty perch.

Mesmerized by the marble design, Grace's hand hunted the wall for the roll of toilet paper. Rather than finding tissue, her hand struck the bare cardboard, and it slapped against the aluminum dispenser to sound its hollow warning.

"Crap," she said when she looked at the torn scrap of soft paper dangling from the empty roll. She scanned her surroundings before stretching her arm around to the cabinet door below the sink. No rolls. Grace considered calling out like she would at home, asking anyone to fetch a roll. *What's the point? No one will hear, anyway.*

She looked around the room again and frowned at the small village of gnomes grouped together and staring at her from the far end of the counter.

"Well, you're no help." She raised her chin in challenge.

A decorative tray sat in front of the gnomes, but no paper hand towels remained. Crumpled and damp, the discarded napkins filled the wastebasket. She huffed and shook her head. She blushed as she sat up tall and nearly called out to attract her mother. She could hear the woman's cackling laughter traveling through the house and breaking through the silence at the far end of the hall outside the bedroom. She stopped when she remembered she had closed the bedroom door for added privacy.

Fixated on the cabinet, Grace noticed a tiny disc of dark metal fashioned into an ornate flower. Upon closer inspection, she realized the oddly positioned blossom on the face of the piece was a miniature handle to access a camouflaged compartment. Once the pattern of the cabinet's calculated disorder was exposed, she found two additional short drawers stacked above the cabinet—each chamber with its own tiny flower attached to the wood according to artistic design rather than traditional placement in the center of a panel.

Reaching forward, she hesitated. *Isn't this intrusive?*

"Screw it. I need some paper, so . . ." Her words trailed off. Again, she reached for the floral knob to tug open the small door.

Wood scraped against polished wood to reveal the dark, cramped storage space within. The weight of memories closed Grace's eyes. She was six years old when she discovered an odd space hidden beneath floorboards in the linen closet of her family's former home. She could still hear the sound of people cheering on football players on the TV her dad watched. He had the volume loud to compete with the unrestrained conversation her mother was having on the phone with her grandmother. Gary was in his room with the door locked after having refused his little sister's request to play Candy Land.

Deciding she would make a tent in her room, she went to the linen closet to fetch a sheet. Standing on her toes and stretching upward, her extended fingers couldn't reach the bedding.

A shift of her weight caused the end of a wood plank to pop up from the floor, revealing a secret space.

Grace removed another board and lowered her feet down into a compartment that had smooth metal walls. She looked around the hall to check if anyone was nearby before snaking her body under two more boards still covering the hole that formerly held a safe concealed there by the previous homeowners. Sitting cross-legged in the spacious hold, her head didn't touch the boards unless she sat up tall.

*Why build a tent when I already have a hiding place?* she thought. She picked up her bunny and whispered to her stuffed companion. "Do you think they will find me in here?" She looked at her floppy friend who offered a blank stare through its jeweled fuchsia eyes.

Grace yanked down some towels off a shelf. She giggled as the fluffy linens rained down and lay scattered. She piled towels to cushion her bottom and reached out from her secret hiding place to close the closet door, but the corner was obstructed by towels. She replaced the wood panels and sat waiting.

She waited and waited, but nobody came looking for her. She didn't chat with her bunny; rather, she studied how the stuffed animal's eyes glowed when struck by a thin strip of light sneaking in through a crack between the wood panels.

After enough time passed, and without noticing, her body sank lower and flatter until she was curled up with her bunny on the bed of towels. She lay there under the dim glow from the strip of light, napping like she was in her own bed.

Time in the confined space passed absent measure when the light extinguished. She awakened in the darkness and had to remember where she was. She pushed up on one of the wood planks but it wouldn't budge. She tried another, but nothing happened.

Two days passed before anyone found the young girl; two days of her parents, her brother, friends, and the police searching for her and believing she had been taken. Surely, she wasn't in the house.

By the time her family noticed she had been missing, there was too much commotion in their home to hear her crying out or quietly sobbing when she wasn't asleep in the metal cavern. There was too much noise to hear her bawling muffled by the wood panels that had been covered by a heavy box of books left out in the hall. She had fallen asleep in the cavity and didn't hear her father placing the box in the open closet. She didn't hear him close the door.

It was a family friend who first heard the weak sobbing. The woman offered to help her friends by taking care of chores so the family could concentrate on finding their little Grace. It was she who heard a strange sound in the closet as she was placing clean towels on one of the lower shelves.

She removed the heavy box holding Grace captive and kneeled down. She banged the floor and called out, "Gracie? Is that you?" The sound stopped. The woman froze.

A wood panel popped up and fell back askew. The woman seized the board and tossed it aside. "Grace! I found Grace!" the woman shouted down the hall. The child lay squinting from the sudden flood of light entering her tomb.

~*~

Trying to shake off the haunting memory, Grace grabbed a roll of toilet paper from the cabinet. She had to get out of that bathroom. She gathered a wad of the paper to use and jumped up from the seat while replacing her pants, but her trembling hands complicated simple tasks.

"Damnit. Come on!" Blood pounded through her veins and her head began to hurt as she tried to press the button through its hole and latch her belt.

She flushed the toilet and turned on the sink faucet to wash up. In the mirror, a girl with panicked eyes looked back at her. Beyond her reflection, a red glow came from that antique cabinet.

Her heart was pounding as she swung around and saw a crimson radiance in the eyes of one of the Art Deco accents on the cabinet. The two brass ram's heads were positioned like protective gargoyles on either side of the top drawer. She squeezed shut her eyes, but the luminous color triggered images of her bunny and that dark trap. Grace felt dizzy and reached for the polished granite counter to steady herself, but her wet hands slipped and she nearly fell over.

She caught herself, slapped away remaining dampness onto her pants, and reached around for the door's handle as she attempted to escape the confined space.

The button lock released as the knob turned, and she tugged on the door, but the warped wood held fast in the bottom corner. She gripped the knob with both hands and tried again, pulling harder this time, but the door wouldn't budge and only slammed back into position.

"Stop this!" she demanded as she pounded her fist on the wood. *You're being ridiculous.* "Breathe." She closed her eyes and tried to soothe her growing anxiety. "You can do this. You know what to do."

197

She pictured a beach—a pleasant setting with calming waves. "You're okay. You're okay." Her body relaxed. She leaned back on the door and laughed at her predicament as the shaggy rug beneath her feet slid toward the sink.

"I did it. I'm okay." Still chuckling as she fixed the rug, she paused when she heard Gary outside the door.

"Grace, are you okay? Mom told me to find you."

"Yes, I actually am."

"Well, are you coming out?"

"Um, I'm stuck. Again. But at least it didn't take too long to be found." Her cheeriness surprised them both.

Her sibling tried the door. "When I say so, pull the door."

Gary rammed the wood with his shoulder and the wood pulled free of its trap, but he didn't hear anything else other than some thuds from the wood slamming against Grace's forehead and knocking her off balance. She fell backward, her weight shifting with the sliding rug, until she heard an odd sound: a "clunk" as the back of her head slammed against the granite. Liquid gushed from her head as her skull lay broken on the cold floor. The bunched up carpet, weighed down by her legs, became lodged against the door. Blood spread out around her body until it met with the rug that soaked up the sanguine flow.

The bathroom was silent. "Grace?" Blood pooled under the door. Gary attempted to press open the door. "Grace!"

No one answered.

"I'm sorry, Grace! I'm sorry! I'm sorry!"

# Glorious Distractions

## William Hillar

His fingers were delicate, almost fragile. He lay on his back, his small frame partially covering the discarded AK-47. He was alive, but several of his fellow mercenaries lay dead, strewn about by the savagery of a close-in firefight. Blood and broken plants lay along the well-beaten jungle path. The seventy mules carrying the raw opium seemed to be oblivious to the noise and carnage.

The picture on his Singapore driver's license said his name was Lee Jing. An inch over five feet tall, he weighed 135 pounds and was two days away from his thirty-fourth birthday. His wallet also yielded a picture of him with his very pregnant wife holding two young girls. His hands, still delicate looking, seemed caring and sensual.

Most of the blood on his uniform was not his. He had hit his head on a small boulder and knocked himself out. He was regaining consciousness as I was getting ready to bind his wrists and ankles. He stared at me as I pulled him into a sitting position. His right hand reached up to grasp my left forearm. "Help me," he said in French. "Please help me," he added in Russian. "Are you American? Do you speak English?" he asked. His hand gripping my arm was as expressive as his language.

We heard others coming through the brush, and I quickly bound his wrists. The abusive language and sinister laughter were a precursor to his fate. His eyes told me that he knew interrogations ended in death, or one wishing he were dead.

Over the years, I had become intimate with the Chinese proverb: Never mount a tiger, because when you get off, it will consume you. Walking around the jungles of Burma, Laos, and Thailand was bad enough. But walking around those jungles, when three or four warlords were trying to steal each other's opium, was a suicide pact with the tiger.

Lee Jing's hands were not those of a mercenary or soldier. They were hands that could heal and give comfort and love. I had little time. "Lee Jing," I said in Mandarin. "I will not hurt you. You will come with me. I am going to roughly pull you to your feet, grab your arm, and lead you off the trail and back into the jungle. Do you understand?"

His eyes never left mine. Almost imperceptibly, he nodded, and I jerked him to his feet.

Passing the men coming through the brush, I jostled my prisoner, and cursed him in Chinese. He was kicked in the legs by two men as we went by. Soon, out of sight, I released his arm. For twenty minutes we walked; the silence broken by small arms fire—three single pops spaced several minutes apart. There was little doubt Lee Jing thought he would be next. Near a large banyan tree, we stopped. I motioned for him to sit. He did but would not make eye contact. "You are American?" he asked in English.

"Yes," I answered. "Hold out your hands." He did and I cut his wrist restraints. "Here," I said, handing him the knife, hilt first, "you might need this later." After a slight hesitation, he took it and set it down beside him.

"Your Chinese is good. How do you know my name?"

"I examined the papers in your wallet while you were unconscious."

He patted his pocket, puzzled it was still there. "I do not understand." He shook his head then put his hands together, palm to palm, looked me in the eyes, and bowed from the waist while still sitting. I returned his blessing.

"Lee Jing, I must get back to the ambush site soon or they will send others to find us." His eyes widened, he rapidly nodded. "You are not a private war fighter, Lee Jing. Your hands gave you away. Quickly now, tell me how you ended up carrying an AK-47 and speaking four languages"

His eyes welled with tears as he told me that almost a year ago, he and his family had been vacationing in Phuket, Thailand. "The men of the Triad came at night. They carried guns and demanded money and jewelry. Some women were raped, and some men and older boys were dragged off into the jungle . . . to be used as slaves or fighters. I was one of them."

He looked away, momentarily, and continued. "I am . . . was a professor of languages at university." His voice broke as he showed me the picture of his wife and children. "My son is long born by now." A groan came from deep inside him. Silent shaking added to his despair.

"Lee Jing, I must get back. You must get home." From my pack I gave him several hundred Chinese yuan, a handful of Thai baht, and some Singapore dollars. He refused to take them. I shoved them into his shirt pocket. Then I stood up, pulling him to his feet. I removed a 9mm military Beretta from my pack. He froze, then opened his mouth, as if to speak. I jacked the slide to show him it was loaded and offered it to him, grip first. He tucked it into his belt. I offered him an extra clip, full of ammunition. He took that as well.

He watched me as I shouldered my pack. Any doubts he may have harbored regarding my intent were now gone. We stood there looking at each other. "How are you called, sir," he asked.

"Friend," I said.

He gave me the picture of his pregnant wife and two daughters. "Friend, keep this for me. They will be much safer with you." I thanked him and placed it in my own wallet. We both slowly bowed low—from the waist.

"One last thing," I said, pulling my own weapon from its holster. Quickly, I fired one round into the ground. "You are now dead." He nodded his understanding, beginning to realize what was about to happen. "Be safe, Lee Jing . . . Be safe," I quietly prayed. We turned from each other and walked back into our lives.

Fifteen minutes later, I re-entered the ambush site. "Let's mount up," I barked, not needing to discuss my supposed interrogation and killing of my prisoner. Within days, the raw opium was delivered to its buyer deep inside northern Laos.

~*~

That was twenty-seven years ago. For the next twenty-plus years, I immersed myself in Southeast Asian cultures where drug and human trafficking are prevalent. I frequently thought about Lee Jing. I would look at the picture of his wife and daughters wondering if he ever made it home. The probability was not in his favor. During those times, in that part of the world, there were more victims than survivors. Later, when in Hong Kong, Bangkok, or Singapore, I would occasionally catch a glimpse of someone who I thought could be him. But they never had his hands.

After several years, the frequency of the memories of Lee Jing was less than seldom. I think, subconsciously, I may have been afraid that I'd sent him off into the jungle knowing it was nearly impossible for him to survive. I didn't want that validated. I was good at compartmentalizing those events that wake you up at 2:00 a.m. and slam you to the floor. I'd learned, early in my career, to hide my feelings and emotions . . . and to lie to myself.

Locking up painful feelings and emotions is helpful when you have to make sound decisions during traumatic events. But it is imperative to periodically revisit them, lest they begin to distort your reality. Especially when you are a trained professional. For most of my adult life, I rarely took the time to unlock them. And it began to show.

I got kudos for being professionally adept. But no one ever congratulated me for trashing two marriages, being an absentee father, drinking too much, or bouts of inappropriate acting out. To get my attention, a clinical psychologist once said to me, "Will, if you live to be a hundred, my guess is you would still be a damn good operative." Before I could smile he added, "But, you'll never be able to engender a true honest lasting relationship with anyone. One of these days you are going to wake up in the morning to find you are on the other side of the mountain . . . never having been to the top." It got my attention.

The following ten months, he showed me how I created and nurtured an inner martyr. I learned that not forgiving myself and others sparked irrational thoughts, leading to irrational behaviors. Slowly my life improved. I discovered I could be equally successful driven by humanitarian and social justice issues as ones driven by politics. Soon, I began to see a route to the top of the mountain. I also re-discovered memories of Lee Jing.

~*~

In 2010, I booked a room at the historic Raffles Hotel in Singapore. Built in 1887, it is a place I frequently stay when in Southeast Asia. I had several days of vacation before flying up the Malay Peninsula to Bangkok. During the eighteen-hour flight from San Francisco, I was bombarded with memories of the years I had spent in what used to be Indochina. Seemingly out of the blue, Lee Jing's name popped into my mind. I briefly searched my wallet for the picture he had left in my care. It was not to be found. I made a mental note to try to find it when I got back home.

From Singapore's Changi Airport, I shared a midsize limousine to the hotel. I loved the Raffles for its quiet elegance, efficient staff, and highly satisfied guests.

I was led to the registration island while my passport, visa, and credit card were examined. The young Asian woman helping me kept up an enjoyable and friendly conversation while she efficiently checked me in. "I see, on previous trips, you enjoyed our Long Bar Steak House and the Writer's Bar . . . oh, and the Courtyard as well." I smiled and was rewarded with complimentary drink and meal tickets at each of these amenities.

"That's very kind. Thank you, Miss Yang."

She smiled and handed me my travel documents. "Enjoy your stay."

I turned to follow the bellman. Out of the corner of my eye, I thought I saw somebody quickly duck behind one of the large pillars in the lobby. I'm not as suspicious as when I was younger, but old habits die hard . . . if at all. The bellman and I walked past the column on the way to the elevator, and . . . nothing. There was no one there. No one hiding or trying to have me not see them.

I awarded myself with a well-deserved, in-room massage. After my requisite cold shower, I dressed and headed for the Long Bar Steak House. In the early 1900s, the exotic drink, the Singapore Sling, was created here at the Raffles Hotel. So, when in Rome, well, you know. The first one was delicious. And being in the bar's cosmopolitan setting meant I could listen to seven or eight languages as there were guests from all over the world.

I ordered dinner to be eaten at the bar and another "Sling." It was one of those bars where all those who waited on you made you feel like you were their first priority. When the bill came, I opened my wallet to retrieve a credit card. Stuck to the back of it was the picture of Lee Jing with his pregnant wife and two daughters. I actually looked around to see if, perhaps, God or one of his minions was messing with my head.

Carefully, I placed the picture on the bar and handed the bartender my card. He took it and glanced at the old photo. Smiling, he said he would return shortly. The old photo flooded my head with memories. I remembered it all. I felt sure I had done the right thing, all those years ago. The bartender returned for my signature. I signed. He grinned and bowed and moved closer. "Excuse me, sir," he said politely. "We are inviting several guests to join us in our private meeting room for complimentary after-dinner drinks. Please follow me."

The private room turned out to be a corner room on the top floor with a 180-degree panorama of Singapore at night. "Make yourself comfortable, sir, the other guests will be arriving soon." I went to stand close to the window. The view was spectacular. About a minute later, I heard a door open followed by whispering and shuffling feet. I turned to see a 60-year-old Lee Jing leading his 90 plus year old mother to meet me. His two grown daughters and their husbands were there too. My bartender was his son. His middle name, Friend, was given to him by his father two years after he was born.

I am seldom speechless and almost never allow myself to cry in public. Lee Jing and his mother put their arms around me. We sobbed and trembled with emotions pent up for a quarter of a century. Later, Lee Jing explained he saw me checking in. It was him who I caught a glimpse of behind the column in the lobby. "I wasn't sure it was you, so I asked my son to use his cell phone and bring me a picture I could examine."

He had made it home. He was now director of sales and catering at the hotel. At his home, we talked for days. I learned how he found his way back to his family. How he found a different line of work. How grateful they all were for my help. His mother would not stop bowing and feeding me. At night, back at the hotel, my face would hurt from the constant smiling.

I began to see how interrelated everything is. And how one act of kindness, even to a stranger, whose hands weren't right, can have far reaching consequences.

# *Home*

## Skye Blaine

The phone rang late at night. Maggie fumbled for the receiver, heard her younger brother's deep tone, and sat up abruptly in bed. "Dad's missing. I think he's lost again." His voice sounded rough with a sharp edge of worry.

Anxiety prickled Maggie's stomach. "Did you call the police?"

A sigh. "No. It's so . . . embarrassing. It was just last week . . ." He trailed off into another sigh.

She strengthened her tone, an older sister voice. "You'd better call them, Sam. I'll take a leave of absence and catch a flight tomorrow. Another vet can stand in for me." She paused. "You know Daddy can't live alone in that big house any more. We need to decide on a place."

There was a long silence. "This shouldn't happen to an old man." Her brother's timbre was gruff.

"We both want him to be safe, right? Please, call me no matter what time they locate him." After her brother hung up, she folded with worry into a chair as the refrain began inside. *Daddy, Daddy, where are you?*

At 2:00 a.m., her brother phoned back. A late night mini-mart attendant called 911; an old man had been standing in the corner of the store for more than two hours. "Three miles from the house," Sam said. "How'd he pull that off?"

"Beats me. I've already made flight reservations. See you tomorrow night."

~*~

Maggie stepped off the Friday-evening commuter plane into the sweltering Midwest humidity. Her long day's journey had included a canceled flight, then rerouted due to severe thunderstorms, and a three-hour wait at O'Hare Airport. Finally, the airplane landed at her destination.

After deplaning, sweat droplets rose on her skin: the signature of high summer in this locale—moisture, humus, and deciduous trees. Cincinnati, Ohio. As she drew in the complex aroma, the day's exhaustion slipped from her. It smelled like home.

Glad she'd worn walking shoes, Maggie shrugged her arm through the backpack strap and made her way into the terminal. Was this the first time she'd come into town and not been met by family? She savored a peculiar meld of feelings, an odd mixture of adult and forlorn, home and homeless, all at the same time.

Close to 10:30 p.m., Maggie dragged herself out of the rental car in front of Sam's Mt. Adams townhouse. Lights on—he was up, thank heavens. For once, she was glad he lived alone. She grabbed her pack. Stuffed fuller than usual, it served as medical kit and overnight bag when she traveled.

Sam met her at the door. She hugged him close, then stood back and took a clear look. He seemed thinner, and a bit drawn, like when they lost their mom a decade before. Deeper lines now. He must be fifty-two. Her baby brother, with gray showing in the curls at his temples that was new since she'd seen him two years ago. She stumbled over niceties for a moment, then chuckled. "I'm too beat for this, Sam. Let's talk in the morning. Get me up, okay?"

Maggie went upstairs to the guest room, undressed, folded her clothes, and plopped them into empty dresser drawers. She'd be settling in for a while. She slid gratefully between the sheets and into sleep.

~*~

Trilling awakened her. She searched for a clock, disoriented. Must be the middle of the night. She heard Sam's voice in the next room.

"Dad? Are you all right? What's up?" A pause. "We'll search for the keys together in the morning, okay? All right, good night, Dad. Sleep well."

Maggie tried to doze off. The telephone rang again. A soft groan from her brother's room. Dad again. Three more times the phone rang. Three more times Sam gently responded to their father.

My God, she thought. No wonder he's exhausted. Maggie pulled herself out of bed, padded across the hall, and knocked softly on his door.

"Come on in," he sang out. He lay on his bed, hair-tousled head propped on his pillow. His hands rested one on top of the other, over his heart. Heartache, she thought. How do you get used to this? She curled up on the end of his bed.

"Is it like this all the time?" She looked at him with a questioning gaze. "Why didn't you tell me?"

"This happens in patches. It's been rough for a couple of months. What could you do? You live two thousand miles away."

"I could come. I came," she said simply. "I'm his child, too." She loved her brother too much to be angry that he hadn't asked for help.

"Yeah." He fell quiet. "Thanks." Then his words came in a rush. "You work full time. You've got a veterinary practice and major commitments. I'm a self-employed potter; I figured I'm the one." He tilted his head and grinned at her.

"I love housekeeping, aprons, lists . . ."

She reached out to touch him. "Has Pop forgotten to be angry at you?"

"Gender preference isn't in his vocabulary anymore. Most of the time he's trying to remember my name. Sometimes he struggles to remember his own. I found him one day, repeating 'My name is Johnathan Braun. My name is Johnathan Braun.'"

Where had she been—so caught up in her own life? Dad had been the one to maintain contact after their mom died. When his memory failed, he'd forget to call. Maggie felt a wrench of guilt. *Daddy, Daddy, where are you?* She hadn't picked up the slack; she'd let phone contact with her father slide. "Will he recognize me?"

"Probably. He recognizes my face. I think he knows I'm his son or at least, someone he loves. He just can't find the name any more."

Maggie looked at her brother for a long moment. They both sighed, and spoke at the same moment. "It's time, isn't it?" Laughter bubbled up. Two such different people, and yet they often finished each other's sentences.

"Your hair looks gray. Is that because you cut it?" he asked.

Maggie ran her fingers through her short-cropped hair. "I kept it long for Bob. Once he left, I stopped dyeing it, too. Guess I'm not trying to look younger anymore."

"Well, thank God for that. Never did like that guy." He paused, and Maggie felt his eyes take her in. "I did make some calls about Dad earlier, before you got here," he said. "Ended up with more questions than answers. Like—do we include him in these decisions? Should he be in a home with only Alzheimer's patients?"

"I've been asking myself questions too. It's easier with animals—guess that's why I'm a vet, not an M.D." Maggie looked at

Sam's drawn face. "Want to make a list before we go see Dad? Not that we'll ask him, but our questions will be fresh for us."

"I've needed your support, Sis. Over coffee in the morning, okay?"

Back in the guest room, Maggie belly flopped on the bed and tried to fall asleep. Her mind was spinning like a computer disk drive. She lay awake imagining scenarios. If he didn't remember her name, should she jump in and offer it? That might feel demeaning. Maggie knew him as a proud man or at least, he used to be. Would he remember the endless phone conversations as he'd struggled to come to terms with Sam's admission he was gay? She and her dad had developed a deeper closeness during that period twenty years ago. Would he look the same, or would his eyes be vacant? Her chest banded with grief at the thought. So many questions. How could she and Sam best meet Dad's needs? Would he accept the help he required so badly? Maggie finally dozed off with a prayer that she and Sam would find just the right solution and agree on what should be done.

The telephone woke her at dawn. She was again humbled by Sam's patience. So little sleep, yet his steady voice conveyed care. "Up already? Calm down, Pop, we'll find them. Want some company for breakfast? Maggie came into town last night." Her brother's voice dropped, but she could make out the words through the wall. "Maggie, Pop. Your *daughter*."

Her hands flew to cover her face, as though to block out the blunt, unrelenting truth, the abrupt and immense sense of loss. She felt physically struck, and fled to the bathroom, fumbled with the shower faucet, then let the spray pound her body. The water and tears flushed out a mix of grief and guilt. She had no one to blame but herself. Finally, Maggie stepped out of the shower and into what she knew would be an unforgettable day.

She followed the scent of coffee down the stairs. Sam glanced up as she entered the kitchen.

"Ready for your morning booster?" He handed her a travel cup. "We're headed over to cook breakfast for Dad. Let's work on our list later. Best not wait too long—he's anxious this morning."

"Yes, I overheard."

"All of it?" His eyebrows shot up.

She nodded. "Guess I'm a fatherless child." Maggie chewed her lip for a moment then took a slow, appreciative sip of her latte. "You're the best, Sam. I'm lucky to have you for a brother." She raised her gaze to his as he leaned against the counter, head tilted to one side, his crooked smile lighting up his face, softening the smudges of fatigue under his eyes.

"Because I make a fine latte? Come on, girl. Let's go. This day isn't going away. Let's hang on to our curiosity and sense of humor as best we can."

Sam drove in silence to their childhood home as Maggie took in the familiar, yet altered, sights along Kellogg Avenue. Where was the polo field? A large seafood restaurant and giant parking lot had taken its place. That hurt. As a teenager, she had cooled ponies on that field every Sunday for years. As they rounded the corner near the little Miami River, another reminder of change—the singing bridge was gone, replaced by a modern concrete one. The sound from her childhood remained with her—the cla-clunk as cars entered the span, the musical ring of tires on open steelwork that allowed the floods to rise and fall, and the final cla-clunk as the cars returned to pavement. Bridge music still nestled in the corners of her dreams.

Sam parked in the driveway and started toward the front door. Maggie hung back, and Sam gathered her close with an arm around her waist. "It's still Dad, you know. But different, just like the scenery on the way here."

He'd always been able to read her mind. Why had they fought so much as kids?

The condition of the house shocked Maggie. The exterior paint was chipped, and the inside needed a deep cleaning. Stacks of newspapers towered in the halls. *Wow. Dad doesn't fix and putter anymore.* They finally located their father in his basement workshop. More hunched, but still sporting a head of glorious white hair, he stood at the counter, apparently sorting screwdrivers. Sam called his name, but he didn't respond. Her brother tried a louder "Hello."

Their dad whirled around, startled. His eyes settled on his son for a long moment. "Nice of you to stop in." He looked toward Maggie. "Who'd you bring, a new girlfriend?" His eyes held mild curiosity and innocence.

Maggie caught her brother's glance. That had been a blow for him, too. She thought she had prepared herself, but her body reacted as though it belonged to someone else. Tremors of shock rushed up her spine, and her hands quivered against her body in their own, uncontrolled rhythm. *Daddy, Daddy, where are you?* Her voice shook as she said, "Dad, it's Maggie, your daughter."

Her father's gaze rested on her. His face changed in minute increments, each shift a tiny window into knowing. "Maggie?"

Puzzlement, remembrance, humiliation? She couldn't be sure. He looked back and forth between them. Sam looked at Maggie and gestured her forward. Propelled toward her father, she opened her arms and enfolded him.

"I love you, Dad." Moisture collected where their skin met. His tears? Hers? She wasn't sure. "Come on upstairs. We'll cook your favorite breakfast." She managed to smile at her brother. "Then we'll all scout around for those keys."

# Lucille's Lesson

## Robin Moore

Lucille was not a stupid woman, but sometimes her impulses took over. She watched her daughter slide off Toby's bare back, and slip the rope from his neck. She left him to graze on the weedy lawn while Maxine, the old mare, grazed contentedly nearby. With no fence around the house, the horses could amble and eat wherever they pleased in the farmyard.

Julia dashed upstairs to do homework. "See you in a bit, Mom."

Free from saddles or halters, the horses were grazing in the farmyard. Lucille sat on the porch swing and watched them. *Julia is so nimble when she swings up onto them bareback. Sheesh. I used to be able to do that when I rode bareback.*

Toby, the young gelding, moved closer to the side of the porch where Lucille munched an apple. Perhaps he was tempted by the smell of the apple. He edged nearer.

"Come on over here, Toby," Lucille called. "You can have the core in another minute."

He sidled closer when Lucille's first impulsive thought struck. If he gets close enough, I can swing a leg over and sit on him bareback.

Lucille snapped the apple core in two and gave half to Toby. He stepped closer yet. She dug her fingers beneath his black mane and scratched his neck near his withers. He curled his upper lip out in a horse grin, happy to be scratched. He leaned in and took another step. *I'd better do it quick before he moves away.*

She fed Toby the rest of the core and swung her leg, clad in shiny green gym pants with a triple stripe down the sides. The slick pants crackled and rustled as she slipped onto his fat soft back.

His head popped up at the sound. She soothed, "That's a good boy, Toby. Just stand there." He sighed, lowered his head, and licked the last of the apple off his lips.

*All is going well,* she thought while sitting on his bare back and scratching his neck. Then impulse struck again.

"Julia." Lucille called loudly, tilting her head toward the second story window. No answer. "Hey, Julia, come take our photo."

Toby's ears and head rose at the timbre of her voice. He was used to Julia's soft voice. Lucille definitely had his attention. She

211

scratched him some more, but she felt his hide tighten beneath her seat.

All of a sudden she realized the fuzzy sheepskin slippers on her feet were about to slide off. In a bit of a panic, she feared the slippers would spook Toby if they slapped the ground beneath his belly, so she curled her toes and wiggled her feet to get them back on. Those actions seized Toby's attention. He rotated his ears back and forth like radar antennae and tensed up. Was she sending him a cue to go? Toby decided she was. He took off at a trot.

"Whoa, Toby." Having no bridle, nor halter or rope to control him, she gulped and grabbed a handful of mane. She held her breath until she saw they were headed for the old mare resting beneath an oak.

*Good. He'll stop by Maxine.*

Toby stopped briefly and Lucille let out her breath. "Whoa." *I'll get off now.*

Grabbing a bigger handful of mane, she tipped forward ready to slide down when Toby took her movements as another signal to move on, faster.

He trotted toward the woodpile while Lucille regained her seat. Visions of being tossed onto the log rounds that lay ready to be split prompted her to press her right leg into him to move away from the wood. He moved all right—into a canter.

Lucille began to bounce, so she clamped her legs on him tighter. Toby knew that as a signal to go faster. He broke into a gallop and raced toward the tractor and farm implements by the far barn. She panicked. *Oh, no. Don't dump me on that mower.*

Pressing the flat of her hand against his bare neck, Lucille tugged a handful of mane with the other hand, and pressed a leg against his belly to move him away from the John Deere. He turned uphill toward the pasture and stopped briefly at the closed pipe gate. She let out her breath again and considered how she could now do a rapid dismount.

That was not to be. Toby wheeled and took off down the corral fence, circling the barn and apparently heading back toward Maxine. He was picking up speed and heading for the downhill rock wall he'd soon have to leap.

*This is it,* she thought. *I have to bail.*

Using both hands, she grabbed for the top board of the fence as it flew by. She vaguely recalled there was a water trough on the other side. *That water sure beats the rocks.*

Toby kept running as she tried to pull herself off his slick hide, but as if they had a mind of their own, her legs remained in a death grip around the gelding's slick belly. She had a good hold of the fence, but her legs were snatched out from under her when he ran on. Lucille crashed on her side on the hard ground with a thud that knocked the wind out of her.

Facing the water trough on the opposite side of the fence, she felt what seemed like thousands of hot needles raking across her skin beneath her tee shirt. She flipped onto her back. She squirmed. *Oh no. Feels like gravel and stickers.*

Still unable to breathe, she rolled herself over and got up on her hands and knees, sucking in a moan for what seemed an eternity until her lungs relaxed enough to take in air. Finally, ragged breathing returned and she took a few gasping breaths. Burning waves continued to rip across her skin. She rocked back on her knees while her breathing returned to normal. "Ow, ow, ow, that stings. Road rash."

Toby had stopped shortly after she fell off. Now, he doubled back to her with a look that seemed to ask, what happened to you? He sniffed her head.

"I'll be all right, Toby."

She reached up and pulled a clump of stickers from her hair. A burning feeling seared her back as if it were scorched by road rash. Lucille brushed away a patch of burr clover seeds from beneath her shirt; their dry spines dug into her skin.

After getting up, Lucille took a few tentative steps and froze. "Ow!"

The feeling of hot stinging needles returned to zip up and down her spine and pierce her side. Her skin felt charred with road rash, but she was grateful to have survived. She stumbled back down the hill circling toward the shade of the barn where Julia caught up with her.

"Mom. Are you okay? What were you doing?"

"Yeah, I'll be fine. Just give me a minute in the shade." Lucille nodded. *Give me a minute to rest and think about what an incredibly stupid, impulsive thing I just did.*

Julia grabbed her mom's elbow and helped her over to the truck where she leaned against the tailgate. She spoke up, "Mom, you always said it was okay to do something stupid now and then, and it's also all right to be impulsive on occasion. But you can't do them both at the same time."

Lucille rolled her eyes and slowly shook her head, unable to believe the stunt she'd just pulled. "Yeah," she mumbled, "impulsive and stupid don't mix."

# Millicent, My Millicent

## Harry Reid

St. Ole's is a smallish college in the middle of Minnesota, founded and funded by the late Simian St. Ole, manufacturer of the St. Ole storm door. It's a gentle sort of place, little known except by those who are interested in apes.

Two years ago, the school received money from the National Science Foundation to study if injecting serums in primates might uncover discernable speech between them. Because of my extensive work in this field, I was given the project.

I chose two chimpanzees for my study: Popcorn, eight years old, and Millicent, ten. Their cages were set side by side. Next to them was a common room.

Popcorn was blustering and excitable. Millicent, a nurturing Bonobo, tended to patch things up with erotic hugging—six or seven times a day—with such enthusiasm I had to separate them when she was in *estrus*.

The two were rigged with microphones and constantly video-recorded while I monitored them from my lab. When twice a day I joined them, they grinned big, toothy grins and jumped all over me. Often, we'd be a threesome whirling in a circle, and people came to watch us through an observation window. Once, a TV station from Minneapolis came to film us dancing around together.

Popcorn shared Millicent equally with me but, when I got too close to her, he'd be jealous. So, I was very careful lest I interject myself into the project. I also didn't want Popcorn to kill me.

Toward the end of my two-year grant, I had taped more than two thousand hours of Popcorn and Millicent, and I felt we were making progress. But one night, a frigid storm rolled over Minnesota and I returned to the lab to check on them. Popcorn was asleep, shrimping noises through his lips but, turning to Millicent, I found her standing at her door, shivering—*without a stitch of fur!*

Not only was I shocked, I was embarrassed—as if I'd wandered into a women's changing room. Apes tend to shed but, except for a tiny wreath of curls around her ears, Millicent had shed *everything*. Naked, her pink skin—typical of the Bonobo—presented an uncomfortable contrast with the human female whom *homo sapiens* had taken more than five million years to adore.

I was sad at heart for her, but was also about to lose a chimp I'd spent hundreds of hours on. With a NSF review just a few weeks off, I had to find out why Millicent had lost her hair, but for now, I had to cover her nakedness.

Grabbing a St. Ole Curling Club lap robe she'd spirited away in her nest, I wrapped her in it. For this, she hugged me gratefully. I looked over furtively at Popcorn, happy I'd not unlocked his cage.

I knew a scandal would soon brew over this. I could see sniggering people lined up at the viewing window, the TV station coming here again from Minneapolis, embarrassed trustees shutting down the college, my academic reputation going into freefall. I had to get Millicent out of the lab.

~*~

The only place I could take her right away was my log house on the outskirts of town. Early-morning air crackled, and a bright moon silhouetted us against the snow as we left the lab. Millicent, scarcely four feet tall, hip-hopped along with me as if I was bringing her home from school.

The log house had just two rooms to heat. One accommodated my bed and a bathtub; the other, my kitchen and a large fireplace I'd banked a few hours before.

The house was toasty when we entered. Delighted, Millicent hop-crawled excitedly all over the place. Finally, when she began to tire, I made her some hot chocolate, then made a nest with the lap robe in the bathtub and encouraged her into it. Wide awake, she lay there looking up at me with shiny eyes while I, despite my anxieties, dropped right off to sleep. The next morning, Millicent was in bed with me.

Awaking, I phoned Prue, who worked with me at the lab. "What happened?" she asked.

In a story barely laced with truth, I said, "I think we've made a breakthrough."

"Wonderful!"

"In the meantime, please look after Popcorn."

"Let him out of his cage! Are you crazy?"

"Just put the food outside his door," I said. "I'll see to it when I come in."

~*~

So, there was a completely hairless female primate hanging out at my house, wearing only a lap robe emblazoned with the seal of the St. Ole Curling Club.

I called my sister, who had a ten-year daughter named Daisy.

"You got some kids' hand-me-downs?"

"What's going on with you?" she asked suspiciously.

"Just a jacket and some leggings."

"You're shacking up with a mom, aren't you?"

My reply was vague, far off.

"Okay," she said. "Drop by after work and I'll have something for her."

Putting one of my winter sweaters on her, I made a cozy spot for Millicent in my bed and gave her a copy of *Good Housekeeping* to tear pictures from.

At the lab I told Prue that Popcorn and Millicent weren't getting along well and needed a vacation from each other. Also, if Millicent lived with me for a while, maybe she'd begin to mimic my words, and I promised to be at the lab three hours every day to look after Popcorn.

When I stopped by my sister's, she had a jacket and leggings ready for me, also a box with a ballet costume in it. "Daisy's into soccer now. Sorry I don't have the slippers."

I shook my head at the box. "Thanks, but it's only for a short time."

Pressing it into my hands, my sister said, "Go ahead. You never can tell."

~*~

Millicent pawed through the jacket and leggings curiously, but when she saw the ballet costume, she was ecstatic. Insisting I help her into it, she hopped over to a mirror and stood there transfixed, looking at a ballerina dressed in white who'd suddenly dropped into her life. That night Millicent slept, not in my bed, but in a nest she made for herself in front of the mirror. From then on, we were a family of three.

For the next two weeks, home-life with Millicent was encouraging. She didn't tear up her *Good Housekeeping* magazine but, sitting in her ballet costume, she thumbed through it, watching me do the household chores and prepare our meals. One day when I returned from the lab, I found her sweeping the kitchen floor. Dishcloths were drying on a line I had strung over the sink. Another night, when she was crouching in a rocking chair in front of the fire, I saw her slowly drop her legs to the floor to copy mine.

With Millicent busily having an affair with her mirror, I now had time for Popcorn. He was taking Millicent's absence very badly. For a day or two, he poked around, looking for her everywhere, rattling her cage so violently we left it open so he could go inside and assure himself she wasn't there. This he did dozens of times a day—convinced she was hiding from him.

Popcorn scared Prue so much that she quit. I had to take over as the lab's janitor until I could find her replacement, and I was unable to proceed with the project. Fearing Popcorn smelled Millicent's scent on me, I carried a dart-tranquilizer whenever I entered the common area.

~*~

Sadly, not long after, Millicent patched up with her mirror so amorously she broke it. Disconsolate, Millicent now demanded all my time.

This was when my sister called.

"How are things working out with your girlfriend and her kid?"

"Who said anything about a girlfriend?"

"Come on, this is your sis. I know what's going on. I just called to tell you there's a hell of a daytime show on—*Desperate Housewives*—and thought about your girlfriend."

"I don't have a girlfriend, and I don't have TV."

"Too bad. She'd get a real kick out of it."

~*~

That afternoon, I bought a sixty-inch TV and hooked it up by satellite. Fearful Millicent might start patching up with the TV screen, I scavenged a display case from Goodwill and mounted it high up above the fireplace. There are more than sixty episodes of *Desperate Housewives*, in case you're interested. For a price, you can play them over and over again.

Millicent took to *Desperate Housewives* with such passion, I kept the sound on so she'd be exposed to simple, mindless conversation.

This gave me time again for Popcorn who once was a high roller at the Cincinnati Zoo. There, his wishes were rarely thwarted. What he wanted, he usually got. In fact, I chose him, hoping his very nature might provoke discernible speech.

Unfortunately, Popcorn and I were now at a stand-off. Whenever I opened the common room door, he'd rush at me, snarl, and beat his breast. Because of this, I began to avoid the common room, which had become such a disgusting mess, I wrote the NSF that their presence at this crucial stage might endanger the project.

Apparently, they'd received a number of letters like this before and insisted their immediate presence "would prove very helpful."

~*~

The only solution was to bring Millicent and Popcorn back together, which wasn't an easy matter because, at the moment I was going to bring Millicent back, she was deep into an episode of *Desperate Housewives*. Bruno Capponi had just socked his Consuela in the eye, and she was down on the floor, clutching his knees, begging him not to leave her, i.e., not spend the night down at the *Sons of Italy*.

When I turned off the TV, Millicent gave out a deafening scream. This meant I had to wait twenty minutes until Bruno finally lifted Consuela off the floor and said, "Okay—Okay," and it looked like they were on their way to patching things up.

~*~

When we got to the lab, a man from the NSF was waiting impatiently for me. He took one look at Millicent, in her ballet costume and sporting a half inch of fuzz, and said, "What the hell is this?"

"It's not what it looks like," I explained.

"God, I hope not!" he said.

"Let her at least go back inside."

The man from NSF looked like he thought I was crazy, but I opened the door to the common area.

~*~

Millicent sashayed into the common room, pink in her ballet costume. When Popcorn saw her, he ran and crouched, horrified, in a corner. I expected Millicent to run to him right off.

She looked at Popcorn. But, seeing the mess covering the entire common room floor, she grabbed a broom and started sweeping.

Not until she'd finished sweeping did Millicent come to Popcorn. If she spoke, it was hard to tell; so quickly did they begin to patch things up.

~*~

Did they communicate?

The guy from NSF and I reviewed the audio tape over and over without success. But the video recorded movement in Millicent's lips. We called in a lip reader. Playing the video back and forth, again and again, he said, "I wouldn't stake my career on it, but I believe she's saying, 'Okay . . . Okay . . . Bruno.'"

~*~

Millicent's fur is slowly coming back. Clothes for her arrive from all over the world. She could be the best-dressed chimpanzee in North America, but she insists on wearing her ballerina costume.

How did Millicent lose her hair? The enzymes I gave her were various. Could it have been a bottle of spot remover that showed up among them?

# One Thousand Words

## Skye Blaine

Jack shoved the yellow pad and tape recorder into his bag. He was due at the cripple's house by five. New uses for the drug Thalidomide had started an uproar and landed on the paper's front page. Here he was, going to interview some Thalidomide "dancer." A woman. He'd griped, but Sam snapped at him to "open his mind" and "get over there." As long as restoring his sports car depended on his paycheck, he wouldn't say no to his editor.

Interviewing a gimp was bad enough, but deformities—he could hardly stomach them. He was a hard news man. Rubbing a hand over his stubble, he decided to let it be, slammed the front door, and headed for his classic silver Porsche.

Cruising the Eugene university neighborhood, he located her house by the ramp leading to the front door. The green-on-green paint job looked fresh. His throat thickened with resentment. Her home looked damn good. His place was shabby compared to this, with peeling paint, a scruffy lawn. He rapped on the door, shuffling from side to side, impatient. One thousand words. Then he could get out of here.

The door opened, and he lurched backward.

"Elevator wheelchair. So I can reach stuff." An impish grin blazed across her freckled face, framed by short blonde curls. "You must be Jack." She wheeled to the right to allow him passage. "Come in. I'm Cindy."

She offered a stubby armlet with three digits. The whole thing was only seven inches long. What the hell was she doing? Was he supposed to touch it? She waited, eyebrows raised. He gathered himself and gingerly shook the proffered limb. Her grasp was firm, but the misshapen fingers reminded him of claws, making him want to pull away.

"Sit here." She gestured toward the flowered couch. As he pulled out his recorder, she buzzed her wheelchair lower. "I made coffee. Isn't that a reporter's deadline drink?"

"Sure, I'll take a cup."

As she poured from the carafe, he made mental notes. She could only use her right appendage. The left looked more like a

221

flipper—no bones, maybe. The cup holder on her chair. Tidy living room. Nothing fancy.

"Why'd they put you on this story?" she asked. "I've read some of your work. You seem a strange choice, considering your style."

"And what style is that?"

She leveled her gaze, as though assessing what he could take. "A bit cynical, and proud of it."

Well, that was a fact. Still, her comment felt like a sharp pebble in his shoe.

She leaned forward in her wheelchair. "Why'd they put you on human interest?"

"I was available." That wasn't true. He was hard-nosed and objective, and Sam didn't want some "I got it so bad" story.

"Cynic and cripple. They both begin with 'C'," she said, and laughed, a free sound, almost like birdsong. "We have *that* much in common. What do you want to hear? My life's probably just like yours—good stuff, hard stuff."

*Just like mine?* His expression neutral, he glanced at her face. Her mouth hadn't quirked up at the corners. She wasn't joking. "Walk me through it," he said, grudgingly. "Orient me."

"I want to approve the article."

"Not newspaper policy." He set his recorder on the coffee table, then glanced up and caught her expression. "If you can't trust me, you'll have to trust my editor to check the facts." She frowned, but finally nodded. He waited while she gathered her thoughts.

"Let's see. From the moment of conception, I made Mom ill. She threw up nonstop for weeks." Cindy sighed, rotating her wheelchair toward the window. "I don't share this story often. The dance troupe knows. They're family." Her mouth squinched down. "My father thought she might turn herself inside out, vomiting like that. So he said, 'Don't these doctors have some new kind of nausea medicine?' They did—that's all history now—Thalidomide, the miracle drug." Cindy paused, her forehead drawn into a frown. "I'm the miracle."

Jack's pen froze on the page. What was her intonation behind that? Not sardonic. He scrawled an asterisk and lifted his eyes.

Cindy's glance settled on the page. "What does a star mean?"

"To listen to this part of the tape again."

She pursed her lips. "For what?"

He hesitated, not liking to disclose his methods. "Intonation."
"That doesn't sound cynical. You must be a teeny bit curious."
She wheeled her chair around. "Wait a minute." She buzzed out of the room. When she returned, she poured some photographs out of an envelope. Jack quelled an urge to help.

"My father wouldn't hold me, didn't even look at me. Mom said he couldn't figure out how. He left us, left the week I was born. I only know his face from snapshots—look here, so young." She rotated and handed Jack a photo, scissored between two of her three digits. "This picture taken while Mom was pregnant? He's real sweet on her."

A lengthy silence. Jack wrote quickly.

"Anyway, she brought us to Eugene after JFK took office. We needed a fresh start, she said." Cindy maneuvered her chair. Her slate blue eyes drilled him. "Now, a big leap. On my fifth birthday, Mom took me to see *Sleeping Beauty*, a ballet choreographed for kids." Her expression sobered. "That day I fell in love with dance, and when we got to her VW bug, I told her I wanted to be a ballerina. She cried and cried until she didn't look like Mom anymore. Finally, she said, 'Gotta have legs to be a dancer, Cindy Lou.'" Cindy dipped her head, and when she looked up again, the engaging grin was back. "She calls me that when she breaks bad news."

Jack's gaze instinctively shifted toward her legs, and Cindy yanked the off lap blanket. Short stubs, and some toes, but no legs really, no proper feet either. As though she sensed his revulsion, she tossed the blanket over the lower half of her body again.

"Still, I knew I'd dance. My heart beat fast every time I watched Nureyev on TV. Mom would prop me on the couch, supported by pillows. I'd raise my wings—she called them that—and pretend to spin and stretch and leap with him."

Jack wrote as quickly as he could, trying to cover his own repugnance. He jotted down what could not be captured on tape— impressions of her mood as it shifted, her longing.

"One day, close to Christmas, we went to Penney's. She wheeled me by racks that towered high over me. I remember the feel of party dresses brushing my face, clothes I would never get to wear. Mom had to sew all mine. I saw the most beautiful turquoise velvet dress and reached to touch the fabric." Cindy's expression darkened. "Then I heard a familiar brat voice say, 'That's the flipper girl from school.'"

"'My name is Cindy, and you know these are my arms,' I hollered. That day it finally sank in. Even people I knew saw me as a freak. It was my turn to cry in the car." She shook her head, as though trying to dislodge the memory. She raised her eyes to him. Jack looked away. An awkward silence fell.

"How about a change of scenery?" she asked. "I'll show you my garden. Bring your recorder." She leaned forward, settled two digits on the knob to reverse her chair, and headed out of the room.

He glanced around as he walked through the house. There were no cupboards under the kitchen sink, probably to allow room for the chair. The faucet had a long extension. "You make it on your own here?"

"I don't do heavy cleaning, if that's what you mean." Her voice held a chuckling lilt. "Think about it. None of us handle life all on our own. It's just a question of degree." She cocked her head. "Do you make or mend your own clothes?"

He snickered.

"Well, neither do I," she said, "so don't feel bad for me."

He followed her down the ramp, shaking his head. At the bottom, a tiny perennial garden in rampant bloom framed the patio. "I didn't prepare the ground," she said. "But I planted every seedling. It just takes longer. A lot longer."

Jack sat on the cedar bench, and Cindy lowered her chair. He tried to imagine her planting. Small birds came to dip and flutter in the stone bird bath. "Chickadees," she said. "I get hummingbirds in the garden, too. They're my favorite." She stretched her arm nubs upward. "Ready for the next chapter?"

Jack set the recorder on the bench, surprised at his curiosity to hear more.

"A modern dance troupe came to my junior high. By that time, Shriners' Hospital had outfitted me with a fancy power chair. Mrs. Vanarsdale told me to park at the back of the gym, but I said, 'No ma'am,' and zipped up to the front row."

She stared at the bird bath. Jack made another asterisk and glanced at the light playing on the big-leafed maple. When her memories were painful, she seemed to patiently sit with them.

She started again. "A woman soloed *Metamorphosis*. Most of her dance took place on the floor. She arched and stretched, did backbends and somersaults. Then she folded her parts, tucked them in, held herself, and rocked. In that moment, her body looked like mine."

He felt the beats of silence.

"That changed me. Forever."

He cleared his throat. "I bet."

She stared, as though she were evaluating him again. "Too much detail?"

"Some of it won't end up in the piece, but I need it for background." Bending down, he flipped over the tape. "Go for it."

"I locked my bedroom door. No one would see my first dance. I rolled my bed against the wall with my chair, and lowered myself to the floor near the stereo. My wings trembled." She paused, then said in a soft voice, "I haven't told anyone this."

Jack waited.

"I put on the Pachelbel Canon, but the rhythm felt wrong, so I turned it off—just dove inside myself and bent and rolled and swayed to what I found there. At the end, I lay on my belly and stretched my wings against the floor. The wood was warm from the movements of my body." She fell quiet, and Jack's heart beat against his ribs.

He leaned over and fiddled with his shoelace. *Christ. I whine about a pinched finger.*

Cindy took a swallow of coffee.

"When I entered Eugene High," Cindy said, "I discovered the after-school dance club, and showed up for the first audition. The kids shuffled and stared. After the teacher got control of his mouth again, he said, 'I'm sorry, Cindy, this isn't possible.' He sent me to the school counselor just because I love to dance."

She snorted and screwed up her face. "Bigot." She looked directly at Jack, but he couldn't hold her gaze.

"There's just a little more. My mom freaked at the idea, but at eighteen, I moved to the dorms at San Francisco State." She whirled her wheelchair in circles. "Freedom. Soon after, Mom came to visit. Checking on me, I think. She slipped up and mentioned my father had phoned her—first contact since he walked out. She smiled when she told me. I wondered if they'd get back together."

He leaned back in surprise. "Wouldn't that make you crazy?"

She stared at him with her brow furrowed, as though she didn't understand his question. "Crazy? You've got your brain on crosswise. Not once I got over the shock. Think about it. Mom gave up everything for me for eighteen years. She deserved some happiness, however she could find it.

"Here's the latest. Dance is my life, ever since that day at *Sleeping Beauty*. I came back to Eugene after college and joined the Dance-Abled Troupe. I've had seven years of traveling the world." She pointed to a photo with one of her digits. "There's eleven of us. James choreographs and performs—he has your standard, two-legged, two-armed body. Susan has cerebral palsy, Frank's an amputee." She rummaged in the bag hanging on the side of her chair and pulled out more papers. "Look at this review we got in the Chronicle. They don't call me a ballerina, and that's all right. I sure don't dance the classical form."

She looked up, her slate eyes bright. "We're dancing at the Hult Performing Arts Center a week from Saturday—would you like to come? I left some tickets in the paper's name. This article will help our publicity, and we appreciate that."

Jack met her gaze. "Okay," he said, startled at his own response. "I'd like to see you dance." He looked over his notes. "Between these and the tape, I have enough material. A few questions, though. What about your mom and dad? Did they get back together?"

"They talk every couple of months. Too much ground to recover, I guess."

"How do you manage?" He flung his arm out, indicating the garden and house. "Does welfare pay for this?"

She laughed out loud, a triumphant, chirping sound. "I was waiting for that question. Nope. We have an endowment and get grants too, like any dance group. I fully support myself. How many artists can say that?" Her smile spread wide, and she whirled her chair again.

Embarrassment seared his belly. "You saw right through me," he said. "I thought you lived on disability."

"Everybody thinks that," she said. "Assumptions—they'll get us all."

"And reporters should not make them." He sighed. "The biggest and last question: how do you feel about Thalidomide going back on the market?"

For the first time during the interview, tears sprang to her eyes. "The human species is careless," she whispered, and cleared her throat. "I can't bear the thought that other innocent children will be deformed like me. Congress is holding hearings and I'm going to D.C. to speak out." She turned her head and wiped tears away. "The public attention will be hard—scrutiny, different than being on stage—but this is something I have to do."

Jack sat quietly, flexing all ten fingers. His one thousand words were in the bag, and he knew he should collect his equipment, say thanks, and goodbye. He hesitated, weighing his choices. "Say," he said, casting about for shared interests, "you seem to know about birds. What are these little brown ones? They hang around my house, too."

Cindy powered her chair back and forth on its hind wheels. "I'll tell you," she said. "Want a beer? Birds and beer go together."

# *Pieces of Dysfunction*

## Pamela Taeuffer

It was one hour before midnight, late for a child of nine to be up on a school night. Then again, the dark family secrets I kept made me grow up quickly. My friends were tucked away and asleep in their beds, but not me.

Mom and I sat on the living room floor in front of the heater vent, one of two in our 1930s San Francisco two-story home. The heater was an antiquated monster with two big arms that reached up from the basement, bringing warmth into the living room and hallway outside of the two bedrooms.

The Monopoly board was spread between us. We rolled the dice, purchased properties, went to jail, tried to get out free, and winced as we landed on each other's high rent districts.

With each move through St. Charles Place, Marvin Gardens, and Boardwalk, we wished we'd hear Dad's sky blue, Chevy step-side pickup pull into the driveway. Even though we played a game, the thing that remained unsaid and just under the surface was the fear that his life, or someone else's, had ended because he'd driven home drunk.

Being in an alcoholic family numbed us. But the wait . . . always the fear of everything ending . . . was like a blade held to our necks until the call from the police, or a friend, or a co-worker let us know in one way or the other, if he was all right.

Then we'd prepare for the next bad thing to happen—Dad walking in.

"How about I make us some fudge?" Mom got up and walked toward the kitchen. "Mark the board so we don't forget whose turn it is."

"Yeah." I shouted with the anticipation of a delicious reward. I felt special that she was cooking a batch just for us. Once again, the answer to the pain of being emotionally abandoned by my parents— Dad because of his addiction, Mom because of her codependency— was the comfort of sugary treats.

As the fudge boiled, we tasted a spoonful every few minutes. She dropped the mixture into a bowl of cold water, pinched it between her fingers, and when it formed the perfect soft ball it meant her fudge was ready to rest and minutes away from being whipped into form.

"Mama?" The intermingling of chocolate, cream, and vanilla were not only delicious, they were intoxicating.

"What is it, honey?"

"I love it when we make fudge. You look happy, and I feel so good when you smile."

When she cooked fudge, I knew I had her love and comfort. Her attention was mine, and she was a mom. Sliding the butter knife into the creamy mixture was like cutting a piece of serenity.

"I love making it for you," she said warmly, completely absorbed in her task and the love she poured into it.

"It's like we're okay, Mommy." Letting the chocolate melt on my tongue took me to a place of pretend. Took me to escape. The worry if Dad was alive was forgotten and a moment of freedom was ours.

"We are okay," she reassured, even as she dropped the glass lid on the floor and it broke in half.

She placed the fudge on the counter to set, and we went back to our game. We rolled the dice, both of us into it, as we tried to win the large pot of money in the center of the board. Twenty minutes later and after midnight, we had to pause to whip the fudge. I loved hearing those beaters whirring. It made me feel like we could be a normal family. Didn't "regular" families cook? Didn't mothers teach their daughters their secrets about baking and preparing meals? It seemed that way with my friends. I wanted that. So whenever I could, I imagined it was happening for me.

Just as I put my hand on her back, bringing our connection closer, the front door crashed open, banged into the wall, and made a slight dent in it.

He staggered inside.

I felt Mom's body tense. Her head jerked around. We spun to look at him. In reality, we didn't have to. Both of us knew what we'd see: his red face, sunken eyes, an expression that sagged, and a body that was out of control.

My father was home.

Soon, we'd find out what horror lay in his wake.

"Making fudge," he slurred. "My fat wife and fat daughter, getting fatter. That all you do is eat?"

Dad crashed, stumbled, and fell into the living room, stepping onto our game, kicking and scattering all the pieces throughout the living room. Just that quickly, normal changed to unpredictable rage.

Again.

My mother's face dulled. I wondered if she could get used to his insults. I winced when I heard his favorite word for us, "fat." It hit me right in the heart with a poisoned tip.

"Let's keep going," I encouraged. I looked up at her to find an expression of both relief and regret. He was home. We'd lucked out one more night. On the other hand, what would it be like to have it be over?

Did she wish my father would not come home? Did she secretly wish him dead?

Sometimes when his hand came down on her, I did.

We'd finally be able to move on instead of staying caught in this dangerous web of waiting for disaster to arrive.

My hand lifted from her back when she turned off the beaters. The big spoon she used to stir the fudge dropped against the porcelain bowl. I knew the candy was at its crucial moment, ready to turn from liquid to creamy chocolate candy. Mom turned off the kitchen and range lights and lay down on the couch.

Our game, our evening . . . broken.

"You do anything around here but lay around?" Dad said to his wife. His words were the usual defense—shoot before you get shot. She said nothing, only looked at her book.

"Damn whore, I should beat the hell out of you."

He took a sloppy step toward her.

I froze. He took another step, but almost fell.

"You." He pointed at me. "Upstairs, or I'll paddle you, too." I didn't move, waiting for the threat to pass. He took another step toward Mom and her eyes glazed. In only seconds, both of them left me standing alone, as if I didn't exist—as if none of us existed as a family.

Dad swung at the air, turned, and crashed his way up the stairs.

"I'll finish, Mama," I cried out, hoping to continue our evening. I turned the lights back on and began to whip the fudge.

It had hardened the same way my mother just had.

I knew I couldn't save it. But I had to rescue something in our house. So I took the big spoon Mom dropped and scooped out the clumps of candy onto three buttered plates: one each for my mom, my sister, and me. Soaking the pot in warm, soapy water, I put the beaters in the kitchen sink and slid the plates of candy in the refrigerator.

Carefully, I put all the pieces back on the Monopoly board.

If I could only keep all the pieces together . . . it might be okay.

But something felt different. Although she was right there, on the couch, she was invisible. She stared at the book without reading and sighed. That's when I felt it—the moment that Mom gave up. Was it one insult too many? Was it the anger on his contorted face? The threat of the punch?

"Mama, I finished everything. The game is back just like we had it, so can we play now?" Was I breathing when I said those words? I'm not sure. Questions were difficult to ask in our household. It often felt like I held my breath until I was certain I hadn't offended anyone. If challenged, Mom and Dad became angry.

I wanted to cuddle against her belly.

Rub her feet.

Massage her back.

She didn't even look at me.

"I don't feel like it," she said wearily. "Would you mind putting everything away?"

The curtain fell and she was gone.

The night Mom and I sat in front of the Monopoly board waiting to see if my father was alive and unharmed, her routine changed—forever. It was the last game we played. The bits of light indulgences that had remained—ended. Her romance novels, once an occasional respite, become her permanent escape. Maybe it allowed her to have the courage she needed to open her bedroom door at night and enter the whiskey-scented air that awaited her. Maybe, by staying up late, she'd be tired enough to fall asleep as soon as she laid her head down on her pillow. Perhaps it was a luxury she indulged in so she wouldn't have to endure the hacking, mucous-filled drunken coughs of her husband. Maybe, she could dream of lost romance—or a possible future—rather than the addiction that held her life hostage.

I cried silently as I packed away our evening. Somewhere deep inside, I knew I was packing away the memories of being a child with my mother.

We never engaged in that way again.

# *Pirouette*

## Robbi Sommers Bryant

I stood behind the curtain waiting for my cue. Pepper, the dancer on the stage, let her skimpy cowgirl get-up drop to the floor. I didn't own a costume, but the manager said my flirty summer dress was "sexy enough." My lingerie, although lacy and black, was no match for Pepper's sequined-covered bra or her eyepatch-sized G-string. Victoria's Secret was the best I could do.

For me, auditioning at a strip club was strictly about the dancing. A woman had seen me tango in a club, said I was a natural, and mentioned the audition. I'd figured, why not? The dreams I'd had as a young jazz dancer were about to come to fruition—the lights, the glory, the applause.

*There was no business like show business.*

I basked in the promise of stardom until the reality hit me like a sudden storm—I was expected to strip. A tingling held my arms and legs hostage. My heart thumped, and I squeezed my fists. To relieve my jittery nerves, I tensed my muscles as tight as I could and then, released. I imagined I was about to perform on Broadway. *This was Times Square, and I was the principle in a show bringing rave reviews. My outfit dazzled. I wore glittery jewels. The audience appreciated the difficulty of my dance moves and stood with a roar.* The promise of the glitz and the glamor of show biz calmed me down. My moment to shine was minutes away.

Rod Stewart crooned "Tonight's The Night," and Pepper writhed on a fake leopard-skin cushion in nothing but her red G-string, plaid scarf, cowgirl hat, and boots. The music stopped, and Pepper's burnt-red hair gleamed under the lights. She grabbed her holster, costume, and giddied up off the stage.

"Our next dancer is auditioning for us today. Let's give her a big welcome." The manager's black hair, pulled tight into a bun, emphasized her tiger-eyes, but it was her bright fuchsia lipstick that stole the show. As she strutted off the stage, her burgeoning breasts threatened to tumble out of her violet corset, and her spiked high heels click-clacked.

While the audience applauded, I chose Marvin Gaye, Al Green, and Maria Muldaur then punched the jukebox buttons. The standard was three songs, three dances. Slow, slower, and slowest.

232

"You're up, kid. Break a leg." Pepper gave me a slight shove.

I took a deep breath and *pirouetted* onto the stage. My heart jumped like a junkie on speed. My breath came in short spurts. I scanned the room. Not quite Broadway, but pleasant enough—with its velvet curtains tied back on each side of the stage, its low-lit lights surrounding the room with a red glow, and the scarlet carpet with gold, floral designs.

Six men in sharp suits jammed around a table to the side. A couple in the back made out like hungry vampires. In the lit doorway, the barker motioned for passersby to take a peek at "the hottest show in town."

Pepper whispered in the ear of Jabba the Hutt's twin who snorted when he laughed. He handed her a fistful of cash, which she stuffed into her holster before sitting on his lap. Directly in front, a penguin-faced man pulled a five from his pocket and dropped it on his table with a wink.

I moved right into a jazz walk—stylized steps with shoulders moving in opposition. I kicked one leg high then the other and switched to a perfect jazz pirouette. A *pas de bourree*—back step, side, front—arms bent and palms to the floor—and again on the right. One stag leap across the stage, and I turned. Jazz hands. Jazz hands Step. Step. Step.

I repeated the routine toward the back of the stage, turned, and snapped my fingers as I headed to the edge. The more I danced, the more complicated my moves.

Caught in the web that Pepper had spun, Jabba was hers. I could have done a backflip and landed on my hands; Jabba wouldn't have cared. The sextet on the side talked baseball, and Penguin's eyes seemed veiled with a glaze.

In the corner, the manager turned her hands in a rolling motion. *C'mon, get going* was what she meant. Marvin Gay finished "Let's Get It On," and I let one spaghetti strap slip down my arm. Penguin ran his tongue across his crusty lips and tapped his pudgy finger on the five-dollar bill.

I did a *mambo*—a front/back, back/front step with hips swiveling in figure eights as Al Green sang "Let's Stay Together." The drunk Giants' fans yelled take it off, and Jabba finally looked toward the stage.

The manager stepped up her signals and rapidly snapped her fingers at me—concern racked her face. I shot her a forced smile and let the other strap fall. Perhaps a jazz split would appease her. I slid to the floor, both legs 90 degrees from my body. The manager crossed her arms and shook her head like a viper watching a fly.

Her explicit instructions: the dress comes off, song one. I moved out of the splits and reluctantly pulled my dress off and swung it in a circle above my head. I glanced at her. *Happy now?*

"Yeah, baby," the Gaylord Perry fan yelled, and the group threw dollar bills onto the stage.

Penguin grabbed a newspaper from a vacant chair and set it on his lap just as a dancer placed two drinks on his table. "The show is free," the barker had called, not mentioning that the two-drink minimum was $12 a pop. If this were Broadway, they'd pay more than $100 a seat. In my opinion, they were getting a deal.

I did a fan kick and made a sweeping arc in front of my body. I knew by the end of the second dance that the bra had to go, but instead, I did a few pirouettes. With each turn, I focused on Penguin's beak-shaped nose. He waved the five in front of his face and blew me a kiss.

"Midnight at the Oasis" now played. It was song three. I should be hitting the leopard cushion with my bra flung to the floor. As I reached to unhook, Penguin shifted his hand from his drink, slid it under the newspaper, and hunched over the table like a hungry rat. There was no doubt in my mind what he planned to do.

Without thought, I screeched to a stop and stared in disgust.

"Jesus Christ," the manager gasped and headed toward the stage.

Pepper stopped kissing Jabba's ear and abruptly turned to see what I'd done.

Maria Muldaur continued her tantalizing song.

"I'll be your only dancer, prancer. And you can be my sheik."

I did a lunge, reached for my dress and waved it like a matador's cape. I twirled from one end of the stage and back. With each turn, I spotted Penguin—the look on his face got creepier, and his eyes blinked like flashing traffic lights.

The room suddenly looked seedy with its tacky red lights, sleazy crowd, and whorehouse carpet. I wanted out. Now.

Into another pirouette, I swirled. Like a slow-motion tornado, I crossed the stage. I spun by the leopard cushion, the velvet curtains, down the stage stairs, and to the side exit. With one more turn, I danced out the side door and into an alley.

Out of breath, I slumped against the grimy brick wall. A rat scurried across the dirty street and hid behind a dumpster. Overhead, a crow on a wire dropped a scrap of moldy bread near my feet.

Holy shit! What had I just done?

"What the hell do you think you're doing?" The manager poked her head out the door. "Get the fuck back in here."

I quickly pulled my dress on. "That was the end of my act."

"Well, you're not hired." She turned and slammed the door behind her.

I took a deep breath, straightened my fabulous summer dress, and headed for the glitz and glamor of everyday life.

# Retribution

## Marilyn Campbell

The moment the group of engineers entered the mission, Eric noticed the placement of relics in strange juxtaposition to one another. There was a glass case filled with robes and other fine vestments in heavy silks and satin brocades across from primitive tools used by American Indians who had labored within the walls of the mission. Next to the tools was a life-size painting of a serene young woman holding a tray on which lay two perfectly formed breasts. The breasts, according to the artist's notes, figuratively belonged to Saint Agnes who was mutilated on the orders of a Roman governor for scorning the advancements of his son.

The disturbing image of the martyred saint stayed with Eric as he moved through the neglected building. He entered the chapel; the last room to be explored during the tour. The space was long and narrow, its thick walls embellished with details of early mission life. *Probably painted with dyes made from native plants*, he thought. It would be difficult to duplicate the colors of the natural dyes, but Eric made a note to talk with a ceramicist he knew who might have some helpful suggestions.

Eric dreaded this project being considered by the engineering firm for which he worked. The company specialized in historic restorations and, until recently, only accepted jobs involving commercial buildings and vintage homes dating back a century or longer. He was part of a team assigned to bid on the job of restoring the crumbling mission.

Eric had voted against the project, but as a junior member of the firm, he held little sway in the decision-making—especially on an undertaking of this magnitude. It didn't help that the boss was a staunch Catholic who later questioned his subordinate's negative attitude.

Eric got the message. He didn't want to jeopardize his job, even though he had vowed to never again step inside this or any other church.

Several members of the team removed their hard hats, crossed themselves, and genuflected as they made their way deeper into the chapel. Eric stood his ground. After all, he was no longer a Catholic—

not even a lapsed Catholic who could return to his faith at any time. *Once a Catholic always a Catholic.*

He was in a separate category of nonbeliever. Eric rejected the faith into which he had been born and in which he blindly participated until he was fourteen years old. Now, he counted himself among the hardcore atheists of the world.

The guide recited various details about the chapel's construction and of the financial campaign to pay for its restoration. When the group moved ahead to study the stained-glass windows, Eric remained behind to stand uneasily in the middle of the Stations of the Cross. The banks of votive candles, glowing in the gloominess, reminded him of the many young acolytes for whom he could light a candle. Regardless, he no longer believed in the rituals and magical thinking of religion, and so he moved on.

As he neared the center aisle leading to the altar, Eric approached a table stacked with brightly-colored pamphlets. Their title drew him in: *Working Together to Prevent Child Sexual Abuse.* Displayed below in smaller type: *Keeping Ministerial Relationships Healthy & Holy.*

A rope of tension tugged between his shoulder blades, but he carefully picked up one of the tri-fold pieces and opened it, anyway. His eyes scanned the text and came to rest on phrases like "children, a valuable treasure," and "clergy abuse scandal." He scrolled down the page to the signature that read, Cardinal Roger Mahony, Archbishop of Los Angeles.

"The bastard," he swore.

The pamphlet, displayed in a prominent position, must have been one of the terms of the lawsuit against the church—a public confession followed by this attempt to atone and educate the public. *Too little, too late*, he thought, as the edges of the tract, folded into sharpness, dug into the sides of his fingers. Eric loosened his trembling grip and watched the words free-fall from his hand, landing on the floor. He stepped over them as if they were something disgusting that had been deposited on the sidewalk.

The overwhelming odor of burning incense stirred his memory. Eric heard rustling robes as the old priest made his way down the row of penitents and administered the rite of Holy Communion. Dutifully, he opened his mouth and received the wafer. "The body of Christ," intoned Father Murphy.

The wafer stuck to the roof of Eric's parched mouth. He tried to dislodge it with the tip of his tongue with no success. His stomach felt queasy like the time when the priest tried to push his privates into his mouth and he gagged. Eric heaved all over Father Murphy's shiny black shoes.

"What's the matter, my son? Don't you want to be whole with Christ?" The florid, fleshy face had turned a deeper shade in frustration—as red as the hairs on his thick, muscular thighs.

Eric forced himself out of the past and rushed to a door leading outside where he fell to his knees and was sick in the rose garden. Waves of revulsion washed over him until he had nothing more to vomit.

"May I be of assistance?"

Eric hadn't heard the priest approach. When he looked up, he was gazing into the dark, fluid eyes of a young man wearing a white robe to match his feminine, white hands.

"No. Go away," he cried.

"Allow me to give you some water," he said. "It may help."

Eric would not look up again until he heard the priest walk away. The cup of water he had offered sat on a garden bench within easy reach. Eric studied the pure liquid a moment and then took a sip, rinsing his mouth, clearing away the taste of bile. After a second sip, he gulped the remainder, swallowing it gratefully.

When he looked around, studying his surroundings, Eric saw the young man standing by the door to the vestibule, his hands folded in front of him. It was as if he were waiting for Eric to give him a sign on whether it was safe to approach. He couldn't quite make out the priest's expression; was it one of compassion or contrition?

Eric stood up with trembling legs and peeled off his jacket, laying it on the bench. He fished a handkerchief from his back pocket and wiped his mouth. From the corner of his eye, he spotted fellow team members in the parking lot boarding the van which had brought them to the mission. He was thankful no one had seen him getting ill.

*It was a mistake to have come,* Eric thought. *I should have tried harder to get out of this assignment.*

He moved away from the roses and the church with its secrets and hard lessons. He had hoped his anger had remained in the past. By not filing a lawsuit against the church as had so many others who sought retribution, Eric figured he would be spared reliving the sordid details. Instead, he expected the stain of shame to fade like the color of a favorite shirt put through the laundry too many times. But he was wrong to assume he could manage his feelings after all these years— years during which the cloying scent of incense made him break out in a sweat, and the sound of church bells gave him a headache.

"Man, what happened to you?" someone asked as Eric boarded the van. He rolled up the sleeves of his sweat-stained shirt and loosened his tie.

"Yeah, we lost you in the chapel," another co-worker said.

"Oh, I went back to check the date on one of the exhibits. Sorry," said Eric. He dropped his gaze to discourage further questions.

Staring out the window, Eric saw the priest rushing into the parking lot, trying to catch up with the van. He held something up, waving it to get the driver's attention. It was the jacket Eric had left behind on the bench. He prayed the driver wouldn't notice because he didn't want the jacket, tainted like his memories. He shifted his gaze forward and slid down in his seat as the van picked up speed and hit every pothole in the lot.

# Spare the Rod

## Cristina Goulart

It's Sunday morning. The phone rings. We all stop eating our breakfast and stare at the clanging wall phone. Daddy has strict rules about meal time. No answering the phone, for one. On the Sabbath, extra rules apply, and he does enforce them with a strong hand.

The four of us are sitting in our Sunday best, back home from church. The table is set with the Sunday best, too; no chipped or mismatched plates. The pancakes, bacon and eggs are piled up in heaps and the Aunt Jemima is warmed and poured into a gravy boat. From where I sit, I can see the steam rising from Mama's black coffee, backlit by the sunlight streaming through the clear windowpane. No matter how hot the day is, she always has to have her hot coffee in the morning. "It ain't breakfast without hot coffee," she always says.

Lately, I've been in trouble more often than I'd like. Bending the rules, as I call it, usually gets me a good smacking. Asking too many questions about religion or about the rules of the house can get me a good smacking, too. There is a fine line between sincere questions and questions that imply disbelief or disrespect, so I am told. I try to walk that line, but sometimes, I fall on the wrong side of it, not even knowing why.

I'm just trying to understand things. If Jesus would rather have a mill stone around his neck than hurt a child, for example, then why does Daddy say, "Spare the rod, spoil the child," and say it's from scripture?

I think that is a fair question. Daddy thinks it's sass.

Mama? She just frets. She asks me not to provoke Daddy. I ask them both to just let me *ask*.

I lean toward the ringing phone. It's on its third ring now.

"Dorothy Marie." My father says my name in a warning tone. "Do not answer that phone."

I lean a bit closer.

"Do *not* pick it up," Daddy says. I don't look at Mama, but I know she's looking at me. I know she's got that fret line digging into her brow.

Fourth ring.

240

"Rebel without a cause," my cousin Jake likes to call me. That boy can irritate. I am not rebellious for the sake of it, and I normally would not tempt my father's ire just for a phone call.

Fifth ring.

I swear I can feel someone reaching to us through that phone, begging us to pick up. I feel it in my gut; this call is coming from the other side of the world.

Sixth ring.

My tongue worries the lump on the inside of my lip, put there by Daddy's discipline a couple days ago. My stomach is nothing but butterflies looking at his stern face, but I leap up and snatch the receiver off the wall with my left hand and sweep my chair in front of me with my right. The chair's wooden feet scrape across the worn linoleum floor.

"Hello?" I say into the phone.

I keep my chair at arm's length between me and Daddy, like I'm a lion tamer and he's the lion. My heart is thumping and my legs want me to run. Daddy's got a look of patience lost on his face. Mama sighs. My little brother says, "Oooh, you are gonna get it." He's a little too gleeful.

"I'm sorry," I say into the receiver. "Who is this, again?"

I hear the name the second time it's spoken and I whoop into the phone. "Rick! Rick!"

My little brother, Joey, hops out of his own chair and squeezes under my lion tamer arm. He jumps up and down grabbing for the phone. Mama is crying into her napkin. Daddy stands frozen.

"Where are you?" I scream the question into the phone.

"Well, I'm still here." His tone indicates that by "still here," Rick means, "still alive." He says he's still in Afghanistan. "We were on a mission for some weeks," he explains. "I couldn't call or get a letter out. We just got back to base. I figured you all would think I was dead by now."

I'm bent over to Joey's height, holding the receiver away from my ear so he can share the conversation. He rapid fires questions and information into the phone. "Hi Rick! Are you coming home? Did you shoot anybody? I can a ride a bike now!"

I cringe. Rick laughs. "Good job, Little Buddy."

My father's legs thaw. He walks the few steps between us, keeping his eyes on the faded linoleum tile. Daddy holds out his hand for the phone. Mama is still sobbing, and she can't seem to get out of her chair.

"Son?" My father says into the phone.

I pick up the munchkin so we can both have our ears at the phone. Daddy holds the receiver out so we can hear Rick.

"Hey, Dad. Sorry if I worried y'all," we can hear Rick say.

"No saying you're sorry, Son. You just do what you got to out there." Daddy shifts into a pretend cheerful voice and says, "We were just sitting down to Sunday breakfast."

"It's near suppertime here," my older brother says. "The sun is just down and the sky is every kind of pink. It's nice out tonight; for once."

My father is working his jaw hard to keep from crying, but a rebel tear spills down his cheek. Joey's eyes get wide. Mine, too. We've never seen our father cry before this moment. I had figured his eyes didn't come with tear ducts.

"Sorry, Dad," we hear Rick say, "but I should let some of the other soldiers have a turn at this satellite phone."

"That's fine, Son. It was good to hear your voice."

"Same here, Dad."

"You just do what you got to out there. Don't you worry about us."

"Okay, Dad. Give Mom my love."

"Mom?" Joey and I mouth the word at each other. Since when does Rick call our Mama "Mom?"

"I sure will, Son."

My father hangs up and stares out the back door window for a spell. When he pulls his eyes from the phone and looks at me, the anger is gone. He reaches for my face and pats my jaw with a tenderness that I just now realize I've been missing.

Daddy's jaw trembles, and his eyes fill again. He is out the back door and into the yard before another tear escapes. He lets the screen door slam, which usually gets Mama irritated, but she doesn't say a word.

Mama has calmed herself now. She walks over to Joey and me and hugs us both hard.

"My brave little rebel," she whispers to me. Her wet eyes are sad but proud. She opens the screen door and steps outside, easing the door closed so it won't slam. She doesn't say a word to Daddy. She

242

goes out to stand with him under the sycamore tree that gives the house so much blessed shade.

Joey and I watch Daddy lean up against the sycamore with one hand and cover his eyes with the other. He's the one sobbing now. We can see his shoulders shake while Mama gives his back a gentle rub. We probably shouldn't be staring, but we are.

"Why is Daddy crying?" Joey asks me.

"'Cause he's so glad Rick is okay."

He looks at me and crinkles his nose in confusion. "Then shouldn't he be laughing?"

Joey's still riding my hip when I swing him around into a hug so tight, he lets out a muffled grunt. I break into a vigorous, bouncy polka like Gramps and Gran would do, but at double-speed. I dance all around the table, singing a loud oom-pa-pa rhythm with Joey's feet dangling behind my back. His sweet giggles fill my ear.

# So Long Shady House

## Michael Welch

There are no trees left on the street, but the park across the way has a picnic shelter that provides some relief on hot August days. The sunlight coming through the green plastic roof resembles light falling through the leaves of a tree. To everyone in Cleveland's Kinsman ghetto—even the K-Barz gang members who hang out there—the shelter is known as Shady House.

Larry Magwire, comes downstairs at one in the afternoon. He is twelve years old. His brothers and sisters are still asleep. They were up all hours last night. It was too hot and noisy to sleep. Larry's mother is sleeping in the back room of the house. Her Friday night bootleg parties have been drawing huge crowds. She buys liquor from the State Store and resells shots to friends who come to drink and play cards. The money is good, but the smell of whiskey and urine are hard to get rid of.

Larry waits for Henry at the Shady House shelter. Henry Shaw is the night manager at Lawson's. He pulls up in a well-preserved El Dorado next to Shady House. "Hop on in," he says, leaning over the wide front seat to push the door open. A big man with a shaved head and goatee, he served in Vietnam as a quartermaster.

Inside Lawson's, Mr. Freed is sitting at a desk back behind the cold beer and wine section. He is going over inventory while the day manager totals receipts at the cash register. Mr. Freed looks over his glasses when Henry and Larry come in. He asks Larry to restock shelves for the weekend rush.

Four teenage boys roll into the store carrying a boombox. It is seven at night. They turn the music down when they see Henry. They are unlikely to attempt a robbery with three men in green Lawson's vests in the store.

Henry looks at a round mirror on the ceiling, which is trained on the aisle where batteries are displayed. "Them batteries ain' none too fresh," he calls out to the boy lurking by the batteries. "Come on up front where the fresh ones is." Henry's voice and his Popeye-sized forearms command respect.

The boy approaches the counter reluctantly.

244

"Here ya go," says Henry sliding a package of four D-sized batteries across the counter. "That'll be $1.19."

The young man's friends jeer at him while he empties both pockets in search of enough change to purchase the batteries. He has the K-Barz tattoo of a knife on his hand. When the boys leave, Henry holds the door for them.

"Ever see them before?" Mr. Freed asks Henry.

"I don't know. Maybe it'll come to me." Henry keeps the door open for an elderly woman who shuffles in pulling an empty laundry cart. "Good evening, Mrs. Taylor," he says smiling.

"Lord Jesus, it's hot out there," she moans. She stops to mop her brow with a Kleenex. "Do you have any of that fresh squeezed orange juice with the pulp in it, Henry?"

Larry appears out of nowhere with a can of frozen juice and hands it to Mrs. Taylor.

"Why, hello, Larry," she says. She holds the can against her temple. "Will you help me with my shopping today, honey?"

Larry patiently follows Mrs. Taylor with a basket. He knows she's improvising. She is pretending to be shopping just to have somewhere to go and someone to talk to.

"My, you've grown up tall, Larry," Mrs. Taylor says as they walk toward the back of the store. "My Houstis was over six feet tall, you know. I made him get down on his knee so I could kiss him goodbye. 'Get down on one knee' I said, 'like you're proposin' marriage,' and he did. I kissed him on the cheek and never saw him again." Her bottom lip trembles. She fumbles in the folds of her housedress for another Kleenex.

"Was Houstis your son, Mrs. Taylor?" Larry asks.

"No, Houstis was just my friend for the longest time." She examines the price on a four-pack of toilet tissue. "Why don't you use those long arms and get me a package of that good toilet paper on sale up there. That cheap stuff is hard on hemorrhoids."

"What did you teach when you were a teacher?" Larry asks, changing the conversation.

"I had fifth and sixth grades mostly, so I taught a little of everything," she says.

The day manager calls, "good night," the door chimes ringing behind him.

Mrs. Taylor spends a great deal of time in the store, and Larry's glad for it. It gives him something to do, and his supervisors appreciate it. "You take care of the old folks," Mr. Freed told him. "Henry and I'll take care of the hoodlums."

The Lawson's store owned by Mr. Freed had been robbed three times this summer. Each of the robberies happened at the end of the last shift between nine and ten. None of the robberies happened on the evenings Henry worked as night manager.

One of the things Larry enjoys about his job at Lawson's is the trust invested in him by Henry and Mr. Freed. They let him see where the big cash receipts are kept—not in the register but in an envelope between the cashier's counter and the Sno-Kone machine. They have also told him where the gun is hidden—not under the counter but on top of the beer cooler.

"We're sharing this with you," Mr. Freed told him, "because we know we can trust you."

Larry is thinking about this when he hears someone shout: "C'mon, fucker." It is a boy's voice. Shrill. Frightened. "C'mon, c'mon, c'mon."

Larry hurries down to the end of the aisle where Henry is sitting at the desk and hears a sharp explosion, like an M-80 firecracker. Mr. Freed staggers out from behind the counter.

"Huuu, huuu . . ." Mr. Freed says. He stumbles down the aisle holding the heel of one hand to his eye. Blood rushes down his arm and splashes to the floor. After several steps, he pitches forward and falls with a thud on his face. Blood pools under his cheek and moves out across the aisle.

The assailant, one of the four boys who'd come in earlier, runs after Mr. Freed and slips in the blood. He falls hard on his backside, but he manages to keep his gun trained on Henry who is sitting horror struck behind the desk.

"Fucker," the boy shouts. He gets back on his feet. "Gimme the money," he screams at Henry, stabbing at him with the gun.

Henry stands slowly. His hands are shaking wildly. He reaches into the desk, pulls out a wad of bills and throws the money down as if he'd found a rattlesnake in the drawer.

"Fucker," the boy screams and lunges at Henry.

"Don't shoot," Larry pleads. "That's all we got."

The boy glances over at Larry. "Pick it up," he shouts.

Larry gathers the bills from the desk and bends down to pick up others from the floor.

Henry glances over his shoulder where the gun is hidden on the cooler inches away.

Larry flattens a few bills on the desk so the boy can pick them up easily. The boy jams the bills into his pocket with one hand while holding the gun on Henry with the other.

He runs out the front door without looking back. The seat of his pants and the back of his jacket are slick with blood.

Henry walks to the cashier's counter. He takes the long way around the bread and condiments aisle to avoid Mr. Freed's body and the blood.

Larry looks down at Mr. Freed. A few minutes ago this man was the closest thing Larry had to a father. Larry wants to cry. Instead he checks on Mrs. Taylor.

"Are you all right?" he asks.

"I'm okay," she says glumly. "Did someone get hurt?"

"Mr. Freed got shot," Larry says. "I'm going to call the police." He pushes Mrs. Taylor's basket to one side, so he can read the Emergency Numbers posted above the phone. He realizes he has no change.

Larry walks around to the front of the store to get a dime from the cash register. Leaning over the counter, he sees Henry crouching beside the Sno-Kone machine with a thick wad of bills in one hand. It is the cash from the register which Mr. Freed had hidden. "I was looking for a dime," Larry tells Henry meekly.

"What you want?" Henry glares up at him.

"I need a dime to call the police." Larry wants to look away, but he can't.

"Why don't you go see if there's anyone else here. See if they're awright 'fore you call the po-lice."

"Mrs. Taylor's still here. I'll go see if there's anyone else." He walks carefully around the aisles, before calling the police.

The police arrive thirty minutes later. Henry is interviewed at length. He leans on the desk in the back and describes what happened with Larry standing at his side. Henry points to where they keep the pistol.

One of the policemen takes the gun from atop the stand-up cooler. He smells the barrel. "Ain't been fired," he says.

"I didn't have a chance ta reach up there an' git it," Henry says. "The boy had his gun on me the whole time. I heard the shot—next thing I know Mr. Freed's comin' toward me bleedin' like hell, an' there's that fool kid behind him with his gun on me."

The policeman in charge, a white man with a red face and piercing green eyes, turns to Larry. "Is that the way the way you remember it, son?"

Larry speaks so softly the policeman cannot hear him over the condenser on the cooler.

"Let's go over in the corner where it's quieter," the policeman says. He leads Larry to Mrs. Taylor's chair next to the pay phone and sits on the window ledge nearby. He reads Larry's Lawson's badge. "Larry Doby Magwire, huh. After the ballplayer. The first Negro in the American League. The catcher."

"That's right," Larry says smiling shyly. "My dad loved the Indians."

"So, what happened?" the policeman asks.

"When I heard the commotion," Larry explains, "I walked around the end of the aisle to where Henry was sitting and saw Mr. Freed coming toward us with his hand on his eye. When Mr. Freed fell down, the boy came running toward us with a gun and slipped in all the blood."

"Then what?"

"He got back up and made us give him what money we had. When he walked out, his pants and his jacket were covered with blood."

The policeman leans back again the window and closes his eyes. "What I don't get is why the kid came after Mr. Shaw. Didn't he already have the money from the register? Hard to believe a boy who'd just shot a man through the head would hang around, unless he hadn't got anything from the register. Know what I mean?"

Larry shrugs his shoulders and acts puzzled. "I guess."

The policeman sits forward, puts a hand on Larry's shoulder and smiles. "I know once somebody gets shot all bets are off. People do crazy things. Just the same, how much money do you take in here on Saturday?"

"I don't know exactly," Larry says. He does not know exactly, but he knows the average take on a Saturday in the summer is more than two thousand dollars.

"Gotta be a thousand bucks, don't it?" The policeman belches under his breath.

"I'm just a stock boy," Larry says. "I don't even know how to open the register."

Larry says nothing about the other robberies and the precautions they had taken—especially the trick of hiding the $20s, $50s and $100s in an envelope next to the Sno-Kone machine, nor does he mention the boy's K-Barz tattoo. He talks instead about Mrs. Taylor.

"I'm not worried about the old woman," the policeman says. "I'm worried about why the boy ran back and stuck up the goddamned night manager."

It is midnight when everyone finally leaves. Henry pays two boys hanging around out front to help clean up the blood while he and Larry close out the register.

"We all squared away with the po-lice?" asks Henry as they walk through the sweltering night to the Cadillac.

"He asked me how much cash we had," Larry says. "I told him I didn't know exactly."

"What did you tell him, exactly?" Henry's voice is cold.

"I told him I didn't know."

"And he believed you?"

"He said there had to be at least one thousand dollars in the register. He wondered why some boy would hang around to rob you, if he already had the money. I told him I thought the boy was surprised. He didn't expect to see you back there. It looked like he tried to shoot you, but his gun jammed. You gave the boy what money you had and he left."

Henry let out his breath slowly. "My Lord! You da man." He pulls up next to Shady House and reaches into the back seat for a carton full of frozen steaks, TV dinners, ice cream and malt liquor. He gives Larry the box and laughs. "So, his gun jammed. That's it, huh? Damn!"

Larry says nothing while Henry drives away. Then he walks over where the K-Barz boys are playing basketball under the one lamp that still works. He puts the box on a picnic table and invites them to divvy up the spoils, warning them the ice cream is melting fast. After a few minutes, he walks across the street. The bootleg party is going strong when he gets home. It will be another long night.

# *Tapioca*

## Susanna Solomon

From the Sheriff's Calls Section of the *Point Reyes Light*, January 13, 2016. SAN GERONIMO VALLEY: At 5:18 p.m. a motorist said a white man with a shaved head had flagged him down to say he had escaped from kidnappers. Deputies placed the latter on mental health hold.

It was Darlene's first real date since she'd moved to Point Reyes two months before. She was in Bernard's car—not the cruiser—but his real car, a 1997 Honda Accord with stick shift. She had always admired men who could drive a stick, but this time, he ground the gears when he slowed down, making her cringe.

She looked up from reading the *Point Reyes Light*. "Doesn't sound like a flat, Bernard; otherwise we'd go kthunk-kthunk and be all crooked." On another date a few years back, Darlene had made the mistake of helping out when he'd had a flat. That had been her last date with him. This time, she kept her hands to herself and hated feeling helpless.

"Nope, not the tire, Darlene. There's a guy in the middle of the road. Wish I had my cruiser. I'll only be gone a minute," he said, and exited the car.

Darlene, a retired P. I., wasn't going to sit still—not when there was some real action in West Marin. Maybe she had made a mistake moving out here; it was too quiet in her estimation. "Anything I can do?" she asked, her head out the window.

"Nope, got this," he replied.

Darlene put down her paper and strained to hear. Doggone, they were just out of earshot. Bernard, a cop in his thirties with thinning hair, was standing on the side of the road talking to a white guy with a shaved head. Skinhead, gang member? Darlene wasn't going to sit this one out, date or no date. There was always something interesting going on with Bernard.

"And there I was, on the side of the road," the bald man said. "I should've told my sister, she knows about these types of things," he muttered, rubbing his hands together. He was wearing khaki pants, a khaki shirt, but no identifying insignia. Not Park Service, that was for

250

sure; they wore a darker shade of green. Darlene came closer, staying on the right side of Bernard's car so the bald guy could see her but Bernard couldn't. He had his back to her, was scratching his bald spot with one hand and reaching for something with the other.

"There were five of them," the bald man said. "Short guys."

"Your name, sir?" Bernard pulled out his badge.

"I didn't do it. I didn't do anything, Officer. Don't arrest me."

The bald man was trembling, but Bernard wasn't intimidating, not really, just a bit tall and goofy. He had a soft side as big as the moon. Darlene had picked that up right away. "Name, sir?" Bernard asked.

"Templeton Fortescu. Mr. Fortescu," the bald man sputtered. "They guys were all small—short like your girlfriend back there."

Bernard turned and frowned when he noticed Darlene. She gave him a little wave.

The bald guy took two fast steps toward the bushes but Darlene ran up to him and caught him just as he was about to fall into a ditch.

"I got this, Darlene," Bernard said.

"Templeton," Darlene said, her hand on his arm. "It's been too long."

The bald man blinked. "There were five of them, two of you now, you wouldn't stand a chance. They were so . . . pretty," he sputtered. "Gray."

"A family of grays, then," Darlene asked. "Squirrels?"

Bernard rolled his eyes. "The movie starts in ten minutes, Darlene."

"Of course I remember you," Darlene chattered. To Bernard she may have seemed loony but to the bald man her attempt worked. He stood up, now out of the ditch, looked her in the eye. Relaxed, some.

"So, you've seen them too?" he asked, bright-eyed.

"Meth, dope, crack, oxy—what'd ya take, Mr. Fortescu?" Bernard asked.

The bald man grabbed Darlene's arm. "They were quick. I gave them all I had, fifteen cents. They screamed at me so I handed over my cell phone and they threw it in the road."

"Too bad," Darlene said, trying to pull away but the guy was too strong. Bernard stepped in closer, lifted Mr. Fortescu's hand off Darlene's shoulder. "If you don't mind, Mr. Fortescu?"

"My sister made me do it. We were in the kitchen, eating leftover mac and cheese, and next thing I know, she's telling me about this car, this vehicle, says people are crying out on the road. She wanted me to save them. My sister's delicate, Officer."

Darlene pulled out her cell phone and pressed record, fascinated. "Then what?"

Mr. Fortescu shook his head when he saw the red light. "No. Mr. Blinky makes me nervous. You can't record me. They'll take my soul. They said . . ."

"Who said?" Bernard asked, pulling out his notebook and pencil.

"The gray guys. All I tell you about is gray guys."

"Like the man in the gray flannel suit?" Darlene asked. "You a movie buff?"

"My sister would say so but she's not here. And what's it to you? You're missing the point."

"Which is?" Bernard asked.

"Their skin was gray," Mr. Fortescu said. "And you don't believe me. Like your pants, Officer. Slate gray."

"I see." Darlene stepped closer. "Did they take your virtue, Mr. Fortescu?"

"What virtue?" Mr. Fortescu laughed, his belly hanging over his belt buckle taking the brunt of it.

"Did they take anything else, Mr. Fortescu?" Darlene asked.

"My sister. They tied me up. By then she had come out of the woods . . . our house is just up there . . . Officers . . . and . . . and . . .," he broke up, sobbing.

"There, there, Mr. Fortescu," Darlene said. "Perhaps you can come with us."

"To the station," Bernard said. "So we can take care of you and put out an APB on your sister."

"Don't bother." Mr. Fortescu came over to Bernard's car, leaned against the hood, took a look at the sky, held one hand over his eyes to shade them from the sun. "You'll never find her," he said. "She went with them. The group. Went with them happy, a smile on her face, skipping, laughing. About fifteen minutes ago."

Bernard pulled out his cell phone, called the station, was about to request a cruiser when Mr. Fortescu tried to yank the phone out of his hands.

"Now, now, now, Mr. Fortescu, we'll have none of that." Bernard snapped.

"That's what did it, Officer," the bald man said. "The signals. They'll swallow you up, just like what happened to Gladys." His face went white and he wobbled a little bit, pulled himself up again.

"Mr. Fortescu, you feeling all right?" Darlene asked. "Your sister, then, she still at home?"

"Making tapioca," Mr. Fortescu replied. "I've always loved tapioca."

"Should we call ahead and ask them to make it for you at the police station?" Bernard asked.

"But there's no stove at the police station," Mr. Fortescu replied. "Only at the fire house. Everyone knows that."

"My dear Mr. Fortescu," Darlene said, taking his arm and opening the door to Bernard's car. "It's been a kind of a tough day for you, hasn't it?"

"My sister's just been abducted by aliens. I should say so, Miss."

"You live with her?" Darlene asked.

"Up until today," Mr. Fortescu sighed. He stopped, looked down the road, his eyes glazed. "Up until the accident. She died a year ago. I keep expecting her to come walking up our drive, carrying a bowl of tapioca, and wearing her favorite coat—you know the color? Squirrel gray, I think. Yes, she just loved that coat."

# The Anniversary

## John Heide

If it were up to me, wedding anniversaries would always be acknowledged in a meaningful way and annually celebrated with pure reverence for the good fortune of having bonded with a mate. But even on the most well intentioned path one can come upon a banana peel.

Subsequent to depositing our youngest at his first-year college dormitory nestled near the northern tip of California's academia, my lovely wife and I took a leisurely drive south, down the incredibly dramatic coastline. "Look at that, Honey," Ingrid said (not my wife's real name), pointing at a small structure perched on an angular spit of land jutting away from our wide spot in the road. The sun sparkled off the setting sun to the west. The waves crashed beyond and sprayed an intoxicating scent of beauty and solitude. "And there's wine," she exclaimed. Sure enough, a handmade wooden sign indicating a previously unknown brand of our favorite grape-derived drink dangled from a post not one hundred yards further up the road. She brightened and indicated with no uncertainty that we were about to drop into this heavenly confluence of spirits and uncommonly beautiful landscape. Of course I responded positively, and we turned onto the gravel driveway and headed toward a larger building with the magic words "Tasting Room" above a doorway.

As we sipped our sample of the proprietor's best, I couldn't help but notice that Ingrid kept staring toward the ocean at the previously spied picturesque cottage. Our host, Samantha (not her real name), was experienced in this reaction from more than a few visitors and raised an eyebrow while leaning toward my wife. "Wine club members can rent our Cliff House. On occasion," she added with a hint of exclusivity. The women locked eyes.

"We're coming back for our anniversary," Ingrid gushed. Samantha merely nodded.

I cleared my throat. "Maybe you should go look at it first," I said in a friendly manner as to not indicate any doubt as to Samantha's hosting competence.

"No need," Ingrid smiled back.

~*~

Exactly thirty-four days later, Ingrid and I pulled into the winery for the second time, the sun low over the ocean. Samantha greeted us with open arms, a decent chardonnay, and few stories of her life. We learned that she loved her wine, her grown kids (somewhere on the East Coast) and most every aspect of her life. Yet . . . with a sweeping arm, she bemoaned the flaky, on-and-off-again boyfriend, the broken winery equipment, and her wine maker, Raoul, who evidently had a bad habit of not showing up.

"And there's also my sheep." Samantha declared loudly and took another sip from her glass. "By the way, don't let them out, under any circumstance." I had not noticed any sheep on my prior visit, and a quick glance toward the cliffs did not reveal any. But I didn't mind sharing the cliff with a few wooly creatures, and I definitely had no problem with leaving them right where they were.

I nodded and touched Ingrid's arm in a "let's go, Honey" sort of manner.

We drove the two hundred yards, parked, and stood for a moment, scrutinizing the cabin. We glanced at each other, shrugged and pushed open the door. The main floor was only nine feet by nine feet and consisted of a "mini-kitchen" with a sink, a small electric toaster oven, an eighteen-inch counter top, one small chair and no room for another. On one wall a fabric curtain concealed a compact composting toilet and a shower stall designed for midgets, the shower head pointing directly at an average sized person's belly button. Our previous expectation of "cozy" was now replaced with "cramped." The available floor space was further taken up by a spiral staircase that wound its way up to a sleeping loft with a thin, small mattress. The loft itself was charming enough, as it featured a stained glass window with some sort of Gaelic symbol. Unfortunately, the non-opening, colored glass blocked the view and guaranteed a stuffy, cloistered environment. The gabled roof angled down to only a few inches above the head of the bed.

But, who's to complain? We had a big deck, two lawn chairs and the sun was setting over a spectacular sparkling ocean with crashing waves all around us. And there was a sauna and hot tub to look forward to. Time to open a bottle of champagne and fire up the barbecue. Having always been on the gas side of the barbecuing divide, I stared at the old, rusty Weber with the half-empty bag of damp briquettes. After a half hour and a can of lighter fluid, I gave up trying to coax them into doing their job. Fortunately, we had brought a cooler with a quart of soup that Ingrid had made the day before. We devised a method of baking one bowl at a time in the toaster oven. At least the champagne worked.

It was during the twenty-minute wait for the second bowl of soup that Samantha dropped by to see how we were doing. A large fluffy cat with a flat face trailed behind her. "He's a doll," she assured us as she stroked his head. "We call him the Boss. But don't let him take over. He'll try. Everything okay?" Without actually waiting for an answer, she spun around and headed back up the path to the winery. The Boss stayed behind and stared unflinchingly at me.

After taking the edge off of our hunger, we wanted to wander and explore. It was dark by now but we had flashlights, more champagne, and the light of a half moon. We walked the hundred yards down to the cliff's edge and inhaled the magic beauty of ocean and rock. With empty glasses, we turned to head back, my flashlight leading the way. We froze. Illuminated in the light we could make out a pair of full-grown sheep flitting gracefully through a previously unnoticed open gate. Another dozen or so sheep were cautiously lining up, probably contemplating whether to follow their friends. I did what any rational man would do under the circumstances. I shouted loudly while running in the sheep's direction. This did not work. In fact, the rest of the sheep bolted at full speed through the gate and into the darkness beyond.

"They'll be slaughtered on the highway," Ingrid shouted.

Ingrid and I flew into action and started vigorously bickering over the best plan to round up the rascals. I took charge and resorted to more running and shouting and was moderately successful in scaring two sheep back through the gate. But because we had to leave it open for the arriving flock, the few that were finally back in the fold decided to simply turn around and go back out with their buddies. We argued some more, but it was finally determined that Ingrid would stay as hidden as she could by the gate and open and close it as I herded the animals closer.

It only took an hour of cussing and stumbling through dark, rock strewn fields to round all of them up. I'd suffered a twisted ankle, and it was officially cold out there now. Damn sheep had a full wool coat to keep them warm. I wanted a hot sauna.

The Boss was waiting for us when we returned to the cabin. We'd left the one downstairs window cracked open and the implacable cat sat lounging in our one chair. He merely stared at me with an "I dare you" look in his eyes. He hissed at me when I tried to pick him up, so I expressed my desire for him to get the hell out of my space by snapping a towel close to his butt. This did not work. The enraged beast sprang up on all fours and swiped a claw-extended paw in my direction. Game on. I girded my stance, fired off another towel snap, and let out a cheer when he sprang out the window. "We have to keep this closed," I yelled over my shoulder.

"I have to have fresh air," Ingrid challenged. This posed a problem as this was the only opening window in the entire structure, and it had no screen. I grunted my considerable displeasure and a few threats into the darkness outside.

Ingrid had had enough. She was ready for bed, and evidently, just fine without me. I was cold, hungry, limping, and ready to get hot. The sauna was in a separate identical cabin across the deck from our main hovel. Whereas the sizes of these structures were totally inadequate as living quarters, they were also way too big for a practical sauna. But it was relatively clean and easy to understand as one only had to light a fire in the wood stove and wait to sweat. I got naked, lit the fire, and waited. And waited. It became apparent wood stoves take a while to heat up in a large uninsulated, drafty space. Thirty minutes later, the fire was roaring and my skin finally got to the clammy stage. After roughly calculating the time required to actually get hot, I grunted some more considerable displeasure and gave up.

When I entered the cabin, Ingrid was asleep and snoring a gentle rhythm five feet above my head. To my relief, the Boss was nowhere in sight, and I narrowed the window's gap to a cat-proof slit. "Keep it open. I need fresh air," came the directive from upstairs. I grimaced and cranked it back open just a bit.

At the foot of the bed, I took a moment and beheld my lovely wife, gingerly stepped over the candles, and wedged my head into the ceiling vertex next to Ingrid's flowing hair. I hesitantly joked about needing bicycle helmets for any sexual activity. Ingrid mumbled back something about my inattention to latching gates and pulled more covers over her. Seconds later, she was again gently snoring. Ah, but sleep was welcome and I drifted off.

"What's that noise?" Ingrid whispered, while shaking my shoulder. I roused rather slowly from a dream and tried to make sense of the flickering shadows on the wall. The candles had burned low and Ingrid had an insistent desperation in her voice. "What is that noise?" I cleared my throat, shook my head, and tried to concentrate. At first, I heard nothing; then, an ungodly noise, somewhere between a whine and a crunch originating much too close to ignore. I bolted upright with the predictable consequences of bonking my head on the ceiling.

"Where's the damn flashlight?" I shouted. We both fished around the sides of the bed with no results. The noise had stopped. I peered toward the foot of the bed. Couldn't see a thing. Ever so slowly, I pulled back my covers and skidded my naked body toward the staircase. My eyes were straining in the candle light. My ears were on full alert.

Another crunch sound. "God! What is that?" Ingrid shouted. I was now semi-vertical and moving forward in that I'll-protect-you-sweetheart sort of mode. Ingrid found the flashlight and waved it around the loft. In the flitting beam, I saw the Boss crouched at the foot of the bed. He raised his wet mouth from the large, dead rat long enough to make sure he and I made direct eye contact.

"What is it? What is it?" Ingrid's voice was getting hoarse.

"It's fucking, him," I growled. I made a menacing motion toward the Boss but he did not move a muscle.

"Get out of here," I yelled.

He studied me with an unsettling measured indifference and took another chomp. With utter clarity I realized I needed to rise to the occasion. I did not take my eyes off the beast; rather I felt around the side of the bed with one hand until I located the discarded Kona brewpub T-shirt from an hour ago. I felt I could take charge of the unfortunate rodent and cast him outside, thus thwarting any feline schemes to the contrary. With Ingrid's rather forceful exclamations and wildly random spikes of light as atmosphere, I threw caution to the wind. Using the cotton T-shirt as protection, I grabbed whatever I could.

The Boss was not going down easy. I had the rat by the tail. He growled and tugged back in the opposite direction. Ingrid shrieked, the shadows undulated on the walls, I hit my head on the ceiling again, and the desperate tug-of-war lasted way too long for anyone's benefit. I finally won, gagging while I hoisted a dead rat trophy. The Boss bolted.

I scurried downstairs, opened the door, and flung the hapless rodent into the darkness. That's when Ingrid agreed to shutting the window, despite any lack of air. I washed my hands three times.

At dawn, we awoke to rain. A steady, persistent, unrelenting, callous drizzle. One cup at a time, we heated hot water in the toaster oven, and poured it through a paper towel pocketed with ground coffee, and took turns sitting in our chair until deep hunger struck. The car sat merely twenty feet away.

We had paid for two nights, but . . . twenty minutes later we zipped past the wooden sign, onto the highway, and headed south. Our own bed felt unusually good that night.

# The Choice

## Malena Eljumaily

Grove Avenue. She didn't want to be here, and he knew it. The street was lined with beer cans, drunks in doorways, head shops, and tattoo parlors. She would never have ventured here on her own. She wanted to run, but she'd promised him. She agreed to do this for the sake of their relationship. Still, shouldn't it be her choice? After all it was her body.

He took her arm and guided her forward. Her hands were sweating. His grip was like a vise. He wasn't letting her go. They were close.

She froze.

"What's wrong?" he asked.

"I can't go through with this."

"Not again. We're twenty feet from the entrance." He sounded frustrated.

She was frustrated, too. It always had to be his way. Why didn't she have a say? "I'm sorry, but I've changed my mind. I can't do it."

"Yes you can," he snapped.

"It's a big decision," she stammered.

"One that we've already made. You promised me."

"I know, but it's harder for me than it is for you. I'm scared."

"Of what? This isn't some back alley operation. It's clean and safe in there. All the equipment is sterile."

"I know, but . . ."

"So, a promise means nothing to you. What else have you said to me that you don't really mean? Do you even love me?"

"Of course, I love you."

*I sound desperate*, she thought.

"Prove you love me and walk through that door." He picked up her hand and caressed it. "I'll be with you the whole time." He whispered.

"I know, I guess . . ." She steeled herself. She had to say it. "I guess I'm just not sure about the skulls."

He looked surprised. Not angry. "We agreed on the skulls."

"I'd rather have roses than flames. How about if you get flames and I get roses?"

260

"That defeats the purpose, babe. They gotta be matching tattoos."

He was right. He was usually right. Not always, but usually.

"Okay," she said, taking his hand.

# The Date, i.e., Cerulean Meatloaf

## Linda L. Reid

I grab the Sonic and get out my toothpaste, a sensitivity brand that my dentist recommends. I turn on the shower and begin brushing my teeth, in a race to when the shower gets hot, without me in it—wasteful. The government, or someone with authority, should make every homeowner install one of those instant hot water systems, so you don't have to run all that water waiting for it to get hot. Is that socialist? Those gadgets cost a few bucks, so maybe I'm being elitist. Whatever. When in the kitchen, I collect the cold water run-off to use for boiling potatoes or watering indoor plants. Proletarian?

"Where are you going?" Clyde says, looking up from his morning paper as I scamper through the kitchen wrapped in a towel.

"Lunch . . . Brenda."

I pour a cup of coffee to take with me to the bedroom. Clyde snaps the paper sharply, so I know that he knows. This is not our comfortable morning routine. Clyde is experiencing a sixth sense moment, like our cat, Gus, who spends most of the day napping on our bed and then miraculously, is up and at his food station exactly on time. We're both retired from mid-management jobs, Clyde with PG&E and I from the telephone company. You could say we are utilitarian, typical, average Americans. Mid-salary retirements, mid-life, and getting bigger around the middle. Well, one of us is.

There's a reason for the scent in the air.

Two sips of coffee, and I slip into the shower. First comes the shampoo, then conditioner. While the conditioner does its thing, I rub my body with Green Apple and Ginger body wash. The aroma is refreshing and exotic all at the same time; perfect for this day. Then, I rinse everything at once, body and hair—in this exact order. One day, when I overconfidently switched the order, I forgot to rinse off the conditioner. When you roll into age seventy-three, you think about things. It's important to create good habits. Drivers who use their turn signal at every turning event when younger, will find, when older, that the habit has taken over and they will get to drive longer than other old, bad drivers.

Some habits are not good. I just broke myself of two annoying practices in one fell swoop. Picture this: I'm driving. The cell phone rings. I answer while pulling off an earring to better press the phone to my ear. I arrive at my destination and, having put said earring into my lap, I now exit the car, forgetting about the earring that tumbles onto the parking lot. When returning to the car, I look into the mirror and gasp. Yikes. I've just sat through an entire whatever with one earring. I look around the seat and floor. Unable to find said earring, I start the car, back up and run over said earring, now smashed on the parking lot tarmac.

Sigh.

As I said, this nasty habit is gone. As recommended by the police, I no longer use my cell in the car and thus, no smashed jewelry, no ticket, and no dead people. All good.

Here's another helpful preparatory hint in preparing for an older age—be nice. You know, be in the "moment" with the person who is chomping your ear off. Several unpleasant experiences with my mother taught me that older folks can no longer hide their personality deficiencies. If a person has managed to, say, hide the fact that they were prideful when younger, it will seep out later in life through careless speech, over phone wires, across the sky, down the lane and into gossip-ready ears. So, let nice be your habit now or be known as a big crab later.

Stepping from the shower, I towel down: head first, arms, back, legs. Same system every time. Then a good grade lotion is applied: Eau de Campagne by Sisley of Paris. I know it's good because it cost a lot. I look at my naked body and wonder what it might look like to someone else. Not Clyde. He always tells me I'm cute. Well, I was cute, but now there's some serious sagging and lumps. I suck in my tummy. Whatever. I put cream on my face so it can soak in while I dress.

My eyes run across the closet rack, taking in the many colors. I'm not an artist, but I know each color has a meaning—purple for royalty, red for passion. Definitely—not red today. I've heard that blue is the favorite color of all people, but the most complex because of the many shades. I'm not a blue person, which makes me feel insecure. However, I am complex, especially lately. I first took note of Steven when he commented on my turtleneck sweater. I was standing in line at the library. "You look great in cerulean blue," he said, and smiled. Cerulean? He's an artist. I tried to see what books he was holding, but no luck.

I reach for my turquoise blouse and my hand shakes from a surge of adrenalin. I shake my head to clear cerulean thoughts. I wonder why I pick turquoise for today. Why was I wearing a cerulean blue sweater when I don't even like blue? See...complex.

As I slip into the soft silk blouse, I'm reminded that silk is dangerous. Once, in another lifetime, when I was a businesswoman wannabe at a meeting with lots of big-shots—all men, of course—I had a traumatic experience with silk. It was bloody hot and the room was crowded. I'd recently started down that long tunnel of madness called menopause. It happened. A hot flash turned my light blue silk dress dark blue...under my arms, around the belt, down my back, between my breasts. What did I do? I'm sure I disappeared because God is good.

I put foaming stuff on my hair to give it body, so they say, and begin the blow-dry. I cut and color my own hair. Most women would assess this as brave or stupid, depending on their pocketbooks. For me it's about *time*. I don't enjoy lolling about the salon or the chitchat that goes with it. I was blond for three years. Now I'm somewhere between auburn and maroon. I smile, thinking of a charming lyric from the "The Judge's Song" in Gilbert & Sullivan's *Trial By Jury*.

"She may very well pass for forty-three
In the dusk, with a light behind her!"

Ha! Hair-wise, it will be a bitch to get back to my original color, which is now, most likely, mousy gray. We have a male friend who, at sixty-five, dyed his hair green. I mean bright lime-green. We all need to act out, make statements about our emotions. Not that I'm ready for green hair, but it's getting close. Certainly, today's plan could use some couch time.

Now, for the face. I wonder if Steven will like what he sees? Don't think about it. I put on anti-aging cream that contains tiny bits of sand and scrub. It is Oil of Olay. Last week, I stopped at one of those new mega makeup stores in the mall. Entering at the same time was a woman my age who was very hip, tall and thin, wearing huge loop earrings and those six-inch fuck-me-dead heels, and a silver jacket with the collar turned up like they do when being particularly chic. She whipped in through the double glass doors and I whipped in right behind. I can't look like her, but I can spend just as much money trying.

I found my way to the makeup area and asked for an excellent face cream. I did not ask for a diet pill to shrink me instantly so I can continue to eat ice cream, or, for better, non-plantar-fasciitis feet, or any other number of cures that would make me look...what? Desirable? Best settle for *interesting*. Wrinkles can be tough. It will cost a fortune. Just the desperate look on my face alone would give the sales girl license to run up the tab. She batted her Avatar eyes and said, "If you've been using Oil of Olay for all these years, you should stay with that." What? Truth and fairness from a salesgirl? Do they know she's peddling honesty?

I look deeply into my makeup mirror and trace what's left of my eyebrows with a dark-brown pencil. I discussed this issue last week with a beautician and she said it was possible to dye them, but I would look somewhat like Groucho Marks for a few days. I decline—Clyde deserves better than that. The same goes for my lips; that crisp shape is fading to a straight line. I'm beginning to resemble a smiley face. After applying lip liner, the entire masquerade is finished off with rouge, because darling, the blush is definitely off this rose.

Gads. Am I really going through with this?

My shoes are new, opened toed, two-inch sandals. My daughters told me at Easter, "You look hot, Mom, but your shoes are way too out of style." I wish them well and buckets of luck to look à la mode at age seventy-three; to know what to wear—to even care. You get out of touch. Magazines show women my age with drama, sex, and energy. I can do this.

I dash for the car keys, always in their trusty bowl. This is a must, or else I'll waste hours running from room to room, madly diving into purses. Heading for the kitchen to say goodbye to Clyde, I find him standing at the front door.

"Have a fun lunch," he says, and kisses me on the forehead. We face each other. I smile, give him a peck, and leave as he stands at the door, finally closing.

When I arrive at the restaurant, Steven is not there. Should I wait, sitting on the chair beside the door like a forgotten, wilting lily? Did he have a reservation? This whole thing is much harder than I'd imagined. The waiter takes me to a small table. I sit. My resolve is melting as my assured chin drops down to stare at the Coach purse gripped firmly in my lap. I don't even recognize it—an expensive gift from my daughters. One I'd have never purchased on my own. "You need to accept our commercialized world," one said while the other nodded. I narrow my eyes and wonder what it will be like when they are calling the shots…taking care of Mom.

My cell phone rings—it nearly knocks me back. I have a special ring for Clyde and for each of the daughters, set up by my ten-year-old grandson. Our anniversary tune, "Always," tinkles out.

"Honey?"

I hear Clyde's voice, which for some reason sounds far away. Honey? He hasn't called me Honey since our twentieth anniversary, when I was twenty pounds lighter.

"Can't find the saltines," he says.

I'd thrown away the Nabisco box and moved the last sleeve of crackers into the kitchen drawer because there was only one package left in a big box, and I'm constantly vigilant to reduce our inventory in the pantry or fridge, or any place where too much stuff collects. I tell him where the crackers reside, but it's not about crackers.

"Thanks," Clyde says, staying on the line, hesitant.

I can see his wrinkled white T-shirt and yet messy morning-hair. We've gotten goodly comfy with each other; perhaps, one might call it, sloppy. Is it his fault? Mine? Is it all my tidiness, making of lists, cracker rearranging that's killing our romance? What am I up to? I think about the loveliness of a long-term relationship, shared memories, years of caring, the children who don't need us anymore. Are we in late-life crisis? I like the sound of that word—*crisis*—at least something's happening.

"Say hi to Brenda," Clyde says. "Oh, and…I'm making meatloaf for tonight." He waits for me to be happy.

"Nice," I say and hang up as the tips of two shoes come into view at my feet. I look up.

"Oh . . . Steven."

# The Doll Museum

## Jeanne Jusaitis

I sat alone in the back seat of Zeke's open Jeep, and observed the old lady as she opened the screen door. She sidled out to the sagging porch of the Victorian house, and fed some seeds to her caged parrot. Her garish clothes shouted carnival fortune-teller.

A hand-lettered sign that read "Doll Museum" hung crookedly from the mailbox. As I read it, I had no clue that things would never be the same.

My friend, Molly, had been dying to visit the Doll Museum in Bodega for a long time. Dying is probably a bad choice of words.

She'd called me that first morning of Spring Break. "Hey Twyla True, Zeke and I are going out to Bodega Bay for a picnic, and I talked him into stopping at that Doll Museum on the way. Wanna come?"

On that sun-shiny day when Molly called, I had nothing better to do, so I jumped at the chance to go along for the ride. I didn't care that Zeke had just gotten his license. But then, the long rural road wound its bumpy way to the coast, and I hadn't taken a carsick pill. So there I sat in the car, waiting for the queasiness to settle while Molly and Zeke went ahead into the museum.

The sight of that ancient house filled me with a whole new kind of queasiness. An old lady turned back toward the door, stopped, then turned around to face me. She gestured for me to come in.

I shook my head no.

She stood there, holding the screen door open, waiting for me.

"Two dollars," said the old crone as she held out her bony hand. A bunch of bangle bracelets dangled from her wrist. She fascinated me.

I walked up to the porch and pulled two wrinkled dollar bills out of my jeans back pocket. She took them, stuffed them into her blouse, and ushered me into the foyer.

"This is a self-guided tour," she rasped. "You like dolls?"

"Yes," I lied. I'd never been into dolls. Force feeding plastic heads and talking to dollies at tea parties always seemed kind of lame.

"Make yourself at home, Dearie."

I entered the dimly lit rooms, probably the former living and dining rooms, but didn't see my friends. As a matter of fact, I saw no other humanoids. The old lady had wandered off.

Frilly dolls sat on the couches, Christmas dolls lined the fireplace mantle, while a host of dolls stood on tables and sat on chairs. Overwhelmed by dollies, I quickened my pace through the rooms and past the kitchen, searching for Molly and Zeke.

Each room felt more crowded than the last, but I finally arrived at a sunny glassed-in porch. Zeke stood there alone, hands in his pockets, looking into the backyard. I followed his eyes, and saw the old lady hanging out some tiny clothes on a line. Her fringed shawl billowed behind her in the breeze and her iridescent turban glimmered in the sun. A big gray cat watched on.

"Zeke," I said. "Finally. I thought you and Molly had been swallowed up in this place." I looked around the porch. A zillion more dolls. "Where's Molly?"

"Uh, she went upstairs. These are all historical down here. Antiques."

"Yeah, hysterical."

Zeke laughed.

Small handwritten cards described each doll.

"Check out this one," he said, pointing to a tin soldier. "You can wind it up and it plays the drum." He demonstrated by winding it up and setting it back down on the table. The mechanism made a groaning sound and the soldier lifted one drumstick. It just stopped there.

"Not impressed."

"See that one, over there? It was owned by Marie Antoinette." He adjusted the Giant's baseball cap that covered his curly brown hair. Was he really getting hooked on the dolls?

"Yeah, Marie Antoinette. And I was the Queen of England. I think I'll go upstairs and see what Molly's up to."

"Maybe you can hurry her along. I hear the beach. It's calling Twyla, Twyla."

"I know. I hear it, too."

I walked up the curving staircase, sliding my hand along the walnut banister. Thick dust and a hint of mildew caused me to stop and sneeze a few times, but I finally got to the second floor landing. I had a choice to make—the room on the right or the room on the left. I chose the left because it looked bright and sunny.

It was a small two-windowed bedroom packed with more dolls. Through the front window, I could see the pink blossoming treetops lining the street, and Zeke's car at the curb. Large dolls, from toddlers to adults, curved along the walls between that window and the other one on the adjacent wall. I felt surrounded by them. An antique wicker baby carriage held a pile of swaddled baby dolls.

Somebody walked into the room. I sensed it, but I looked around and saw no one. When I saw the bed, I started feeling the creepy-crawlies.

A single bed, covered in red silk, was pushed up against the wall, close to the door. Dolls sat all along the bed, with their backs to the wall. I had the distinct feeling that somebody, a real person, was in that room with me.

Was he or she hiding among the dolls, like that closet scene in *ET?* The creepy crawlers turned creepier, starting in my stomach, spreading up my spine, and moving to a prickly hair feeling at the top of my head. Then, I don't know if it was the dust motes in the light from the window, or a trick of my eyes because I was near fainting, but I saw a swirling, whirling transparent whiteness near the head of the bed. Distinctly, I felt like I was not wanted in that room—that I was being pushed out. Drops of perspiration slid down my back, and my heart beat an erratic rhythm as panic overwhelmed me. I tore out of the room, across the hall, and into another small bedroom. Zeke and Molly stood there, laughing about one of the dolls

"Take a look at this one, Twyla. Her face is so ugly it could stop a truck." Molly's new nail polish, blue and sparkly, caught the light as she pointed at the unfortunate doll. My stomach retched, and I was afraid that I was going to throw up.

"Molly, I have to get out of here. I don't feel good. There's something way too spooky about this place."

I was halfway down the stairs when I heard Molly say, "Okay, go on down to the car. We'll be there in a few minutes."

The old lady was nowhere to be seen, but I knew she was watching me. I could feel her eyes.

I charged out the screen door, past the parrot, down the porch steps, and through the open gate of the picket fence to Zeke's car, feeling that I had escaped something awful. I leaned on the warm car, shaky and nauseated.

If I had it to do over again, I would insist that Zeke and Molly leave with me. But I didn't know then what I know now. It might have been too late anyway.

The sun felt glorious, and I couldn't get enough of the fresh ocean air into my lungs. I took a little walk down the old, broken sidewalk, wanting to get away from the house and shake the spell. I needed to feel normal again.

My mom always said that I had a wild imagination. So, I tried to talk myself down—talk some sense into myself.

"Twyla."

I turned around to see Molly and Zeke, standing by the car.

"Where are you going?" asked Molly.

"Nowhere special," I said, attempting a normal expression as I walked toward them. I didn't feel normal at all. "Just waiting for you guys. I had to get away from that house. Really. Way too weird for me. I thought I was going to puke." Molly laughed and tossed her long hair back with her hand. "What set you off?"

"That bedroom with the red silk bedspread. I swear, something didn't want me there. Did you go in?"

"Yeah," said Zeke. "Molly and I even tried out the bed." He wiggled his eyebrows up and down.

"You what?" I shrieked.

Molly laughed again, giving Zeke a little shove. "Only for a minute. We were just goofing around, fighting over his cap."

"Until the dust almost choked us to death," said Zeke.

Now, that was the part that I really should have paid attention to. But I didn't. It was only later . . .

We went to the beach and there was no more talk about the Doll Museum.

After that day, life went back into normal mode, pretty much, but there was one difference. It seemed to me, that whenever the three of us were together, I'd get that sick tingly feeling. Sometimes, I even imagined that I could see that white energy swirling around Molly and Zeke.

And then Molly got sick. The doctors didn't know what it was. It seemed that one day she was hanging out at the square with the gang after school, and the next she could barely sit up and visit without falling asleep. I visited her every day. Zeke did, too. She slept more and more, until the day she didn't wake up.

I cried for days. I missed Molly's laugh and couldn't believe that she was gone. It just didn't make sense. Zeke and I drifted apart. It seemed that all we had in common was Molly, and now that she was gone we had no reason to hang out.

And then, through the grapevine, I heard that Zeke was sick––some kind of respiratory illness. Again, the doctors didn't know what caused it. I went to see him and we had a short visit, but he went into a coughing fit, and his mother told me that I needed to leave and let him get some rest.

He got some rest, all right. He died, choking to death.

I kept thinking about the day that Molly, Zeke, and I visited the doll museum. I was haunted by the memories of the staring dolls, the old lady, the whole experience.

Every day, I started taking my temperature, and if I sneezed once or twice, I would stay home and take extra care. Would I be the next one to go? I tried to talk to my mom about it, but she gave me the old, "What an imagination you have, Twyla. Don't let it get the best of you."

And then one night, in the middle of my homework, my mom called out, "Twyla. Come here. You've got to see what's on the TV. Hurry."

I rushed into the living room where our big screen dominated the fireplace. A TV news magazine's feature story was about a ghost hunter from Michigan, who came all the way to California to visit a doll museum in Bodega.

"Can you believe this?" asked my mother.

I just stared at the TV.

The ghost hunter took her equipment into the doll museum and snooped around. She finally got a reading when she went upstairs and into the room on the left. I watched as the old lady in the shadows lurked behind her.

Oh my God. I had to sit down.

At this point, the ghost hunter let her psycho-whatever skills take over and told her findings to the reporter. A child had been very sick in that bed, and had eventually died. The mother had been in and out of that room, caring for the child. The ghost hunter said their ghosts were still there—the child in the bed, and the mother moving in and out.

The camera panned across the dolls on the bed. One boy doll wore a Giants cap. A few dark curls sprung out from under the cap. The girl doll next to him had sparkly blue nails.

"No!" I cried. It couldn't be.

Several years later, my boyfriend and I rode out to Bodega Bay. I had told him my story and he wanted to drive through the town of Bodega to see the Doll Museum. I don't think he believed me. I didn't want to go.

"We'll just do a drive-by," he said.

This time I'd taken a carsick pill, but when we turned onto the street, that familiar queasy feeling rose up in my throat.

The old Victorian stood there still, the picket fence leaning more than it had in my memory, the house paint chipped and worn. A rusted cage sat on the front porch. No sign hung from the mailbox. A couple of Hitchcock's crows sat on the telephone wire. The place looked deserted.

"Are you sure this was it?" he asked, pulling up on the opposite side of the road.

"Yes, I'm sure." But there were no witnesses left to back me up—no proof. It was then that I noticed a gray cat sitting on the porch next to a weather-beaten wicker chair. "There was a gray cat," I said. "But that was so long ago. It's probably not the same one."

"Twyla, is that a doll sitting on the chair?"

I removed my sunglasses and squinted, but it was too far away. "I don't know. There's something on that chair, though."

"I'll turn around so we can get closer."

We drove slowly down the street, made a U-turn, and stopped right in front of the house. Yes, it was definitely a doll. The doll wore a fringed shawl, a green iridescent turban, and bangle bracelets.

I thought of the first time I'd seen those bracelets.

A voice from the past whispered in my ear, "Make yourself at home, Dearie."

# The Drop-off

## Marilyn Lanier

Her two young children skip alongside her this chilly March morning in Seoul. They pelt her with questions as they marvel at the brass pots hanging above their heads and the food stalls heaped with dried fish, raw mussels, ginger root, apples, and bins of rice.

"Oma. Oma," they exclaim. "Is that fish soup? Can we have some?" The enticing smells draw them to the stainless steel cauldron. But Jeong Yeob charges ahead through the morning throng, tightly clasping their hands and ignoring their chatter. The trio skirts bicyclists, taxis belching diesel fumes, and crowds heading cross directions through the alleys and narrow streets of the busy Myeongdong district.

The congestion and clamor of the street remind her of how much she dreaded this trek with her children through downtown Seoul when she found the address of the adoption center in the phone book a few weeks ago. At the same time, she was relieved that the Yosu branch of the international adoption agency was within walking distance of her house. She could get the children there without taking a taxi and, more importantly, without drawing her husband's attention.

She had practiced what she would say to him if he asked where they were going.

"To the market," she told him. "We need eggs. The baby's asleep," she said, nudging the children toward the front door.

Her heart was beating hard and fast as she helped the children with their coats. They must have detected her nervousness because neither said a word. Her husband didn't respond either. In fact, he didn't look up when they slipped out.

Their march to the adoption center was a solution to the problem that had consumed her ever since her third child, a boy, was born eighteen months ago. He was the first child of her marriage to Lee Kyung. She had moved to Seoul to find work after the father of Chul Moon and Yoora had died at sea. Actually, she still wasn't certain whether he was dead or not. But he never returned to her parents' farm south of Seoul after leaving for a month-long commercial fishing voyage, so she figured he must have died or taken up with another woman. Either way, she knew she had to find employment, and Seoul was the center of commerce and jobs in South Korea. A year later, she

273

moved there with her two children. Chul Moon was four years old, and his younger sister, Yoora, was two and a half.

She met Lee Kyung at the shoe factory on the outskirts of Seoul, not far from the East Gate, where she got her first job. He was her line supervisor. Although he was a taskmaster, she was attracted to his rugged good looks, and she readily agreed to his proposal after dating him for only a few months, certain that marriage would give her and her children a better life.

After her second son was born, she registered herself and the new baby as part of the Korean family registration process, a tradition called *Hojuk*. She learned, however, that neither Chul Moon nor Yoora could be registered under their stepfather's name, and the same was true for their father since she had never married him. Her heart sank. Chul Moon and Yoora would be forever considered bastard children, without social recognition in their native land.

As they walk past slabs of fresh meat strewn over blocks of ice covered by gunny sacks, she is reminded of the night she and Chul Moon had endured the frigid night air as they waited for her husband to unlock the front door when they returned from the neighborhood meat market. She sought help at the nearby police station, where a policeman agreed to accompany them home. After a lot of shouting and pounding on their front door by the officer, it suddenly flew open, her husband bracing himself and snarling at them in a drunken stupor.

"He's a mean man." Chul Moon declared later, after her husband had dozed off on the futon that was shoved against the living room wall for the night. She squeezed her son's small hand and looked away. Her husband had locked them out of the house before. Another time, Chul Moon was upset over the belting he had received for refusing to eat moldy kimchi. "It's rotten," he had insisted, pointing his shaking finger at the offending food. But her husband was furious at the young boy's challenge to his order. There were other incidents like this, always focused on Chul Moon.

More than once she had encountered Chul Moon and his young sister arguing about her husband, usually after Chul Moon had been struck by him or received a belting for misbehaving. Chul Moon would call him a "mean man" while Yoori would insist he was a "nice man." So far, Yoori had been spared his abuse. Kyung had taken a liking to her little girl. Must be her chubby cheeks or that she always obeyed him.

At first, she had confronted Kyung about his heavy drinking and his upsetting behavior, but he threatened that worse things would happen to all three of them if she complained again. As his drunken episodes grew more frequent, Jeong Yeob didn't trust that he would continue to spare Yoora from his outbursts. However, she was sure the baby was safe because her husband was clearly fond of him, his own child.

Could she find a way out? She didn't have the means to raise all three children on her own, and Kyung was clearly not going to accept her two older children as his own. Gradually, she became convinced that foreign adoption would offer Chul Moon and Yoora a chance for a good home where they could be well cared for and get a good education. Someone told her that most of the children placed by the international adoption agency were sent to families in America. She is counting on that as she quickens her pace to get to her appointment on time.

As she rounds the next street corner, the two-story, pale-yellow stucco office building wedged between an alley and two busy boulevards suddenly appears. Jeong Yeob sighs. A large sign, "Eastern Child Welfare Society," marks the building entry. She cautiously approaches the reception desk, her children clinging to either side. "I'm here for an interview," she says in a subdued voice, hopeful the children will not understand.

The receptionist finds the appointment on a piece of paper filled with names and times. "Here it is. You can have a seat in that room," she says, pointing to a small room with bare walls where a rectangular table and two side chairs are set up in the middle.

"My children?" Jeong Yoeb asks her, not moving.

"They can go to the playroom during your interview." Jeong Yoeb can hear children's high-pitched voices through an open doorway down the hall.

The receptionist motions to a young office worker standing nearby. "Please show these children the playroom. Help them pick out some toys."

As soon as Jeong Yeob is seated, the intake worker begins asking questions, one after another, about her children and the family history. As she responds, the intake worker feverishly jots notes in her rudimentary English. She pauses to explain, "My job is to capture your family history. Your answers will be typed into a document called the "Initial Social History" for the agency's official adoption records."

Jeong Yeob responds that both she and Park Kwi Shik, the father of her two older children, were born five years apart to farm families in Chollanam-do province of South Korea. He was the third of a large family of five boys and three girls. "He is one hundred and seventy centimeters tall or rather, he was one seventy centimeters tall. He had a handsome face. He was honest."

In contrast, the intake worker notes that Jeong Yeob stands "one hundred and fifty-eight centimeters tall with a medium build, ordinary looking, active, and extroverted."

Jeong Yeob continues quietly, showing little emotion. She recounts how she and Mr. Park, a commercial fisherman, lived together on her parents' farm in the South Korean countryside after the births of their two children. "We quarreled frequently. Neither of us was sincere with each other."

She clasps her hands tightly. Her head droops.

"In September 1983, he left for a month-long fishing trip and never returned. I tried to rear my children in hardship without financial support, but I decided I couldn't do it any longer. My parents were struggling to live on their small farm and they were unhappy with me that I had not married my children's father."

Jeong Yeob recounts the rest; her move to the big city with her two young children in tow to find a job in Seoul, and how she met and married Lee Kyung a few months later.

Her voice falters for the first time as she finishes the story of her long journey to the adoption center. "I thought it would be better for the children to be raised and educated by a stable family in America. My friend told me that I would be able to see them again when they are grown."

The intake worker shifts in her chair, hesitating before nodding her head. "That's right. As soon as we find a suitable family for your children, they will go to America."

Jeong Yeob's voice hardens. "They won't split up my children, will they?"

"Oh, no. We will make sure they stay together. It's the agency's policy. Their new American family will have to decide to take both of them. "

Jeong Yeob heaves a sigh and stares at the intake worker, wondering if she has children herself, but is afraid to ask because the answer might change her mind now that the interview is coming to an end.

After explaining how the adoption process works and asking more questions about the family health history, the intake worker asks Jeong Yeob to sign some release papers. She stands up and hovers over her trembling client. "Here's a pen."

Jeong Yeob's hands shake as she scratches her signature on the paper.

"You may say goodbye to your children now," the woman says without expression.

Pausing at the playroom doorway, Jeong Yeob sees her children playing with Disney toys pulled from a big square box placed in the center of the room. She shivers, hesitating to step forward.

"Children." she says. They rush toward her with wide grins. She hugs them tightly, not wanting them to see her face or feel her tears.

Yoora wriggles out of her mother's arms. "I need to go potty." The worker whisks her away to the bathroom down the hall while Chul Moon stays behind with his mother.

Joeng Yeob turns to him. "I will be leaving soon. I can't take you and Yoora with me."

"When will you come back for us?" he demands.

"You must understand. I won't be back. I can't take care of you and your little sister any longer. You will soon be going to live with a family in America who will take good care of you both. They will make sure you go to college someday. When you become a doctor, you can return to Korea and I can see you again."

Chul Moon listens intently, trying to grasp what his mother is saying. He knows she is saying something important. He remembers that America is a place far away where they give you cookies.

Leaning close to him, she whispers with a deep sense of urgency, "You must take good care of Yoora. She will need your help."

She hugs him tight to her chest before reaching for her heavy wool coat hanging on the door hook overhead. Coat in hand, she bolts out of the room toward the reception desk, not glancing back at her son.

Chul Moon is distracted by Yoora's boisterous return from the bathroom.

"I'm back." she says. She searches the room for their mother. "Where's Oma?"

Chul Moon tugs her shirtsleeve. "She is gone," he says solemnly. "She said we must stay here and go to America where they have cookies."

Yoora stares at him in disbelief. Where could her mother have gone? She was only in the bathroom a little while. She pouts, and stomps her feet. "But I didn't give her a hug goodbye." Chul Moon clutches his sister's hand as the adoption worker steers them back to the playroom.

Jeong Leob walks home through the crowded, narrow streets, past the taxi stands and the food stalls and steaming cauldrons, numb to everything, her hands in her coat pockets. When she walks in the door, she looks at her husband and informs him about the day's events in the same detached voice she used with the intake worker.

"Tomorrow morning, the children will leave for the Pyeongtaek Children's Center, an hour-and-a-half train ride from Seoul. They will stay there until the agency finds them a new family in America."

He jerks his head around, jolted by the news. "Why'd you do that? I wondered why you were gone so long."

"I want them to have a good home. A loving home."

He spits in a bowl on the kitchen counter. "You must think you know what you're doing. No other reason for doing something that crazy."

"Yes. I know what I'm doing."

He turns away. "Yeah. Maybe so."

She cradles their baby in her arms, seeking reassurance from his warm body.

# The Invisible Delivery Man

## Marilyn Lanier

When he returned home that mild November day, James plunked a sack of clothes on their bed and pulled out a pair of used dark blue pants and matching shirt with the FedEx logo on the right pocket.

"I'm going to help FedEx drivers deliver packages downtown this holiday season."

She skewed up her eyes at him. "Downtown?"

"Yeah. The Financial District. Commercial deliveries."

He can't be serious, she thought. Downtown San Francisco is crazy congested. Streets chock-a-block with cars, taxis, bikers, tourists, business people, shoppers, and the homeless hunkered down in threadbare sleeping bags in recessed doorways night and day. Gina shrugged her shoulders, consoling herself with the thought that it was a temporary job, bound to lift his spirit after months of spinning wheels on job applications.

"It'll be a good chance to lose that ten pounds," he added. He wanted to return to one hundred and seventy-five pounds, his weight as a Masters swimmer back in the day. She pictured his six-foot-two-inch frame slimmed down a bit, though his weight seemed about right for a sixty-four-year-old man his height.

It brought back memories of the tall, lanky guy who stood alongside her at Amanda and Joe's wedding in Denver over twenty years before, a model of fitness and casual confidence. She was distracted by his long limbs. She pictured how his arms could engulf her. That thought proved a prelude to their first date. James was taller than her first husband, and kinder. He represented a new direction in her life.

Before starting his new job, James pulled his bike out of storage to get to the Daly City BART station three miles away from their home in the Sunset District. He left before dawn each morning to begin his twelve-hour day.

He quickly established his routine. After arrival at the Daly City station, he loaded his bike onto the six-car train, and rode it again the final two-mile stretch through the industrial section of South San Francisco to the gigantic FedEx dispatch warehouse near the airport. The whole trip from home to the warehouse took him over an hour.

279

He had gulped when he first saw the sea of FedEx trucks inside the warehouse, each positioned for loading of boxes nearby. After checking in, he was assigned a delivery truck for the day. A supervisor showed him the rows of boxes stacked almost to the ceiling marked for his truck. He couldn't imagine how he was going to get all those boxes into the twenty-five-foot bed, ready for his thirteen-mile drive on the 101 North to the Financial District. Somehow, with help from fellow workers, he always managed it.

Within days, he grew accustomed to the scene, though he came home exhausted every night. He was still amazed at how different it felt to drive a rickety truck so high above multiple lanes of merging commuter traffic on the 101. And Gina couldn't get over his huge appetite now that he was loading and delivering boxes instead of working on the computer every day.

Riding his bike to work was a good solution until the first Pacific winter storm blasted the city five days before Christmas.

"Do you mind dropping me off at BART tomorrow?" he asked that night. "I got drenched on my bike this morning."

The next morning, Gina jumped at the chance. Better than James navigating his bike through heavy traffic on 19th Avenue in the pre-dawn on a blustery day.

Two days later, she got his panic call about six o'clock in the evening.

"My loaner truck is stalled in the middle of Sacramento Street. The ignition key just broke in half. I can't pull over and commute-traffic is backing up as far as I can see. Damn it."

Gina shivered at the thought of him on the steep, narrow street trying to coax the truck to life, his feet on the loose floor plates offering views to the ground below.

"I can't reach the dispatcher. Guess his phone is down. People are leaving stalled buses to walk up the hill instead. They're threading around my rattletrap giving me dirty looks."

She pictured harried commuters exiting the big city buses that tied to overhead electrical lines, all scrambling from the Financial District over Nob Hill to points west.

"Can't you get roadside assistance from FedEx?"

"It's Eddy's truck. Doesn't belong to FedEx. It's his responsibility." He paused. "Hey, I'm getting a call. Gotta hang up."

He called her back again a few minutes later. One of Eddy's men had come to his rescue after thirty minutes of torment.

They celebrated the day James weighed in at one hundred and seventy-five pounds of pure muscle. It brought back sweet memories of the lanky guy who always outpaced her on weekend hikes.

His newly trimmed physique was a silver lining for a highly physical job that demanded all his energy every day. He figured he was walking between five to seven miles a day, and lifting or hauling over a thousand pounds of goods on average. She understood why he soon quit going to the fitness center with her. It was quite a contrast with his former life as a high-paid computer software executive who traveled first class and dined with international customers at fine restaurants around the world.

But his new stories were riveting; vignettes about loading stacks and stacks of boxes each morning onto his truck, wondering how they could all fit; about him schlepping boxes on dollies up crowded elevators to the workspaces designed for high tech millennials in the office towers. San Francisco was enjoying its second dot-com boom.

James couldn't believe how different things were from his life as a software exec. He felt thrust into a business world of hipster programmers, casually dressed techies who created "shoot 'em up" war games, and mold-busting social media apps aimed at the under-thirty crowd. They worked for companies with quirky names like Entropics, Pocket Gems, and Tiny Company—high-energy start-ups exploding with growth. One day he encountered a young woman in black leggings and army boots who appeared to be talking to herself. When he noticed the earbuds in her ears, he finally figured out what was going on. He laughed at his naiveté.

James slowly realized he was the invisible man with access to whole floors of office space unhampered by cubicles or interior walls. The cavernous spaces reminded him of refurbished warehouses; albeit with all the accoutrements of game areas in local bars featuring Ping-pong and pool tables at one end, as well as large coolers filled with exotic soda drinks and microbrews.

Receptionists sometimes offered him sparkling limewater and chunks of Ghirardelli chocolate before he departed for the next delivery. They had to act fast after James unloaded a heap of boxes in their office and obtained their signature on the scanner. Maybe they also sensed that he needed a little extra nourishment to keep his baggy FedEx pants from falling off his hips as his weight continued to drop.

Their thoughtfulness contrasted sharply with the hip young professionals who wouldn't stop their conversations or pull out their earbuds for a few seconds to help him find a suitable place to drop off his heavy load.

But these slights didn't bother him. What offended him was an encounter one day with two attorneys, former business colleagues, who glanced away when they saw him.

"They refused to recognize me," he exclaimed to Gina later that evening. "I couldn't believe it."

"They were caught by surprise," she said, her voice barely audible. "You were out of place, not in your usual business suit and tie. Seeing you in your FedEx uniform hauling delivery boxes made them uncomfortable."

He glanced down, wincing at his callused fingers. Gina knew he'd dealt successfully with many professionals over the years, including lawyers. He shrugged, "Maybe so."

She took his hand. "Look, honey. You're a friendly guy. You're used to everyone welcoming you. Embracing you. Trusting you. This is a big change. Now you're walking into these places as a deliveryman. You're the "FedEx Man," not James Britton, the high level software guy."

He slumped onto the nearby armchair, exhaling with the cushion as it released air. His eyes caught hers. "Guess you're right. This is the reaction in a lot of places, especially the big banks and financial firms—Wells Fargo and Bank of America. When I ask who can sign for a delivery, often no one knows. They don't even know the name of their colleague in the next cubicle."

She perched on his knees and wrapped her arms around his neck. "It's okay. You haven't changed. Your job has. You'll make something good out of this, I'm positive."

He smiled and nuzzled her neck. She sensed his optimism returning.

James talked a lot about Pablo, a second-generation immigrant who was studying to become an EMT and working part-time as a loader at the Terminal. His Portuguese father had returned to the Azores after his divorce from Pablo's mother.

"Pablo's smart, strong. A hard worker who presents himself well. He has to wake up at three in the morning to begin work at 4:30—a four-hour shift that pays a low flat daily rate with no benefits."

He asked James how he could get "field work"—work outside the vast cavern of the FedEx Terminal where he was an entry-level loader. James promised to put in a good word for him to his supervisor.

One day James encountered Pablo at the terminal, all dressed up in FedEx clothes for his new delivery job. Fellow loaders were jokingly calling him "traitor." It was tongue-in-cheek, an expression of their own aspirations. James began to realize his value as a mentor.

In bed late one night, James woke Gina with his constant pecking of keys on his laptop.

"What are you doing?" Gina asked, annoyed at the invasion of computer light and keyboard tapping.

"Making some PowerPoint slides. Roger asked me to put together a five-minute driver safety program for tomorrow morning."

"At this hour?"

"It's kinda important."

"So important that you have to use your laptop in bed?"

He hesitated. "There was an accident a few days ago. A bad accident during morning commute."

"Oh!" she said.

"One of our drivers ran over a motorcyclist who was trying to squeeze between the FedEx truck and an 18-wheeler on the 101 going toward Market."

"Oh my god. Sounds terrible. I didn't hear about it."

"It was terrible. The cyclist lost his balance and fell off his bike, but our driver didn't see him below. The driver was really messed up about it. Ended up quitting. Yesterday, Roger asked me to put together a safety program. He's determined his drivers learn how to prevent this kind of tragedy."

"How many drivers do you expect?"

"Maybe twenty. Twenty-five."

She looked away, chastened by the news. But a pattern was emerging. The franchise owner was starting to tap into James' business know-how. Another approached James about forming a specialty lighting company. Workers were benefitting from his mentoring. These overtures came as a welcome surprise to him, and reinforced her earlier prediction that he would find a silver lining in his new role.

Toward the end of the holiday season, James expressed concern about staying with the package delivery business. "I'm not sure I can continue this," he said. "It's causing some problems with my foot." He'd had surgery for a badly pronated right foot a couple of years before.

Late at night, he began to study for an insurance licensing exam—property and casualty. He passed it with a score of 95 percent and promptly applied for the certificate. Days later, he was back at the computer studying for an additional licensing exam in life and accident/health. Once again, he passed it with good scores and applied for the next certificate.

"Why not?" he asked her. "I want to be able to sell it all."

"Yes, why not?" she nodded, looking at the tall thin man flashing his ever-optimistic smile at her.

# The Island

## Marilyn Wolters

Two long days of driving through hazy mountains, flat desert scrub. A truck-stop night, Jenna folded into the front seat of her car. Driving until exhausted, eyes straight ahead. No glancing to the side. Not yet.

Jenna pulled into the dirt parking lot at three o'clock, much later than she had planned. She swung herself out from the small sedan and shook the stupor from her head and the crimps from her body, jittery from too much road and too much coffee, yet pleased at her restless muscles and numbed thoughts.

She had hoped for a dreary day shielded by clouds, but a willful sun lit the sky. With no wind to stir the sea, she could be back before nightfall. Her kayak waited atop her car.

Jenna's fingers worked the stubborn knots until she could pull the boat free from the roof rack. Straining, she eased it onto the caked mud. From inside the car she grabbed the paddles and the life vest and placed them in the boat. She checked the main pouch of her backpack for her warm jacket and lunch, and the front pocket for the plastic bag zipped tight. Everything in order, she slammed the car door shut.

On the long trudge to the shoreline, one hand clutched the backpack while the other dragged the kayak by a rope tied to its bow, bouncing it along the uneven ground. At the top of a dune, she stopped to let her bare feet tunnel into the heaped sand, welcoming the cool underneath. In front of her stretched a wide beach and beyond, the teal-blue bay.

And the island.

A photo of the island in a magazine had lain open all day on her mother's lap; her bony, spotted hands resting on the glossy image. Whenever Jenna leaned over the recliner to wipe her mother's face or clean spilled drink, her mother blinked, smiled at the photo, and whispered, "Beautiful." Her last word.

Jenna saved the magazine pressed open to that page on a shelf in the guestroom, now her room. She wished she had brought it along. The island in front of her was flat-topped and barren, not the deep warm-sunset color of the photo, but as bleached as the sand by her feet. She recognized the rocky bluffs that raised the land above the ocean, but they seemed smaller and farther than she expected. And,

285

unlike in the photo, the sea surrounding the island was empty of boats. But all for the better. She would be alone to let the harsh terrain scold her sorrow into silence.

Not much afternoon left. Winter, she reminded herself. The wind remained calm and she was ready. She retied her long, brown hair into a ponytail, tightened her jaw, and resumed her steady march.

When she reached the shoreline, she pushed the kayak into the water with her foot, holding the rope tight. There was no champagne to mark her maiden voyage, just a large aluminum bottle filled with water. She slid it under the kayak's deck. For later, she insisted, despite her thirst. Setting the paddles on top of the seat, she lowered herself and her backpack into the boat. She checked the front pocket again for the bag, still intact.

Her paddle pushed against the sea floor. The boat floated, a red-orange chunk of shiny plastic, not sleek like the other kayaks in the bay. She had studied videos of paddlers, and now copied the movements of those nearby, setting an easy rhythm. The squat boat did not always obey her paddling, but she learned to steer it against its will, swerving back and forth toward the island.

As her arms circled, images reeled through her mind of her mother, her friend, disappearing inside her drooping skin, sinking into her recliner, muscles that refused to work, a mind that refused even more. Jenna had stayed by her side, vigilant, feeding her painkillers. For months they waited together for death.

Meanwhile, other kayakers smiled when she passed, and she forced a smile back, an intruder into their festivity of sun and water. Before long, she left them behind. Waves rose from the water's surface. Wind ruffled her hair and grazed her skin. Jenna glanced toward shore. The wind was up, but she was bound to her silent promise, no retreating now. Paddling harder. And harder. Spasms of thought between heavy breaths. Tomorrow, the drive home, the wounded house. Purge the sickroom stink. Scrub away the pain.

A gust of wind powered a large wave. Water splattered inside. I am strong, she convinced herself and paddled furiously as the waves ripped the sea. She melded with the boat as she struggled to hold her course. At last, she steered onto the island's closest beach.

Her hair, loosened, blowing against her face, divided her view as she dragged the boat out of the water and onto the sand. She slogged to the base of a cliff where she found a recess in the rocks, a spot of

286

calm. She slid down against the stone, wincing at the pain in her arms and back.

The ocean puckered into hills of breaking waves capped in white foam. The air blew colder. She opened her backpack and traded her life vest for her jacket. Her gaze moved from the churning ocean to her paltry boat. She sighed and muttered, "Looks like I'll be here a while." Reaching for her sandwich, she broke off a small piece and sipped a little water. Enough for now.

She opened the front pocket, removed the large bag and set it by her side.

All that was left. Years and years, reduced to dust and traces of memory. She looked at the sky and imagined her mother gazing at the island, seeing her on what, in the photo, had been empty beach.

"Okay, Mom," she said. "We'll sit together a few more minutes, and then it will be time."

At last the roiling sea beckoned. Jenna stood, clutching the bag to her chest. Gusts of wind pushed her toward the shallows of the shore. Sprays of saltwater pelted her as she tore the bag open. When the bag was empty, she watched the ashes bob on the waves. The wind carried her tears out to sea along with her soft goodbye.

She raised her head toward the mainland. A harsh land of bony black mountains profiled against the sky and against the desert plain leading to the beach, all separated from her by the turbulent bay. No going back today, she groaned, impatient for morning.

A sliver moon interrupted the cloudless sky. Later, there would be little light. She wondered what might emerge from the rock cracks to stalk her as she tried to sleep. Forcing one deep breath, then another, she imagined the floating spray of ashes ascending, each one nesting in a different star that would soon be visible and travel with her as she lay in the cool of the sand.

She would leave in the early calm and see the island distant, lit warm by a low sun as in the photo her mother admired. She chuckled at the odd way things work out, how she would manage with her jacket, the cave, and even the kayak turned upside down.

When she returned to her rock shelter, she set the empty bag on the sand by her side. Remnants of ashes clung to the plastic. She picked it up and stroked its worn skin. Tonight she would rest with her head nestled on the bag. Tomorrow it would be trash.

# The Necklace

## Marilyn Campbell

"Any distinguishing marks?" The officer produced a one-page form and pulled a ballpoint pen from his shirt pocket that he clicked repeatedly.

Jeffrey found the clicks distracting as he turned the word "distinguishing" over in his mind, picturing a distinguished Englishman in proper gentleman's attire.

"No," he finally answered. He felt confused. He hadn't slept all night.

"Nothing then? No scars?"

"Actually, Tiffany does have a scar. Under her left knee cap—from a fall off her bike when she was nine years old."

The officer checked a box with a flourish. "Any tattoos?"

"A small one." Jeffrey splayed his thumb and index finger apart to indicate the size. "A butterfly. On her left hip." He had seen it when his daughter tried to sneak out of the house wearing a skimpy bikini. When he forbade her to wear it, she refused to talk to him for a week. For all he knew, she had multiple tattoos by now.

"We see lots of butterflies. Anything special about your daughter's?"

"I don't know." Jeffrey shrugged. "I only saw it the one time." He acknowledged that tattoos were no big deal anymore. In his day, only sailors on shore leave got them or longshoremen working the docks. Now, everyone was sporting them—especially kids wanting to emulate their favorite rock star or athlete emblazoned in body art. *Tats* they called them.

"Anything else?" the officer said. "Any piercings?"

Jeffrey wasn't sure. He raised his eyes to the ceiling, trying to concentrate when he noticed one of the asbestos panels had a large water stain. The image of his daughter's pink flesh yielding to a piercing gun, and later scabbing over the way her earlobes had after she pierced them, made his stomach turn. The practice of self-mutilation belonged to a different tribe—not the one to which Tiffany ascribed. The officer checked off some more boxes, scribbled a word in the margin, and clicked his pen a final time before returning it to his pocket.

"I don't think so," he finally said.

288

"We'll do what we can. Add her to the list of runaways."

"Aren't you going to do more than just add her to a list?" Jeffrey cried. "We don't know that she ran away. She could have been kidnapped or—what about issuing an Amber Alert?"

"Well, she is under seventeen, but you have no information that leads us to believe she was abducted. So . . ." The officer tilted his head toward one shoulder.

"You don't assign someone to investigate?"

"I'm afraid not. This isn't television, buddy. Sorry."

Jeffrey opened his mouth to protest, but thought better of it.

"Look," the officer said more sympathetically, "We've got the picture you brought in and a description. We'll issue a bulletin with the information and our officers will be on the lookout for her."

Jeffrey left the precinct in despair. He worried that his attempt to give an accurate description of his daughter had failed. Tiffany had adopted a Goth look in recent months that included pale white skin in contrast to her dyed black hair, heavy eyeliner and black lipstick. He couldn't help think back to when she was a toddler with a rosy complexion, the plump skin in the crook of her arm always a little moist and ticklish to the touch. How easy it was to reach down and run his mustache across the spot, causing her to collapse into helpless laughter. Peals of giggles filled the room as she yelled, "Daddy, stop!" But, she always came back for more.

As she grew older and thinner, Jeffrey noticed how she had become self-conscious. So much was being written about young girls struggling with body image and self-esteem issues, but he was unable to think of the right words to make her feel better about herself.

"My neck is too long," she had complained as she arched her head and pulled her neck up like a tortoise emerging from its shell. As she examined herself in the hall mirror, it did appear long and thin sitting atop her torso with her collarbones jutting out.

"It's just a phase," his wife Marie told him. "She'll fill out later." To Tiffany she had said, "Quit looking in the mirror so much."

Why hadn't Marie been more sensitive? Wasn't that what mothers were supposed to be? In fact, he had not found his wife's attitude helpful at all. Shouldn't she have been bothered more by the physical transformation of their only daughter? As her father, Jeffrey had felt unqualified to comment on Tiffany's appearance. Now, their troubled daughter was just a number on a list of runaways.

That was another thing. Marie hadn't thought that they should report Tiffany missing right away. It had been twenty-four hours before she agreed to Jeffrey filing a report.

"Give it a day or so," she had said. "It's not like she hasn't pulled this crap before. Remember when she lied about staying overnight at Felicia's house? The two of them left with those older boys from a party and stayed out all night." Marie bent over the stove's gas burner to light her cigarette. She inhaled before continuing. "Tiffany eventually showed up. It's not like she did something I hadn't done myself as a kid." She laughed and exhaled a stream of smoke toward the ceiling.

*She's too permissive,* Jeffrey had thought at the time, resenting her calm when his nerves felt like loose wires shorting out, spitting sparks.

"Times are different, Marie. There are predators out there. We don't know that Tiffany is out with other kids. What if she was taken by someone, stuffed in a van?"

"Okay Jeffrey, let's do it your way. I'll call all Tiffany's friends while you take another drive through town to look for her."

"Better call their parents, too," Jeffrey suggested. "You know kids don't answer their phones if an adult is trying to reach them." Ironically, he and Marie had been unable to call Tiffany when they first realized she was missing; Jeffrey had taken her cell phone away as punishment for breaking curfew.

"Check out all the drive-ins and convenience stores," Marie said.

"I'll cover the bus station too. Just in case." He felt better now that they were doing something.

"You might drive up to the lookout," she added. "I hear it's still a make-out spot just like it was when we parked there." Jeffrey thought he heard a smile in Marie's voice, but when he looked her mouth was set in a firm line. She was all business now, issuing orders.

Jeffrey had sunk heavily behind the wheel and cruised through main streets, and then through the alleys crossing them. He spotted the usual—garbage cans brimming with the detritus of over-consumption—much of it broken toys like the cracked plastic gym set he spied. It didn't seem that long ago when Tiffany had one of those clumsily constructed playthings too large for her tiny bedroom. Hers was a plastic mini-kitchen. He remembered that everything in her kitchen had been in shades of pink—not the soft pink of bubble gum, but in the orange-pink of gaudy flamingo lawn ornaments. She had baked warm fruit tarts in the oven, serving them on small plates edged in blue bells. How old was she then? Five? Six?

Jeffrey had found nothing alarming, so he headed outside the city limits, meandering up and down country lanes looking for clues— a sweater or schoolbook lying in a ditch. To his relief, he saw nothing.

When he arrived at the look-out, it seemed smaller. *A trick of light?* He had never been there in the daytime. The trees lining the road had grown so tall and thick that they blocked the view. You could no longer see the city from here. But it was the same spot all right. He and Marie spent many nights here when they first began dating. In fact, he remembered Marie giving herself to him on this very spot.

There was nothing much of interest here. A few plastic bags caught in brambles moved back and forth in the breeze. He got out of his car and stepped closer with the intent of releasing the bags from the clutches of the junipers, but they held on tight and ripped in his hand when he tugged at them.

Below one of the bushes something shiny caught his eye. A necklace. Jeffrey inched closer and scooped it up, studying it carefully. It was a simple heart-shaped pendant hanging on a gold-colored chain. His heart beat an extra measure, and he felt flushed. *Does Tiffany have one like this?* He couldn't remember. It looked like it had been there a while or was that wishful thinking? A bird probably dropped it. Birds were attracted to shiny objects, weren't they? *Or maybe,* Jeffrey thought. *I've found a clue.*

He pocketed the necklace and drove home quickly, wanting to confirm its link to his daughter and, at the same time, hoping to rule it out.

"I called everyone, but no one knows anything," Marie said in exasperation, when he returned home. "What now?" she challenged.

"I didn't learn anything either," Jeffrey admitted. "But I found this." He slowly pulled the necklace from his pocket and dropped it in Marie's palm.

"Where did you find this?" she said.

"At the lookout. In the bushes. Do you recognize it?"

"Should I?" She looked blank as her eyes met his.

Jeffrey's throat was dry and felt as if it were closing up on him. "Does Tiffany have a necklace like this?"

"I don't know," she said barely above a whisper.

"How can you not know?" he yelled, startling them both.

"I don't remember us buying it for her. And you know girls. They're always borrowing or trading stuff. It could be hers, but I just don't recognize it."

"I'm taking it to the police and asking them to check the area for other signs."

"How can you when we don't even know if it belongs to Tiffany?"

"Well, we can't rule it out, either, Marie. I'm going down to the precinct."

In all the confusion of answering the police officer's questions and filing a report, Jeffrey forgot to show the officer the necklace. It was such a thin clue. Probably meant nothing. The cop was right. This wasn't television and answers wouldn't be forthcoming like they were on shows where everything was wrapped up in an hour. Maybe the next step would be to look at photos of Tiffany to see if she was wearing the necklace. That would be proof of—something, wouldn't it?

"Well?" Marie asked when Jeffrey returned home. "What did they say about the necklace?"

"I forgot to show it to them."

"Forgot! How could you forget? You were the one making a big deal over it."

"Well, they kept asking questions about tattoos. And piercings."

"Jeffrey, for God's sake. You got me so worked up that I started going through Tiffany's things."

"Like what?"

"Her clothes, her jewelry, her backpack of unfinished homework."

*Finally, Marie is taking things seriously.*

"I even tried to find information on her cell phone and laptop. It was all kid stuff. No stranger was trying to lure her into a secret meeting."

"You might have missed something. Let's look at all the photos on her computer and any new ones we have here in the house." Jeffrey was still hoping the necklace would provide a clue.

After staring at pictures for an hour, Marie stood up and stretched.

"I can't stand looking at any more photos of Tiffany's freaky friends on Facebook."

"I know it's a strain on the eyes. Take a break and I'll keep looking," Jeffrey said, hunching over the keyboard. "I just want to download some older files. See what comes up."

"Suit yourself."

An hour later, he was still at it when he heard a door slam and loud voices coming from the kitchen.

*Tiffany?* Jeffrey slammed down the laptop lid just as Tiffany rounded the corner from the kitchen to her bedroom. She stopped short in her tracks when she saw him.

"Dad? What are you doing in my room? Her face was void of the dark-circled eyes she painted on each morning and her lips were a natural pink.

Rushing to her side, Jeffrey pulled Tiffany into his arms. "You okay, honey?" he croaked in a weary voice.

"Sure, I'm okay," she said into her father's shirt.

"Where the hell were you for the last twenty-four hours?" Marie shouted as she came down the hall.

"Didn't I tell you I might stay overnight at Lindsay's?" Tiffany slipped out of her father's arms, avoiding eye contact. "I could have called, but you took away my phone, remember? Wait," she said, scanning the room. "Were you guys snooping in my stuff?"

"You bet your ass we were snooping." Marie said.

Jeffrey stepped between the two. "Let's stay calm, shall we? Tiffany, your mother and I need to know where you were and with whom."

Tiffany inhaled, puffing up like a hot-air balloon about to be set aloft.

"This is a very serious matter, young lady. The police have been called."

"You called the police? Gawd!"

"We were afraid something bad happened to you. We were looking at pictures trying to find out if this necklace belonged to you?" Jeffrey held up the pear-shaped pendant.

Tiffany clutched her throat and then tried to cover up by pulling close the collar of the blouse she was wearing.

"Why do you need to know?"

"I found it at the lookout under some bushes."

"Your father thought you lost it during a struggle," Marie interjected.

"Oh man. You two sure get dramatic." Tiffany plopped down on the side of her bed. "Yeah. It's mine. I was up there with some kids, but nothing happened to me."

Jeffrey and Marie looked at one another and then Marie began to cry. Tiffany made a tentative gesture toward her mother.

"Aww, Mom."

"We have lots to talk about later, but right now I'd better call the police and tell them you've returned," Jeffrey said, turning to leave. "But, before I do, we need to know if you've added any new tattoos or piercings?"

"Why? What's that got to do with anything?"

"Well, if you continue your risk-taking behaviors, we should know so we can give the police a *full* description of your body. That way, if you're ever missing again and you turn up—unrecognizable—we'll at least be able to identify you by your markings."

"Oh," Tiffany said.

Marie cried louder.

"Think about it," Jeffrey said, as he left the room.

# The Pilgrimage

## Jack Fender

The circle of light gradually grows as we approach the exit of the south bore of the Waldo Tunnel. I gasp in surprise at my first glimpse of the bridge. How can that be? The bridge looks as majestic as it had the last time I viewed it, more than seventy years ago. I am dumbfounded. No one could have climbed that stately structure to apply paint.

I survey the scene before me, the butterflies in my stomach itching to fly free. The hills of the Marin Headlands are covered with new green carpets of early spring growth. I guide my mare Nellie toward my goal—the Golden Gate Bridge. As sure-footed as always, she carries me and my precious package across the cracked, weed-infested remains of the old roadway. It is difficult to discern where the lanes had once existed. Grass, shrubs and other types of vegetation have taken hold of any advantageous place to thrive and grow. A windblown seed finds a small crevice to live in; in time it becomes a majestic tree. Mother Nature soon reclaims her territory once the hand of man is stilled.

It takes the best part of an hour to get onto the bridge. My earlier surprise gives way to muted acceptance. It's not layers of international orange paint coating this steel wonder; it is of course, rust. The towering and once pristine structure is now covered with layers of orange rust. Only a few areas bear any traces of paint. Just above my head the huge suspension cable curves down to mid-span. It then continues on in a graceful arc upward to disappear into the fog-shrouded morning.

I stand beside the eastern handrail, at the exact center of the bridge. I look out over the Bay toward the shattered La Isla de los Alcatraces. The crumbled concrete ruins of the old prison are sprawled across its rocky, forgotten surface. It is, again, a haven for the flocks of pelicans from which it got its name. To the southeast lies San Francisco—the "City of Lights" as some called it. Now though, it's a place of darkness and utter devastation. Little or nothing remains of the lofty spires and imposing grand architectural edifices built by its inhabitants.

The view before me resembles early photographs I'd seen in my youth of ancient ruins in Mexico, the vast Maya cities buried for centuries by the jungle of vines, creepers and trees. The parks and gardens which had survived the infernos had grown and spread out to engulf the remnants of homes and buildings. I wonder if people still dwell there, cloistered in their fortress homes.

Below the bridge, the ebb and flow of the tide into and out of the Bay continues, just as it has for untold millennia. A steady, dependable force of nature, it cares nothing for the fortunes or foibles of people. As far as I can see, not a boat or craft of any kind floats upon that expanse of churning blue water.

It's strange standing here on the most famous bridge in the world. Strange because, apart from my horse, I am alone. For a moment, I close my eyes. I recall a day when I was very young, just a boy. I stood at this exact place with my father.

He and I had ridden in his car to San Francisco. It was the day I turned eight. As a birthday surprise, Dad had decided to take me to the city. I had been there a few times before, but I was younger on those occasions, too young to recall anything about the visits.

During the drive through Marin County, my father talked about his childhood memories growing up in the outer Mission, and how he loved San Francisco, but my mind was elsewhere. I wanted to see the bridge. In my classroom at school, there were large pictures on the wall of the two San Francisco bridges, the Bay Bridge, and my favorite, the Golden Gate.

It was sunny that day as we approached the twin tunnels on the Marin side. At sixty miles an hour, we raced into the tunnel bore, dad sounding the horn several times as other drivers did likewise. It was frowned upon by the Highway Patrol, but I thought it was a fun thing to do.

"Can I sound the horn on the way back, Dad?"

"You betcha," he replied.

The car burst from the semi-darkness of the tunnel into the light on the other side. There stood the Golden Gate Bridge, shrouded in fog, the morning sun illuminating the upper portions of the two orange towers standing straight and tall. It was a moment of pure joy. Minutes later, we drove onto the bridge, the tires thrumming a beat as we passed over the sections of roadbed.

After a great afternoon of driving around to witness the sights of my dad's youth, we headed home. This time though, Dad drove through the Presidio along a road that teetered on the edge of a steep cliff. The ocean swells crashed against the jagged rocks below. After several twists and turns, I caught a glimpse of one of the two bridge towers. Ahead, the road sloped downwards and then curved to the right to pass under a bridge. We made a quick left turn and parked in the lot beside the toll booths. Dad revealed a beaming smile.

"C'mon then. Let's take a walk part way over. Get a breath of that salty air. What do you say, Benjamin?"

I was speechless. In seconds, I was out of the car. Then we trotted along the path toward the bridge, my father's hand clasped mine.

"I haven't been here since I was a kid myself. It's changed quite a bit since then."

We strode onto the bridge; tourists of every race and culture walked and ran beside us. As we strolled, I looked upward, my attention drawn to the top of the south tower. I imagined myself walking along one of the cables, up toward its connection at the top. The farther you traveled, however, the steeper it became. Closer to the tower it seemed, from my vantage point, the cables rose almost vertically.

At the base of the south tower, we stopped to admire the marvel of its construction. I counted the rivets which held the steel plates together. After a hundred though, I gave up. There were thousands upon thousands of them all geometrically placed and rounded. They receded into the distance till it was impossible to resolve them individually. I noticed a large bronze plate mounted to the steelwork of the tower. Engraved upon it are the names of eleven men who died during the bridge's construction. I read each name aloud to my father who remarked that the bodies of some of them were never recovered from the waters beneath the bridge.

At the midway point where the two giant cables dip to their lowest point, we stopped to take in the view eastward. I gazed out toward Alcatraz, the East Bay hills, and beyond, the wonder of it all enthralled me. Glistening in the afternoon sun, the towering skyscrapers of San Francisco mingled with the tree-studded hills and public parks. In the distance, the gray towers and cables of the Bay Bridge receded toward Yerba Buena Island. I closed my eyes and savored the sounds about me—children laughing, the voices of people all around talking in different tongues, the incessant sound of car engines, and the thrumming of their tires on the roadbed. It was a perfect day; one I would cherish for years.

Just a few weeks later in mid-August, one morning dawned like most other days for that time of year. In the East Bay, the first rays of sun glinted over the peak of Mount Diablo and the surrounding hills. Without warning, a newer and different sun arose; it cast a blazing, white light coupled with searing heat and noise. Soon, other blossoms of nuclear horror grew and cast their radiant death upon the innocent populations of the Bay cities.

The months that followed were a torturous hell. My family and I moved from one refugee camp to another. Nuclear winter was upon us with all of its savagery. I recalled the numerous "disaster shows" on television about how the world would end. The world didn't end; the planet still lived, still existed. It was the population that ended, reduced to a few million I supposed.

I've travelled to many places in the years that followed "The Annihilation," as many still call it. Scorched, flattened cities and towns by the score I've witnessed. However, none as eerie and quiet as the cities of the Bay. The surviving populations moved toward the mountainous regions of the Sierras and the Rockies as the Plains and other agricultural regions were devastated by hundreds of warheads. Strategic planning by our enemies decided that targeting the food-producing regions was much more effective than hurling missiles at all the cities. Pure economics I suppose. After all, starvation is cost-free.

After my travels to discover encampments of other survivors, I returned to Sonoma. I lived there with my beloved wife, Sarah, and our children. Sarah lived to be almost seventy—an old age in these times. Before she passed, she asked me to promise to take her ashes to the bridge and scatter them there. As a girl, she had lived in San Francisco with a view of the bridge. She loved it as much as I did.

And that's why I'm here.

A sudden nuzzling warmth against my cheek rouses me from my reverie. Nellie desires to be off this desolate expanse of steel and concrete. She nickers nervously. She longs for her pasture, the feel of soft grass under her hooves. I pull my jacket closer to my neck to ward off the chilly morning.

With care, I unpack my sacred cargo—Sarah's ashes. It seems the wind has acknowledged my somber task; it ceases to blow so fiercely. I pour her remains out and down into the flowing waters of

298

the gate, far below. I recite a simple blessing. The wind, anxious to return to its ever-present, restless buffeting, resumes its chilling embrace.

For many years I have yearned to return here, to linger awhile amid the memories and ruin of what had once been for me, a place of joy. I know that I will never return here again. I am an old man. At seventy-eight, I'm too old to be riding a horse back and forth over miles of countryside. With luck and a prayer, I can get back to my shack in old Sonoma County. Back to my bed, back to my books.

I will remember this place with fondness every day I have left on this glorious earth.

# The Stick House

## Janice Rowley

There she is.

Under that first big tree at the edge of the woods. Hair still blond. Must be five, six years old? So serious, left hand cupping her right elbow, index finger stroking her bottom lip, focused on that small clearing where the sun has gained a hold through the canopy of oak and dogwood sharing the Mississippi bottomland with the pine and the sweetgum. The resinous smell of dry needles and sap and the mustiness of decayed leaves fill the air. No breeze, must be ninety degrees.

She has a plan. I can feel it.

She moves toward the clearing now with a firm step, stops, comes back to the tree, stoops, and picks up—what? Hard to make it out from here. She tucks something under each arm and, with elbows close to her body, stoops again. She picks up a good-sized rock with both hands and walks to the center of the clearing, drops the rock and—oh, I see—the rock is for the two corncob dolls, dressed in matching calico dresses and caps. She props them just so against the rock, points a stern finger, and says, "You stay right there and don't move until I get back."

A short backward glance and she's off, foraging among the trees, picking up small logs and limbs discarded by age or wind. Arms full, she returns to the clearing. The dolls have been obedient—they haven't moved.

"I'm back," she announces. "The new house will be ready before suppertime."

How methodical she is.

I watch as she lays the foundation walls and divides the space into rooms with the smaller limbs. Back out she goes, gathering rocks.

"What a busy little girl you are," I say, knowing she can't hear me from this distance. How strong she is to carry such big ones, and to find so many in this Delta forest.

Twittering birds are scattered through the trees, cheerleaders spurring her on. A squirrel pauses halfway up the spruce to watch this small, inspired human. There is an intermittent rustling under the litter layer and in the short growth around the clearing. Birds digging for worms in the softer soil? It's early yet for possums or raccoons, but maybe a rat.

She's picked out her rocks and arranged them to furnish the stick house.

"This is your room in here," she says, carrying the two dolls to the small square with two small rocks against the outside wall. "You have to share, but you have your own bed. Now you stay in your room while I make supper."

As she steps through the small gap from the dolls' bedroom into the front room, she stops, and stares at the perimeter walls a foot in front of her.

"I forgot the door," she exclaims, flips her face to the sky and flaps her arms to her sides. "Well, we don't want to get shut in here and not be able to get out." She stamps over the wall, turns, picks up the log, walks away from the clearing, and disappears from view.

The silence fills with insect flicks and heat waves. How long has she been out there?

Oh, good, I hear her shuffle through the leaves, closer now. She's back, with one medium size and one very small piece of wood. She places the larger one in the vacant space, and the smaller one at a ninety-degree angle away from the foundation.

Hands on hips, she considers her handiwork and, with a smile, declares, "There. Now it's done."

She walks through the new doorway and into the kitchen, digs her hand into the pocket of her green, polished-cotton pants. I know those pants have deep pockets; her mother always put deep pockets on her pants because of the collections she found on washday.

She pulls out a handful of split pecans, eats the sweet meat, and lays the shells on a rock at her feet. The shells now empty; she fills two with dirt, spits in them, and stirs it around in the shell with a twig. A shell in each hand, she enters the doll's bedroom.

"You get to eat first, Sandra. You have been very good today," she says, picking up the closest doll. She dips her little finger into the shell and offers it to Sandra, but withdraws her arm in hesitation. Something has caught her attention. She stops mid-feeding, jerks her head toward the deeper wood.

What's out there?

I hear the crackle of dry leaves and brush, too heavy for a bird or even a squirrel.

"Uh oh," she says. "That big, old pig, I bet."

She sure moves fast. With Sandra and friend in hand, she's out of the house in a second, without going through the front door. But she's not running, no, she's skipping fast, head down, skirting each cow patty on her path through the pasture. She approaches the fence and cautiously reaches through the barbed wire, places the dolls on the other side, lifts two of the strands, and moves through headfirst.

Will she safely make it through this time, no cuts on her arms or legs, no tears in her clothes? I hold my breath as she barely makes it without injury, picks up the dolls, and moves off at a slower pace.

She's approaching her grandfolk's farm. The goat ignores her, munching away in the front of the house. Doesn't look like he'll chase her today.

How I love the climbing roses around the porch of the old house, except for their plentiful sharp thorns as dangerous as barbed wire. She stops at the nearest trellis, holds the dolls to her chest, and moves her face to the small brilliant red and yellow petals.

I breathe in their deep, rich perfume with her. Even at this distance in time, it fills my nose, rising to my eyes, bringing tears of sweet nostalgia.

"Janice? Where are you? Come on in, and wash up. It's almost suppertime."

A beautiful woman—raven hair, brown eyes, and that warm, sweet tone—appears from the back of the house. She was so young when I was so young. My heart and breath catch with the memory.

"I'm here, Mother. I'm coming," she calls and walks on through the yard to the back of the house, swinging a doll in each hand, scattering the Bantam hens pecking at the corn in the dust, and out of sight into the kitchen.

I smile and sigh.

~*~

Journal Entry—May 2, 1987

"Country sounds bring visions of summers spent with grandparents, wandering as only my child did, imagining the world as I wanted it to be. Building my future home with sticks laid out in the dust to be my walls, rocks for furniture, and the sky and boughs of trees as my roof. The corncob dolls were my family, and I raised them with care, and of course discipline. The birds were my companions, and the squirrels, the chickens and the cows. And don't forget the goat, what a stubborn one he was. Country roses smelling so sweet, the cow dung in the fields reminding me where I was, and not to step there."

# The Tax Man and Me

## Don Dussault

In the paneled interview booth in not-exactly gray, not-exactly beige, a color trying hard to be no color, I sat across from the fiftyish man perusing the papers spread across the table between us. In desperate need of diversion, I studied the movements of his gray eyes and how his gray suit jacket separated from his shirt collar, denoting an imperfect fit. I imagined a coroner's description of him as "a well-nourished white male."

As he concentrated on the documents I'd brought, turning over one after another, scribbling numbers on a legal pad, I tried to appraise his mood and whether he had a kind disposition. After two hours, the best I could come up with was *businesslike, hopefully fair.* That's as favorable as you can get in an IRS agent, but then my habit is to look toward the bright side.

At last he raised his gray eyes to meet mine. "You keep excellent records. Five years of receipts, bills, taxes, postage, home office costs, DMV, a writing conference, all there, every expenditure accounted for." Ready to launch a big grin, I maintained a circumspect attentiveness.

He had more to say. "Your deductions are appropriate and reasonable for a self-employed writer. For all five years." Here comes the verdict, I thought, unable to suppress my rising hopes a minute longer. He looked again at his notes. Frowning, he scratched the gray hair at his temple. My hopes hovered, straining to stay aloft. Many people frown when they're thinking. "However," he said, "you pose a dilemma for me. I hate dilemmas."

I managed not to stammer. "Is anything wrong?"

"If I adjudicate these five years as deductions for a hobby, you'll owe us some back taxes. With interest, of course. You did enter two writing contests. Your email and postal records list queries to 386 literary agents, a serious number. Of those, you received twenty-one replies, all form letter rejections. Your submittable file lists sixty-seven rejections for five story titles."

He paused. Was he assuring himself I'd heard his numbers correctly or commenting on my production of a mere five stories over five years? He went on, "Here's my dilemma. Your five years of claims could be a scam to reduce your taxes." He paused again to let that sink in. "You know, queries for a book that's a bunch of typed pages, titles slapped on old college essays. We at the IRS don't present ourselves as literary critics. We're damned good with numbers."

I could have nodded to let him know I understood and respected his skills. I could have launched a firm denial of any scam, leaning heavily on injured innocence. Best to maintain an unadulterated diffidence, meaning keep my face blank and my mouth shut.

"In five years you've sold no fiction, nonfiction, or poetry. You've given none away. Self-published nothing. You've won no contests, not one honorable mention. You haven't earned one cent from your writing. If you really are a writer, you're the lousiest writer I've ever audited."

I was stunned. No agent or editor had dared utter or write such a judgment. Some of their most terse rejections had a soft, almost kind, tone. I had to reply to this man. "Writing is a tough field to break into. It's more competitive than . . ." (what would he know about?) "NFL football. It takes time. You've got to admit I'm tenacious."

"Hmm. Yes, you are tenacious. As a working hypothesis, we can qualify you as a hobbyist. We'll look forward to the next tax return you'll submit. But as a sample of a writer's endeavors, sorry, these returns are not what we're looking for."

# The Thinker

## Janice Rowley

Evelyn Powers' intuition told her this was not just any job interview. A burst of anticipation pushed her through the revolving doors and into the lobby of the Hammersmith Building. *Smack in the middle of San Francisco's Financial District*, she thought, jaw tensed.

Evelyn's specialty in statistical analysis made this little-known, even secretive, research group appealing. Their intense pursuit of Evelyn, coupled with her current employer's disinterest in her latest passion (the effects of intention on ambient fields, including gravity) fired her determination. But here, a short elevator ride away, was interest, maybe support, and maybe more.

"Maybe my destiny," Evelyn whispered as she walked a little faster, held her head a little higher. This lobby echoed success. The click of heels on marble, the myriad ring tones for calls and alerts, the pitch of confident voices. Leather and wool, soap and cologne.

Evelyn passed the main bank of elevators and turned right to find that one restricted to the fourteenth floor, stepped in and entered the private code provided by Human Resources. A rare smile played on her full, unpainted lips and spread over prominent cheekbones and up to eyes that shifted from green to blue and settled on hazel as the doors closed.

~\*~

A ten-minute walk north, Adam Penseur returned his cell to the antique bedside table. For the first time in over twenty years, he called in sick to his employer on the fourteenth floor of the Hammersmith Building. As he disconnected, a chill gripped him. This was not just a cold. This felt different. Penseur buried his head under a pillow to block out the fog and the pain.

~\*~

The elevator doors opened and Evelyn faced a notice on the wall opposite that read "Reception" with an arrow pointing right. She stepped out; her chestnut bob lightly rippled as she crossed the gap into the corridor. A definite change from the atmosphere in the lobby. Beyond quiet, close to silence. Carpet hid footsteps. No phone sounds. The only smell was that of warmed vents from forced air.

There were more frequent turns than Evelyn expected in a building this size. And no signs. She passed one door for each turn of the corridor with no clue of what lay behind them. Empty or secretive? She walked, she turned, and she arrived at a dead end where she found, as promised, a reception desk. It fronted a wall graphic spread over fifteen feet of pale gray background: a muted white shadow outline of a perpetual motion machine overwritten by *Thought in Motion – Reinventing Tomorrow* in bold black script.

The receptionist, who blended into this background, directed Evelyn to a door tucked, as if by afterthought, into the far corner. She was to wait inside. From the doorway, Evelyn saw it was a small office, square but for an alcove in the extreme right corner filled with a ladder-back chair. The only other chair, a once-black leather swivel with a worn head-sized discoloration below the top edge, adjoined the desk.

One long, two-drawer, gray metal file cabinet sat just within reach from the alcove chair. *Someone lacks organizational skills*, she thought, disgusted by the jumble of manila folders atop the cabinet sharing the space with a Starbucks' Go-Cup and a small graphing calculator with the black cover open to a blank screen.

Evelyn felt a fleeting moment of disquiet as she considered what might be behind the unmarked doors off the corridor that brought her here. She moved to the window, behind the desk and stretching almost to the popcorn ceiling. Slats of white metal blinds sat flat at the top, dingy cords hung down the side, and on the ledge sat a nameplate: Adam Penseur. Evelyn considered the view and made a mental note to add office requirements to her contract demands.

The brilliant September San Francisco sun streamed over the nameplate and flooded the room, intruding into the grayness. Below the sun and beyond downtown, out past the Avenues sat a bank of fog, offstage awaiting its cue. Evelyn turned back to the interior and recognized the black and white poster on the wall to her right. It was the facade of the Musée Rodin in Paris. It reminded her of her own visit with her grandmother (and namesake) on Evelyn's twenty-first birthday. She owned a similar poster of the Orsay Clock.

The desk, more gray metal, supported another disorganized mass of files, a bright yellow smiley-face coffee mug (the only color in the room), and the remains of a sculpture with a brown, stinky piece of banana peel atop a rough rounded section. She wrinkled her nose and inspected the piece. She thought it might be *The Thinker*. Time and use had erased much of the sculpture's details, as if used as one large worry bead.

As Evelyn settled into the chair in the alcove, the door opened inward. A large man crossed the worn brown carpet in three strides, breathing noisily as big men do. He reached the file cabinet, leaned down and opened the bottom drawer before sensing Evelyn's presence. His head jerked right and his gunmetal blue eyes widened, but otherwise his expression did not change. He ignored her, flipped through several file folders, withdrew one, closed the drawer, walked back across the room, and out. Evelyn closed her mouth. The man had not looked like her vision of an Adam, (she pictured him as slim and muscular, even if sloppy), this surely was not his office, and if he were her interviewer wouldn't he have acknowledged her?

Evelyn checked her watch, and as she did so, she had an uncomfortable thought: what if this was part of the interview, a test? She opened her laptop on her knees and typed with her head lowered to the screen while her eyes scanned the room. She saw no evidence of a camera.

Evelyn's interview, scheduled for nine forty-five, was overdue. Her computer clock glowed ten fifteen. The slight by the intruder, along with the unexplained wait, grated on Evelyn. Her feet tapped to an unheard rhythm, and she felt her pulse rate quicken behind her ear. Knees did not make a stable surface for typing even when still, and the desk didn't have an inch of clear space. She stepped out of the room in search of the receptionist.

Evelyn found an empty chair and corridor. She returned to the office, stood with hands on hips in frustration when the door opened, and, again, the man appeared.

"You're still here?" he glared at Evelyn.

"Obviously," she blurted, and then caught herself, and continued in a softer tone, "Is the receptionist back at her desk? My appointment was scheduled for a half-hour ago."

The man moved the file folder in his hand to cover a smile, and said, "You had an appointment with Penseur?"

"I had an appointment with Human Resources. An interview. If I have to wait much longer, I need a place to work with my laptop," Evelyn waved her arms to encompass and draw attention to the desktop clutter and the small office space, "and away from that banana smell."

"Oh. I'll find someone from HR and send them in. Clean off the desk. Penseur is a slob. He's sick today and you'll be doing him a favor. I'll just return this file and get out of your way."

"Thank you. Sorry for the rant. I'm a little nervous and this office is . . ."

The man flapped a hand to wave off her comments as he exited the office.

She chased after him, calling "Where's the bathroom?"

The man pointed to the door on his right as he sped down the hall.

Evelyn, hands back on hips, lips pursed, studied the desktop, then visited the bathroom, returning with a mountain of paper towels. She grabbed the banana peel with a triple layer of paper towel and wrapped it in a tight bundle and wiped off the residue on the sculpture with another sheet and tossed all in the trash. She then arranged the desk's surface items into categories and stacks. The sculpture was a mess of nicks and gouges, and Evelyn questioned why anyone would want to keep it, but it wasn't hers to discard. She laid it on a paper towel on the floor next to the desk, using its former space for her laptop. A quick swipe over the chair and she settled in. As she began work on a project, Jake from Human Resources opened the door, introduced himself, and invited her to follow him.

~*~

Two days passed before Adam Penseur breached the thinning fog in his head and the streets outside his Bush Street apartment to return to the fourteenth floor of the Hammersmith Building. He approached his office door and paused, hand stretched toward the knob. A beat had been missed; something had been lost. He wrinkled his brow in confusion and after a few seconds, opened the door and stood on the threshold. Head to one side, like a bird catching the sound of a cat's whiskers, his face in concentration and his deep brown, usually expressionless, eyes focused on the desk across the room. It was wrong. Penseur glanced behind him at the empty reception desk, down the hallway at the unmarked doors and shook his head to clear the fog. He was in the right place, but it was wrong. His feet moved forward one reluctant step at a time, torso angled in resistance, until he reached his desk.

Penseur removed a banana from his coat pocket and placed it in the middle of the desk, where the *something missing* should have been.

The middle fingertips of his left hand touched first one stack of folders then another as if they might disappear if awakened. Mouth slack, his round wire-framed glasses slipped down his nose, his eyebrows jittered as he stared at the center of the desk. It was gone. *The Thinker* was gone.

Penseur reeled from one part of the small office to another, opening drawers, searching corners, under the chairs, in the desk kneehole. It was nowhere. He sagged into the chair, placed his elbows on the desktop and his head in his hands. If anyone heard his keening, they did not interrupt, but he was used to not being heard.

Penseur was paid to think. To think. To collect and analyze data. He worked alone, well, almost alone. He needed *The Thinker*. And, now, it was missing. They had been together since Penseur was seven years old. A gift from his grandfather. On the bottom of the sculpture's base, Penseur had taped a John Dewey quote:

*"Every thinker puts some portion of an apparently stable world in peril."*

That quote, and the sculpture ruled Penseur's life. He had changed his name to match his passion, his life's focus – scouring the past to invent the future. His work, quantified and qualified by the files in this room, the analyses he'd spent thirty years amassing, always with *The Thinker* to touch and to share his soul.

Penseur's keening ceased, his face reflected firm resolve; he pulled out his laptop along with his cell and began an urgent search for a duplicate sculpture. He ordered overnight delivery for six possible replacements, but he worried. What if they are too big or too small, the wrong color, the wrong material? It had to be identical or it wouldn't be the same, not for Penseur.

Penseur left his office with the orders on their way, told the receptionist he still did not feel well, didn't ask who had been in the office, and didn't ask why his desk was rearranged. Penseur didn't ask where the sculpture was; it was too late for that. A trace of a smile and a hard-edged glint in the receptionist's eyes did not fail to register with Penseur. He believed she hated *The Thinker*; she pestered him to replace it. Well, now he had to.

Penseur did not return to his office until noon the following day after which time he expected the deliveries. By four o'clock he knew that none of the sculptures were right.

The receptionist, leaving for the day, opened the door to see if he was still there, and saw him sitting at his desk with the only smile she'd ever seen him wear. It was disconcerting, and the sight so disturbed her she turned and closed the door behind her, shook her head and left the building. Penseur had just made a phone call to a small collectibles shop in Sonoma, two hours north. He was so certain this was the duplicate sculpture he felt something close to happiness. Penseur almost slept well that night.

*The French Connection – all things collectible*, would open at ten o'clock. Penseur crossed the Golden Gate Bridge at eight-thirty that morning. He didn't remember the fog being this thick when he left his apartment; it seemed to close in behind him as he drove. The spires of the bridge were now obscured in his rear-view mirror. The further he drove, the thicker the fog, hiding the landscape of Marin County as he passed by Sausalito, San Rafael, and Novato into Sonoma County, then heading east from Petaluma. He almost missed the turn onto Arnold Drive; the fog was closing. Once on Broadway, the storefronts became hazy.

Just a few blocks to go, Penseur thought, as he began to experience lightened gravity and blurred surroundings. The shop window with its white, italicized French script and pilaster borders floated in a gray mist, beckoning.

~*~

*Thought in Motion* hired Evelyn Powers. The company was growing, as predicted by the analyst, Adam Penseur, who had walked out one day and never returned.

Office space was in demand, but Evelyn was assigned Penseur's old office, and her contract included specific stipulations regarding that space. She was met on her first day by a painter with buckets of pale yellow paint, a handyman with bright window coverings, a carpet representative with samples, and the delivery of a desk, plush chair, and locking upright file cabinet.

Four special items she hand-carried: a framed poster from the Musée d'Orsay depicting the Orsay Clock, a 12-inch replica of Rodin's Eve, and an apple. The fourth was a nameplate, which she placed on the front of the desk facing the door: Eve Power.

The door opened. A large, familiar man followed. Eve watched as he glanced at the sculpture, the locking file cabinet, and the nameplate, grinned, winked, and said, "Ah," closing the door behind him.

# The Walking Wounded

## Ian Nevin

Michael woke in a homeless shelter in San Francisco. It was November 11, 2008; Veterans' Day, and five years after his deployment to Iraq. He needed a job and he needed to get out of the shelter. Perhaps, today would be his lucky day since it was a holiday for men like him.

Michael shaved, dressed in his best clothes, and set out to find a job. He walked the streets for hours before he saw a small convenience store with a "Help Wanted" sign posted on the window, and "Bless our Veterans, Show a sign of service for a discount." Seeing these, Michael walked into the store and asked for the owner.

"Can I help you sir?" The owner asked.

"I'm looking for a job. You have a help wanted sign and you have a Bless our Veterans sign. I'm a veteran," said Michael.

The store owner studied Michael from head to toe before saying, "Sorry, I made a new hire yesterday, we're not looking for anyone else."

As Michael turned to leave, a young, beautiful woman walked in.

"Emma," said Michael, surprised and happy.

The woman turned, looked at him, and replied, "My name's not Emma, you must have me confused with someone else."

"I'm not confused," said Michael. "I know you. We dated a few years ago. I'm Michael, Michael Kimble."

"I never dated a Michael Kimble. I'm sorry you must have me confused with someone else," said the woman, who now looked scared and moved toward the owner.

"Sir, I'm going to have to ask you to leave. You're making this woman and me uncomfortable," said the owner, with a touch of anger.

Michael left the store having lost some of his earlier optimism and continued his walk. He found a bench and as soon as he sat, a young beagle walked up and nuzzled his leg.

"Hey boy, what are you doing here?"

Michael noticed the dog didn't have a collar, but an indentation in his fur indicated he had once worn one. "Do you want to stay with me?"

The dog barked his agreement.

312

"Ok, let's stick together," said Michael. "Since we're gonna be pals, I might as well tell you my story. I'm a veteran, which means I was in military service. I never meant to be in a war, though. "War, war never changes." That quote by Ulysses S. Grant stuck with me when I was deployed into Iraq."

He scratched the dog behind his ears.

"I graduated high school back in June 2001. I needed a way to pay for college, and my best friend, Johnny, talked me into joining the reserves. Johnny said, 'Michael, man, we have no chance of any scholarships. What do we do? We play video games and smoke pot. We don't have rich parents who can pay for college, but we could do like my older brother, Freddy. He served in the army reserves and they helped pay for his college.' The government would help me pay for college. That was my hope anyway."

The dog sniffed at Michael's pocket. He had forgotten about the jerky he'd been given at the shelter this morning. He pulled out a piece and gave it to the pooch.

"When I joined the reserves, I thought . . . no, I *believed* I would never need to take a life, nor go onto a battlefield. One weekend a month and training during the summer, that was it. Oh, how wrong I was. After the terrorist attacks on September 11, I knew it was only a matter of time until I had to disrupt my education at Sacramento State. I got my letter in 2003 saying I was deployed to Iraq. My girlfriend Emma, told me, 'I will always be there for you, Michael. I love you, and I'll stick it out with you.' If only she had really meant it."

Michael gave the dog another hunk of jerky. "Before going to Iraq we had to go to a real boot camp. Unlike the reserves training program, this drill sergeant was cruel and humiliated everyone. He told me every day that my family hated me. He told me that I had no future. He said I would die. He gave me nicknames to further dehumanize me. Basic training was true hell."

Michael's mind went back to those horrible days as if a video played in his head. The drill sergeant's crew cut atop a purple face appeared inches away from Michael's face.

"What's your name private?"

"Sir, Michael Kimble, Sir."

"Bullshit. It's Scumbag now. Do you like that name, Private Scumbag?"

"Sir, No, Sir."

"Look what we have here, a frickin' Einstein. Listen up, Shit for Brains. I got your name, I got your ass."

Michael shuddered as he came back to reality and stroked the dog again to calm himself. "I was told the purpose of boot camp was to break you down in order to build you up. That was true in every facet of this hell. My squad was sent to Iraq on September 11, 2003, two years after the anniversary of the 9/11 attacks. For the first six months, we led border checks, led the security forces.

"The day that changed my life forever was the day we were sent to stop a group of insurgents and liberate a compound. I went there armed with a .50-caliber sniper rifle and three squad mates who turned into my best friends."

Michael closed his eyes and could once again see the desert compound that was far away from any known city. "As we entered the outskirts of the compound, we split up into two teams: Recon and Assault. I was on Recon, the safer team at the time. As I scouted the base, I saw fifteen armed guards with AK-47s. I was terrified. I did not want to kill anyone. I did not sign up to kill. I just wanted to go to college. Fear coursed through me and I shivered from head to toe. I reported to Assault that there were fifteen guards armed to the teeth. I called Base to order back up as we were outmanned and outgunned. As I waited for them to respond I readied my sniper rifle and gazed down the scope aiming at a man's head."

Michael mimicked holding a rifle and pointed his right arm in front of him. A teenage boy across the street quickened his pace, giving several looks over his shoulder at Michael.

"Soon I heard a large explosion from a breaching charge, and saw the Assault team rush in with guns blazing. We killed three people trying to escape. Then one man went to ring the alarm. I blew his head clean off his body." Michael shook his head and looked around the bench as if seeing the bone and blood everywhere.

"After the gunfire subsided, we left our surveillance post to go down in the compound. Only one person was left unharmed. That man had a bag over his head. I didn't know if he was one of ours. When I pulled off the bag and took the gag out of his mouth, he screamed in Arabic. My commanding officer put the gag back in his mouth, handcuffed him, and threw him over his shoulder. We boarded the Humvee that had taken us there. I was worried and scared. Anderson, the driver, was ordered to take us to the base. We had not gone far when there was a large explosion from a roadside improvised explosive device. I passed out from that explosion."

The dog looked up at him with sad eyes. Michael gave him another nuzzle around the ears. "It's okay, boy. I woke up in the hospital. I was hazy at first, but I soon saw there were medical machines all around me. I felt a breeze, a cold breeze run across my scalp. I touched my head and felt bandages. I started to freak out and tried to pick myself up and couldn't. My left arm would not respond. I looked down, and screamed when I saw a stump instead of an arm.

"A nurse rushed into the room and put her arm on my shoulder. She said, 'Michael, you are going to be okay. You were found in a wrecked Humvee and your left arm was crushed. We had to amputate. Let me get Dr. Morton for you.'

"I was brave though, little pooch, and wanted to be selfless and forget my own pain. I needed to find out about my buddies. I yelled, 'To hell with me. What about the rest? What of my squad mates? What of the other men who fought?'"

The dog winced at the sound of Michael shouting.

"Sorry, Boy. I'll try to keep my temper in check." Again, he petted the dog who lowered his head onto Michael's lap.

"Now, where was I? Oh, yes. Dr. Morton came to my bedside. His face was glum, and he said, 'Michael, the important thing is you're alive. It could have been much worse.' When I heard that, I knew the worst of what had happened. No one else survived. The men I spent over six months of my life with were now gone. They were dead. Anderson, Peterson, Miller, Kowalski, and Cook. I had to live with the guilt that I was the only survivor." He gave a deep sigh.

"My other injuries were third-degree burns on my face, right arm, and legs. I was awarded a Purple Heart for being wounded, and a Medal of Honor for my mission. Then after I returned home, I received a broken heart from my girlfriend, Emma, who could not deal with the changes to my body and looks."

The sound of her voice haunted him. "Michael, I think we need to breakup. I was just accepted to Harvard, and I can't take care of you anymore, I'm sorry. Besides, I met someone else while you were gone."

"Emma's voice was as cold to me as my aim toward those I killed. I was not able to continue schooling due to my PTSD. I could not concentrate. The waiting list for counseling by the VA was just too long, a year for an appointment, and I gave up. The burns never fully healed, so I look deformed and sick. Without the ability to take a job, I became homeless. My family couldn't take care of me. My mom died of lung cancer while I was gone, and my dad has kidney disease and lives in a nursing home. My distant family didn't feel obligated to take care of me. Hell, strangers won't even look at me. Little children run away screaming, I look like a monster to them."

A large black SUV parked across the street. There were American flags strapped to the antenna.

"So, that's my story. What about you? I need to come up with a name for you, little guy. I'm going to call you Fifty," said Michael, as he petted the sleeping dog on his lap.

A well-dressed middle-aged woman and her small daughter walked hand-in-hand across the street.

"Jesse." yelled the little girl who ran up and hugged the sleeping dog.

As she raised her head, a look of terror crossed her face when she saw the burn scars on Michael's face.

"Mommy!" she screamed. "He has our doggy."

"That's our dog. What are you doing with him?" asked the mother.

"He must have run away. He came to me and I gave him a new name, Fifty, like my bullets. He likes me. He's the only thing left in my life. Please don't take him away from me."

"I wouldn't expect a bum to understand," she said, as she looked down at him. "I bet you wasted your life on drugs and alcohol. If I gave you any money, you'd probably spend it on booze. Jesse is our dog. He doesn't deserve to be with you."

The woman picked up the dog, set him down on the sidewalk and put a collar and leash on him. She walked the dog to her SUV with the flags waving. As they drove away Michael saw a "Support our troops" bumper sticker.

"God damn hypocrite," Michael yelled, waving his fists in the air. "That's it. I can't take it this anymore. Veterans' Day is supposed to be a day meant to honor people like me, yet I'm treated like a piece of shit. My drill sergeant was right; I am a piece of shit. I've had enough, enough of this disparity, enough of the discrimination."

Michael pulled out his combat knife and stashed it in his jacket, then waited for a city bus. He waited for two stops then pulled out his knife and started swinging. People ran to the back of the bus and cowered in fear. The bus driver pulled over and radioed for help.

A few minutes later, two uniformed police officers boarded.

"Sir, put the knife down. Put it down now, sir," said the older officer who looked like he was in his fifties.

"No," Michael screamed. "I fought for this nation, and now this is all that's left—my knife. That's it, I have had enough."

The demeanor of the cops changed. The younger one's face softened and looked Michael straight in the eye. "Thank you for your service."

Michael lowered his knife as tears of gratitude streamed down his face.

# The Window

## Rebecca Smith

Paint splattered across the canvas, beyond the easel, and onto the floor as brushes dipped, paint arched, and a new creation emerged. Sunlight flared in from high windows, but the best spot was next to the bay window. It offered a view of the harbor, boats, sunsets, and memories.

She dipped her brush into the pool of colors and watched the sunlight roll across the sable. Burnt copper curls bounced as Elizabeth staccatoed paint on top of paint in time to Paul McCarthy's "Nod Your Head." She had to complete this commission today. Rent was past due, and the landlord would come knocking on her door any day now.

Elizabeth took a breath and stepped back to evaluate her painting. She turned the music off and opened the window for fresh air. Dappled light skipped across the water and flashed when it hit the chrome whirly-bob on her deck. She tuned in to the harbor sounds. Gentle waves lapped on fiberglass hulls, and lines clanged against steel masts. A lonely wind pushed distant chimes into service. She took melodies and translated them into acrylic images. The paintings captured sights, sounds, light, and magic. They weren't just pictures. They were tactile, experiential.

Lingering on the cusp of anonymity, she sold barely enough to pay the rent while her name remained unknown. She preferred it that way.

Now, they wanted more.

Not just one painting, but a series of pictures—a story. She told the galleries that each picture *was* a story.

"Then we want a book," they said.

But the story didn't come. The paintings wouldn't come. All she could do was look at the stark white canvases and blobs of paint with no inspiration to pull out the brushes. The canvases sat there, blank, taunting her for months. Barely able to do more than get out of bed, she made tea, wrapped a shawl around her shoulders, and stared out to the bay for hours. The searches, pleads, and whispers to her muse—fruitless. She only saw birds flapping about and scavenging for bones.

The bald-headed hyena of a landlord was done with waiting for his meal; he wanted that rent check or he wanted her gone. She'd come home to an eviction notice on her door. Elizabeth ripped it down and barreled into her flat, rushing to get inside before the vertigo hit.

Elizabeth dropped her groceries on the counter and braced herself. When the room started spinning, she slid down the cabinets and collapsed on the floor in tears. She knew she'd done this to herself. Her muse was unreliable. She'd banked on a mutually beneficial relationship with the creature, but the muse turned out to be a flake and only showed up when it wanted. Mostly when she was happy. But she couldn't remember the last time she smiled. Her mood was like a damp coastal fog hanging low. Sounds, sights, and smells lost their appeal.

Joel leaving had taken the wind out of her sails. Alone and adrift, currents of despair carried her along in a downward spiral. For the first few days, she wondered how she'd survive without breathing. The tight band across her chest was like a boa constrictor, taking more space away with each exhale. Her heart, shattered into pieces, was useless. And she was cold, so cold. The fog crept inside of her, seeping apathy to all extremities.

The only thing that kept her going was the care and feeding of her dog, Pony. A pint-sized Pomeranian, Pony had never really liked Joel and was delighted to have Elizabeth all to himself, once again. Joel hadn't much fondness for Pony either and had the bloody ankles to prove it. Unbeknownst to Elizabeth, Pony's ankle biting days ended with a punt across the room by Joel. After that, Pony just kept to his crate until Joel left.

It started out innocently enough. They met while walking along the harbor in Bodega Bay. Joel tossed a tidbit of fish to Pony, who dragged Elizabeth over to him.

"Dog walk you often?" Joel asked.

"Only if there are treats involved," Elizabeth replied.

"And I was figgurin' those fiercely toned arms came from your Pommy-flex," Joel teased.

Elizabeth turned to look at his boat so he wouldn't see the blush.

"Name's Joel. And this little fellah is . . . ?"

"Pony."

"Pleasure." Joel tossed Pony another scrap.

"This is yours? She's beautiful." Elizabeth ran her hand along the taunt bowline.

319

"Earns her keep chasin' salmon." Joel fondly slapped the bow.

Elizabeth's gaze drifted past Joel, past the bay, and out to the open sea. "Long way out there, eh?

"S'pose so. Gives a man pause to reflect on opportunities. Don't like to let 'em drift by." He grinned at her.

Elizabeth held tighter to the leash as if a ten-pound dog could help her balance. Images of Jane Wilder typing novels on a boat danced in her head. She could romance the paint, create cliffs rising from the sea on her canvas.

The tug on her arm pulled her back to the dock. Pony darted toward the boat, unable to resist the alluring smell of fish and promises of treats.

Elizabeth began to walk to the dock every day. Then, she brought an easel. Joel was an easy subject. He told stories while he worked on the boat and wrapped her in dreams that carried her away.

Her best paintings came during this happy time. She got into the galleries, gained clients, and won best of class at the fair. With her heart wide open, her business flourished and money flowed.

Elizabeth took Joel's critiques as encouragement and strove to do better. His suggestions pushed her to explore fresh aspects of her art. When the galleries wanted more, he praised her. She spent less and less time with her friends and family and more with his. They were a wonderful, loving family, and she adored them.

One day, she came home with something shiny on her finger. Elizabeth confided to Pony how she'd fallen in love with not just Joel but his whole family. They were a warm bundle of love and smiles. Now, she and Joel were going to start a life together.

Pony was none too pleased about this family talk and decided to plot against Joel. Pony hated being deserted each night—left with just a bowl of food and water. He missed snuggling up in Elizabeth's bed. His spot at the crook of her knees had been usurped by a hairy human, and now this? Banned from her bedroom. What was next, a doghouse?

Pony scratched furiously at the door, begging to be let back in. The whining and scratching wouldn't let up until Elizabeth finally opened the door and scooped him in her arms, only to lock him in his crate. Elizabeth saw the way Pony had gone after Joel's ankles. The little Napoleon was furious about his out-of-favor status.

Joel put the pillow over his head to shut out that damn mutt's incessant yapping. He picked this broad because she had money, and he needed cash to keep his fishing boats afloat. The more sunshine he brought, the more she painted. The more she painted, the bigger the boat of his dreams.

He wove the enchantment around her like a modern stinkin' fairy tale, and she bought it as if under a magic spell. Joel played the romance like her favorite movie, *The Jewel of the Nile*. They'd live on the boat in exotic harbors, he told her. He'd sell fish and tours. She'd sell paintings. They'd be independent, chart their destiny. They'd be free.

They'd get married. Buy the boat. As long as she kept selling those little nuggets, they'd be grand. If she started losing her trim or her talent, they'd go chumming.

Elizabeth felt the chill in the air when she returned to the room. She'd put Pony in his crate. Joel should be happy. But something felt off. She chalked it up to the noisy pommy, but the feeling unsettled her. She tucked back into bed only to face a mountainous back. She turned away, as well, and felt a rift.

She didn't go to the dock the next day or the day after that. Her muse had left for sunnier climes, and she didn't give notice as to when she'd return. Pony started getting more possessive and Joel moodier. When the sales started to slip, Joel encouraged her to paint. However, the encouragement felt forced, not fun like before. The galleries had clients lined up for her paintings, but when she dried up, they did too. And oddly, so did Joel.

At first, she thought it was just her imagination. His sharp criticisms weren't meant to hurt, right? How could someone who cared so much for her suddenly notice all of her faults? She must have done *something* wrong. They were starting a life together. They should be sharing, talking, and preparing to join as one. But the rift grew. A strangeness came between them, and she couldn't shake it.

He blamed it on the dog and told her to get rid of it.

Just the thought of it caused her to grieve. How could he make her choose? She'd promised Pony she'd always be there for him. But would she be considered a fool if she chose a dog over a husband? It wasn't that. It was the fact that he made her choose. How could she live with someone who could be so cold?

"Lizzy, for Christ's sake, can you put that dog outside? I have to get up at 3 a.m. and that whining ain't helpin'," Joel snarled.

321

"I can't put Pony outside. It's too cold. Maybe I can put a blanket over the crate to muffle the sound," Elizabeth defended.

"You need to get your priorities straight." Joel glared at her.

Elizabeth suddenly saw the revolting truth. She clutched the blanket to her and stared at this stranger. Pony whined again. Joel threw the clock against the door.

"That's it. I'm going home where it's quiet. Give you some time to think about what's important here," Joel said.

Elizabeth watched him go without a word. She already knew what was important, and it wasn't Joel.

Elizabeth withdrew into her flat and drank only sips of tea. The chamomile calmed her frayed nerves and sense of failure. She declined all calls, pulled the curtains tight, and refused to see Joel.

When Joel realized he lost the jackpot, he baited hooks for a fresh catch. He cast off the lines, headed out of the harbor, and raised a flag as he chugged past her. The diesel belched when he pushed the throttle forward. He left her without so much as a backward glance.

It was when PG&E shut off her power that Elizabeth pulled up her robe, sipped cold tea, and looked around. She no longer wanted to sit in darkness; it was time to move on. She threw open her window. The sea breeze came in with a fresh breath of spring, a little pink tongue licked her ankles in glee, and Elizabeth picked up her brush to paint.

# Wings

## Susanna Solomon

From the Sheriff's Calls Section of the *Point Reyes Light*,
August 13, 2015. NICASIO: At 3:13 p.m., someone watched
a man exit his car and walk down the middle of the road,
barefoot, shirtless, and dressed in white jeans. He was gazing
at the trees.

"What are they calling me for?" Mildred asked. "This isn't about your
brother. Henry doesn't own any white jeans."

"Oh, my dear little wife, hand me the phone," Fred said,
cupping his hands over his ears as her voice got louder and louder. "No
need to shout."

"Turn down your hearing aids." Mildred said, slammed the
phone into his hands, and stormed out the bedroom door.

Fred had been taking a nap. Feeling groggy, he put the phone
next to his ear. "My brother doesn't drive, and he certainly doesn't go
shirtless or barefoot." The officer asked him, only too kindly, to come
to the station. At the same time Mildred charged through the door, her
Easter hat on, her purse over her arm, and twirling the keys.

At the station, Officer Linda Kettleman helped them into a
cruiser and with lights flashing, the three of them sped out of town,
the cruiser burning up the asphalt along Route One.

Mildred, excited, clutched her purse and whispered, "Faster,
faster," while Fred, in the front seat, asked the deputy to give him more
information.

"It could be Henry," he muttered, feeling sad. Henry had been
doing better lately, or so Fred had thought. He had been taking his
meds and living in a studio in Inverness Park. He even had enough
money for a cup of coffee every Thursday when they met at the
Bovine.

"He may be gone by the time we get there," Linda said, "or he
may be confused, on the side of the road, or lost."

"Or worse," Fred said. A moment later, he brightened. "Maybe
it's not Henry."

"Oh, it's him, all right," Mildred said, from the back. She would
have clocked him on the shoulder, but there was a wire-mesh grill

323

between the front seat and the back. "That old fool should be in a rest home."

"Like you?" Fred said, under his breath. She didn't hear, which was good. Or was it that he hadn't heard her? He didn't know the difference.

They pulled up in front of Rancho Nicasio at the Square. The afternoon was a cool one. The clouds blocked the sun and a hush had come across the landscape. The little church stood sentry over the peaceful setting.

Fred stuck his hearing aids deep in his ears. He'd have to be on double alert to hear his brother in the silence.

"I'll take a walk to the church," he said, easing himself out of the front of the cruiser. Linda had already stepped out.

"Hey. What about me?" Mildred cried, stuck in the back where there were no door handles. "Somebody could die back here."

Fred opened the door. "I'll take the church; you want to wander around the Square?"

"I'll bet a whole quarter I'll find your brother first," Mildred said, and climbed over a rail fence into tall grass.

Fred liked the little church. He checked the front step. There were no clothes and no shirt. But there was a gathering of breadcrumbs near the front door. Henry—or whomever—couldn't have been gone too long, otherwise, birds would have eaten the evidence. He wandered back behind the church, steering clear of blackberry bushes and murmuring, "Henry? Henry, is that you?"

"I made the call a little over an hour ago," the proprietor of Rancho Nicasio said, when Linda came through the door to the bar. "He was barefoot, shirtless, and mumbling something about his beloved gone these twenty years." The proprietor, a guy with an after-eight mustache, wiped down the bar. "We get plenty of interesting people out here, Officer, but usually not someone that old showing off his pecs with a full head of white hair. He headed to the church."

"Henry," Linda muttered, and gave him her card. "Call me if he comes in, please."

The door banged open. Mildred came to the bar. "Drinking already, Officer Kettleman?" She threw her purse and coat on the counter. "Whiskey, neat, and make it snappy, bartender. My brother-in-law's missing, and it's chilly out there."

Linda left Mildred at the bar, climbed back into the cruiser, and drove around the Square. She knocked on the doors of the few houses, then took a ride at least four miles out of town in all three directions. She drove slowly, calling Henry's name, but she didn't see any pedestrians at all. Disappointed, she drove back to the Square and checked the bar again. She looked in the church and felt despondent. A man in his eighties, shirtless and shoeless, could get cold and disoriented if he wasn't brought inside soon.

Fred tiptoed around the back of the church, muttering to himself, calling out Henry's name and fiddling with his hearing aids. It was brushy back there. Tall grass pulled at his pants. A coyote yipped in the distance. "Henry?" he called. Nothing.

Sure it would be locked. Linda pressed on the latch to the front door. It opened with a whisper. The sanctuary looked inviting. She walked the pews, checked the floor and hiding spaces, and left the door unlocked as she walked out. "Henry?" she called out to a darkening sky.

At the back step, Fred sat his bulk down. What would Mom say? Even though she'd been gone forty years, she always insisted that Fred take care of his older brother. "He's special," she'd say. "He needs a little more than you do, my beautiful boy." *I failed*, Fred thought, and pressed his head into his hands.

Something swished the grass near his feet. "Henry?" He looked up to recognize Marmalade, the orange parish cat, whose picture had recently been in the *Light*. Fred stood up and on creaky legs meandered into the church. The front door was open and candles flickered on a table by the door. Fred wasn't a religious man, but he could use some help today. He sat in a pew, begged God's forgiveness, and prayed the best he could, using shreds of phrases he remembered from Sunday school. A few minutes later, he felt a hand on his shoulder. "Linda? Officer?" he asked and opened his eyes.

"Imagine my surprise. There I was feeling out of sorts, and bang, here's my little brother, sitting in a church, for God sakes. Fred, have you lost your mind, or have you been saved?"

It sounded like Henry, and looked a bit like Henry. But he wasn't wearing his usual clothes: beat-up, blue jeans, and red and black plaid flannel shirt. He had on a thick, puffy, white top. "You okay, big brother?" Fred asked.

"God asked me to put on wings," Henry smiled and smoothed the feathers on his arms. "You like?"

"We've been worried about you," Fred said. "How'd you get here? Are you wearing shoes?"

"God's little sandals," Henry replied, showing off his feet. "White pants, angel wings, and sandals. Seems like I'm ready for the Holy Ghost."

"You're ready for the asylum, buddy boy," Fred said, taking his arm. But the arm felt ethereal, as if nothing were there.

"Oh, it's me, all right, Fred," Henry laughed. "I'm no ghost. The Holy Father called and I came running. I listen well, these days, Fred. I listen to Him."

"For heaven's sake," Fred sighed. "Anything broken? You off your meds?"

"Never felt better, little brother." Henry twirled in the candlelight. "Mom would be proud, don't you think?"

"Will you come see Mildred?" Fred asked, feeling he'd lost control of the situation. She'd know what to do. "She's at the bar."

"Drunk, I bet," Henry said. "I swore off booze when the Lord called."

"Jesus," Fred said, putting his head into his hands.

"He called too, but I didn't answer," Henry said. He looked up at the ceiling. "But he's watching over me," he said. "And if you sit in the pew with me and pray, maybe he'll listen to you, too." He grinned. "C'mon, Fred, make me happy for a change."

Fred would've gotten up and dragged Henry out of there, but Henry was a bigger man who could hold him down.

"Come, sing a hymn with me," Henry said.

Fred's head swam.

"You remember 'You Have a Friend in Jesus,'" Henry said. "Sing, little brother, just sing."

Feathers fell from Henry's costume onto Fred's lap, but he sang in a crackly, gravelly voice. And he sang the next hymn as the door burst open, and he sang again while Henry squeezed his fingers ever tighter and insisted, "The next verse, Fred. Don't forget the next verse." And Fred kept singing, as his voice rose with his brother's and two female voices joined them. One his wife's, Fred thought, but she slurred her words, and a fourth voice joined them. They all sang, "You have a Friend in Jesus."

Henry loosened his grip on Fred's fingers.

Fred opened his eyes. No one was there. Goosebumps ran up and down his arms. The church was empty except for one white feather on his lap.

The door opened.

"Fred?"

It was Mildred. "You coming, Sweetheart? Your brother's in the car. We just found him there, grinning in the back seat, his flannel shirt in his lap. It's getting late, and my roast has been cooking all afternoon."

"Yes, Dear," Fred said, clearing his throat. It felt a little constricted. "I'll be there in a minute."

# AUTHORS

**Inga Aksamit**. Inga is a travel writer whose passion is adventure and exploration around the Pacific Rim. Publications include *Highs and Lows on the John Muir Trail* and stories in *Travel Stories from Around the Globe*, *Coast* and *Kayak* magazines and *Journeys: On the Road & Off the Map*.

**Carmen Appell**. Carmen is a retired personal injury litigation paralegal. She writes both fiction and nonfiction with an emphasis on mental health issues for children and adults. She volunteers as a Court Appointed Special Advocate (CASA) for children who are in foster care or the juvenile court system.

**Mary Lynn Archibald**. Mary Lynn is a freelance editor and author of two memoirs: *Briarhopper: A History,* one woman's story from 1913 Kentucky to 1945 California; and *Accidental Cowgirl: Six Cows, No Horse and No Clue,* the award-winning story of two greenhorns who inadvertently find themselves in the cattle business.

**Sandy Baker**. Two of Sandy's passions are writing and gardening; she combines those into children's gardening books, having been inspired by her sixteen years as a Master Gardener. Sandy co-wrote the thriller, *The Tehran Triangle,* in 2012, and writes poetry for teens. She is president of the Redwood Writers and chaired two conferences.

**Wendy Bartlett**. Wendy won the top writing prize in the 2007 San Francisco Writers Conference for her novel, *Cellini's Revenge*. She is taking a marketing course online and will be publishing the rest of her books as an indie author. Her latest novel, *Good-bye with a Kiss,* is a possible movie.

**Elspeth Benton**. Elspeth is the author of the mystery *Crucial Time*, and a limited-publication, the memoir, *The Apple's Core,* from which several chapters have been anthologized. She chaired a Redwood Writers short story contest, and she serves as a copy editor for *The Redwood Writer.* Elspeth loves writing, and enjoys hearing her fellow Redwood Writers read their work.

**Skye Blaine**. Skye writes memoir, fiction, poetry, and blogs. Her writing explores themes of aging, coming of age, disability, and awakening. She received an MFA in Creative Writing from Antioch University. *Bound to Love: a memoir of grit and gratitude* was published last year. Her novel, *Call Her Home*, is almost complete.

**Laura Blatt**. Laura has worked as a laboratory technician, an editor and manager at a publishing company, and as a website writer. Her work has appeared in *Tiny Lights, California Explorer, Vintage Voices* and in *Touch: A Journal of Healing*.

**Harker Brautighan**. Harker lives and writes in Sonoma County, California. Her work has appeared in *Music in the Air*, edited by Whitney Scott, where her piece, "The Best Seat in the House," placed third. She has been published in a number of anthologies.

**Robbi Sommers Bryant**. Robbi's award-winning books include a novella, four novels, five short story collections and one book of poetry. Her work has been published in magazines including *Readers Digest, Redbook,* and *Penthouse* and in several anthologies. She is past president of Redwood Writers, and currently works as a developmental and copy editor. Robbibryant.com

**Joelle B. Burnette**. Joelle is an award-winning journalist, author, and artist. Aside from writing television news in San Francisco, she wrote for a New York Times daily newspaper. She holds a master's in journalism/communications from Stanford University. Aside from her writing appearing in magazines and anthologies, her published books include her nonfiction memoir, *Cancer Time Bomb: How the BRCA Gene Stole My Tits and Eggs*, and a children's holiday book, *Freedom Doesn't Just Come Along with a Tree*. Joelle's writing experience also extends to her work on Capitol Hill and media relations on presidential and regional campaigns. JoelleBurnette.net.

**Marilyn Campbell**. As a former social worker in Adult Protective Services, Marilyn put her knowledge and observations to good use. She published *Trains to Concordia*, a YA novel in 2015 and has contributed to every Redwood Writers anthology since 2008. Her poetry was included in *Stolen Light*, the Redwood Writer's 2016 poetry anthology, and she was a featured reader of this year's Author Spotlight Fiction Book Club series at Copperfield's Books. She is currently working on a sequel to her novel.

**Simona Carini**. Born in Perugia, Italy, and a graduate of the Catholic University of the Sacred Heart (Milan, Italy) and Mills College (Oakland, CA), Simona writes nonfiction and poetry. She has been published in various print and online venues. She lives in Northern California with her husband. Her website is simonacarini.com.

**Fran Claggett**. Fran is the author of two poetry books, *Black Birds and Other Birds* and *Crow Crossings*. Her poems deal not only with birds, but with life events, love and loss. After years of teaching, consulting, publishing and writing, currently Fran is an instructor of memoir writing and poetry at Sonoma State University's Osher Lifelong Learning Institute. She has written a number of books for teachers and students on critical thinking, literature and composition, and has received many teaching and writing awards. She lives in Sebastopol with her Saluki and whippet.

**John Compisi.** John is a freelance travel, adventure and lifestyle writer focusing on California and Italy, who resides in Sonoma County. He loves nothing more than getting out there and experiencing the world; no matter if it's a destination close to home, a road trip, or a journey to romantic international destinations.

**Roger DeBeers, Sr.** Roger has self-published a mystery/thriller *Murder Is Forever*. DeBeers also writes mystery/thrillers, slice of life vignettes, poetry, and memoir. DeBeers is a single custodial parent of his musically gifted seventeen-year-old son. DeBeers earned his B.A. in history, M.A. in english, and his M.F.A. in creative writing from Goddard College.

**Don Dussault**. Don has a B.F.A., B.A., and M.A. He did postgraduate coursework in International Novel and Linguistics. Don has taught, done government work, including social work, and has lived abroad. Don is wrapping up a fictional family saga spanning over a century set in numerous U.S. and foreign places.

**Malena Eljumaily.** Malena has been a member of Redwood Writers since 2008. She is treasurer on the board of directors of Redwood Writers and co-chair of the workshop committee. "Threshold" was adapted from a one-minute play that was part of the 2015 Gi60 Play Festival put on by Brooklyn College in NYC. She lives in Santa Rosa.

**Pamela Fender.** Pamela is the author of her memoir, *Beside Myself: Recovery From My Family Betrayal and Estrangement*. Pamela received her degree in English at Sonoma State. She's a substitute teacher and notary public. Raised in the suburbs of Los Angeles, she returned to Sonoma County after losing her home in the 1994 L.A. earthquake.

**Jack Fender.** Jack is from London, England. A former actor and theatre entrepreneur in San Francisco, he now lives in Sonoma County. Jack spends his spare time writing short fiction as well as plays. He is a member of Redwood Writers. He is currently working on his first novel.

**P. H. Garrett.** P. H. Garrett is a journalist and public relations professional. She has authored numerous fiction and non-fiction pieces. Her work appears in several anthologies, including *Sisters Born, Sisters Found*, newspapers, and magazines. Her first novel, *Trail of Hearts*, set in the 1850s American West, is due out in 2016. Wordwranglingwoman.com.

**Cristina Goulart.** Cristina's prose and poetry have appeared in several Redwood Writers anthologies, and her articles addressing environmental issues have appeared in the *Windsor Times* and other community papers. Her short story, *Saffron Street Woman*, won first prize in the 2014 Redwood Writers Conference prose contest.

**Marcia Hart.** Marcia is a retired physical education teacher. She is a new member of Redwood Writers who hopes to develop her writing muscles. She's interested in memoir and, very occasionally, poetry. And, she's looking forward to benefitting from the all the writers helping writers.

**Pamela Heck.** Pamela is a special education teacher, artist, and writer of picture books, memoir, short stories, and poetry. She made her Redwood Writers club début in the 2015 anthology, *Journeys*. Her work also appears in the recently released poetry anthology, *Stolen Light*. Pamela is currently illustrating her children's book, *Amazing Animals*.

**John Grayson Heide.** John lost his life savings in the crash of 2008 but was also given the gift of a powerful dream. He began to write the story and his life changed. His debut novel *The Flight of the Pickerings* was released in March 2016.

**William Hillar.** Bill's interests are travel, history, reading, cross species communication, languages and human resiliency. He has been a father, husband, boy scout, referee, soldier, psychologist, cook, cab driver, and a negotiator. He has been a writer for over thirty years.

**Laura McHale Holland.** An author, editor and storyteller, Laura has published three award-winning books: the anthology *Sisters Born, Sisters Found: A Diversity of Voices on Sisterhood;* *The Ice Cream Vendor's Song*, a flash fiction collection; and *Reversible Skirt*, a childhood memoir. Her new book, *Resilient Ruin: A memoir of hopes dashed and reclaimed,* is a coming of age tale set for release in November 2016. WordForest.com.

**Mara Johnstone.** Mara grew up in a house on a hill, of which the top floor was built first. She lives in California with her husband, son, and laptop-loving cats. She enjoys writing, drawing, and spending hours discussing made-up things.

**Leigh Jordan.** Leigh was born in Waltham, Massachusetts, but spent her childhood in New York City and teenage-hood in Sacramento. She went to San Francisco State University and was just in time for love-beads and acid rock. She reads a lot. Poetry made the most sense to her. She took to writing poetry, and, at first, it shunned her. Poetic inspiration was like the princess' pea—it was always there but difficult to find. Over the years, however, she has come to an understanding so she can say, I am friendly with inspiration and I am a poet.

**Jeanne Jusaitis, MA.** Jeanne is the author of *Journey to Anderswelt, Lilah Dill, and the Magic Kit*. She lives in Petaluma, California, where she writes poetry and fiction for children. Jeanne draws from her memories of growing up in the bay area, and her many years of teaching and traveling through Europe.

**Valerie Kelsay.** Valerie is researcher and writer. She threads her varied career experiences through her memories of people, places, and the discoveries of her heart.

**Sue Kesler.** Sue Kesler's (Estee Kessler) books include: *My Partner Jakup the Jay: An Untold Story of the Napa Valley (Jakup and Riley: A Most Unusual Duo Book 1)* and *J & R Rides Again: A Tale from San Francisco to Paris and Back (Jakup and Riley - A Most Unusual Duo) (Volume 2)*, two tongue-in-cheek paranormals featuring the unlikely duo of Riley (a guy) and Jakup (a scrub jay). The third book in the series is in progress. Sue is a news junkie, walker, traveler, and aficionado of the mighty pun.

**Molly Kurland.** Molly sees life as a great experiment. She writes about taking risks and the crazy moments that evolve into funny stories and wisdom gained from lessons learned. Her book, *Successful Strokes*, is a guide to creating a fulfilling and lucrative massage practice. Her book and blog are available at Successfulstrokes.com.

**Marilyn Lanier.** Life on a 1950s Wyoming ranch inspired Marilyn's debut novel, *Hardpan*. A short film based on a chapter was selected for the Director's Award at the 2008 UCLA Film Festival. Lanier has an M.A. in English, CSU East Bay, and has taken creative writing courses from UCLA's Extension Program.

**Betty Les.** Betty grew up in Texas, served in the Peace Corps in Latin America, lived the big middle of her life in Wisconsin, and moved to California for the fourth chapter. She is a lifelong writer, focusing on poetry and creative nonfiction.

**Jing Li.** Jing taught high school ESL in China. After earning her Master's in America in 1989, she taught twenty more years of high school Mandarin Chinese in San Francisco. She won First Place in 2015

Redwood Writers Memoir Contest. A self-proclaimed gourmet cook, Jing makes the best Chinese potstickers.

**Venus Maher.** Dr. Maher is a chiropractor, writer, singer, and life coach. She has been published in six anthologies. Her writings in progress include *Light Weaver*, and *The Wild Years*. She is the founder of "Life Spark! Transformational Tools for Living," designed to free the creative loving genius within.

**Juanita J. Martin.** Juanita is Fairfield's first poet laureate. She is the author of *The Lighthouse Beckons*, a poetry collection. Juanita serves as the acquisitions editor for *The Redwood Writer*. She has published in *Blue Collar Review*, *SoMa Literary Review*, *Vintage Voices*, & others. She is the winner of the 2011 Poet Laureate Honor Scroll, the 2014 Helene S. Barnhart Award and she featured in 100 Thousand Poets for Change, the Berkeley Poetry Festival, and the Petaluma Poetry Walk. Jmartinpoetwriter.com..

**David Mechling.** Dave has been writing for about eight years, after realizing poetry didn't need to be stuffy. He has had poetry and prose published in *The Sitting Room, Healdsburg Alive, Water, Vintage Voices: The Sound of a Thousand Leaves, and Vintage Voices: Words Poured Out.* He will be promoting his collection of work titled, "Daveisms; miscellaneous ramblings from a suburban kind of guy sometime after he hits retirement age."

**Marie Millard.** Marie is the author of the Canterbury Tales based young adult novel *Anaheim Tales* and the fairy tale comedy *Littlefoot Part One.* She blogs at Mlmillard.wordpress.com and Wereyoualwaysthisfunny.wordpress.com.

**Robin Moore.** Robin has a B.S. in journalism from Cal Poly. She has worked as a newspaper editor, reporter, and photographer. She has had numerous newspaper articles published including full page spreads. Several of her short stories and poems have appeared in the Redwood Writers Anthologies. Currently, she writes mainly for children and young adults.

**Dmitri Rusov-Morningstar.** Dmitri is a ripe old hippie with good humor. During the 1960s and 1970s, he worked tirelessly for peace. He became a union carpenter and has been a residential designer for the past thirty-three years. Writing is his passion. He writes memoir and stories about his Maine Coon Cats.

**Ian Nevin.** Ian is a senior at Windsor High School. His short story included in this anthology was used in a speech competition and awarded third place. Ian also competed in the National Catholic Forensic League's national tournament in May 2016. He enjoys debating, chess, video games, anime, and travel.

**Jan Ögren, MFT.** Jan is a developmental editor, international author, public speaker, and licensed psychotherapist. She loves helping people rewrite their lives both through therapy and as an editor. She especially enjoys introducing writers to the magical world of developmental editing where creativity multiplies and readers transform into intimate friends. JanOgren.net

**Renelaine Pfister.** Renelaine's stories, essays and poems have been published in her native Philippines and in the U.S., including *Vintage Voices: Call of the Wild.*, *Water, And the Beats Go On*, *Cry of the Nightbird*: Writers Against Domestic Violence, *Filipino Fiction for Young Adults*, and *Healdsburg and Beyond*.

**Leena Prasad, M.A.** Leena received her M.A. from Stanford University. She has authored two books: *iT felt Like A kiss*, an exploration of art in the Mission district of San Francisco, and *not exactly haiku*, a collection of short poems. Her writing portfolio is at FishRidingABike.com. In her other life, she is a software executive.

**Harry Reid.** Harry is an architect, author, playwright, and MIT grad. He received his M.A. in anthropology and history from Sonoma State University. Harry's plays have been performed in San Francisco and elsewhere in the Bay Area. His seventh novel, *The Coming of Charlotta*, is about a dysfunctional family living on an island off the coast of Maine. HBReid.com

**Linda Loveland Reid**. Linda is author of two novels. She is past president of Redwood Writers and chairs the Play Contest & Festival in conjunction with 6th Street Playhouse. Linda is instructor of art history at Sonoma State University's Osher Lifelong Learning Institute. She is a figurative oil painter and directs local theater.

**Belinda Riehl**. Belinda is a winning haiku poet. She writes fiction, memoir, and essay. She is a vice president on the board of directors of Redwood Writers, and chair of the 2017 retreat committee. Belinda was awarded the Redwood Writers 2015 Pullet Surprise (say it aloud) for her volunteer work. Her musings can be found at belindariehl. wordpress.com.

**Lilith Rogers**. Lilith writes in various mediums—poetry, prose, plays, and children's stories. Her work has appeared in numerous anthologies and periodicals, and she has self published several books. Lilith also is a performer and loves presenting her show, *Rachel Carson Returns*, in which she becomes the author of *Silent Spring*. Rachelcarsonreturns@gmail.com

**Janice Rowley**. Janice's writing is included in *And the Beats Go On*, *Stolen Light*, and *Water*, anthologies published by Redwood Writers. Jan served on Redwood Writers board of directors and as membership chair for three years. She is retired with time to enjoy the fruits of northern California's wine country.

**Rebecca Smith**. Rebecca is a renaissance artist who writes fiction, screenplays, and poems to awaken, enlighten and inspire—or at least give food for thought, and hopefully some entertainment along the way. She loves Sonoma County where the men are kind and the women wild, the bees happy, and children play in golden fields of green.

**Susanna Solomon**. Susanna is the author of *Point Reyes Sheriff's Calls*, (HD Media Press 2013). She has had numerous stories published in the *Point Reyes Light*, *The MacGuffin Literary Review*, *Meat for Tea – the Valley Review*, and on line in the *Mill Valley Literary Review* and in *Harlot's Sauce Radio*.

**Pamela Taeuffer.** Pamela writes coming of age and women's contemporary fiction books. Pam's book series *Broken Bottles* is about the effects of growing up in a family battling alcoholism. Her book *The Introverts Guide for Attending Conferences and Business Networking* is the first in her Introvert series. She has published poems in *And the Beats Go On*, and a short story in *Sisters Born, Sisters Found*. She runs a property management/vacation rental business with her husband and son.

**Patsy Ann Taylor.** Patsy is the author of *Stealing Home*. She is a founding member of Los Angeles-based Cottage Poets. Numerous literary journals, including Redwood Writers anthologies, have published her poetry and fiction. She is a member of California Writers Club Napa Valley and Santa Rosa branches, SCBWI, and Sisters in Crime.

**Deborah Taylor-French.** Deborah writes mysteries full of dogs and positive dog leadership. Awarded a California's Artists in the Schools, Guest Artist in Residence, Deborah has led hundreds of teachers workshops. Deborah facilitates the Redwood Writers Author Support Group. She blogs to "save dogs' lives & dog lovers' sanity" at Dog Leader Mysteries.com.

**Kathleen Thomas.** Kathleen writes fiction, non-fiction, prose and poetry. Her work has appeared in *The Sun* magazine, California Writers Clubs 2015 Literary Review, and *1000 Words - Summer 2016: playa*. She is president of Napa Valley Writers (CWC), and active on Facebook, Twitter, and her blog: WriterPaints.

**Barbara Toboni.** Barbara is a writer, blogger, and poet. Her work has appeared in literary journals, and anthologies, including *Wisdom Has a Voice, Water, And the Beats Goes On*. She is the author of two chapbooks: *Undertow*, published in 2011, and *Water Over Time*, published in 2013.

**Michael Welch.** Michael grew up along the Whetstone River in Ohio. He retired from the non-prophet (profit) world to philosophize on life back home behind the corncob curtain. Informed by Dickens, Twain, and Updike, he is inspired by his daughters Katrin and Dylan, both of whom are better writers than he.

**Jane Wilder.** Jane retired in 2008 after many working years, and now enjoys more time to pursue her lifelong passion, fiction writing. Along with her wife, Mardie, she also enjoys traveling, photography, operating a crafts-festival business, attending movies, socializing with friends, and reading as much as time allows.

**Marilyn Wolters.** Marilyn has lived in Sonoma County for over thirty years. Many of her working years were spent helping disabled community college students develop skills in essay writing. Now retired, she is an enthusiastic writer, gardener, hiker, and volunteer. Her published works include poetry, short fiction, and non-fiction.

**Jean Wong.** Jean is an award winning author writing fiction, memoir, poetry, and plays. Her work has been produced at Sixth Street Playhouse, Petaluma Reader's Theater, and Off the Page. She is the author of *Sleeping with the Gods,* and her memoir *Hurtling Jade* is soon to be published.

**Taryn Young.** Taryn spent her working career as a technical writer, workplace investigator, and human resources manager. In her semi-retired state, Taryn enjoys hearing, and telling, a great story.

# EDITORS

**Roger C. Lubeck, Ph.D.** Roger was the editor-in-chief for Redwood Writers 2016 Anthology, *Untold Stories*. Roger is the president of It Is What It Is Press and Corporate Behavior Analysts, Ltd. Roger's published works include business articles, business books, six novels, half a dozen short stories and poems in five different anthologies, and "Lean and Hungry," a ten-minute play performed by the 6th Street Playhouse in Santa Rosa, California. His stories and photographs have appeared in the *Sonoma Valley Sun* and the *Press Democrat*. Roger edited three anthologies by The Writing Journey and a memoir by Sam Chandler. His most recent novels are *Key West* in 2015 and *Overland* in 2016. His blog RogerInBlue.com features writing, photography, and art.

**John P. Abbott.** John is a writer, editor and marketing consultant based in Petaluma, CA. His fiction has appeared in *Frisko, Fence* and five Redwood Writers Anthologies. He served as editor for the 2013 Redwood Writers Anthology *Beyond Boundaries*. Email: JPAbbott@sonic.net.

**Catharine Bramkamp**. Catharine is the writer part of Newbie Writers Podcast (NewbieWriters.com) that focuses on newer writers and their concerns. She is a successful writing coach and author of a dozen books including the five book Real Estate *Diva* Mystery Series and most recently, *Future Girls* (Eternal Press). She holds two degrees in English, and is an adjunct professor of writing for two Universities.

**Robbi Sommers Bryant**. Robbi's award-winning books include a novella, four novels, five short story collections and one book of poetry. Her work has been published in magazines including *Readers Digest, Redbook,* and *Penthouse* and in several anthologies. She is past president of Redwood Writers, and currently works as a developmental and copy editor. Her website is robbibryant.com

**Joelle B. Burnette**. Joelle is an award-winning journalist, author, and artist. Aside from writing television news in San Francisco, she wrote for a New York Times daily newspaper. She holds a master's in journalism/communications from Stanford University. Aside from her

340

writing appearing in magazines and anthologies, her published books include her nonfiction memoir, *Cancer Time Bomb: How the BRCA Gene Stole My Tits and Eggs*, and a children's holiday book, *Freedom Doesn't Just Come Along with a Tree*. Joelle's writing experience also extends to her work on Capitol Hill and media relations on presidential and regional campaigns. JoelleBurnette.net.

**Fran Claggett**. Fran is the author of two poetry books, *Black Birds and Other Birds* and *Crow Crossings*. Her poems deal not only with birds, but with life events, love and loss. After years of teaching, consulting, publishing and writing, currently, Fran is an instructor at Sonoma State University's Osher Lifelong Learning Institute. She has written a number of books for teachers and students on critical thinking, literature and composition, and has received many teaching and writing awards. She lives in Sebastopol with her Saluki and whippet.

**Marlene Cullen**. Marlene is the founder of Writers Forum of Petaluma and creator of Jumpstart writing workshops, hosts The Write Spot Blog, a place for writers to share their writing, receive commentary and inspiration to keep writing. Her writing workshops and blog provide essential elements for successful writing. TheWriteSpot.us.

**Cristina Goulart**. Cristina's prose and poetry have appeared in several Redwood Writers anthologies, and her articles addressing environmental issues have appeared in the *Windsor Times* and other community papers. Her short story, "Saffron Street Woman," won first prize in the 2014 Redwood Writers Conference prose contest.

**Susan Gunter, Ph.D.** Susan has published poetry, three books on the James family, and a memoir, *My Vacation at the Beach*, about her transformation from college professor to full time nanny for her granddaughter. She studied poetry with James Dickey, and her poems have appeared in journals around the country, including *Poet Lore*. She held the William Dean Howells Fellowship in American literature at Harvard's Houghton Library in 2005. Currently she is finishing a suspense novel about two women college professors, *The Juke Joint; or, The Life and Times of Mrs. Ann James*.

**Crissi Langwell.** Crissi is the author of eight published books, including *Reclaim Your Creative Soul*, a nonfiction guide to making room for one's craft, and the recently published novel, *Loving the Wind*, a Peter Pan fan fiction. She is the newsletter editor for Redwood Writers. Find her at crissilangwell.com.

**Juanita J. Martin.** Juanita is Fairfield's first poet laureate. She is the author of *The Lighthouse Beckons*, a poetry collection. Juanita serves as the acquisitions editor for *The Redwood Writer*. She has published in *Blue Collar Review*, *SoMa Literary Review*, *Vintage Voices*, & others. She is the winner of the 2011 Poet Laureate Honor Scroll, the 2014 Helene S. Barnhart Award and she featured in 100 Thousand Poets for Change, the Berkeley Poetry Festival, and the Petaluma Poetry Walk. Jmartinpoetwriter.com.

**Eugene McCreary.** Eugene's love of writing has persisted through varied careers ranging from college professor to carpenter and real estate appraiser. He has written several screenplays, and his first novel, *Madame President*, a political thriller, was optioned by Milestone Productions in Los Angeles and formed the platform for an ABC series. His new book, *Gift of the Tiger*, set in China during World War II, was a finalist in the 2015 Indie book Awards in historical fiction. Gene also won the Grand Prize at the San Francisco Writer's Conference 2015 Contest.

**Jan Ögren, MFT.** Jan is a developmental editor, international author, public speaker and licensed psychotherapist. She loves helping people rewrite their lives both through therapy and as an editor. She especially enjoys introducing writers to the magical world of developmental editing where creativity multiplies and readers transform into intimate friends. JanOgren.net

**Belinda Riehl.** Belinda is a winning haiku poet. She writes fiction, memoir, and essay. She is a vice president on the board of directors of Redwood Writers, and chair of the 2017 retreat committee. Belinda was awarded the Redwood Writers 2015 Pullet Surprise (say it aloud) for her volunteer work. Her musings can be found at BelindaRiehl. wordpress.com.

**Janice Rowley.** Janice's writing is included in *And the Beats Go On*, *Stolen Light*, and *Water*, anthologies published by Redwood Writers. Jan served on Redwood Writers board of directors and as membership chair for three years. She is retired with time to enjoy the fruits of northern California's wine country.

**Helen S. Sedwick.** University of Chicago Law School graduate Helen Sedwick is a business lawyer with 30 years of experience assisting clients in setting up and running their businesses, legally and successfully. A published author herself, she wrote *Self-Publisher's Legal Handbook* to help other writers publish and promote their work while minimizing legal risks and errors.

# REDWOOD WRITERS

## Redwood Branch of the California Writers Club (CWC)

Jack London, George Sterling, and Herman Whitaker, among others, eventually formed the Press Club of Alameda. In 1909, a splinter group of writers formed the California Writers Club. Early honorary members included Jack London, George Sterling, John Muir, Joaquin Miller, and the first California poet laureate, Ina Coolbrith.

In 1975 Redwood Writers was established as the fourth CWC branch. Informally known as Redwood Writers, the branch owes a debt to Helene S. Barnhart of the Berkeley Branch, who had relocated to the North Bay. She and forty-five charter members founded the Redwood Branch of the CWC.

Redwood Writers is a non-profit professional organization whose motto is "writers helping writers." The club's mission is to provide a friendly and inclusive environment in which members may meet and network; to provide professional speakers who will aid in the writing, publishing, and marketing of members' endeavors; and to provide other writing-related opportunities that will further the club members' writings.

In 2006, Redwood Writers published its first anthology. This anthology is the thirteenth in that series. From 2010 - 2016, Redwood Writers sponsored a short play contest in which winning plays were performed at 6th Street Playhouse in Santa Rosa.

Today, the club features professional speakers at monthly meetings that are open to members and the public. Every other year, the club holds a day-long Writers Conference offering seminars on all areas of writing, taught by area professionals. In addition, the club sponsors a book club at Copperfield's bookstores, public readings, open mic nights, salons, workshops, seminars, writing contests, a monthly newsletter, and a website. For more information about Redwood Writers, visit redwoodwriters.org.

# PRESIDENTS OF REDWOOD WRITERS

The Redwood Branch of the California Writers Club is indebted to its founders, charter members, board and club members, and volunteers who make the Redwood Writers a success. The Redwood Branch could not have developed into the professional and successful club it is today had it not been for the leadership of our Presidents.

| | |
|---|---|
| 1975 | Helen Schellenberg Barnhart |
| 1976 | Dianne Kurlfinke |
| 1977 | Natlee Kenoyer |
| 1978 | Inman Whipple |
| 1979 | Herschel Cozine |
| 1980 | Edward Dolan |
| 1981 | Alla Crone Hayden |
| 1982 | Mildred Fish |
| 1983 | Waldo Boyd |
| 1984 | Margaret Scariano |
| 1985 | Dave Arnold |
| 1986 | Mary Priest |
| 1988 | Marion McMurtry |
| 1990 | Mary Varley |
| 1992 | Barb Truax |
| 1997 | Marvin Steinbock |
| 1999 | Dorothy Molyneaux |
| 2000 | Carol McConkie |
| 2001 | Gil Mansergh |
| 2003 | Carol McConkie |
| 2004 | Charles Brashear |
| 2005 | Linda C. McCabe |
| 2007 | Karen Batchelor |
| 2009 | Linda Loveland Reid |
| 2013 | Robbi Sommers Bryant |
| 2015 | Sandy Baker |

# JACK LONDON AWARD

Every other year, CWC branches may nominate a member to receive the Jack London Award for outstanding service to the branch, sponsored by CWC Central. The following members received the Jack London Award for service.

| | |
|---|---|
| 1975 | Helen Schellenberg Barnhart |
| 1977 | Dianne Kurlfinke |
| 1979 | Peggy Ray |
| 1981 | Pat Patterson |
| 1983 | Inman Whipple |
| 1985 | Ruth Irma Walker |
| 1987 | Margaret Scariano |
| 1989 | Mary Priest |
| 1991 | Waldo Boyd |
| 1993 | Alla Crone Hayden |
| 1995 | Mildred Fish |
| 1997 | Mary Varley |
| 1998 | Barbara Truax |
| 2003 | Nadenia Newkirk |
| 2004 | Gil Mansergh |
| 2005 | Mary Rosenthal |
| 2007 | Catherine Keegan |
| 2009 | Karen Batchelor |
| 2011 | Linda C. McCabe |
| 2013 | Linda Loveland Reid |
| 2015 | Jeane Slone |

# HELENE S. BARNHART AWARD

Inspired by the first president of the Redwood Writers, the Helene S. Barnhart Award was instituted in 2010 as a way to honor outstanding service to the branch. It is awarded in alternating years of the Jack London Award.

| | |
|---|---|
| 2010 | Kate (Catharine) Farrell |
| 2012 | Ana Manwaring |
| 2014 | Juanita J. Martin |
| 2016 | Robin Moore |